LEGEND OF THE GALACTIC HEROES

VOLUME 3
ENDURANCE

YOSHIKI TANAKA

HAIKA
SORU
SAN FRANCISCO

LEGEND OF THE GALACTIC HEROES

VOLUME 3
ENDURANCE

WRITTEN BY
YOSHIKI TANAKA

Translated by Daniel Huddleston

Legend of the Galactic Heroes, Vol. 3: Endurance
GINGA EIYU DENSETSU Vol.3
© 1984 by Yoshiki TANAKA
Cover Illustration © 2007 Yukinobu Hoshino.
All rights reserved.

Cover and interior design by Fawn Lau

HAIKASORU
Published by VIZ Media, LLC
P.O. Box 77010
San Francisco, CA 94107

www.haikasoru.com

Library of Congress Cataloging-in-Publication Data

Names: Tanaka, Yoshiki, 1952- author. I Huddleston, Daniel, translator.
Title: Legend of the galactic heroes / written by Yoshiki Tanaka ; translated
   by Daniel Huddleston.
Other titles: Ginga eiyu densetsu
Description: San Francisco : Haikasoru, [2016]
Identifiers: LCCN 2015044444I ISBN 9781421584942 (v. 1 : paperback) I ISBN
   9781421584959 (v. 2 : paperback) 9781421584966 (v. 3 : paperback)
Subjects: LCSH: Science fiction. I War stories. I BISAC: FICTION / Science
   Fiction / Space Opera. I FICTION / Science Fiction / Military. I FICTION /
   Science Fiction / Adventure.
Classification: LCC PL862.A5343 G5513 2016 I DDC 895.63/5--dc23
LC record available at http://lccn.loc.gov/2015044444

Printed in the U.S.A.
First printing, November 2016

MAJOR CHARACTERS

GALACTIC EMPIRE

REINHARD VON LOHENGRAMM
Commander in chief of the imperial military. Imperial prime minister. Duke.

PAUL VON OBERSTEIN
Chief of staff of the Imperial Space Armada. Acting secretary-general of Imperial Military Command Headquarters. Senior admiral.

WOLFGANG MITTERMEIER
Fleet commander. Senior admiral. Known as the "Gale Wolf."

OSKAR VON REUENTAHL
Fleet commander. Senior admiral. Has heterochromatic eyes.

FRITZ JOSEF WITTENFELD
Commander of the Schwarz Lanzenreiter fleet. Admiral.

ERNEST MECKLINGER
Deputy manager of Imperial Armed Forces Supreme Command Headquarters. Admiral. Known as the "Artist-Admiral."

ULRICH KESSLER
Commissioner of military police and commander of capital defenses. Admiral.

KARL GUSTAV KEMPF
Fleet commander. Admiral.

AUGUST SAMUEL WAHLEN
Fleet commander. Admiral.

KORNELIAS LUTZ
Fleet commander. Admiral.

NEIDHART MÜLLER
Fleet commander. Admiral.

ADALBERT FAHRENHEIT
Fleet commander. Admiral.

ARTHUR VON STREIT
Reinhard's chief aide. Rear admiral.

HILDEGARD VON MARIENDORF
Chief secretary to the imperial prime minister. Often called "Hilda."

HEINRICH VON KÜMMEL
Hilda's cousin. Baron.

ANNEROSE VON GRÜNEWALD
Reinhard's elder sister. Countess von Grünewald. Lives in seclusion at her mountain villa.

ERWIN JOSEF II
37th emperor of the Galactic Empire.

RUDOLF VON GOLDENBAUM
Founder of the Galactic Empire's Goldenbaum Dynasty.

DECEASED

SIEGFRIED KIRCHEIS
Died living up to the faith Annerose placed in him.

FREE PLANETS ALLIANCE

YANG WEN-LI
Commander of Iserlohn Fortress. Commander of Iserlohn Patrol Fleet. Admiral.

JULIAN MINTZ
Yang's ward. Civilian employed by military; treated equivalent to lance corporal.

FREDERICA GREENHILL
Yang's aide. Lieutenant.

ALEX CAZELNES
Administrative director of Iserlohn
Fortress. Rear admiral.

WALTER VON SCHÖNKOPF
Commander of fortress defenses at
Iserlohn Fortress. Rear admiral.

EDWIN FISCHER
Vice commander of Iserlohn Patrol Fleet.
Master of fleet operations.

MURAI
Chief of staff. Rear admiral.

FYODOR PATRICHEV
Deputy chief of staff. Commodore.

DUSTY ATTENBOROUGH
Division commander within the Iserlohn
Patrol Fleet. Yang's underclassman. Rear
admiral.

OLIVIER POPLIN
Captain of the First Spaceborne Division at
Iserlohn Fortress. Lieutenant commander.

NGUYEN VAN THIEU
A fierce commander in the Iserlohn Patrol
Fleet.

WILIABARD JOACHIM MERKATZ
Highly experienced admiral of the Imperial
Navy who defected to Iserlohn. A "guest
admiral" who is treated as a vice admiral.

BERNHARD VON SCHNEIDER
Merkatz's aide.

ALEXANDOR BUCOCK
Commander in chief of the Alliance Armed
Forces Space Armada. Admiral.

LOUIS MACHUNGO
Yang's security guard. Warrant officer.

JOB TRÜNICHT
Head of state. Chairman of the High
Council.

DECEASED

JESSICA EDWARDS
Representative in the antiwar faction of the
National Assembly. Died in the Stadium
Massacre.

DWIGHT GREENHILL
Frederica's father. Ringleader of a failed
military coup.

PHEZZAN DOMINION

ADRIAN RUBINSKY
The fifth landesherr. Known as the "Black
Fox of Phezzan."

RUPERT KESSELRING
Rubinsky's chief aide.

LEOPOLD SCHUMACHER
Former captain in the Imperial Navy.
Defected to Phezzan.

BORIS KONEV
Independent merchant. Old acquaintance of
Yang's. Working in the office of the Phezzan
commissioner on Heinessen.

MARINESK
Administrative officer on board *Beryozka*.

DEGSBY
Bishop dispatched from Earth to keep an
eye on Rubinsky.

GRAND BISHOP
Ruler in Rubinsky's shadow.

*Titles and ranks correspond to each
character's status at the end of *Ambition*
or their first appearance in *Endurance*.

TABLE OF CONTENTS

CHAPTER 1
FIRST FLIGHT   9

CHAPTER 2
THE FORTRESS TAKES
FLIGHT   35

CHAPTER 3
ONE SLENDER THREAD   63

CHAPTER 4
THINGS LOST   93

CHAPTER 5
COURT OF INQUIRY   117

CHAPTER 6
A BATTLE WITHOUT
WEAPONS   147

CHAPTER 7
FORTRESS VERSUS
FORTRESS   175

CHAPTER 8
RETURN   205

CHAPTER 9
RESOLVE AND AMBITION   237

CHAPTER 1:

THE BOY HADN'T ALWAYS LOVED the stars.

One winter's night, when he might have been most accurately called a toddler, he sat on his father's shoulders and looked up at the sky. Above snow-capped peaks tinged blue by starlight, a cold, hard expanse of utter blackness had spread out above him. Seized with terror, he had clung to his father's neck tightly, fearful that invisible arms were about to reach out of that endless darkness, scoop him up, and carry him away.

Now his father was gone. So was his fear of the depths of space. What he had now was someone greater than his father and a heart that longed for wings to carry him through the vast sea of stars.

It was January. SE 798, IE 489.

Julian Mintz was about to turn sixteen.

Rear Admiral Dusty Attenborough had departed Iserlohn Fortress leading a 2,200-vessel division composed of warships both large and small. Operating far away from both the fortress and the rest of the Iserlohn

Patrol Fleet, Attenborough's division was deployed inside the Iserlohn Corridor, like a bayonet pointed toward the Galactic Empire's territory. It was in this formation that Julian Mintz was presently serving.

Their mission was to run security patrols along the front, although this doubled as large-scale training maneuvers for new recruits as well.

The Alliance Armed Forces' human resources pool had been drained to no small degree last year by the so-called Military Congress for the Rescue of the Republic, whose coup d'état had rocked the FPA to its core. Under the command of Admiral Yang Wen-li, the Iserlohn Patrol Fleet had weathered many battles in that conflict, and in the civil war's aftermath a significant number of its veterans had been headhunted to fill key positions in new or expanded units.

This meant that the fleet's most experienced personnel had been replaced by raw recruits, and although the numbers remained the same, it was hardly surprising that the fleet's overall quality as a fighting force had declined. No matter what latent abilities these new faces might conceal, efficient use of those talents could only come with time and experience.

It's gonna be no easy job makin' soldiers outta these kids...

Such thoughts were never far from the minds of the instructors as they contemplated the long road ahead for their young charges. Moreover, Iserlohn Fortress was on the very front line of the Free Planets Alliance's defenses, so every time the Galactic Imperial Navy made a move, it was those so stationed who stood to take the first blow. In spite of that, the battle-hardened warriors of this vital military installation had been poached, then replaced with untrained recruits.

What do those imbeciles in government think they're doing?!

After much verbal abuse of the powers that be, Iserlohn's officers had set about dealing with the reality in front of them. These newbies had received only about a tenth of the training required to become fully functioning soldiers. To raise the odds of victory and increase their likelihood of survival, it was essential that they have at least 50 percent of the recommended training before it came time to face combat.

Accordingly, from the moment they arrived at Iserlohn, the recruits were subjected to an overwhelming barrage of intense training, as well as blistering rebukes from veteran soldiers and angry, red-faced instructors.

"Did you scumbags just come here to goof off?! All you are's a buncha good-for-nothing puppy dogs!"

"You want to live, you improve your skills! The enemy won't be giving you any handicaps!"

"Understand? The one who wins is the one who's stronger, not the one who's right. Losing out here doesn't just disqualify you from some debate about right and wrong—you're disqualified from breathing, too. Don't you ever forget that."

"Focus less on shooting early and more on shooting accurately! And even when you do shoot first, timing is everything. Remember: when you open fire, you're also giving the enemy your position."

"Your responses are slow! Do it over, from the beginning!"

"Go back to military school! I don't see how you ever graduated in the first place! Don't come here until you're at least out of diapers!"

The voices of the instructors grew ever louder and more heated. Whenever someone responded too sluggishly or failed to grasp an explanation, merciless abuse was sure to be heading their way.

Although it was rare to find a youth with reflexes and powers of comprehension on par with Julian, not even he was able to make it through a training session without a baptism of invective—and not just once or twice, either. One of the more reprehensible characteristics of the military's specialized hierarchical society was that recruits too far above average earned the same angry glares as those who underperformed.

Nobody in Attenborough's division got punched, but that was only because it was part of the Iserlohn Patrol Fleet; that was not the case in other regiments. In most matters, Yang, the commanding officer, was rather soft when it came to military discipline, but there were two areas in which he was so strict as to seem another person altogether: when soldiers harmed civilians, and when senior officers inflicted unfair or "creative" punishments on their subordinates. He had once demoted an officer decorated for valor on many a battlefield—and also sent him back to a post on Heinessen. It hadn't been the first time the man had used violence against subordinates, and Yang had ignored the cohort of officers who'd said they hated to lose his abilities.

"Subordinates can't do a thing to resist their CO's punishments. If a CO goes around hitting his men and we hold him up as a model soldier, that just makes soldiers an embarrassment to humanity. We don't need a man like that. At the very least, I don't."

Yang had neither raised his voice nor shouted. Both his expression and his voice had been rather soft. He was always like that when he was sticking to his guns about something.

Yang Wen-li was Julian's legal guardian, and when the boy had told him he wanted to be a soldier, Yang had not looked pleased. With the look on his face and his voice alike, he'd said, "There's all kinds of careers out there to choose from. Of all things, surely there's no need to pick the military."

Yang Wen-li was a military man himself. Although he was young, he was a full admiral already and was viewed as the number three man in uniform after Admiral Cubresly—director of Joint Operational Headquarters—and Admiral Bucock—commander in chief of the space armada.

Most in his position would have gladly offered assistance if Julian wanted to join the military; Yang, however, didn't feel that the military life was his own calling and decided that it would be a poor fit for Julian as well. At the same time, however, he couldn't just obstinately deny the free will of a young boy. As things stood presently, he was giving Julian his silent, if reluctant, assent.

Although Yang was Julian's legal guardian, holder of parental authority over him, and his guarantor, none of that gave Julian any advantage whatsoever in training. On the contrary, it provided once-in-a-lifetime grist for mean-spirited junior officers to use when calling him names and making fun of him. *Don't think you'll get any special treatment here because you're Admiral Yang's adopted son...Just look at you—you're an embarrassment to the admiral's name...If you think we're gonna go easy on you, you've got another thing coming...You probably think you can run crying to the admiral and he'll take care of everything, but that isn't gonna happen here…* Comments like these infuriated him, but they never pushed Julian beyond the bounds of his endurance. The boy knew that, despite the abuse, he was still in an enviable position. The attitude pervading Iserlohn Fortress and the patrol fleet was still without a doubt the best in all the armed forces of the alliance. That the air here could not be completely purged of such negative emotions was perhaps simply a cross that had to be carried—not only by the military, but by any other group of humans as well.

II

Triglav was the flagship of Attenborough's division. Named for the war god of Slavic mythology, the warship was beautiful—graceful, even—in its refined functionality, and in that respect exceeded even Yang's flagship, *Hyperion*. *Triglav* had arrived at Iserlohn as a brand-new, top-of-the-line warship, and at the time many had wondered aloud whether Commander Yang might move his commander's seat. That speculation hadn't panned out, however, at which point other voices supposed that Yang was simply the type who couldn't recognize the need for beauty in military vessels.

"If I may ask, sir," his chief of staff, Rear Admiral Murai, had asked, "Why didn't you make *Triglav* your flagship? It has that sort of *presence* that suits a flagship, I think…"

Yang's reply had left Murai speechless. This is what the dark-haired, dark-eyed young commander had said:

"Yeah, *Triglav* sure is a pretty ship to look at. And that's precisely why I *didn't* make it the flagship. After all, how am I supposed to admire it from the inside?"

Julian had had his doubts as to whether Yang had been answering seriously. Knowing Yang, he might have just thought it was too much of a chore to move his command from a ship he was familiar with. It was always a hassle for him when subordinates wanted to argue issues that were really beside the point, so maybe he had just given a totally out-of-left-field answer to see if it would shut Murai up. That was what Julian thought, though at the same time, he also had a feeling that Yang could have been entirely serious. In short, Yang was still a difficult person for Julian to read.

Aboard *Triglav*, the operators' movements were growing more hurried. The enemy-detection system had picked up a group of more than one thousand unidentified vessels.

If one set aside the minuscule chance that this was a massive fleet of defectors, the only other possibility was a Galactic Imperial Navy fleet. Rear Admiral Attenborough received the report and had orders relayed to all ships' captains to cease training exercises and go to alert level two. By that time, everyone in the forward group could already feel the enemy approach in their bones, due to the disruption of their transmission signals.

Warnings rang out from the intercoms. *Enemy fleet detected! Fifty minutes till contact! All hands, battle stations!*

Tension raced at the speed of light into the mind of every officer and soldier. Those who had been sleeping jerked awake, and mess halls were left vacated in moments. As for the new recruits, they were in a pathetic state, going through all the panic, confusion, and dread of the unknown that the seasoned crew did not. Taking twice as long as their battle-hardened brethren to get into their combat suits, they stood in corridors looking back and forth, not knowing what they were supposed to be doing until at last they were shoved out of the way by senior crew who looked like they were ready to kill them.

"Good grief, what a mess! How am I supposed to fight while leading *boy scouts* into combat?!"

Looking at the shipboard monitor, Rear Admiral Attenborough grabbed his iron-gray hair through his black military-issue beret. At twenty-nine years of age, he was one of the youngest admirals in the Alliance Armed Forces and had been two years behind Yang at Officers' Academy. He didn't lack for broad-mindedness or courage, and the confidence Yang had in him was evidenced by his entrusting Julian to him, albeit temporarily.

Commander Lao, chief staff officer for this division, frowned. "You're saying you intend to take these raw recruits and trainees into battle?" he said.

"Of course!" yelled Attenborough. After all, even the trainees had been assigned to this division in order to fight. They had to experience their first battle sometime. For most of the new recruits—nearly all, actually—this battle had come too early. However, avoiding combat was no longer possible at this stage, nor was it possible for the experienced crew by themselves to protect the newbies from all harm. Most importantly, without those new recruits positioned in every department, it would mean crucial shortages of combat personnel.

"I'm going to have them fight as well. We don't have the leeway to have them sitting in box seats watching the rest of us play war games. Mobilize them."

As he was giving that order, Attenborough couldn't hold back a sense of gloom as he wondered how many of them would make it back to their beds in the Iserlohn Fortress barracks. At least until relief arrived, all he could do was try to hold casualties down to the barest minimum. The young commander decided to adopt a "rather than win, don't lose" policy. Not that circumstances had given him another option.

∴

"The Attenborough division has made contact with and engaged imperial forces at Corridor Point FR—"

When the communications officer gave that report, Admiral Yang Wen-li, mighty commander of the FPA forces, was not in the fortress's central command room. He was hardly a man of such diligence as to hang around his workplace outside of regular working hours. Still, he had been diligent in communicating his expected whereabouts—even if in nothing else—so his aide Lieutenant Frederica Greenhill was able to find the young commander in short order. He was pretending to be asleep on a bench in a botanical garden.

"Your Excellency, please wake up."

At the sound of her voice, Yang laid one hand on the beret that was resting on top of his face. Without moving from that position, he said in a sleepy, muffled voice, "What is it?"

After his aide had reported, he took his beret in hand and sat up.

"Not a day's peace at the frontier fortress. Spring comes late to these northern climes, eh? This is gonna be trouble. Hey, Julian—!"

Yang had called out for the boy out of habit. He looked around the park, rested his gaze on Frederica's face, and then, with a little sigh, scratched his head with one hand. Then he rose to his feet, grumbling to himself as he put his beret back on. "I sent him out there 'cause I thought it'd be safe . . ."

"I'm sure he'll come back safely. That boy has a lot of talent and a lot of luck, too."

Frederica spoke knowing full well just how powerless words were. Yang looked at her with a cryptic expression. He must have taken her remark as a mixture of both official and personal sentiment.

"There're a lot of raw recruits on those ships," he said. "This won't be easy, even for Attenborough. We've gotta get out there and reinforce them ASAP."

Even so, Yang's scowl and his ill-tempered words were nothing more than a cover to hide the awkward embarrassment he felt at her concern.

On Janary 22, fleets from the Galactic Empire and the Free Planets Alliance randomly encountered one another at coordinates closer to the empire's side of that narrow, tunnel-shaped region of space called the Iserlohn Corridor. It occasioned the start of a battle that was, for all practical purposes, strategically meaningless.

This was a textbook example of a chance encounter between hostile parties. Neither the imperial forces nor those of the alliance had expected the other to be out this far from their home base.

The border between these two states and their very different political systems was wherever their territories happened to collide. Since neither side recognized the other as an equal partner in diplomacy, no official border existed, and danger swirled through that region of space like a silent, formless cyclone of tension, unease, and hostility. It was a pipe dream to think that peaceful intentions were behind any eyes turned toward this region. Yet even so, moments did occur from time to time when people let their guard down. Caught up in the daily routines of their respective patrols, neither side had been expecting to run into an enemy force. Some might call it carelessness, and carelessness it was. But human beings were simply not furnished with such powers of concentration that they could stay fully vigilant all the time for such random occurrences.

Julian's supple limbs were enveloped in the combat suit he now wore as pilot of a single-seat spartanian fighter craft. He was waiting in the mother ship's hangar, listening intently to the intraship broadcasts for his launch order.

"Enemy force strength estimated at 200 to 250 battleships, 400 to 500 cruisers, approximately 1,000 destroyers, and 30 to 40 mother ships."

Not exactly a huge fleet, thought Julian. Still, there must be as many as two hundred thousand crew trusting their lives and futures to the space inside those vessels, just a few walls away from hard vacuum. Were some in that number heading into their first battle, just as he was? Julian looked around at the other pilots nearby. The confident—even cocky—expressions of the seasoned warriors were in sharp contrast to the pale faces of the greenhorns. Maybe it was all empty bluster. The new pilots, however, didn't even have the confidence to spare for that.

Suddenly, the voice of the space traffic controller came pounding on his eardrums through his headphones. "Sergeant Mintz! Board your spartanian!"

His was the first name they called among the rookies.

"*Ja!*" Julian shouted, and took off running for the spartanian engraved with the number 316—the one reserved for his use, and his alone.

He pressed his ID card—imprinted with his name, rank, FPA Armed Forces serial number, DNA sequence, both ABO and MN blood type, fingerprints, and voiceprint—up against a certain spot on the cockpit. The spartanian's computer read it and popped its hood open for the first time, welcoming its new pilot.

Julian settled into the cockpit, fastened his safety belt, and put on his helmet. The helmet joined tightly to the combat suit's neck with an electromagnetic seal. This helmet was connected directly to the onboard computer by two cords that transmitted the pilot's brain wave pattern. If that pattern did not match the one the computer had on file for its pilot, the pilot would be rendered unconscious by a low-output, high-voltage shock. Unlike on some children's action show on solivision, a real spartanian could not be stolen and piloted by an enemy soldier. It used a pseudo imprinting system created to allow only a single pilot to fly any given spartanian.

With his helmet now on, Julian quickly checked his instruments and inspected the provisions inside his machine.

Salt tablets—sodium chloride coated in pink fructose—along with plastic bottles of concentrated vitamin fluid, tubes of royal jelly mixed with gluten, and more. They were part of a set of nutritional supplements that could keep him alive for a week. There was also a resin spray that hardened instantly for use in the event of hull cracks, signal flares with a hand catapult for launching them, and even calcium injections. These were included because the human body lost calcium while in a weightless state, and calcium couldn't be supplemented by food or oral medication. All these things, together with fast-acting painkillers, pills to lower body temperature and induce artificial hibernation, organic germanium pills, assorted other medications, and a compression syringe made up the complete set.

Effective and beneficial items all, at least so long as the pilot didn't die instantly. Through them, the FPA Armed Forces seemed to be loudly declaring that they did not view soldiers as expendable and always did their utmost to preserve them. But could that really be reconciled with the way they were always glorifying the idea of death in service to the state?

Everyone feels a premonition when they're about to die—Julian had heard that somewhere. Wondering if it was true, the boy had decided to ask Yang Wen-li, who had been inches from death on any number of occasions. This is what Yang had said:

"Julian, don't tell me you're buying a bunch of hot air about death from some guy who's never even died once himself."

The harsh edge in Yang's voice at that time had not really been directed toward Julian, of course, but all the boy had been able to do was turn red in the face and withdraw.

"Control Officer, I'm ready for takeoff. Instructions, please."

Following protocol, Julian spoke first, and then the reply came, giving him his instructions.

"Very well. Proceed to launch gate."

Already, more than ten fighters had launched into the void from the mother ship. Julian's spartanian slid along the wall toward the launch gate. The wall itself was magnetized by an electric current running through it, making the spartanian's chassis adhere to it.

When it reached the edge of the gate, the current stopped, and the wall lost its magnetism.

"Launch!"

Julian's spartanian cut loose from the mother ship.

III

All around Julian, the world was spinning.

The boy swallowed his breath. He knew what was happening. In the instant he transitioned from artificial to zero gravity, his sense of up and down went haywire and he lost track of where he was. He had been through this countless times in training. Still, no matter how many times he practiced, he just couldn't seem to get the hang of it.

His breathing and pulse accelerated, and his blood pressure rose. His adrenaline-secretion reading was probably on the way up as well. His head started to feel very hot, both inside his skull and out. His heart and stomach felt like they had taken off running in opposite directions. The three canals of his inner ear were blaring out an anthem of rebellion. It took more than twenty seconds for that fanfare to soften, settle down, and at last fade away. That was when his balance and equilibrium were restored.

Julian inhaled deeply and was finally able to spare some attention for his surroundings.

He was right in the middle of a war zone. As the two sides struggled to seize the area from one another, lights were blazing in and out of existence by the second in the darkness. The darkness buried these lights in infinite depths, and the lights almost seemed to be fighting back in momentary bursts of life.

One sight stole Julian's eyes: a friendly mother ship took a hit just as it was about to release its spartanians, and all were engulfed in the explosion. The ball of light swelled outward, and after it had vanished, all that remained was an empty region of eternal darkness.

A chill ran down Julian's spine. *Thank goodness I wasn't shot the instant I cut loose*, he thought, feeling grateful for the superb timing with which the control officer aboard his own mother ship had released him.

Julian's fighter raced through spaces filled only with death and destruction. The giant shredded hulk of a damaged battleship continued to pound the enemy with beams of energy from cannons that had escaped damage, even as it buckled on the brink of death itself. Scattering the faint white light of its remaining energy, a wrecked cruiser that had lost its pilot swam right past Julian, then disappeared into the blackness. Beams seared the darkness with flashes of brilliance, missile trails threaded their way across the battlespace, and the light of exploding warships formed stars of exceedingly brief life span that illuminated all around them. Silent bolts of lightning were crisscrossing everywhere. If sound had existed in that world, eardrums would have burst from the roar of those malevolent energies, and madness would have claimed every listener as its eternal prisoner.

Suddenly, a walküre—a single-seat imperial fighter craft—swerved into Julian's field of view. He felt his heart skip a beat. It was moving so fast that by the time he did a double take, all that remained was the ship's afterimage.

Its turns were so sharp—its movements so swift and savage—it was hard to believe that it wasn't a living thing. Whoever was piloting it must have been an experienced veteran. Julian felt he could almost visualize the man's eyes, glistening with murderous intent, with certitude of victory, at the sight of the inexperienced foe before him. Even while that thought was crossing through Julian's mind, his hands were moving even faster than their owner willed. The spartanian responded with movements so sudden that its frame vibrated in protest. As abrupt, sharp changes in trajectory threatened to make him nauseous, Julian got an up-close look at the trail left by the high-power shell that had just slipped past him.

Had it just been good luck? What else could he call it? Julian had just dodged the first shot fired by a far more experienced pilot.

Underneath his flight suit, his whole body broke out in gooseflesh. He had no time for relief, however. He had to keep both eyes locked on the enemy's position on his main screen, take in data simultaneously from multiple readouts displayed on subscreens to the right and the left, and "erode enemy fighting strength with the greatest efficiency possible." *Easy for you to say!* What were the spartanian's designers and technical writers thinking—that pilots had compound eyes, like bugs? Did the survival of the other pilots—and of the empire's walküren pilots too, for that matter—depend on meeting their excessive demands? If that were the case, then all they could do was set themselves to their tasks knowing that it was hopeless.

Julian had slipped past the walküre's surefire kill shot, and its pilot, now driven by an amplified bloodlust, raced to challenge him again. Beams raced toward Julian like white-hot fangs. There were no direct hits this time either, though. Had he missed . . . or had Julian dodged?

Insofar as it was possible, Julian had to avoid moving in straight lines. Whether moving or at rest, the basic shapes of things in space were circles and spheres.

Pitch upward, pitch downward. Imagine the void as an invisible curved surface, and race along that surface as fast as possible. Though Julian didn't necessarily move according to the path he had calculated, that had the unexpected effect of throwing off the enemy's predictions as well. The two craft passed close enough to graze one another, and in the next instant, Julian was looking down on the walküre below him and pulling the trigger on his neutron beam.

Direct hit! Really? Yes, really!

White light flared out in the blackness, and chromatic splendor erupted across his whole field of view. Fragments of the destroyed walküre were thrown clear of the fireball and glittered with reflected light, turning one tiny corner of space into a kaleidoscope of rainbow hues.

Julian Mintz had just sent his first enemy pilot to the grave. Most likely, that pilot had been a warrior forged through many battles, on whose sword many comrades had no doubt fallen. Most likely, he'd never imagined that his life would be cut short by some kid who was out on his first sortie.

The rush of agitation was intense—it was like the cells in his body were being burned up from the inside. But in the same way that masses of solid rock stick up from a flow of lava, parts of Julian's heated mind felt chilled. The pilot he'd just killed—what kind of man had he been? Had he had a wife and family? A girlfriend...? That single walküre had been tied to a particular human life, from which innumerable ties must have branched out into every corner of his society.

This was not sentimentalism. It was something that ought to be etched in the mind of anyone who took it upon himself to end a human life, and remembered until the day came when the same was done to him.

Aboard the Imperial Navy vessels, people were starting to cock their heads sideways in bewilderment. At present, they had the advantage. That was a thing to be welcomed, but at the same time, they couldn't shake the feeling that something was amiss. An imbalance had appeared on the enemy side. Word had it that the Iserlohn Patrol Fleet was the cream of the FPA's crop, yet among their spartanian pilots, many were piloting their craft so poorly that their deaths seemed almost voluntary. What could be the reason? Rear Admiral Eichendorff, commanding officer of the imperial force, had been considered a first-rate tactician when he had served under Admiral Kempf, but right now he was avoiding any sudden charges, trying to secure his advantage while pressing the battle forward cautiously. This was partly because Yang Wen-li's reputation was putting him on his guard, but this stance—praiseworthy under normal circumstances—would soon be faulted for indecisiveness due to the result it led to.

Yang's executive staff had gathered in the meeting room at Iserlohn Fortress. "Admiral Yang sure loves his meetings," they often griped. But Yang had to hold meetings; if he didn't, people would say he was acting arbitrarily, had dictatorial tendencies, and so on. From Yang's standpoint, he was just giving an ear to his subordinates' opinions—he liked to think it was less trouble to do so than not.

In this case, though, there was no disagreement about the need for a swift, smooth deployment of reinforcements; the sticking point was about how large a force to send. After listening to everyone's opinion, Yang turned to Merkatz, who was working for him as an advisor.

"And what does our guest admiral have to say?"

A palpable tension filled the room, though its source might have been the executive staff, rather than either the questioner or the questioned. As a senior admiral in the imperial military, Wiliabard Joachim Merkatz had made his living working for the enemy until just last year. When Reinhard von Lohengramm, a young and powerful vassal of the empire, had crushed the confederated forces of the aristocracy, Merkatz had been talked out of suicide by his aide, Lieutenant Commander von Schneider, whereupon he had fled to the Free Planets Alliance and was named advisor to Admiral Yang.

"Reinforcements, I think, should be sent as quickly and in as great a number as possible...This allows you to deliver a single blow that the enemy can't return, recover your allies, and then quickly withdraw."

When Merkatz had spoken the word "enemy," the faintest shadow of a spirit in anguish had been evident in his aging features. Even if they were under Reinhard's command, they were still Imperial Navy, and it just wasn't possible for him to be entirely detached.

"I agree with our guest admiral's opinion. This time, committing our forces piecemeal would actually lower our chances of recovering the division and invite an escalation of the fighting. We'll go with the whole fleet, attack, and withdraw. Prepare to mobilize immediately."

The executive staff rose to their feet and saluted their commander. Even if they did have their complaints about other things, their trust in Yang's tactics was absolute. Among the rank and file, it was fair to say this trust had already become a sort of faith. After watching them file out, Yang said to Merkatz, "I'd like you to join me aboard the flagship if you don't mind. Would that be all right with you?"

Within the alliance military, Merkatz was officially being treated as a vice admiral, so there was really no need for the higher-ranking Yang to ask so nicely. Still, Yang was giving him VIP treatment.

Yang's intent, put in extreme terms, had been to accept whatever proposal Merkatz gave him, no matter how stupid it might be. When Merkatz had defected, Yang had become his guarantor. He respected Merkatz despite his having come from an enemy state and, furthermore, was willing to make some sacrifices if it would strengthen Merkatz's position in the Alliance Armed Forces.

No matter how dire the tactical situation, Yang had always achieved the maximum success possible under whatever set of conditions he was given, and he felt confident he could do so again, even if Merkatz's advice turned out to be less than top-notch. Of course, past achievements did not necessarily guarantee future successes, so in this Yang might have been overconfident.

But Merkatz's opinion was in agreement with Yang's. Yang was glad to confirm once again that he was an orthodox, reliable tactician. He felt just a little bit ashamed of himself—it really had been rude of him, thinking "no matter how stupid" in regard to this tried-and-true master tactician.

On the other hand, Yang had been considerate of Merkatz's feelings in not wanting to drag him out into direct combat with the Imperial Navy. However, if Yang were to lead the fleet out and leave Merkatz behind, there would certainly be voices raised in concern over possible dangers that might arise while the commander was away.

A ridiculous thing to worry about, Yang thought.

Yet even so, he couldn't just ignore it. It was a problem of balance in his consideration of his subordinates. Merkatz was well aware of the position Yang was in, and of his own standing as well.

Keeping his answer short and to the point, the defected guest admiral replied, "Certainly."

IV

Julian was now in the midst of an even more intense battle.

In the same instant his friend-or-foe monitor caught the weak signal, Julian was reflexively swerving his spartanian downward to port. A split second later, the empty space he had occupied was pierced by a silver lance of brilliance. Before its energies had even had time to dissipate, Julian had located the position from which it had been fired. Taking aim, he squeezed off two shots from his beam cannon and scored a direct hit on the walküre. Its frame blew apart in a swollen sphere of white-hot light. The photoflux adjustment system activated, causing the main screen to display the pulsating, expanding ball of light as though it were drawn by the tip of an illustrator's pen.

"That makes two," Julian murmured inside his helmet. He could hardly believe it himself—this was success on the battlefield. This, despite the fact that a good many new recruits were coming nowhere near to killing their opponents and were instead experiencing their last battle as well as their first. Were Julian's results merely the fruit of good luck? No. He couldn't be this lucky. At the very least, his skills had surpassed those of his foes.

His dark-brown eyes were sharp inside his helmet and gleamed with confidence. It occurred to him that he might have earned his wings already. With two kills on his first sortie, even Admiral Yang was sure to praise him.

When a new enemy appeared in front of him, he became aware of just how calm he felt. It felt like he could respond to any situation in the best way possible.

A light flared out from the walküre's rail cannon, near where its diagonally crossed foils met, but while it was still nothing more than a speck of distant light to Julian, he was already flying to port. The round missed his spartanian by mere centimeters and flew off toward eternity through the ultralow-temperature void. Julian pulled the trigger on his neutron-beam cannon, but the walküre dodged with such suddenness and speed that it seemed to have kicked off from the empty space itself. The javelin of light pierced nothing but infinite darkness.

Tch—!

The frustration Julian felt at having missed was no doubt shared by the enemy pilot. The boy was watching for a chance at a second shot, but then a group of allied and enemy fighter craft came racing into the space where he was dueling. A torrent of light and shadow filled his field of view, and Julian lost sight of his opponent.

The battle grew chaotic.

Anger at the intruders boiled up in the young man's heart. If he had just had another two or three minutes, he would have had another mark on his scorecard. That other pilot had just been lucky—

And the instant that he caught himself thinking that, Julian felt like he'd been punched in the gut.

Inwardly, he turned beet red. He had just become aware of the conceit that had taken hold of him—the illusion that destroying a brace of enemy fighters his first time out somehow made him a battle-hardened war hero. That was a joke. Hadn't his duties up until a few hours ago consisted of getting shouted at by instructors and veteran soldiers? Wasn't he just a greenhorn whose concept of battle came from imagination rather than experience? Clashes between massive fleets he had witnessed up close at Yang Wen-li's side. But at those times, it had been Yang doing the surmising, inferring, and deciding. No matter how excited and earnest he may have felt, Julian had been nothing more than a bystander with no duties of his own. To go into battle was to bear the weight of duty. Duty to carry himself properly, as well as to fight the enemy.

That was something Julian should have learned from Yang. Yang had taught him that lesson not with words, but through his attitude and actions. Yet even though Julian had reminded himself repeatedly to never forget those lessons, here he was now, getting a big head at his first taste of success. Julian felt miserable. While one man bore the duty to protect millions of subordinates and fight millions of enemies, Julian could hardly even bear his duty to himself. When would he be able to close that gap? Would that day ever come?

Even as he mused on these things, Julian continued overworking his trusty spartanian. He dodged enemy beams and avoided allied craft, saturating the empty spaces with his exhaust trail. He fired off a few dozen shots as well, but he didn't manage to score a killing shot with even one of them; maybe his guardian angel was off taking a nap now or something, or maybe he was now fighting to his actual ability.

Presently, a red light started flashing on the control panel. It was his signal to return to the mother ship. Both the spartanian itself and its neutron-beam cannon were almost out of energy. Ten minutes later, Julian docked inside the mother ship. This was accomplished by Lullaby—the special response system that operated between the mother ships and the fighter craft they carried. Julian reported to the control officer while he watched the mechanics come running.

"Sergeant Mintz, reporting. I've landed."

"Acknowledged. Permission granted to stand down during reenergizing. Please act only in accordance with regulations…"

The time given was thirty minutes. During that period he had to take a shower, eat a meal, and get ready for his next combat sortie.

The water in the shower alternated between freezing cold and hot enough to turn him red, and Julian's fresh, youthful skin contracted tightly. He got dressed, went to the mess hall, and was handed a tray. Its contents included protein-fortified milk, chicken au gratin, noodle soup, and mixed vegetables, but Julian's stomach, it seemed, was bearing the full load of his mental and physical stress, leaving him with practically no appetite at all. He drank down all of his milk and was starting to get up when, from across the table, a soldier who had also touched nothing but his milk spoke to him.

"That's the ticket, kid; it's best not to eat. If you're shot through the stomach when you're full, your abdominal wall's sure to get infected. Peritonitis. You can't be too careful."

"You're right. I'll be careful."

That was all the answer Julian gave. How effective was a warning like that when it came to combat in outer space? The greater part of the casualties out there were blown to bits instantaneously, just as Julian's opponents had been. Even if someone did get shot only through the abdomen, the pressure differential between the inside and outside of his body would push out his organs, boil his heart and brain cells with the blood in his own veins, and send fountains of blood spraying from his mouth, ears, and nose long before any abdominal-wall infections could bring about the onset of peritonitis. There was no way he would survive. Still, if a soldier could move his odds even a micron closer to surviving, it was his duty to make every effort to do so. That was the real lesson Julian had just learned from that soldier.

Twenty-five minutes had elapsed by the time he left the mess hall. He ran to catch an electric car bound for the flight deck. It was about to depart with five or six soldiers. He leapt lightly aboard and jumped off three minutes later.

His spartanian was already prepped and ready for relaunch. Julian put his gloves on while walking quickly toward the fighter craft. One of the mechanics called out to him: "Break a leg, kid! But don't get yourself killed!"

"Thanks!" Julian called back.

But as he answered, his mood soured just a little.

He didn't want to die, after all. Not while he was still young enough to be called "kid."

The second launch went well—at least compared to the first one.

The instant the mother ship cut him loose from its gravity control system, his sense of up and down was still thrown completely off-kilter, yet even so he was able to shake off the disorientation in about ten seconds this time.

Like flowers blooming in a night-black garden, the lights of energy beams and explosions were blossoming and scattering their petals, all of them proof of humanity's passion for murder and destruction. The dregs of that wasted passion gave rise to tumultuous swells of chaotic energy that came rolling in to pitch and toss the tiny spartanian about.

Julian wanted to know how the battle was progressing overall, but with the battlespace currently roiled with invisible billows of EM waves and jamming signals, it would be useless to try to get anything out of his comm system. The fleet was somehow maintaining an organic, flexible posture by using all manner of transmission signals and—perhaps a bit amusingly—shuttlecraft bearing message capsules. In ground-based battles, allies had communicated using relayed orders, and sometimes even messenger dogs and homing pigeons, which meant that the clock on this battlefield had in a sense swung back almost two thousand years.

In any case, Julian didn't think his allies had the upper hand. Rear Admiral Attenborough was a capable commander, but in this battle his subordinates wouldn't—no, couldn't—act according to his wishes, aside from a small number of exceptions like Julian. Their newest recruits were probably proving ideal sacrifices for the enemy's gruesome carnival. For his part, at least, all Julian could do was pray for the safety of his mother ship, *Amərətāt*. The word *amərətāt* meant "immortal," he had heard, and Julian sincerely hoped that would prove an apt description.

A surprise arrived just as he was thinking that, as a huge wall rose up in front of his spartanian, blocking the way. If he hadn't instinctively put his craft into an emergency climb, he would have slammed right into it and met with certain death.

It was a cruiser. Compared to a battleship it was small, but next to a spartanian it could be only be described as a mobile fortress. A conglomeration of geometrical shapes formed from metal, resin, and crystalline fiber, it was a palpable mirage born of bloodthirsty engineering technology. At just that moment, it was basking in the glory of having turned an alliance cruiser into a ball of flame.

Julian knew instinctively that he dare not make any careless moves. If he took a direct hit from a cruiser's main cannon, he would be wiped from the universe before the pain could even register. That might, in a sense, be an ideal way to die, but Julian had no desire to go down that road. He adjusted his speed to about the cruiser's and maintained a cautious distance of around three meters from its outer hull. He was practically touching the energy-neutralization field emitted by the cruiser.

Suddenly, one of the gun turrets on the hull began to swivel toward him, but its muzzle failed to lock on. Julian had probably been spotted by its enemy-detection system momentarily but had now ducked into its blind spot. From the cruiser's standpoint, a tiny, vastly inferior foe had flown right up next to it while it was busy slaughtering an enemy its own size. Moreover, it was precisely because no real eyes were actually used in sighting enemies that the cruiser was having such a hard time judging whether that shrewd little foe had run away or was right up against it.

Julian waited. Taking no action of any sort, and with the beat of his heart his only companion, he waited for the scales to tip in his direction. After a few moments that seemed to last an eternity, a small slit opened in the back side of the gigantic enemy vessel, and from it rose the silvery-gray warhead of a photon missile. Its malicious, hemispherical tip was taking aim at an FPA destroyer. Julian held his breath. Just as the missile launched—in the instant that it penetrated the force field from the inside—Julian emerged from his formless hideout, fired his neutron-beam cannon, and launched immediately into a steep emergency climb. Behind him, a burst of light exploded, and a rolling wave of energy scooped up his spartanian, tossed it up high, and then scooped it up again...

"Cruiser *Rembach* has just been destroyed."

Operator reports often left Commander Eisendorff feeling unpleasant. Whether the report was delivered with robotic calm or with a hysterical sense of emergency, both styles had a way of scrambling his nerves. *So what?* he wanted to shout back at them. The solitude of command—that inability to delegate judgments and decisions to anyone else—was making him want to lash out at these people who had no such responsibilities.

"Stop reporting every needless detail!" he said, rewarding the operator with not only a shout, but a blow to the back of the head as well. Perhaps the operator too could now be numbered among Julian's victims.

Over on the Alliance Armed Forces' side, however, Rear Admiral Attenborough was feeling a similar sort of irritation. Although possessed of outstanding qualities as a commander, someone else might indeed be better suited to the challenge of leading this "troop of boy scouts" into battle.

For Attenborough, Rear Admiral Eisendorff's excessively circumspect attitude came as an unexpected salvation, and yet at the same time, it was slowly but surely increasing his fear that their fatal weakness might be discovered at any moment. It was then that Attenborough, who had been shouldering the nigh-unbearable weight of command, saw an allied vessel flit calmly across his main screen as though it hadn't a care in the world. Doing a double take, he asked his aide, "That was *Ulysses* just now, wasn't it?"

"Yes, sir. Battleship *Ulysses*."

At the sound of that name, a smile spread across Attenborough's youthful features. Even in the midst of fierce battle, it was still possible to tickle humanity's undying sense of humor. *Ulysses* was the leading "brawler" of the Iserlohn Patrol Fleet, surpassing almost all the other vessels in terms of both its number of combat flights and its distinguished military successes. Nevertheless, *Ulysses* was most widely renowned as "the battleship with broken toilets," which was why its name never failed to draw a grin when spoken or heard. The nickname had no basis in fact, but to most people, a falsehood dressed up to suit their own tastes was far more enjoyable than a prosaic fact, no matter how annoying that falsehood might be to its target...

"I'd like some of that ship's good luck to rub off on the rest of us," said Attenborough. "All hands, stay alive, even if you look bad doing it."

The sound of laughter broke out around the bridge, and if only for a moment, a feeling that things would be all right drifted through the air. Though the crew of *Ulysses* might prefer otherwise, the ship's nickname was clearly effective in easing the tension of fleet personnel and revitalizing them in both body and spirit.

Nine hours had already passed since the battle had commenced. During that time, Julian had flown four sorties from his mother ship, *Amərətāt*. On his third time out, he had destroyed neither fighter nor warship. This had probably been because the spartanian squadrons, having lost fighter after fighter, were becoming easy prey for walküren gunfire, and a gap had appeared between the two sides in terms of numbers of surviving fighter craft. Coming under fire from two walküren at once, Julian had been forced to desperately flee this way and that just trying to stay alive. Julian had soon given up on useless counterattacks and focused only on escaping. The two walküren had competed over their prey, both relying on solo moves rather than cooperating. If not for both of these factors, Julian would have been dead. But instead, the two walküren had interfered with each other. After Julian had shaken them off and just barely managed to flee back to his mother ship's womb, he had sat in the cockpit for a while afterward with his head down, unable to say so much as a word.

And then there had been his fourth sortie—or more properly, his escape from the mother ship after it had taken a hit. In defiance of its name, the "immortal" *Amərətāt* had fallen prey to fusion missiles and broken in half across its center. Both pieces had exploded separately. After Julian, nearly engulfed in the huge, expanding fireball, had at last escaped into empty space, a walküre had appeared in front of him. He had been just a fraction of a second faster in pulling the trigger that blew it to pieces. The walküre's enemy-detection functions had been severely impaired by the ball of fire at Julian's back. Although he had been victorious, his recharging aboard the mother ship had been incomplete, which meant that his energy reserves were still nearly depleted. With despair clouding his dark-brown eyes, he had turned to look at the monitor, staring at it as he held his breath and gave a nervous laugh. Countless points of light had appeared from the direction of Iserlohn Fortress, forming a rapidly expanding wall of light.

On the bridge of the battleship *Triglav*, the comm officer stood up and shouted, "Reinforcements have arrived! Reinforcements have arrived!" He considered it his duty to show a bit of an overreaction and drum up morale among his comrades.

And the effect was spectacular. Cheers rose up, and countless berets flew into the air. To inform allied vessels, and at the same time rub their enemies' faces in it, EM signals whose interception was fully expected went racing across the comm channels of the FPA forces.

Meanwhile, the imperial forces were in shock. Operators aboard every vessel had gone pale in the face as they stared into their monitors, paralyzing their commanders with reports that bordered on screams.

"Over *ten thousand*?!" the commanders groaned. "That's not even a contest!" The word "withdraw" was flashing brightly in their minds. They had not lost the part of their reason that calculated advantage and disadvantage, and they had just enough flexibility to sound a withdrawal when the answer came up "disadvantage." The imperial fleet's own reinforcements would not be long in coming, but they lacked the huge force strength of the enemy, and more importantly, it was almost certain that once they themselves had been wiped out, it would be their reinforcements' turn to be destroyed separately. Eisendorff, setting an example for the others, began the retreat.

"The enemy has lost the will to fight and is taking flight. Shall we pursue?"

On the bridge of the battleship *Hyperion*, Lieutenant Frederica Greenhill awaited instructions from their dark-haired commander.

"No, let them go," Yang said.

If the imperial force retreated and their allies were saved, then the goals of this mobilization had been achieved. It would serve no strategic purpose to surround and annihilate a numerically inferior enemy force that didn't want to fight, nor would it give him any pleasure as a tactician to do so. The main reason he had brought such a large force out in the first place had been to scare off the enemy without fighting.

"In that case, Excellency, shall we recover those whose ships have been destroyed and head back together as soon as emergency repairs are completed?"

"That'll be fine. Oh, and to prevent something like this from happening in the future, we should probably deploy a few surveillance and relay satellites in this area as well."

"Yes, sir, I'll see to it right away."

Merkatz looked on with gentle approval as Frederica briskly executed her commander's instructions. Even in his long record of service, he couldn't remember many aides as competent as she.

"Also, about Sergeant Julian Mintz—"

As Frederica prepared to give a new report, she saw the outline of Yang's body appear to stiffen just slightly.

"He's returned safely." Looking on with warmth as the strength drained out of Yang's shoulders, Frederica continued. "He destroyed three walküren and one cruiser."

"He destroyed a cruiser? In his very first battle?" It wasn't Yang who had spoken; it was the commander of fortress defenses, Walter von Schönkopf, who had come aboard saying he wanted to see the results of the new recruits' training. He was also Julian's instructor in marksmanship and hand-to-hand combat. Frederica nodded, and he clapped his hands together, looking pleased.

"That kid is all surprises. He's a natural at this. Not even I got to show off that much on my first outing. I'm actually kind of worried about just how much he'll grow in the future..."

"What are you talking about?" said Yang. "All he's done is blow through a lifetime's worth of good luck in one go. If he ends up taking a light view of battle now, this won't have been good for him. The real test starts now."

Yang had intended to speak with the attitude of a strict instructor, but when he saw Frederica and von Schönkopf's faces, he knew right away that he could claim no success in that. Their faces seemed to be telling him, *You really don't have to try so hard.*

It was in this manner that Julian Mintz concluded his first combat outing.

He had emerged alive.

CHAPTER 2:
THE FORTRESS TAKES FLIGHT

WHILE THE FIGHTING that erupted in the Iserlohn Corridor in January of Space Era 798—or Imperial Year 489—was large in scale, it actually concluded as nothing more than a border skirmish.

Admiral Yang Wen-li, commander of Iserlohn Fortress and the man responsible for the FPA military forces in the conflict, had returned the fleet to the fortress right afterward, making no attempt to escalate the fighting.

On the imperial side, Karl Gustav Kempf was responsible for security in this region of space. Although Kempf apologized for failing to wipe out the enemy, the military's supreme commander, Imperial Marshal Reinhard von Lohengramm, had waved the matter away, saying, "In a hundred battles, we can't expect a hundred victories. You needn't apologize for each and every setback."

It would have been one thing if the loss had been in a huge battle with the fate of the nation hanging in the balance, but Reinhard, in his other role as imperial prime minister, had to devote most of his time and energy to improving domestic affairs and expanding his own power base. He didn't have time to spend harping on a localized battle that had little strategic or diplomatic significance.

Reinhard had turned twenty-two, and both a shade of melancholy and a ruler's dignity had been added to his natural comeliness, giving him a presence of late that called to mind that of some demigod. To the soldiers, his was a presence worthy of awe—awe made of the same stuff as religious faith. One of the reasons for that was the manner in which he lived.

After his sister Annerose had moved out, Reinhard had vacated the estate in Schwarzen and moved into military officers' housing. True, it was a house built for a high-ranking officer, but for a lord who ruled over twenty-five billion citizens and several thousand star systems, it was positively frugal. It had a study, a bedroom, a bathroom, a living room, a dining room, and a kitchen, as well as a private room for a personal attendant—and that was all, aside from accommodations for his security detail, located in one corner of the garden.

"This is too modest for one serving as imperial prime minister. I'm not suggesting extravagance, but don't you think something that would display your authority a little more is in order?"

Such comments were naturally heard in Reinhard's circles, but a faint, indifferent smile was the only answer he ever gave.

Poverty of desire when it came to material goods was one point where Reinhard and Yang Wen-li's natures intersected. Though his soul hungered after glory and earthly power, these things didn't take tangible form. Power, of course, promised material fulfillment. If he had wanted to, Reinhard could have lived in a marble palace, had beautiful women in every room, and owned gold and precious jewels piled as high as his waist, but doing so would have only made him an unseemly caricature of Rudolf the Great. Rudolf had been a man with an irresistible compulsion for manifesting his vast, incomparable power as material riches. In addition to Neue Sans Souci Palace, the pinnacle of his magnificence, he had kept wide manor houses and hunting grounds, countless chamberlains and ladies-in-waiting, paintings, sculptures, precious metals, gemstones, a private orchestra, personal guards, extravagant passenger ships for touring the empire, portrait artists, wineries . . . Rudolf had monopolized the best of everything. Aristocrats had crowded in around him, holding up before their delighted faces whatever baubles his large hands threw their way. In a sense, they had known their place quite well, living in subjection to a giant—the first to make himself despot of all humanity—in a manner more like slaves than like cattle. The only reason they hadn't wagged their tails for Rudolf had been that they'd lacked them. From time to time, Rudolf would bestow beautiful women from his harem on his courtiers. Because these women usually came with manor houses, titles, jewels, and more, the courtiers would accept them gladly and go to boast to the other nobles of the favor they had found in the sight of His Imperial Highness.

Reinhard, at present, lived completely divorced from such spiritual rot. There was not a soul alive who could show Reinhard to be anything other than a creative and enterprising statesman, no matter how deeply they might despise him.

"Two things are essential for getting people to trust in the system: fair courts and equally fair taxation. Just these two."

In these words, Reinhard demonstrated that he had a gift for ruling the nation as well as for waging war. Even if both of his essentials had sprung from the same well of personal ambition, he was nonetheless giving voice to exactly what the multitudes were longing for.

While Reinhard was pushing forward tax reforms and working to establish fair criminal and civil codes, he gave sprawling manors that had once belonged to the old aristocracy away to farmers free of charge and freed the serfs on those manors. The mansions of many of the nobles who had been wiped out after aligning with Duke von Braunschweig's camp were opened to the public and became hospitals and public-welfare facilities. The aristocrats had kept their paintings, sculptures, chinaware, and precious metal craftworks all under lock and key, but now these things were appropriated by the state and placed in public museums.

"...Lovely gardens are trampled underfoot by mean fellows of low birth, thick carpets bear the stains of muddy shoes, and canopy beds where only the noble were once permitted to lie are now sullied with the drool of filthy children. Now this once-great nation has fallen into the hands of half beasts, incapable of comprehending either beauty or nobility. Ah, that this disgraceful and wretched spectacle were but a single night's ill dream..."

With anger and hatred dripping from the tip of his pen, one of the aristocrats had written thus in his journal after being stripped of his wealth and privilege. The nobles had refused to so much as consider the fact that the bountiful lifestyle they had enjoyed up till now had been thanks to an unjust societal system, supported by the labor and sacrifices of "mean fellows of low birth." Nor did it occur to them that their failure to reflect on that system had undermined the ground beneath their feet and brought about their fall.

As long as his enemies were those longing only for glories past, Reinhard would have no need to fear them. The most they could possibly do was launch plots against society or terrorist attacks, and outside of the proaristocracy extremists, such tactics would find no support or backing among the people.

At present, the people were on Reinhard's side, and they were watching the former aristocrats like hawks, eyes burning with hostility and thirst for revenge. Their former rulers had been shut up inside an invisible cage.

Reinhard's hands of ruthless reform extended not only into the financial and legal systems, but into administrative organizations as well. At the Ministry of Domestic Affairs, the Bureau for the Maintenance of Public Order—that infamous executor of imperial policy that had long dominated the public and suppressed independent thought—was shuttered after nearly five hundred years. Bureau chief Heidrich Lang was placed under surveillance by von Oberstein, and all thought and political criminals—with the exception of terrorists and radical proponents of republican government—were released. A number of newspapers and magazines that had previously been banned were also given permission to resume publishing.

Special financial institutions that had been exclusive to the nobility were abolished and replaced with Farmer's Safes, which provided low-interest farming loans to freed serfs. "Reinhard the Liberator!" "Reinhard the Reformer!" The praises of the citizenry swelled ever louder.

"Duke von Lohengramm isn't just skilled on the battlefield—he really knows how to ingratiate himself with the public, too," whispered Karl Bracke, a VIP in the "knowledge and civilization" movement who was helping Reinhard with his reforms, to his comrade, Eugen Richter.

"That's true. He may well be trying to win favor with the people. Still, the old aristocratic regime wouldn't have done even that. All they ever did was unilaterally squeeze the people for everything they were worth. Compared to that, this is without a doubt progress and improvement."

"Still," said Bracke, "Can you really call it progress if it doesn't lead toward self-rule by the people?"

"Progress is progress," said Richter. A mild note of irritation lurked in his voice, directed at Bracke's dogmatism. "Even though a powerful authority above is what's pushing this, once the public has been given greater rights, he can't just suddenly take them away again. Right now, the best option for us is to back Duke von Lohengramm and propel these reforms. Don't you agree?"

Bracke nodded, but there was something in his eyes that was neither satisfaction nor agreement...

II

Tech Admiral Anton Hilmer von Schaft, the imperial military's commissioner of science and technology, was a fifty-year-old man who held doctoral degrees in both engineering and philosophy. His hairline had retreated to the top of his head, but his dark-red whiskers and eyebrows were thick and fluffy. With a reddish nose, a plump, rounded body, and the sheen of a well-nourished baby, he might at first glance be mistaken for the proprietor of a beer hall.

However, the glint in his eye was no mere barkeep's. R&D skills aside, rumor had it that this tech admiral had reached the position he held today not only through raw talent, but also through combativeness in driving out bosses, leapfrogging over colleagues, and holding back subordinates. It was also said that his ambition was to become the first imperial marshal in history to reach that rank as a military scientist rather than as a fleet commander or operations advisor.

On the day that von Schaft paid a call to the Lohengramm admiralität, Reinhard had just finished his morning's work and was in the middle of eating lunch. He scowled when he heard the name of the visitor. During von Schaft's past six years of lording over the Science and Technology

Commission, he had maintained his position and privileges by making full use of political power—all the while achieving little aside from the development of directional Seffl particles. Reinhard certainly wasn't fond of the man.

More than once, Reinhard had considered dismissing him and reshuffling the lineup at the Science and Technology Commission. Over the last six years, however, those regarded as competitors to von Schaft had been driven to the sidelines without exception, while von Schaft's supporters had monopolized all the important posts within the commission. To be sure, Reinhard could have dismissed von Schaft and reorganized his faction, but doing so would have certainly caused numerous disruptions in the day-to-day operations of the organization. There was also the fact that von Schaft had long shown a willingness to cooperate with Reinhard, and not with the boyar nobles only.

So in short, Reinhard wanted to cut von Schaft loose but had thus far been unable to find a good enough reason to do so. He was quietly having his people search for a replacement, while biding his time to see if von Schaft might make some huge blunder or get caught mixing public and personal business. Still, von Schaft was just one man, and there was little room in Reinhard's busy schedule to spend on his disposition. The state of the empire desperately called for the constructive side of Reinhard's genius.

On that day as well, Reinhard's afternoon schedule was packed with meetings with various high-ranking domestic officials slated to explain a number of thorny issues relating to such things as property rights over lands formerly owned by the aristocracy, rules at the planetary level regarding taxation and police judiciary powers, and the reorganization of central government offices. Because these were matters for the imperial prime minister, Reinhard had to leave the admiralität after lunch and go to the office of the prime minister. Although he could have simply said the word and had those high-ranking officials come to the admiralität, something either fastidious or stubborn in the young man refused to make things easier for himself in such matters.

"I'll see him, but for fifteen minutes only."

Von Schaft, however, had other ideas about that. Hoping to enthrall the young imperial marshal, he launched into a long, impassioned monologue that disrupted Reinhard's schedule, forcing those officials to wait on their young ruler at the prime minister's office.

"...So in other words," said Reinhard, "you're saying our military should construct a fortress, which would serve as a stronghold for our forces directly in front of Iserlohn?"

"Precisely, Your Excellency," the commissioner of science and technology said gravely, nodding his head. He had clearly been expecting to be complimented, but what he discerned in the handsome face of that young imperial prime minister were shades of disgust and disappointment.

Reinhard felt like saying that even a scant fifteen minutes with this man was a waste of his time.

"As a plan, it isn't bad," he said, "but there is one condition that would have to be met in order for it to succeed."

"And that is?"

"The alliance military would have to sit there and quietly watch while our forces were building it."

The commissioner of science and technology fell silent. He seemed to be at a loss for an answer.

"No, Commissioner," Reinhard added. "I don't mean to say the idea's unattractive—it's just hard to call it realistic. How about making another proposal later, once you've addressed what needs to be fixed."

With a lithe movement, Reinhard started to get up. If he had to deal with this haughty, unpleasant man for even another minute, the stress was going to get to him, and he'd say something he shouldn't.

"Please, just one moment," said von Schaft. "That condition is unnecessary. Why, you ask? Because my idea..."—here the commissioner of science and technology raised his voice to considerable theatrical effect— "...is to bring an extant fortress into the Iserlohn Corridor."

Reinhard turned and looked at von Schaft head-on. The face his gaze pierced was a lump of confidence, kneaded and kilned. A flicker of interest appeared in his ice-blue eyes, and he lowered himself back down onto his couch.

"Shall we hear the details?"

The gleam of victory added another layer of gloss to the commissioner of science and technology's too-ruddy complexion. Though the sight was hardly pleasing to Reinhard, his interest now exceeded his annoyance.

III

No one had ever described Admiral Karl Gustav Kempf as possessed of a deeply jealous nature, nor was anyone ever likely to hereafter. He was a broad-minded and fair individual, deemed outstanding both in leadership ability and in courage.

Even Kempf, however, had pride and a competitive spirit. In the Lippstadt War last year, the battlefield achievements of Mittermeier and von Reuentahl had been remarkable, and both had advanced to the rank of senior admiral, while Kempf himself had remained at the rank of full admiral. Even if he hadn't felt slighted about that, he had felt it was a pity. After all, he had turned thirty-six this year and was older than either of them.

Then, no sooner had the new year begun than one of the fleets under his command had been subjected to some difficult combat during a border skirmish in the Iserlohn Corridor. His pride couldn't help but be wounded, and Kempf had begun to look for a chance to reclaim his honor—in other words, for another battle. Still, he couldn't start another fight simply to salve his wounded pride, and so unfulfilling days had rolled past as he attended to his duties of training personnel and patrolling the border.

That was what he had been doing when a message arrived from Reinhard, telling him to return to the imperial capital of Odin and present himself at the Lohengramm admiralität.

Kempf, along with his aide Lieutenant Lubitsch, was greeted at the admiralität by sublieutenant von Rücke. Von Rücke, still a young man of twenty-two, had served under Kempf for a time but had been attached to the admiralität since last year. He showed Kempf to Reinhard's office, where the admiral spied the handsome young imperial marshal with golden hair and ice-blue eyes, and one other person besides: Tech Admiral von Schaft.

"You're early, Kempf," Reinhard said. "Von Oberstein and Müller will be with us shortly. Have a seat over there while you wait."

As he did as Reinhard said, Kempf couldn't help feeling a little surprised.

He was very much aware of the young imperial marshal's distaste for the snobbish tech admiral.

At last, Senior Admiral Paul von Oberstein arrived, followed by Admiral Neidhart Müller.

Von Oberstein doubled as both acting secretary-general of Imperial Military Command Headquarters and chief of staff of the Imperial Space Armada, and as such, there was nothing unusual about his attending an important gathering. He was, as it were, representing rear operations. On the other hand, the combat commanders would normally be represented by von Reuentahl or Mittermeier; however, neither of them were present today. Even among the full admiral stratum of the admiralty, Müller was lower in the pecking order than Kempf or Wittenfeld, and was younger as well. His successes in battle and an outstanding ability to get the job done were the reasons he wore the rank of admiral at such a young age, but he had not yet established an unshakable reputation comparable to those of his colleagues.

"Well, everyone seems to be here now," said Reinhard. "Shall we have Tech Admiral von Schaft explain his proposal?"

At Reinhard's prodding, von Schaft rose to his feet. The sight of him reminded Kempf of a bantam chicken, comb bristling triumphantly. He seemed like the sort for whom mental exhilaration would lead straight past confidence and on into overconfidence.

Von Schaft gave a signal, and a three-dimensional image, controlled from the operator's room, appeared in midair. It was a gleaming silver sphere—entirely unremarkable at a passing glance. However, its shape was unmistakable to anyone serving in the military of either the empire or the alliance.

"Admiral Kempf, I wonder if you could tell us what this is?" Von Schaft spoke in the tone of a teacher, not a soldier. The fact that he was about twenty years older than Kempf was probably one reason he assumed that tone of voice.

"It's Iserlohn Fortress," Kempf said politely. He restrained some vocal inflections of his own due to Reinhard's presence in the room. Probably for the same reason, Müller also seemed a bit more formal than necessary.

Von Schaft nodded and stuck out his thick chest.

"Our home, the Galactic Empire, is the sole governing body of all humanity, but violent rebels refuse to recognize it, and have continuously wrought destruction and bloodshed across the galaxy for the past century and a half! Presumptuously, they dare to call themselves the 'Free Planets Alliance,' while in reality they are nothing more than the descendents of an extremist mob who strayed from their path as imperial subjects long, long ago. They are playing out a farce, resisting something whose scale they can't imagine."

What in the world does this conceited boor want to tell us? Kempf wondered silently. *He hasn't the slightest trace of humility about what he's saying.* Although their faces and attitudes were all different, none of the four listeners were impressed in the slightest by this unoriginal speech.

Von Schaft continued: "For peace throughout the universe and for the unification of the human race, we must destroy those rebels of the Free Planets Alliance. In order to do that, we can't just respond to enemy incursions; we should attack from our side and take control of the enemy's home territory. However, that territory is far too distant, and the lines of supply and communication far too long. Furthermore, there is only one path connecting them—the tunnel that is the Iserlohn Corridor—and because of that, the defending side has the advantage of being able to concentrate its forces. This means that the attacking side, on the other hand, is particularly limited in its tactical options.

"The imperial military was once able to strike deeply into enemy territory because we had Iserlohn Fortress as a bridgehead and could also use it as a station for resupply. However, Iserlohn is at present in the hands of the enemy, and thus the imperial military is unable to pass through the corridor to strike at the enemy's strongholds. At present, the alliance's military has not recovered from its crushing defeat at Amritsar or from the blows that it took during last year's internal uprising. If only we could recapture Iserlohn, it would be possible for our military to seize all of the alliance's territories in one fell swoop. Moreover, Yang Wen-li, the most brilliant admiral in the alliance's military, is at Iserlohn, and if we can capture or kill him at the same time we bring down the fortress, we will be able to deal a fatal blow to their military, from a human-capital perspective.

"However, from the standpoint of hardware alone, Iserlohn is impregnable—an artificial sphere sixty kilometers in diameter, wrapped in four repeating layers of superhardened steel, crystalline fiber, and superceramic, and each layer plated with a beam-resistant mirror coating. We can't scratch it—not even with the high-powered cannons of a giant battleship. That's not merely theoretical; it has been proven by the fact that the alliance military was never able to take it by attacking from the outside.

"If Iserlohn can't be captured by fleets of warships, what, then, can we do about it? The only way to retake it is to bring to bear armor and firepower rivaling that of Iserlohn itself. In other words, to strike a fortress with a fortress. To move a fortress capable of opposing Iserlohn to a point right in front of it and attack Iserlohn from there."

When Tech Admiral von Schaft stopped speaking and looked around at the other four men, Reinhard, who had known already what he was going to say, did not appear surprised. As for von Oberstein, even if he were inwardly surprised, it didn't show in his face or his movements. That wasn't the case for the others, however. Kempf took a deep breath. He was tapping his powerful fingers on the armrests of his chair, while Müller kept shaking his head as he mumbled something inside his mouth.

Von Schaft began to speak again.

"If you're looking for a fortress within the empire that could stand up to Iserlohn, look no further than Gaiesburg Fortress, which was used as the stronghold of the aristocrat confederation during the civil war last year, and remains abandoned even now. Repair it, attach warp and conventional navigation engines, move it ten thousand light-years, and challenge Iserlohn to a duel of fortresses. The output of current warp engines is not enough to send a gigantic fortress, though, which means we must attach a dozen of them in a ring configuration and activate them simultaneously. It's perfectly feasible with existing technology; everything else will depend on the commander's leadership and ability to carry out the operation."

Von Schaft sat back down, practically bursting at the seams with his inflated ego. In his stead, Reinhard rose to his feet.

"This is why I called you here."

With his spirited, ice-blue eyes fixed upon them, the two admirals straightened in their seats.

"I name Kempf as commander and Müller as vice commander. Following the commissioner of science and technology's plan, you are to recapture Iserlohn."

The appointment of Admiral Karl Gustav Kempf as commander and Admiral Neidhart Müller as vice commander for this new operation made a few waves in the imperial military. This was because it was natural to assume that one of the senior admirals—either von Reuentahl or Mittermeier—would be taking command of such an operation so vast in scale and so isolated.

Naturally, neither of the two senior admirals made any public remarks about the matter, but when they were alone, they couldn't help voicing their disappointment to one another.

"In any case," said Mittermeier, "it was probably decided by *His Lordship*, Chief of Staff von Oberstein."

It was prejudice rather than guesswork that led Mittermeier to make that assertion, but he wasn't all that far off the mark. When Reinhard had asked von Oberstein's advice regarding the appointment of operational command, the man had not answered right away but had instead asked the opinion of Captain Ferner, who was on his team of advisors.

"If admirals von Reuentahl and Mittermeier are successful," said Ferner, "the only rank left to reward them with is imperial marshal, and if they get that, it would make them equal in rank to Duke von Lohengramm. That wouldn't be good for keeping order in the ranks. If, on the other hand, you choose from among the full admirals, you can promote them to senior admiral if they succeed and at the same time avoid letting von Reuentahl and Mittermeier stand too far apart from the rest. And even if they fail, you won't have used up any trump cards, so the loss would be comparatively light."

That opinion had been a match for von Oberstein's thinking. To maintain order in the ranks—and to elevate the authority of the one at the top—it was vital to avoid creating a number two. That was what had worried von Oberstein when Siegfried Kircheis was alive. Kircheis had been rewarded with countless honors after he had died protecting Reinhard. There was no problem at all with bestowing excessive honors on the dead, but it was a different situation with the living. Now that Kircheis was gone, it would make no sense to let Mittermeier or von Reuentahl fill his vacant position. It was vital to create plenty of number threes but no number two, to scatter the organization's power and functionality, and to strengthen Reinhard's dictatorial system.

That being the case, if von Oberstein were to ever try seizing the number two spot himself, he could never avoid the criticism of opportunism. Yet even Mittermeier, who despised von Oberstein, acknowledged the fact that the man harbored no lust for position. What he wanted was something else.

"Let's make it Kempf," Reinhard had said when von Oberstein advised him to choose from among the full admirals. "He's been wanting to wash away the shame of that previous defeat. Let's give him the chance."

For vice commander, Reinhard naturally needed someone below Kempf, and so he had chosen Müller, who was both younger and less experienced.

⁙

At that time, somewhere in the world of Reinhard's psyche, a veil had come down between himself and the fierce passion that had brought him to this point, and he was developing a point of view by which he coldly, distantly regarded even himself. He didn't know whether to call it a cold passion or a dry emptiness. He felt as if his legs—created so he could leap to the very heights of heaven—had suffered a striking reduction in power.

He knew the cause; he just couldn't bear to face it head-on. Reinhard kept telling himself that he was a strong person who didn't need the help or understanding of others. Before, it had taken no effort at all to think such a thing. All he had needed to do was turn and look back every once in a while, and Siegfried Kircheis would be right there, following behind at a half step's distance. That had always made everything clear. *That was it!* The dream had been worth something because it had been shared. And that was why he'd had to realize that ambition: because it wasn't his alone.

All of space would be his. Even if he lost his shadow, even if one of the wings were ripped from his back, still his fangs would remain. If Reinhard von Lohengramm were ever to lose those fangs, the fact that he been born into the world would lose all its meaning. Right now, he needed to sharpen them, even if they were doomed to break in the end.

IV

After the death last year of Siegfried Kircheis—that bulwark of unparalleled loyalty, insight, and ability—it had been Wolfgang Mittermeier and Oskar von Reuentahl who had emerged as the two pillars of Reinhard's admiralty.

Both were deemed virtuoso tacticians who lacked for nothing when it came to valor and clever planning. If the circumstances demanded it, they could run a frontal breakthrough and a backward expansion, launch an all-out onslaught head-on, or take an exclusively defensive posture around a base, employing the highest standards of strategic technique. The deadly swiftness with which Mittermeier carried out his operations and the coolheadedness and persistence von Reuentahl displayed both offensively and defensively were not easy qualities to come by; when it came to reading situations accurately, standing firm in the midst of crisis, adapting flexibly to changing circumstances, and preparing for all contingencies, it was hard to say who was better.

Senior Admiral Wolfgang Mittermeier was exactly thirty years of age, with unruly honey-blond hair and light-gray eyes. While he was somewhat small of stature, he had the firm, well-balanced body of a gymnast and moved like speed itself made flesh.

Senior Admiral Oskar von Reuentahl was a tall man of thirty-one with dark-brown—almost black—hair and an aristocratic sort of handsomeness, but his most striking feature was his eyes—his right eye was black and his left eye was blue. He was a heterochromiac.

In terms of reputation and accomplishments, the two of them were an even match, but neither had ever created a faction to oppose the other. In fact, they had shared many of their accomplishments by operating jointly on the battlefield. Off the battlefield, they spent a great deal of time together as friends, and to onlookers it seemed both mystifying and utterly natural that they could maintain this relationship despite their equivalent ranks and very different temperaments.

Mittermeier was of common birth, and his family was fairly average in terms of social standing and standard of living. His father was a landscaping engineer and had long been doing steady business with a clientele of aristocrats and wealthy commoners.

"In this kind of top-down society," he had taught his young son, "the way for common folk to get by is to get a trade."

He had surely been hoping that his son would become a technician or artisan and lead a life free of any turbulent ups and downs. And an artisan was in fact what his son had grown up to be, reaching a level at which he was even called a master. However, the field through which he had advanced was not gardening or handicrafts—but the tumultuous field called "war."

When Mittermeier was sixteen, he had enrolled in the Imperial Armed Forces Academy. Oskar von Reuentahl had been one year ahead of him, but they had had no chance to meet one another while still in school. At the academy, upperclassmen often ganged up on underclassmen, interfering with them and applying pressure in all kinds of ways, but von Reuentahl had cared not a whit for that sort of group activity.

During the summer of his second year there, Mittermeier had returned home from the dormitory after a long absence to learn that his family had increased in number by one. A girl distantly related to his mother had lost her father in the war and come to live with them.

This girl of twelve, Evangeline, had cream-colored hair, violet eyes, and rosy cheeks, and while she may not have been an incomparable beauty, her smile never faded as she went busily about her work, lively and brisk. Whenever she trotted off somewhere, she would leave a feeling of lightness and cheer in the air behind her, like when a swallow soars through a spring sky.

"*Michél, Michél, Michél. Stehe auf—es ist heller lichter Tag.*"

The sound of her singing had resounded pleasantly in Mittermeier's ears: *Michél, Michél, Michél. Wake up—the weather's bright and clear*…

"She's such a cheerful, honest girl, isn't she, Wolf?"

The academy cadet had replied to his mother in perfunctory monosyllables, as if he indeed had not the slightest interest in this newcomer. From that point on, however, he had started to make a lot of trips home when he had leave, which gave his parents a clear window straight down to the bottom of his heart.

At last, Mittermeier graduated from the academy and was made an ensign. His parents and Evangeline saw him off when he departed to the battlefield. As a soldier, this swift and courageous youth had clearly found his vocation. In very short order, he managed to distinguish himself enough to rise within the hierarchy. But although he was decisive and swift to act in every other matter, he agonized over that violet-eyed girl for seven years before he made up his mind to seek her hand in marriage.

That day, Mittermeier had taken leave and headed off into the city. Looking this way and that, he ran between surprised pedestrians who wondered what in the world he was up to, and then, for the first time in his life, he pushed against the door of a flower shop. When the shop-keeper saw a young man in uniform come barging into her store, she feared for a moment that she was going to have a heart attack. A soldier, red in the face, jumping frantically into one's shop was hardly considered an auspicious portent.

"Flowers! Flowers! Give me flowers! Don't care what kind—no, that isn't right—I need really, really pretty ones, flowers a young girl will be happy to get."

The shop owner, relieved that he hadn't come to impose some inspection or put down a riot, recommended yellow roses. Mittermeier bought half the yellow roses in the store, had them made into a bouquet, and then headed over to a confectioner's shop, where he bought chocolates and a Frankfurt crown cake made with rum. When he passed in front of the jewelers, he thought about buying a ring, but he soon gave up the notion, figuring that that would in any case be getting ahead of himself. Most importantly, his wallet was almost empty by that point.

Mittermeier arrived at his parents' house carrying the bouquet of flowers and the box containing the cake. Evangeline had been in the garden trimming the lawn, and when she looked up to see the young officer standing there all stiff and formal, she rose to her feet in surprise.

"Wol—Master Wolf?"

"Eva, take these, please."

The tension he had felt in battle had been nothing compared to that moment.

"For me? Thank you very much."

To Mittermeier, the gleam of her smile was almost blinding.

"Evangeline—"

"Yes, Master Wolf...?"

Mittermeier had concocted all manner of clever lines for wooing, but at the sight of the girl's violet eyes, all his literary and rhetorical flourishes flew a hundred light-years off into the distance, and all he was able to think of was what a fool he was.

Mittermeier's father clucked his tongue, watching from off in the distance. "Whaddaya think you're doing?" he shouted. "Get ahold of yourself, ya big good-for-nothing!" He had never seen how his son fought on the battlefield, so he had been endlessly frustrated by the indecisiveness of a son who took seven years to propose. As he looked on with hedge clippers in hand, his son, gesticulating all the while, spoke to her in faltering, incoherent ramblings, while the girl, looking downward, listened without moving a muscle. Then, suddenly, the landscaper's son threw his arms around the girl, pulled her near, and summoned up all his courage to clumsily kiss her.

"Well, he actually went and did it," his father murmured with satisfaction.

That day, the young, blond-haired officer had fully understood that there was something in the world more precious to him than himself. Moreover, she was right there in his arms.

A modest wedding ceremony had been held. Wolfgang Mittermeier had been twenty-four, and Evangeline nineteen. Six years had passed since that day. They remained childless, but that didn't put so much as a scratch on their happiness.

Unlike the late Siegfried Kircheis, Oskar von Reuentahl had never made any woman the idol of his heart's temple. Unlike his colleague Wolfgang Mittermeier, he had never had a proper romance with any lovely young girl.

Ever since his boyhood, von Reuentahl had drawn the attention of women. Something about his noble features and heterochromatic eyes—black like a deeply sunken well, blue like the keen gleam of a knife—gave an almost mystical impression that drew sighs from young girls and middle-aged ladies alike.

In recent years, this young man had come to be called a great admiral of the Galactic Empire, who combined both wisdom and courage. But even before he had become feared as a soldier for his ruthlessness in dealing with the enemy, he had been known among his acquaintances for his coldness toward women. They would fall for him one-sidedly, and once relations were consummated, he would cast them aside.

Within a few years of graduating from the Imperial Armed Forces Academy, he and Wolfgang Mittermeier had gotten to know each other and fought side by side in many battles. Despite their differing backgrounds and personalities, they took an odd liking to each other and came to be quite close. During that period, Mittermeier married Evangeline and began a happy home life, while von Reuentahl remain single, continuing a string of dalliances that to onlookers looked like nothing more than indiscriminate womanizing.

"You shouldn't treat them so heartlessly." Mittermeier, unable to simply watch what he did in silence, had cautioned him about this, and not just once or twice. To this, von Reuentahl had always nodded his head and then done nothing in the way of heeding his advice or reforming his behavior. As for Mittermeier, it had finally hit him that something was fundamentally twisted in von Reuentahl's personality, and eventually he stopped bringing the matter up.

In Imperial Year 484, both had participated in the fighting on Planet Kapczelanka. In that dreadful environment of bitter cold, high gravity, and mercury-laced atmosphere, a horrific ground battle had unfolded in which von Reuentahl and Mittermeier, both of them still at the rank of commander, had fought an uphill battle amid chaos and confusion, with even the whereabouts of the front line uncertain. They had fired their particle-beam rifles until the energy capsules ran dry, then, gripping their guns like clubs, had beaten alliance soldiers down into the subfreezing mud. The swings of tomahawks had split the icy air in which fountains of blood had flash frozen, unfurling crimson blossoms in that colorless world of bitter cold.

"Hey, you still alive over there?" Mittermeier had asked.

"Somehow, I seem to be," von Reuentahl had replied. "How many did you get?"

"No idea. What about you?"

"Don't know. I counted as far as ten, but after that . . ."

Surrounded by the enemy, tomahawks lost, blood-splattered rifles bent so badly that they were useless even as clubs, the two men had braced themselves for an early death. They had fought so bravely, so fiercely, and had inflicted such extraordinary losses on the enemy that mercy had seemed unlikely, even if they threw down their arms. Mittermeier had whispered a farewell to his wife in his heart. That, however, was when an imperial airborne fighter had swooped down low with a thunderous roar and fired a missile into the midst of the closing FPA troops. Dirt and ice were blasted high into the air, completely blocking out the weak sunlight. Radar was confused, one corner of the encirclement collapsed, and the pair finally managed to escape in the darkness and confusion.

That night, in a bar on post, they had raised a toast to their safe return.

Perfumed showers had washed the blood from their bodies, but nothing beat alcohol for washing the blood from their minds. They were drinking as they wished, exceeding all moderation, and then suddenly von Reuentahl had sat up straight and stared at his friend. Something more than mere drunkenness had been lurking in his mismatched eyes.

"All right, Mittermeier, you listen here—you may have gotten married, but women . . . women are creatures born to stab men in the back."

"No need to jump to that conclusion," Mittermeier had said, offering restrained disagreement as Evangeline's face appeared in his mind's eye.

His heterochromiac friend had shaken his head fiercely, however. "No, it's true. My mother's a prime example, and I'm gonna tell you all about her. My father was lowborn—aristocracy in name only—but my mother . . . she came from a count's family . . ."

Von Reuentahl's father had graduated from university and become an official in the Ministry of Finance, but very early on, his prospects within that enclosed and very class-conscious bureaucracy had run up against a wall. Afterward, he had invested in niobium and platinum mines, enjoyed five years of success, and built up a fortune that, while not exactly boundless, would have fed a family through his grandchildren's generation.

He had remained single until he was almost forty, then purchased reliable bonds and real estate with the money he had saved. It was only when he was fully secure in life that he thought of taking a bride and raising a family. He was thinking of finding someone of average fortune and average lineage, but the arrangement his acquaintances found for him was with Leonora, third daughter of Count von Marbach.

In the Galactic Empire, distinguished noble families were taken very good care of in both political and economic terms, but that still couldn't prevent every family from getting into trouble. The von Marbachs had produced debauchers as clan heads for two consecutive generations. Not only had they been forced to part with all of their spacious manor houses and villas—to stabilize their livelihood, they had even had to sell off the high-interest bonds received from the von Goldenbaum family.

When von Reuentahl's sensible and calculating father had seen a soligraph of Leonora in all her beauty, he had been dumbstruck. After paying off the von Marbach family's debts, he had moved into a brand-new house with a beautiful bride twenty years his junior.

The marriage had brought grief to husband and wife alike—even though the problem had been nothing more than a temporal gap. The husband felt inferior because of his age and birth, and had tried to make up for those shortcomings materially. That, most likely, had been a crucial mistake, but it was his wife who encouraged it. Again and again, she had nagged her husband for expensive gifts, only to lose interest in them as soon as they were given to her.

As was occasionally the case with women in the closed-off world of high society, von Reuentahl's mother had put her faith not in science, but in fortune-telling and the study of destiny. She had blue eyes, and when a heterochromiac child was born to her and her blue-eyed husband, it wasn't genetic probability that occupied her mind, but rather the face of the dark-eyed man she had been having an affair with.

Believing that the gods meant to destroy her, she had been overcome with terror. It had been her husband's finances that allowed her to live in luxury—and also to have her lovers. Although she was beautiful, she lacked the skills needed to live on her own; what would happen if she were to be cast out into the world, together with that young man presently living a life of leisure thanks to her secret financial support? It was certain that in the end she would lose not only her material stability, but her lover as well.

"…And that's how I nearly had my right eye gouged out by my own mother. I was a newborn, just starting to open my eyes, and my father hadn't seen them yet."

A twisted little smile had played about the corner of von Reuentahl's lips as he told the story. Mittermeier had stared at his friend, not saying a word.

One scene had been floating in the back of von Reuentahl's mind:

A young, graceful woman sits up in bed. Her delicate features stiffen, and flames dance in her eyes as she tries to stick the point of a fruit knife into the right eye of the infant she is clutching at her breast. The door opens, and a maid arrives, bringing warm milk for her mistress. She gives a piercing cry. Milk splashes onto the carpet. Shards of a broken cup scatter across the floor. People charge into the room. The woman's fair-skinned hand loses hold of the knife. It falls to the floor, and the baby cries out, ripping the muffled air apart...

It was a scene he could not have possibly remembered, and yet it was burned into his retinas and his heart, and had all the substance of something he could reach out and touch. That image had put deep roots down in the topsoil of his mind, from which had sprung his deep distrust toward all women.

Mittermeier had learned for the first time what lay behind his friend's casual womanizing. Unable to find the right words, he took a sip of black beer. Assaulted on both flanks by sympathy toward his friend and a desire to mount a defense of women for his wife's sake, he had looked away. At a moment like this, intellect and education were no help at all in deciding how to respond. Mittermeier had been happy in his own life, and in that moment, that had made him feel small.

"Listen, von Reuentahl, this is just me thinking, but..."

Mittermeier had closed his mouth, though, when he turned back toward his fried. The young officer with the mismatched eyes was slumped facedown on the counter, having surrendered himself at last to the sweet caress of Hypnos.

The next day, the hungover pair had sought out one another in the officers' mess. Mittermeier, who still hadn't felt like eating, had been poking at his potatoes and bacon with the tip of his fork when his sullen-looking friend spoke.

"Last night the booze got the better of me. I said some things I shouldn't have. Please forget about it."

"What are you talking about?" Mittermeier had said. "I can't remember a thing."

"Hmm. Is that so? Well, in that case, it's for the best."

There was an irony in von Reuentahl's smile. Whether it was a wry grin directed at Mittermeier's transparent lie or a scornful one aimed at his own inebriated confession, von Reuentahl wasn't quite sure himself. In either case, though, from that day forward, neither of them ever brought up the matter again.

That was how it was between the two of them.

Siegfried Kircheis had long served as Reinhard's top aide, and when he had departed to command an independent regiment of his own, a number of officers had tried to fill the vacancy he had left at Reinhard's side. None of them, however, had lasted very long in the job. No one else in all the universe had shared Reinhard's heart the way Kircheis had, and furthermore, the officers themselves had often been hesitant. They had lacked that mental synergy with Reinhard, and the job had a tendency to become nothing more than receiving and relaying his one-sided orders.

Back when Kircheis had been alive and well, Reinhard, in search of staff officers, had taken on Paul von Oberstein. Now he would be glad to find a top aide with even one ten-thousandth the talent and fidelity of Kircheis.

One day, Arthur von Streit came to see him.

Von Streit had served under Duke von Braunschweig, the head of the boyar aristocrat confederacy, and had come to him with a bold proposal: "Instead of causing a large-scale civil war that would plunge the whole empire into chaos, we should resolve this problem by assassinating Reinhard alone." For this, he had incurred his master's wrath and been cast out. When he had later fallen into Reinhard's hands, the young imperial marshal had taken a liking to the man for his confident attitude and set him free.

Reinhard was extremely sensitive to the beauty or ugliness of people's actions, and he wouldn't hesitate to praise a man like von Streit, even if he were an enemy.

In September of the previous year, when he had lost the one who to him had been closer than a brother, the shock and the sorrow had been such that he'd almost crumbled. Oddly, though, Reinhard had felt no hatred toward Ansbach, the man who had killed Siegfried Kircheis. His own feelings of guilt had been far too deep and far too wide, and at the same time, he had found beauty in the actions of Ansbach, who had thrown away his own life in an attempt to avenge his lord.

On the other hand, it was anger mingled with contempt that he felt toward his late enemy, Duke von Braunschweig. Unable to put capable subordinates like Ansbach and von Streit to good use, he had been a contemptible man whose vanity and pride had led him to a miserable death.

"He was a man doomed to perish. I didn't deliberately set out to bring about his ruin." Reinhard believed that. In that matter, he felt not the slightest twinge of conscience.

One day, von Streit came to see Reinhard. One of his relatives had begged him to do so, and since he had owed a favor to that individual, he couldn't overlook the fact that he and his family were out on the streets, their assets having been confiscated.

"If you bow your head to Reinhard, he's sure to leave something for us—maybe not everything, but at least some of our assets."

Von Streit, having promised to do what he would never do again, swallowed his embarrassment and bowed before his former enemy.

After hearing him out, Reinhard smiled faintly and nodded. "Very well. I'll not do ill by him."

"I'm very grateful."

"However, I do have a condition." Here Reinhard's smile disappeared. "Come and work for me at Imperial Military Command Headquarters."

Von Streit didn't answer at first.

"I hold your good judgment and clever schemes in high regard. I've let you roam wild for nearly a year now, but a new year has come. Don't you think it's about time to put an end to this loyalty toward your old lord you so cling to?"

Von Streit, who had been listening with his head hung low, at last looked up. His brow shone with determination.

"I've no words for Your Excellency's generosity. In return for such kindness toward a fool like myself, allow me to offer my full and wholehearted loyalty."

Arthur von Streit was given the rank of rear admiral and made Reinhard's top aide. One other, Sublieutenant Theodor von Rücke, was made a secondary aide and teamed with the newly minted Rear Admiral von Streit. Thus it was confirmed that no one man could fill Kircheis's shoes alone. In von Rücke's case, rank and age made no difference; he was essentially von Streit's aide.

It was no secret that von Streit had once been an enemy of Reinhard's, so Reinhard's decision to put him in such an important position surprised a lot of people.

"Well, that's a bold thing he's gone and done." Mittermeier, second to none when it came to boldness himself, couldn't help feeling deeply impressed.

The viewpoint that "Chief of Staff von Oberstein isn't going to like this..." was also prevalent, but in this case that prediction missed the mark, as von Oberstein was fully accepting of his senior officer's daring appointment. He was aware of von Streit's capabilities and was also considering the political value of von Streit bending his knee to Reinhard, despite having been a loyal vassal of Duke von Braunschweig. That said, should he acquire too much power in the future, von Oberstein would be sure to start whittling away at it...

Von Oberstein was not a family man. At his official residence, he had an attendant, and at his private residence, he had a butler and a maid—they were a married couple—in early middle age. There was, however, one other member of his household who saw to his personal needs.

This was not a person but a dog—a dalmatian that anyone could tell at a glance was very old. In the spring of the previous year, when the Lippstadt War had not yet escalated to the stage of all-out combat, von Oberstein had gone out for lunch one day and had been on his way back to Reinhard's admiralität. He had climbed up the steps to the building and been about to step into the atrium when an odd look had appeared on the guard's face as he was presenting arms. When von Oberstein turned to look back, he saw that a skinny, dirty old dog had been following right at his heel, amiably wagging its lean tail.

The chief of staff, well-known for his cool and ruthless nature, had spoken in an unamused tone. "What's this dog doing here?"

The guard's face had stiffened—a look of panic appearing on his face as inorganic, artificial eyes turned on him, flashing with their ominous light.

"Ah, er—isn't it Your Excellency's dog...?"

"Hmph, does it look like a dog I would own?"

"Y-you mean it isn't?"

"Oh, so it *does* look like it's mine?"

Looking oddly moved, von Oberstein had nodded his head. And from that day forward, the nameless old dog had become a dependent in the household of the chief of staff of the Galactic Imperial Space Armada.

The aged canine, although rescued from a life of aimless drifting, had virtually no praiseworthy qualities and would eat nothing but chicken meat that had been boiled until it was soft.

"We've got a senior admiral of the Galactic Imperial Navy—one who could silence a screaming child just by looking at him—running out to the butcher shop in the middle of the night to buy chicken for that mutt." Neidhart Müller had revealed this tidbit at the admirals' club one evening, after having spotted von Oberstein doing so while on the way home from work.

Mittermeier and von Reuentahl had both looked like they wanted to say something but had exercised silent restraint in the end.

"Huh. So our chief of staff is hated by people but loved by dogs, then? I guess dogs get along with one another."

That insult had come courtesy of Fritz Josef Wittenfeld, commander of the Schwarz Lanzenreiter fleet.

Wittenfeld was highly regarded for his ferocity in battle, and it was said of him that "if the fight were limited to two hours, even Mittermeier and von Reuentahl might have to retreat from him."

However, this evaluation also testified to Wittenfeld's short temper and lack of endurance. Wittenfeld was at his best when it came to single-blow assaults and all-out attacks, but if his opponent endured that first strike, he wasn't able to maintain the same intensity. Not that there were many enemies who could withstand his first strike....

"Wittenfeld is strong, certainly," von Reuentahl had once said to Mittermeier, brimming with confidence. "If the two of us ever tangled on the battlefield, he'd definitely have the advantage when the fighting started. When the fighting ended, though, the one left standing would be me."

Naturally, they had been alone when he said that. The number of enemies the heterochromiac admiral did not believe he could beat could be counted on one hand.

Reinhard's reforms acknowledged no sacred cows. Waste and luxury had bloomed in wild profusion at the imperial court, but not even those blossoms lay outside his reach.

While the emperor's palace of Neue Sans Souci had managed to escape outright demolition, its vast gardens had been closed and half its stately buildings shuttered, with a great many chamberlains and ladies-in-waiting let go in the process.

Most of those who remained were elderly. Duke von Lohengramm hated the palace because of its splendor—or so it was rumored; Reinhard had his own ideas about that. The elderly chamberlains and ladies-in-waiting had spent decades at the palace by this point, and it was too late for most of them to adjust to life in the outside world. As for the young ones, they had strong backs and adaptability, and there was also demand for them in the labor market. They would be able to find other jobs to support themselves.

Reinhard concealed this sort of kindness—or lenience—behind a mask of ruthless ambition. The late Siegfried Kircheis had been the only one who could have understood without ever a word spoken. Had Reinhard been the sort to stubbornly refuse those who did speak up and ask him his reasons, his actions could have only been interpreted as malice toward the emperor. After all, the malice he felt toward the emperor was a very real thing...

When would this young, powerful vassal do away with the young emperor and set upon his own brow that most venerable of crowns? Not only the empire, but all the universe seemed to be watching with bated breath to see.

Throughout the five centuries that had passed since Rudolf von Goldenbaum abolished republican government and founded the Galactic Empire in SE 310, "emperor" had been another word for the von Goldenbaum family head. When one family—one bloodline—makes a nation its property and monopolizes its highest seats of power for five hundred years, it comes to be thought of as the orthodox system, acquiring an air of holiness and inviolability.

But where was it written that usurpation was any worse than hereditary succession? Wasn't that just a self-justifying theory that rulers used to protect the power they already had? If usurpation and armed rebellion were the only way to break up a monopoly on power, then it should hardly be surprising if those who were passionate for change took the only road available.

One day, when von Oberstein had come to see Reinhard, he asked him in a roundabout way what sort of treatment he had in mind for the young emperor.

"I won't kill him."

In the crystal glass Reinhard was holding, barely visible undulations ran through a fragrant liquid the color of blood. Its reflection gleamed eerily in Reinhard's ice-blue eyes.

"Keep him alive. He has value I can exploit. Wouldn't you agree, von Oberstein?"

"Most certainly. For now."

"Yes, for now…"

Reinhard tilted his glass. As the liquid poured down his throat, a warm sensation spread out through his body. It burned hot within his breast but came nowhere close to filling the empty space therein.

CHAPTER 3:

THE CENTRAL COMMAND ROOM at Iserlohn Fortress was a vast affair, with a ceiling sixteen meters high and walls roughly eighty meters long on each side. When entering from the hallway, one came first to a guards' anteroom. Then, after passing a second door farther in, screens came into view, spreading out over a portion of the forward wall. The main screen was eight and a half meters tall and fifteen meters wide. To its right were twelve subscreens, and to its left an array of sixteen tactical intelligence monitors. In front of the main screen were twenty-four operator boxes arranged in three rows, and a three-dimensional display on the floor behind them. Even farther back was the commander's seat and desk, where Yang Wen-li could usually be found sipping tea while wearing a bored-looking expression. Using a special hotline on his desk, it was possible to speak directly with Joint Operational Headquarters on Heinessen or with the patrol fleet while it was out on maneuvers. To the left, right, and rear of the commander's seat were another twenty seats, which belonged to the fortress's top executive staff. Most of the time, the seat next to Yang on his left was occupied by his aide, Lieutenant Frederica Greenhill, with Rear Admiral Murai, his chief of staff, taking the seat on his right. Rear Admiral von Schönkopf, the commander of fortress

defenses, sat behind him. There were also seats for Guest Admiral Merkatz, Patrol Fleet Vice Commander Fischer, and Fortress Administrative
Director Caselnes, though Caselnes spent a lot of his time in the offices
of Administrative Management Headquarters, and Fischer was often away
in the spaceport's traffic control room.

All announcements, instructions, orders, and official conversations in
the room were transmitted by headset. Two monitor cameras set in the
walls fed video to two different monitor control rooms. In the unlikely
event of the central control room being overrun by the enemy, either of
these rooms could become a new command center.

In later years, when Julian Mintz would think back on his days at Iserlohn, the first thing that would come to his mind was Yang Wen-li sitting
in the commander's seat. Ill-mannered Yang, with his feet propped up on
his desk, or perhaps sitting on top of it cross-legged, a perennial object of
criticism from that cross section of the military that believed real soldiers
had to exemplify the stately beauty of solemn formality. Yang had never
been a cookie-cutter soldier, though, and solemn formality had been
something there was no point in expecting from him . . .

Julian, as yet without a seat of his own in this room, would sit facing
the screen on the inclined, stair-step floor in those days, leaping to his
feet and running over to Yang whenever he was called for. It was only
after he advanced to officer rank that he would secure a seat for himself
in the command room.

A faint tinge of ozone lingered in his olfactory memory, along with the
aroma of coffee rising from paper cups in the hands of crew. Yang was
partial to red tea—a minority in the control room—and the fragrance of
it had usually been drowned out by that of the coffee, a fact that Yang
seemed to find rather irritating. It had been a trivial matter, of course;
Yang had had all sorts of other large and small irritations to deal with.
Included among these had been Julian's first time to go out into battle.

When Julian met Yang for the first time after returning from his combat mission, Yang greeted him with an expression that was hard to put into words, and after a long moment of not saying anything, he said something spectacularly unsoldierlike:

"How many times have I gotta tell you, Julian, don't do dangerous things like that."

Both Julian and Lieutenant Frederica Greenhill, who was standing nearby, had trouble keeping straight faces.

Afterward, Julian headed back to officer country, where he put Yang's domestic computer to work on peaceful everyday chores. He was just working up a menu for dinner when the visiphone sounded and Frederica appeared on the screen.

"Fighting the battle on the home front now, Julian?"

"My CO can't exactly be trusted with this kind of mission. How may I help you?"

The boy's attitude was perhaps a little on the formal side. If anyone had suggested he was at the age when young boys often idolize older women, though, he would have vehemently denied it.

"Yes, Julian, I have an important message to relay. As of tomorrow, you're going to be a chief petty officer. Report to the commander's office at noon sharp tomorrow to receive your letter of appointment. Got that?"

"I'm being promoted? Me?"

"Of course. You did a great job out there. Very impressive for your first time out."

"Thank you very much. But what does Admiral Yang think about it?"

A slight look of surprise appeared in Frederica's hazel eyes. "Why, he's happy for you, of course. Though he'd never admit it . . ."

It was probably the only way she could have answered him. After the call ended, Julian sank into thought for a while.

Yang had never wanted to turn Julian into a soldier. Julian himself, however, wanted to be a soldier. As for Yang, he didn't feel he should force his own wishes on the boy, but at the same time he wanted to keep him close by. This was one matter in which the words and the deeds of the most brilliant admiral of the alliance had been highly inconsistent.

In any case, Yang's own vocational choice had been an extreme case of life not following its intended script. After looking around for a school where he could study history for free, he had entered the Department of Military History at Officers' Academy—only to have his department abolished along the way, to be transferred against his will to the Department of Military Strategy, and then to enter the military without so much as a spark of enthusiasm.

In contrast, Julian was really taking the initiative in his martial ambitions, and being true both to his chosen profession and to himself. This shouldn't have been any of Yang's business. It shouldn't have been, but Julian really *did* want Yang's blessing on the course he had chosen.

Julian's father had been a soldier, but if Julian had not been raised by Yang after his death, it was far from certain that he would have set his sights on the military. For good or ill, Yang's personality had exerted a powerful influence on Julian, and if Yang were to criticize the boy's career choice now, he would only end up scowling at himself in the mirror.

Remembering that look on Yang's face, Julian smiled to himself. He had no doubt that he would understand eventually.

That year, Yang Wen-li turned thirty-one. "Not because I want to!" he had fervently insisted.

"You're still young," Julian had said consolingly.

In fact, Yang really did look young enough to pass for someone in his mid-twenties, though to hear Alex Caselnes—his upperclassman from Officers' Academy—tell it, he only looked young because he wasn't doing the hard work of raising a family.

"Well, with a husband like you," Yang shot back, "I'd say it's *Mrs.* Caselnes who's doing all the heavy lifting. The patience that saintly woman must have. With a tyrant like you for a husband, a normal lady wouldn't last a year under the same roof!"

Julian had chuckled when he heard that. If he hadn't known what a warm family atmosphere there was at the Caselneses' house, or that Yang and Caselnes were friends who enjoyed insulting each other for fun, Yang's words couldn't have sounded like anything other than a stinging indictment of Caselnes's character.

As a soldier, Yang was an awful marksman, average in terms of physical strength and reflexes, and completely useless on the battlefield. In Caselnes's pitiless estimation, he had "nothing vital below the neck." Not that Caselnes had much room to talk. Master of desk work and outstanding military bureaucrat he may have been, but he was hardly first-rate material as a combatant himself.

Caselnes's duty was to manage and run both the hardware and software sides of the gigantic battle station that was Iserlohn Fortress. Facilities, equipment, communication, manufacturing, distribution—all of the many functions indispensable for the smooth, organic operation of the fortress were kept running thanks to his skills.

"When Caselnes sneezes, all of Iserlohn breaks out in a fever," soldiers sometimes said, and there was a kernel of truth in that joke. In fact, when Caselnes had been down for a week with acute gastritis, Iserlohn's administrative offices had become unable to do anything more than their usual work, and found themselves surrounded by a chorus of angry soldiers:

"Do you even have a clue what you're doing? That's way too inefficient! Can't you do something about all this red tape?"

Yang was good with letters but bad with numbers, so just like his aide Frederica, Caselnes was immensely valuable to have around.

Yang delegated his more prosaic work entirely to them; he only came alive when concocting battle plans for fighting massive war fleets and when putting them into action on the battlefield. Contrary to Yang's own wishes, his talents seemed geared for times of upheaval and emergency. Had it been peacetime, he would have died a nobody—at most, a second-rate historian known to only a handful of people. What had made him one of the most important people in a vast interstellar nation was the simple fact that the times had made his talents necessary.

Among the varied talents of the human race, military genius fell into an extremely specialized category. In certain periods and circumstances, it became utterly useless to society as a whole. In times of peace, some people probably lived out their whole lives without ever having a chance to put their immense skills to use. Unlike scholars or artists, they left no lost works buried amid their effects to be posthumously discovered and appreciated. Not even their potential would ever be acknowledged. Only results mattered. And young though he may have been, Yang had already accumulated more than enough of those results.

II

That night, Yang and Julian were visiting Alex Caselnes at his official residence. They had done this from time to time in the past back on Heinessen, but since moving to Iserlohn it had become a custom of theirs to get together once or twice a month. Mrs. Caselnes would serve a homemade meal, and after that her husband and guest would usually enjoy a game of 3-D chess over a glass of brandy.

That night, the Caselneses were hosting a modest but warm dinner party in particular to celebrate *Chief Petty Officer* Julian Mintz's promotion, his first combat flight, and his first heroic deeds on the battlefield.

When the two guests arrived, they were greeted by Charlotte Phyllis, the eight-year-old eldest daughter of the Caselnes household.

"Come in, Julian!" she said.

"Good evening, Charlotte," Julian replied, returning the little girl's greeting.

"Come in, Uncle Yang."

"Er...good evening, Charlotte."

Carrying his five-year-old second daughter in his arms, the head of the Caselnes clan favored Yang with an unkind smile as he noticed the slow response. "What's the matter, Yang? Something bothering you?"

"I just got my feelings hurt. I was kind of hoping to do without the 'Uncle' as long as I'm still single, you know? Can you do something about that?"

When they were alone, Yang would speak to Caselnes as if he were an underclassman at the academy.

"You're spoiled rotten, Yang. Past thirty and still single—how much longer do you think we can let such antisocial behavior slide?"

"There are plenty of people who stay single their whole life and still contribute to society. I can name off four, five hundred for you right now if you like."

"And I could name even more than that who've contributed to society while raising families."

And the point goes to Caselnes, Julian thought.

Agewise, Caselnes had six years on Yang, and was far ahead of him as well in both 3-D chess and venomous contests of wit. Yang didn't attempt another counterstrike—although that probably had more to do with his attention having been diverted by the aroma of dinner.

The dinner was a lot of fun that night. Mrs. Caselnes's specialties—chicory omelets and a fish and vegetable cream stew called *vachiruzui*—were delicious, but what marked the occasion for Julian was being offered wine for the first time. Until that night, he had always gotten the same apple cider as Charlotte.

Though naturally, this only resulted in him turning beet red in the face and being mocked by the adults...

After dinner, Yang and Caselnes moved to the salon like always and started up a game of 3-D chess. After one win and one loss, however, the look on Caselnes's face grew a bit formal.

"There's something serious I'd like to talk about, Yang."

With a nod that promised nothing, Yang glanced over Caselnes's shoulder. Julian was drawing a picture for the girls on a piece of drawing paper spread out on the floor. *A picture-perfect kid himself*, Yang thought. Whether protected by a combat suit on the field of battle or sitting at ease in a peaceful household, Julian just seemed to *belong*, the way a figure in a great painting did. It was probably a disposition he was born with. Yang knew one other person—not directly, of course—who had that same kind of disposition: Reinhard von Lohengramm of the Galactic Empire.

"Yang," Caselnes said, after searching a moment for the right words, "for a vital piece of our organization, you seem to be very unconcerned about your personal safety. And this time, I don't mean that in a good way. It's a fault."

Yang subtly shifted his line of sight and gave his upperclassman from the academy a serious look.

Caselnes continued. "You're not some hermit living alone in the wilderness. You're responsible for the security of a whole lot of people. So how about paying a little more attention to your own?"

"I've got my hands full as it is. If I was thinking about that kind of thing too, then..."

"Then what?"

"Then I wouldn't have time for my afternoon nap."

Yang had taken a stab at being funny, but Caselnes was having none of it. He poured brandy into Yang's glass and his own, crossed his legs, then straightened in his seat.

"Your problem isn't free time or the lack thereof—you just don't want to do it. You know good and well that you need to think about these things, but you don't want to. Am I wrong?"

"I'm just not that detail oriented. It's a pain in the neck to deal with. That's all."

Holding his glass in one hand, Caselnes let out a sigh.

"One reason I bring this up is that our esteemed head of state, His Excellency Chairman Trünicht, worries me."

"What about Chairman Trünicht?"

"The man is bankrupt in terms of ideals and policy, but he's very calculating, and schemes he's got in spades. Now, you can laugh if you want, but to be honest, he scares me a little these days."

Of course Yang didn't laugh. He was remembering that unearthly feeling of terror he had felt welling up last autumn when exchanging an unwanted handshake with the man amid the roar of a cheering crowd.

Caselnes continued. "I'd always thought of him as a two-bit political huckster with nothing to peddle but sophistry and flowery words, but lately I'm feeling something almost monstrous about him. I keep wondering more and more if he's going to do something horrible, and not even hesitate. How can I put this? It feels like he's made a deal with the devil."

There were a number of things bothering Caselnes, and one of them was the growing influence of the pro-Trünicht faction on the military. Admiral Cubresly, director of Joint Operational Headquarters and the number one man in uniform, had endured an assassination attempt, long hospitalization, and arrest by the coup d'état faction before returning to his present post, but word now had it he was getting sick of the ongoing friction and passive disobedience he had encountered since coming back. He had found that the critical positions at headquarters were all occupied by members of the Trünicht faction—chief among them Admiral Dawson.

"When it comes to staff selections and fleet operations, I hear even spry old Mister Bucock's been running into interference at every turn, and that he's had just about enough. At the rate things are going, the upper echelon of the military will eventually end up a 'branch family' of the 'Trünicht clan,' as it were."

"If that happens, I'll tender my resignation."

"Don't look so happy when you say that. Let's say you retire and start leading that pensioner's life you've always dreamed of. That may be fine for you, but put yourself in the shoes of all those soldiers and officers you'll leave behind. Once someone like Dawson has been installed as fortress commander, this whole installation'll end up like the dorm at some seminary. He might even say, 'Hey, let's pick a day and have all hands clean out every last garbage chute on Iserlohn.'" Regardless of whether Caselnes was joking or serious, his point was no laughing matter. "Anyway, think about your safety, Yang, even if just a little. Julian's lost his parents once already. No matter how useless a foster dad he may have now, it would be a shame for him to have to go through that again."

"Am I really that useless?"

"You thought you were doing a *good* job?"

"Four years ago, who was it who forced Julian on this useless foster dad?"

Caselnes didn't have an answer for that one. After a moment, he said, "You up for another brandy?"

"I humbly accept."

Several refills later, Yang and Caselnes both turned to look at Julian, almost as if they had planned it in advance. Both of the little girls had been getting sleepy, and Mrs. Caselnes and Julian had just picked them up to carry them to their bedroom.

"Now there's a good kid—nothing at all like his guardian."

"If his guardian's lagging behind, it's because his guardian has a rotten friend. Julian doesn't have any friends at all, though."

"What do you mean?"

"At that age, you need friends of your own generation—friends to get in fights with, buddies to cheat on tests with, teammates, rivals—all kinds. In Julian's case, there's only adults around, and messed-up adults at that. It's kind of a problem. When we were on Heinessen it wasn't like that, of course."

"Yet for all that, he's growing up to be honest and straightforward."

"I believe he is," Yang said, fully serious now. But after a moment, he added, "It helps that he's got such a good foster dad." Anyone could have seen at a glance that he had tacked on the joke as cover for his embarrassment.

"That kid's disobeyed me exactly one time," Yang continued. "We were taking care of the neighbor's nightingale for a day. I told him to feed it, but he went off to a flyball practice match without doing it."

"And? What happened?"

"I gave him strict orders to go without dinner that night."

"Well, well. I guess that was bad news for you, too."

"For me? How come?"

"Because I can't imagine you making Julian go without dinner and eating your fill by yourself. You'd just end up skipping the meal with him."

Yang paused a moment before continuing. "It's true I had an appetite come breakfast time."

"Oh, did you? An appetite."

Yang sipped his brandy and made an attempt at a recovery. "I'm well aware that I've got a long way to go as a family man. But even I've got my reasons for that. After all, I'm single, and I grew up in a single-parent family myself. There's no way I could ever be a perfect fa—"

"Copying perfect parents isn't how kids grow up. It's more like they see the negative examples their imperfect parents show them and use those to cultivate their spirit of independence. You copy, Your Excellency?"

"I copy that some pretty awful things are being said about me."

"Well, if you don't like being talked about, how about this: go find yourself a wife so you can try and get closer to perfect."

That sudden sneak attack left Yang momentarily speechless.

"Even though the war's not over yet?" he said.

"I figured you'd say that. But still, what's our number one duty as human beings? It's the same as for all living creatures: to transmit our genes to the next generation and preserve the race. To give birth to new life. Am I right?"

"Yeah, which is why the worst sin a human can commit is to kill somebody, or cause somebody to be killed. And that's what soldiers do for a living."

"You don't have to keep thinking like that. But okay, sure, let's say somebody's committed that sin. If he's got five kids and just one of them embraces humanitarianism, then someone just might come out of that who can atone for his father's sin—a son who can carry on the aborted ambitions of the father."

"You don't need a biological son to carry on your ambitions," Yang said, glancing over at Julian. Then, turning his eyes back to his upperclassman from Officers' Academy, he added, as if he had only just remembered, "And what you said assumes that the father has ambitions to carry on in the first place."

Yang got up to go to the toilet, and Caselnes called Julian over and had him sit in the chair that Yang had occupied until just then.

"What is it?" said Julian. "You said there was something important..."

"You, young man, are Yang's number one loyal retainer. That's why I'm telling you: your guardian knows all about yesterday, and tomorrow he can see pretty clearly. But people like that have a bad habit sometimes of not knowing a whole lot about what's on the menu today. You follow?"

"Yes, sir, I certainly do."

"This is an extreme example, but suppose this evening's dinner was poisoned. No matter how much Yang knows about tomorrow and the day after, it won't amount to squat for him personally if he doesn't realize what's going on now. Still with me?"

This time, Julian didn't answer right away. The light of one deep in thought danced on the surface of his dark-brown eyes. "In other words, you're telling me to be his food taster, aren't you?"

"That about covers it," Caselnes said, nodding.

A trace of a smile appeared on Julian's face. It somehow made him look very intelligent. "You make good personnel choices, Admiral Caselnes."

"I don't think I'm too bad a judge of character."

"I'll do everything I can. But still, is Admiral Yang really in that dangerous a position?"

Julian's voice had dropped an octave.

"Right now, things are still all right. Being as we've got a powerful enemy in the empire, Yang's talents are essential. However, nobody knows how quickly the situation could change. Now, if someone like me has thought this, there's no way that Yang hasn't, but something about that guy…"

"Don't go brainwashing innocent boys into believing your weird theories, Alex," said Yang, flashing a wry smile. He had just returned from the bathroom. He told Julian to start getting ready to leave and then looked at Caselnes, shrugging his shoulders somewhat exaggeratedly.

"Anyway, don't worry so much, please. It's not like I've never given this any thought myself. I have no intention of becoming Mister Trünicht's plaything, and I do want to live long enough to enjoy my golden years."

III

Phezzan. The Phezzan Land Dominion.

It was a most unusual country. Strictly speaking, it was not even a country at all. It was nothing more than a special unit of regional government under the suzerainty of the emperor of the Galactic Empire, whose internal self-rule and freedom of trade was permitted by his grace. At the same time, however, its name carried all manner of associations to people—of brisk economic activity, amassed wealth, prosperity, and opportunities for success, pleasure, and the exercise of ability. It was Carthage, Basra, Córdoba, Chang'an, Samarkand, Constantinople, Genoa, Lübeck, Shanghai, New York, Marsport, and Prosperpina—every paradise for adventurous and ambitious souls in the history of the human race—all rolled up into one.

Originally a barren wasteland, this planet was painted with colorful legends of success—and tales of failure many times as numerous.

Phezzan was in the midst of the stream. At any inhabited point in the universe, people, supplies, money, and information flowed in and then flowed back out, accompanied by a markup in price.

In the flow of information, even gossip was an important category. At a watering hole called De la Court—a bar widely known as a gathering place for independent traders—it was said that there existed countless "conversation rooms" and "card rooms" in addition to the spacious main bar, in which all kinds of information could be exchanged behind the security of soundproof walls and a formidable anti-eavesdropping system.

Most of the rumors circulating were dismissed out of hand as irresponsible hearsay or simple jokes, but sometimes they contained nuggets of information that were worth more than gold. One example was the case of the man named Valentine Kauf, whom merchants still spoke of with respect despite the passage of half a century since the days when he'd been active.

Kauf had been born the son of a trading-ship owner who had hardly been middle-class; however, not long after inheriting a fortune from his father, he lost it all on reckless speculation. With the help of an understanding friend he bought a small ore transport vessel and tried to make a fresh start. That vessel, however, had ended up shipwrecked in a magnetic storm, and even the friend who had cosigned for Kauf had been driven to bankruptcy along with him. Kauf, backed into a corner, had felt there was nothing left he could do but take out an insurance policy on himself, name his friend the beneficiary, and commit suicide to pay back a portion of what he owed. And so one night he had been sitting alone at the main bar of De la Court, nursing a drink he had decided would be the last he would ever taste. As he sat there, fragments of a conversation one table over had made their way to his ears.

".... so the marquis is putting forward the emperor's younger brother... On the other hand, the minister of military affairs..."

".... self-destruction and self-abandonment... backed into a corner... need soldiers... won't win, but... Now that you mention it, they do look like pigs…must be rebelling 'cause they're drawn to the slaughterhouse…"

These snatches of conversation had been followed by raucous laughter, but it never reached Kauf's ears. He had slammed payment for his drinks down on the counter and gone running out of De la Court.

One week later, news of an uprising had brought merchants scrambling to the marketplace, where they learned that a number of strategic supplies had been completely bought up by a young, unknown trader named Kauf. Kauf had investigated the characteristics of the people mentioned in those fragments of conversation he'd overheard, worked out their names and territorial holdings, looked into what ores were produced by those territories, and predicted what shortages the chaos would cause. Then he had twisted every arm he could for loans, raising capital to buy up those supplies. Although the war itself was unlikely to last even a month, the things he had bought would be essential during that period. It was as if a condemned man had leapt from the twelfth step of the gallows and landed on a kingly throne—Kauf's gambit had succeeded. He made enough off the deal to buy a dozen trading ships at once and gave half his earnings to the friend who had helped him before.

After that, Kauf's exploits had continued, completely free of the bad luck that had been with him till that day. He became a three-time winner of the Sindbad Award, and when he died in his mid-fifties, he left behind six sons and a vast store of wealth. Today, not a pillar remained of the Kauf Financial Group, however. Just because his six sons had inherited his fortune didn't mean they'd inherited his talent and energy as well. Still, even if it was only for one generation, the spectacular success of Valentine Kauf was a historical fact—and more than sufficient to foster the dreams and ambitions of Phezzanese merchants.

"Today you're a nobody just starting out. But tomorrow you could be Valentine Kauf II!"

That slogan was posted at Phezzan's largest school of commerce, and while its message could hardly be described as refined, it did resonate in the hearts of the young. That university, incidentally, was founded by a grant from O'Higgins, the lifelong loyal friend of Valentine Kauf, so one could say that O'Higgins had, in a way, contributed more to Phezzan than

Kauf ever had. Kauf's vast fortune had vanished like a heat mirage, but the university O'Higgins had founded remained to this day, producing many free merchants, economists, and bureaucrats, and providing Phezzan with its greatest resource—talented people.

One day, at a table in the main bar at De la Court, a group of merchants just back from an interstellar business trip were enjoying drink and gossip. The topic of conversation was how society in the empire was changing day by day.

"It seems that the nobles are selling off real estate, jewelry, and securities very quickly, now that they've lost their special rights. Everyone can see they're holding a weak hand, so the prices have really been beaten down low. Even if they'd like to protest what's going on over there, they're afraid of what might happen to them afterward, so all they can do is sit in their beds and cry."

"When power changes hands, the ones who got fat off the old order will always become targets for revenge in the new. That's an ironclad rule of history."

"In other words, descendants are connected by blood to their ancestors' misdeeds. Don't get me wrong—I do feel a twinge of pity for them, but..."

"Save your pity for all those commoners the nobles have been feeding off of for the last five hundred years. Even if they were set to be punished for the *next* five hundred years, I wouldn't feel a hint of sympathy."

"There you go again—you got ice in your veins or something? You've been able to lead a pretty sweet life thanks to the nobility."

"Everything I do, I put my all into it, and I'm ready for what'll happen if it blows up in my face. But they think money just bubbles up out of the ground without having to use your brain or your body. That's what I just can't get over."

"All right, all right. By the way, I picked up an odd bit of scuttlebutt from officials at the dominion capital."

"Oh? What'd you hear?"

"That the landesherr's been seeing a lot of a certain weird hood lately."

"He's meeting with a hood? That doesn't quite fit my image of the Black Fox."

"Oddly enough, it might fit better than you think. Cause apparently, this is the kind of 'hood' that comes with a long black robe attached."

At the dominion capitol building where Adrian Rubinsky did his work, staffers' eyes turned toward the waiting room as they furtively whispered to one another.

With his extremely busy public and private lives, the landesherr was always saying he needed two bodies to keep up (or failing that, fifty hours in the day), so his staff couldn't fathom what had gotten into him to make him spend the past several days in confidential talks with some mysterious religious leader. Few Phezzanese were aware of the extraordinary relationship that existed between the dominion and Terra, and of those, only a scant handful worked in the central hub of government.

The black-robed figure stood unmoving in the midst of the staffers' converging, disapproving lines of sight. At last the secretary came out and escorted him to the landesherr's office. Visitors who had requested meetings with Rubinsky prior to this man's arrival could only watch his departing form with irritation as their own audiences were delayed.

This bishop, dispatched by the Grand Bishop of Terra to observe Rubinsky, was called "Degsby." It was both his status and his name.

As he entered the room, Bishop Degsby lowered his hood.

The face that appeared from beneath was surprisingly young—probably not yet thirty. His thin, pale face bespoke a life of strictly regimented abstinence from worldly pleasures, as well as a bit of nutritional imbalance. His black hair was long and unkempt, and he had a gleam in his blue eyes that was like the sun in a tropical rain forest—a fervent gleam that made others uncomfortable, suggesting a clear imbalance between reason and faith.

"Please, Your Grace, be seated," Rubinsky said. He had assumed an attitude of humility that was evident in his every movement. It was all a refined act, however, not something that welled up naturally from inside his heart. Degsby lowered himself into the proffered chair with a bearing that was not so much haughty as uninterested in observing the niceties.

"Was what you told me yesterday the truth?" he demanded, apparently seeing no need to exchange greetings.

"Indeed it was. I'm about to start placing an increased emphasis on economic cooperation with the empire, as well as on financial assistance. Albeit not too abruptly."

"By doing so, you'll upset the balance of power between the empire and the alliance. How do you plan on using that?"

"By allowing Duke Reinhard von Lohengramm to unify the whole galaxy, after which I will eliminate him and obtain his entire legacy. Is there some problem with that?"

On hearing the Landesherr's words, surprise appeared first on the bishop's face, followed by a silent unfolding of the wings of suspicion. After taking a moment to collect himself, he said, "It's a fine idea, though perhaps just a little selfish. But the golden brat won't be that easy to trick, and he's also got that scoundrel von Oberstein with him. Do you really think they're going to just go along with what you have in mind?"

"You seem quite informed about the situation," Rubinsky said amiably. "However, neither Duke von Lohengramm nor von Oberstein is all-knowing or all-powerful. There's sure to be an opening we can take advantage of somewhere. And even if there isn't, I can make one."

Had Duke von Lohengramm been omnipotent, he would not have let himself be targeted by an assassin last fall, nor would he have lost his top advisor, Admiral Siegfried Kircheis.

"The thing about authority and the functions of government," mused Rubinsky, "is that the more you centralize them, the easier you make it to manipulate the whole system simply by taking over small portions. In the new dynasty that's coming, we kill one man—Duke von Lohengramm...

or should I say, Emperor Reinhard—and take over the nerve center of his government. That alone will make us the rulers of the entire universe."

"However," said Degsby, "the ruling authorities of the Free Planets Alliance aren't exactly far from our grasp. You Phezzanese have got them by the throat with your wealth, and during the coup d'état their head of state Trünicht was saved by some of our own disciples. Side with the Galactic Empire if you like, but doesn't it seem a waste to let our pawns in the alliance die? To put it in your terms, we'd lose our investment, would we not?"

The bishop's point was incisive. Mental balance notwithstanding, he certainly didn't lack for intellect.

"No, no. Not at all, Your Grace," said Rubinsky. "The alliance's leadership can be used as a corrosive agent to cause the alliance itself to collapse from within. Generally speaking, there's no such thing as a nation that's so strong internally that it can only be destroyed by an outside enemy. And internal decay encourages external threats. And here's the important thing: decay in a nation never starts from the bottom and works its way upward. The rot begins at the very top. There isn't a single exception."

As Rubinsky underscored that point, the bishop looked at him with an ironic gleam dancing in his eyes.

"Phezzan may be called a dominion, but it, too, is a de facto nation. Surely its pinnacle isn't starting to rot like the alliance's."

"That's rather harsh. I'll have to bear in mind my responsibilities as a statesman. In any case, I think that's enough of this formal talk for one day..."

The Landesherr told him that preparations were being made for a banquet, at which point the bishop brusquely refused and departed.

In his place, a young man appeared. He looked like he was fresh out of college, but there was no youthful naïveté in the gleam of his eyes, and although he did have a handsome face, there was something dry and emotionless about it as well. He was a little on the thin side, and his height, while on the upper end of average, was not enough to be considered tall.

He was Rupert Kesselring—installed as Rubinsky's aide last fall. His previous aide, Boltec, had been dispatched to the Galactic Empire as a commissioner, where he was presently engaged in a certain operation on Odin.

"It must be terribly hard on you, Excellency, *babysitting* that bishop."

"Indeed. A fanatical dogmatist is harder to handle than a bear fresh out of hibernation . . . What in the world is 'living for pleasure' supposed to mean?"

The landesherr—a self-described hedonist—sneered at the young bishop's puritanical behavior.

"Thousands of years ago, Christians succeeded in taking over the old Roman Empire by religious brainwashing of its highest ruling authority. And the dirty tricks they pulled afterward to suppress or wipe out the other religions! And thanks to that, they eventually ruled not just an empire, but civilization itself! Nowhere else will you find such an efficient invasion. I said before that I was going to make that bit of history repeat itself, but that was when the plan was to bring down the empire and alliance together . . ."

The Black Fox of Phezzan clucked his tongue with irritation. There was a very good reason why he had finally had to give up on his initial plan. It was because of the rise of Duke Reinhard von Lohengramm. His genius encompassed governance as well as warfare, and under his guidance the empire was now undergoing drastic internal reform. The old and feeble Goldenbaum Dynasty was about to flicker out forever—as was only natural—but from the ashes of its corpse, a young and powerful Lohengramm Dynasty was about to be born.

To defeat both the alliance and this new dynasty simultaneously would be no easy feat. And even if that went well, what came next would be political chaos and a collapse of security on a galactic scale. Restoring stability would require vast military forces and a lengthy interregnum, and during that time, Phezzan's rights and interests would likely be nibbled away to nothing by the legions of petty political and military forces that would arise before a new order could take shape.

And we mustn't have that, thought Rubinsky. *So, then, what should we do?*

What Phezzan should do was rule jointly over a partitioned galaxy, together with this new Galactic Empire. That was the conclusion

Rubinsky had arrived at.

"Partitioned" didn't mean that he wanted to draw up national boundaries in space. No, the whole human family would be unified under this new Galactic Empire, and political and military sovereignty, with all accompanying authority, would be vested in its emperor alone. Phezzan would be subject to him. However, economic sovereignty would belong to Phezzan. By partitioning control over society's functions, as opposed to its three-dimensional space, the "New Empire" and Phezzan could coexist and engage in reciprocal development. The decadent and hopeless Free Planets Alliance would have to play the role of fertilizer, tilled into the soil of a new age.

However, Rubinsky had shared only an edited version of his plans with the Church of Terra's young bishop. The Church of Terra's goal was not merely religious supremacy but a theocracy, in which the political and religious leadership would merge completely. If they made Earth a temple for all humanity, if their pilgrimages never stopped—well, there was no real problem with that. After all, that weak frontier world was indeed the cradle of the human race. But the thought of Earth as the seat of a theocracy, of it once again becoming the center of authority over the whole human race—that was too horrible a thought to even contemplate.

It would only mean the rise of Terra's Grand Bishop in place of the "sacred and inviolable Emperor Rudolf"—a second sense in which history would be running backward. To prevent that, and to make Rubinsky's intentions a reality, he had to give false obedience to the Church of Terra, and then, at the point when the double ruling systems of the empire and Phezzan were established, use the empire's military might to suppress and destroy Terraism. It went without saying that plenty of care and caution would be necessary. In the past, no sooner would a landesherr show signs of throwing off the yoke of Earth than he would pay for it with his life. He mustn't follow in their footsteps—only a perfect victory could make the fetters of Earth disappear for good.

IV

Count Jochen von Remscheid, once a high-ranked commissioner of the Galactic Empire, was now living the life of a defector in an out-of-the-way cranny of the main world of the Phezzan Land Dominion.

As a high-ranking official in the old system, the judgments of the new would be waiting for him should he return to the empire. If he repented of past sins and swore allegiance to Duke Reinhard von Lohengramm, he might be forgiven, but his own pride and the traditions of his distinguished house would not let him bend the knee to an upstart like the golden brat. He had left his official residence and decided on a new house in the Izmail District, half a day's journey from the capital. The artificial sea in front of him brimmed with persian-blue water, and behind him rocky mountains that looked like they were made of agate closed in around. The flat land that lay between was a jumble of cypress groves and grassland. In the midst of it, a building made of granite and heat-resistant glass displayed its quiet presence.

Ever since the young count lost his official livelihood he had been living in a shell of loneliness and boredom, but now, for the first time in what felt like ages, he was sitting in his reception room and greeting a guest. His guest was a young Phezzanese aide by the name of Rupert Kesselring.

Two or three disparaging comments about Reinhard's new system of government served as an exchange of greetings, and then his guest immediately launched into the reason for his visit.

"If you'll forgive my saying so, Count von Remscheid, Your Excellency is presently in an extremely difficult position. Is that fair to say?"

After an uncertain pause, von Remscheid said, "I don't need you to tell me that." There was a shade of anguish in his eyes that his irises' thin pigmentation couldn't conceal. Although he had yielded the use of his assets to a Phezzanese trust company and had no inconvenience in his daily life, he could not deny the existence of a psychological void inside himself. Hatred and anger toward the new system, a longing for home and the old ways—though these passions were negative, they were indeed passions of a sort. A passion for the restoration of the old ways radiated from Count von Remscheid's beady eyes, spreading out before him. Rupert Kesselring, more than twenty years younger than the count, was observing this with a blend of coolness and sarcasm in his eyes, but when he finally opened his mouth, he was very courteous.

"Actually, I'm here as the landesherr's unofficial messenger. He wishes to propose a certain plan to Your Excellency, so if I may have your attention..."

Fifteen minutes later, the count was staring at Kesselring with a look of shock and disbelief.

"That's quite a bold suggestion. And it has its attraction. But I do have to wonder if this is really in accordance with the landesherr's wishes, or if it's in fact just you getting carried away with yourself."

"I am but the landesherr's devoted servant." The young aide was making modesty his virtue, despite its being only lip service. For just an instant, a steely glint flashed in his eyes.

"Be that as it may," von Remscheid said, "there's still something I'm having a little trouble understanding. Don't get me wrong—this proposal of yours is music to my ears personally, but what's in it for Phezzan? I'd think that, going forward, it would be in your best economic interests to try to get along with the golden brat's new order."

Kesselring flashed a gentle hint of a smile. Assuaging the misgivings of the former commissioner was child's play. All he need do was make a show of reaffirming his prejudices.

"Duke von Lohengramm is trying to transform not only the politics, but the society and economy of the empire as well. His actions are radical, and what's more, he's acting arbitrarily on no one's authority but his own. Already, he's begun to infringe on a number of the rights and interests we Phezzanese have enjoyed in the empire. Change is fine—but change in the wrong direction is something we can't ignore. That's an extremely simple explanation, but basically, that's where Phezzan stands."

Von Remscheid thought it over for a moment.

"Naturally," Kesselring continued, "once this plan has succeeded and the Goldenbaum Dynasty's been saved from the hands of that despicable usurper, Phezzan will receive compensation commensurate to its services. But fame as the savior of the nation will be yours. How about it? Don't you think it's an attractive deal for both parties?"

"A 'deal,' is it . . ." Count von Remscheid smirked just a bit. "Everything's grist for deals to you Phezzanese—even the life or death of the nation. And that's the height of strength. If the empire could recover that kind of vitality and spirit, we'd have another five centuries of order and stability . . ."

As Kesselring casually turned to look at a pastel painting on the wall, he was fighting off the impulse to burst out laughing. A wise man recognizes difficulty, but a fool sees nothing as impossible. Ordinarily, Count von Remscheid shouldn't have been such an incompetent, but the idea of an Empire Eternal, drilled into him since early childhood, was no easy thing to overcome. And as long as the partisans of the old order continued to live in that fantasy, the government of Phezzan could use them, whether they defected to Phezzan or remained in the empire.

The landesherr's young aide was wasting no time that day. After leaving Count von Remscheid's residence, he headed straight over by landcar to the home of another man, named Henlow. Henlow had been dispatched to Phezzan as the Free Planets Alliance's commissioner, which put him in charge locally of the alliance's diplomatic mission to Phezzan. Unofficially, he had one other duty as well. That was his role as leader of the alliance's anti-empire spy ring on Phezzan. He thus occupied a position of great strategic importance for the alliance. However, position, responsibility, and capability do not necessarily all go hand in hand.

It was said that the quality of alliance commissioners had been in decline for the past several years. Every time administrations changed, top officials would reward their supporters with lucrative positions in government. Business leaders and politicos who knew very little of diplomacy would show up, having gladly accepted commissionerships in order to burnish their reputations. Henlow's father had been the founder of a well-known corporation, and though Henlow was now its owner, word had it that his incompetence and unpopularity had exhausted all the affection there was for him, until at last management had tactfully sent him off into exile.

When Henlow, with his sagging cheeks, large belly, and tiny eyebrows, greeted Kesselring, he wasn't quite able to hide his embarrassment. He had had it pointed out to him recently that some government bonds

Phezzan had purchased from the alliance were already past their dates of redemption.

"The total value comes to approximately five hundred billion dinars. Normally, we should ask you to redeem them for us immediately, but..."

"All at once? But that's entirely—er...I mean..."

"Yes, it most certainly is. Pardon my rudeness, but it's entirely outside your country's ability to pay. So I'd like you to consider our dominion's forbearance in the exercise of its legal rights as proof of the friendship and trust we feel toward your nation."

"I can't thank you enough."

"However, that extends only so far as your country remains a stable, democratic nation."

The commissioner sensed something ominous in the voice and expression of Rupert Kesselring.

"By which you mean Phezzan is harboring doubts about my nation's political stability? May I interpret your words that way, sir?"

"Does it sound like I'm saying anything else?"

At this sharp retort, the commissioner sank into an embarrassed silence. Kesselring softened his features and assumed a more polite tone of voice.

"Phezzan truly does want to see the Free Planets Alliance continue on as a stable democracy."

"Quite right."

"Disturbances like last year's coup d'état put us in an extremely awkward position. If the coup had succeeded, the capital we had invested there might well have been confiscated without compensation in the name of national socialism. Freedom of industry and the protection of private property are indispensable to Phezzan's ongoing survival, and it would be highly irritating if your country's government changed in such a way as to deny those things."

"I certainly agree with what you're saying. But that reckless conspiracy failed, and my country continues to protect its traditions of freedom and democracy to this day."

"Regarding that, Admiral Yang Wen-li's contribution was...exceedingly great."

Kesselring's words implied that Henlow and those like him had made no contribution at all, but unsurprisingly, Henlow didn't notice.

"Yes, indeed. He's quite a commander..."

"In terms of raw talent, reputation, and ability, there is no one in the FPA military who can stand shoulder to shoulder with Admiral Yang. Isn't that so?"

"Well...certainly, but—"

"And how long do you think such a man is going to tolerate being ordered around by this present administration? Have you given any thought to that, Commissioner?"

For a time, the commissioner seemed to be cautiously mulling over the meaning of the young aide's words. Then, at last, a look of surprise and horror spread out over his face.

"You—you can't be suggesting he would..."

In answer, Rupert Kesselring smiled like a student of Mephistopheles. "I see you're a man of penetrating insight, Excellency."

It was not entirely without effort that Kesselring was able to say those words. Inwardly, he was actually cursing the man's thickheadedness. Naturally, he would do nothing that might reveal his honest feelings, though. Right now he had to patiently guide the commissioner, as if training a forgetful dog to perform a trick.

"But, but...last year during the coup d'état, Admiral Yang sided with the government—he put down the uprising. Why would a man like that turn on the government now?"

"Last year is last year. At least consider this: it was because of Admiral Yang that the coup could be crushed so completely and so quickly. But if he ever grew ambitious himself, who would there be to stop him once he'd mobilized his forces? Weren't both Iserlohn and Artemis's Necklace completely powerless before him?"

"But..."

Henlow started to mount a defense, but he trailed off without continuing, pulled out a handkerchief, and wiped the sweat from his face. Doubt flavored with fear was making his stomach churn. Kesselring could see that clearly. Sprinkle in a little more spice and his doubt would take a decisive turn into suspicion.

"I'm sure what I'm saying sounds slanderous, but I do have some grounds…"

"By which you mean?"

Jowls tensed, Commissioner Henlow leaned forward. He was now just a cheap marionette dancing to Kesselring's flute.

"Artemis's Necklace. Twelve attack satellites in stationary orbit over Heinessen, and Admiral Yang destroyed all of them. But do you really think it was necessary to destroy all twelve?"

"Now that you mention it…" Henlow said after a moment.

"What if he viewed them as an obstacle to his own capture of Heinessen later on and so eliminated them early while he had the chance? I'm speaking solely out of affection for the alliance's government, and if I'm wrong, I'm wrong, but I do think it would be best to have Admiral Yang explain himself."

Having exhaled all sorts of rhetorical poisons, Kesselring took his leave of the Henlow residence. After reporting on all that had happened to the landesherr, Kesselring was looking a little down.

"What's the matter? Something seems to be bothering you."

"I'm happy that things went well, but there's some subtle something that just feels like it's *missing* when they're that easy to manipulate. I'd just like to do a negotiation sometime where the sparks really fly."

"You just can't please some people. Before long, you'll say you want someone easier to negotiate with. And even if today's negotiation was easy, don't think it was because of your superior diplomatic skills."

"I understand that. It was because the commissioner is in a very weak position…both publicly and privately."

Rupert Kesselring laughed in a low voice. The commissioner was a man filled with worldly desires, and in accordance with the landesherr's orders, Kesselring himself had provided the man with both money and beautiful women, taming and domesticating him for future use. Corrupting foreign diplomats did not violate the moral code of the Phezzanese. Things that could not be bought with money certainly existed, but things that were for sale were to be bought at their fair market prices—and once bought, to be used.

"By the way, Your Excellency, I hesitate to bring up such a small matter, but could we speak for a moment about a man called Boris Konev?"

"I remember who he is. What about him?"

"We've received a somewhat hesitant complaint from the office of our commissioner in the Free Planets Alliance. He's not very cooperative or hardworking, it seems, and above all he is terminally unmotivated."

"Hmm..."

"As an independent trader, he seems to have had a passable head for business. But tying him down with the status of public employee... Wasn't that a bit like ordering a nomad to go and till a field?"

"So what you're saying is that he's not the right man for the job?"

"Please forgive me if I've annoyed you. While I do believe the measures Your Excellency takes are without fail the product of deep consideration..."

Rubinsky rolled a sip of wine with the tip of his tongue.

"There's no need to worry. Indeed, Mr. Konev may well have belonged out in the wild. However, I've got pawns that may look useless right now but whose purposes will become apparent later on. Just like with bank accounts and bonds, the longer the term, the better the interest rate."

"That's certainly true, but..."

"How many hundreds of millions of years did it take for oil to form in the Earth's strata before it became something that was usable? Compared to that, give a human being fifty years and he's sure to show results, no matter how late a bloomer he may be. It's nothing to fret over."

"Hundreds of millions of years... you say?"

In the aide's murmured words was the ring of a strange sense of defeat, as if the gap in what the two men were made of had just been driven home. Kesselring turned again to look at the landesherr.

"Even so, the direction that pawns on a chessboard have to move in is decided, but that doesn't apply to people. They move whichever way they like, and making them into something useful may be surprisingly difficult..."

"Don't ruin my metaphors when I'm on a roll. It's true that human psychology and behavior is vastly more complicated than pawns in chess. So to make them move like you want, you just have to make them simpler."

"What do you mean?"

"Drive the other person into particular circumstances and you can take away his options so there are fewer moves he can make. For example, take Yang Wen-li in the Alliance Armed Forces..."

Yang's standing was a little uncertain at present. The alliance's authorities were in what could best be described as a love-hate relationship with him. It made them uneasy to think that Yang might jump into the realm of politics with his present level of support and legally rob them of their authority. But they also had fears—fears Rubinsky had inflamed by way of Kesselring—that Yang might use his vast military forces to establish his own supremacy extralegally. Given these two concerns, the authorities, for their part, would have liked to have had Yang eliminated. However, Yang's military genius was absolutely essential to the alliance. If Yang weren't there, the Alliance Armed Forces might well fall apart without even fighting. Ironically, one could even say that Yang was protected precisely because of the empire's dictator, Duke Reinhard von Lohengramm. If Reinhard were not a factor, the alliance's authorities would have run wild with glee and gotten rid of Yang, whose presence would no longer have been needed. That didn't mean they would go so far as to take his life, but they wouldn't think twice about making up some political or sexual scandal to drag his reputation through the mud and rob him of his civil rights. A first-rate leader finds purpose in the question, "What can I accomplish with my power?" Whereas a second-rate leader's only purpose is to perpetuate that power for as long as possible. And in its present state, the alliance clearly had leadership of the second-rate variety.

"Yang Wen-li is at this moment standing on a slender thread. One end hangs from the alliance and the other from the empire, and as long as this balance holds, Yang will be able to stand, albeit unsteadily. However..."

"You mean to say we of Phezzan will cut that string?"

"We won't even have to—just causing it to fray a little will be plenty. As we do so, Yang's options will steadily decrease. Another two, three years and Yang will have only two paths left to choose from: either be purged by the alliance's ruling authorities, or overthrow the present authorities and take their place."

"It's also possible he'll be killed in battle by Reinhard von Lohengramm before it comes to that."

The landesherr's aide just wouldn't stop pointing out potential problems.

"I can't allow Duke von Lohengramm the pleasure."

Rubinsky's tone was plain and easygoing, but something murky was at work at its bottom. Kesselring had a feeling that Rubinsky was dodging his questions. "There's also the possibility that Yang Wen-li will defeat Duke von Lohengramm on the battlefield. How would you deal with that situation?"

"Mister Kesselring..." the Landesherr said with a subtle change in the tone of his voice. "It looks like I've said too much and you've heard too much. We both have lots to do besides sitting here and talking philosophy. This plan will require us to set up Count von Remscheid as leader, of course, and we still haven't picked the members of the team that will put it into action. First, I need you to take care of that."

After a moment's pause, Kesselring said, "My apologies. I'll complete the selections soon and then return with my report."

The aide left the room, and Rubinsky's powerful body sank down deep into his chair.

When this project was put into action, the Galactic Empire, under von Lohengramm's dictatorship, and the Free Planets Alliance would be made mortal enemies. This plan had to be executed, however, before some politician of great insight arose and tried to negotiate peaceful coexistence between the two powers.

On the firm jaw of the landesherr of Phezzan, there was a faint smile like that of some carnivorous beast.

He mustn't give them the chance to realize that the enemy of the Free Planets Alliance was not the Galactic Empire but the Goldenbaum Dynasty. The moment that the empire and the FPA recognized the Goldenbaum

Dynasty as a common enemy that they should bring down together, peaceful coexistence between von Lohengramm's new order and the FPA would be possible. And so they must never realize it. The struggle between the two great powers must go on for a bit longer. Not forever. Another three years, or maybe four, would be enough. Then, when the flames of war had at last died out, those benighted fools would never imagine who it was who ruled all inhabited planets, as well as the space that tied them together...

CHAPTER 4:

IT WAS THE END OF FEBRUARY when Rupert Kesselring, aide to the landesherr of Phezzan, visited Leopold Schumacher in Assini-Boyer Valley, some nine hundred kilometers north of the capital. In a nation centered on commerce and trade, this region was one vast tract of arable land. It had long been left fallow, but just last year Schumacher's group of settlers had opened up a collective farm there and begun developing the land.

Leopold Schumacher had held the rank of captain in the Imperial Navy up until last year, when he had joined with the nobles' confederated forces in the Lippstadt War, serving as a staff officer under Baron Flegel—one of the hardest of the hard-liners. The baron, however, had continually ignored Schumacher's advice and opinions and, ultimately, had flown into a rage and tried to murder him, only to be shot dead himself by soldiers who'd had more faith in the advisor than in the commander. Afterward, Schumacher had taken charge of the crew and defected with them to Phezzan. In this new land, they had abandoned their pasts to start over. The thirty-three-year-old Schumacher had had a promising career ahead of him in the military, but now he was tired of war and conspiracy, and sought a life of quiet satisfaction.

To that end, Schumacher had disposed of the weapons systems in the battleship they had ridden to Phezzan and then sold off the ship to a Phezzanese merchant. The money he had distributed among the crew, and then he tried to depart, leaving the future of every man in his own hands. His subordinates, however, wouldn't disband. Although they had abandoned their homeland and defected to this place after their defeat in battle, they lacked confidence that they could survive in the dog-eat-dog world of Phezzanese society, where quick wits and craftiness were not optional and you couldn't let your guard down for a minute. Tales of the Phezzanese people's shrewd pursuit of profit were exaggerated in the empire, and the crew, made up of simple soldiers unfamiliar with how this world worked, didn't feel like they could rely on their own abilities here. The only things they trusted in were Schumacher's prudence and sense of responsibility. For Schumacher's part, he couldn't abandon the soldiers who had saved him from the muzzle of an enraged Baron Flegel's sidearm.

The soldiers had left the question of how best to use their shares completely up to Schumacher, and the wise former staff officer—also lacking confidence that he could do business with the Phezzanese and come out a winner—had chosen to go into agriculture. It wasn't glamorous work, but it was steady. Not even a people as business oriented as the Phezzanese could live without food, and generally speaking they were willing to pay premium prices for fresher, more delicious produce. By supplying quality foods to merchants who knew how to enjoy the finer things in life, they could probably make it on Phezzan, Schumacher had figured.

Schumacher had made effective use of the funds obtained from the sale of the battleship. He had purchased land in the Assini-Boyer Valley, installed a plain but well-equipped mobile residence, and acquired seeds and seedlings. For the defectors, a long, patient battle with the land was just beginning.

And then Kesselring had showed up.

Schumacher seemed to view their unexpected guest as nothing more than a troublesome intruder. When the landesherr's aide said he had an important message regarding their homeland, Schumacher replied, "Please, sir, you need not concern yourself with me further." His courteous tone couldn't completely mask a ring of evasiveness. "Whatever's happening with the empire and the Goldenbaum Dynasty has nothing to do with me. I've got my hands full building a new life for me and my friends—I don't have time to spend thinking about a past I've thrown away."

"Throw your past away if you wish," said Kesselring. "But don't throw your future away in the process. Captain Schumacher, you're not the sort of man who should live out the rest of his days smeared in dirt and fertilizer. If you had the chance to change the course of history, wouldn't you rather do that instead?"

"Please leave." The captain started to rise from his chair.

"Wait, please. Calm down and hear me out," Kesselring said. "You all can probably produce crops with your farm. Assini-Boyer is unused and abandoned, but it does have the potential to produce bountifully. Sadly, however, crops mean nothing if you can't sell them in the marketplace. A sensible man like yourself understands, I'm sure."

Kesselring was inwardly impressed that not a muscle in Schumacher's face so much as twitched. The landesherr's young aide realized what a strong and clever man Schumacher was. However, this game had been rigged against him from the start. Schumacher had only one pawn to play against an opponent with a full set of pieces.

After a long silence, Schumacher said, "So this is how you do things on Phezzan?" The note of anger contained in his voice was not directed at Kesselring; it was just ineffectual sarcasm aimed at his own powerlessness.

"Correct. This is the Phezzan way." Kesselring showed not a trace of shame as he acknowledged his victory. "We bend the rules when the situation calls for it. Despise me if you must . . . though a loser's contempt for a winner is, I think, one of the most futile emotions in existence."

"While you're winning, you'll probably think so," Schumacher shot back offhandedly, fixing Kesselring with a discontented stare. The aide was almost exactly ten years his junior. "Well then, let's hear it. What exactly do you want me to do? Assassinate Duke von Lohengramm or something?"

Kesselring gave him a smile.

"Phezzan has no taste for bloodshed. After all, peace is the only road that leads to prosperity."

It was clear to see that Schumacher didn't buy a word of that, but what the young aide needed was Schumacher's compliance, not his belief. He gave him the same speech he'd given Count von Remscheid the other day, and noted with satisfaction the look of shock on Schumacher's face.

Count Alfred von Lansberg was also on the main world of the Phezzan Land Dominion, complaining about his ill luck as a defector. Only twenty-six years of age, he was already experiencing vastly greater changes in his lifestyle than his great-grandfather had seen in a lifetime four times as long. His great-grandfather had enjoyed feasting, hunting game, and womanizing till his dying day, but before accumulating much experience in any of those areas, Alfred had gotten mixed up in that grand uprising that had split the empire in half, and as a result had lost every last mark of his inheritance. His only bit of good fortune was that he was still alive.

Alfred had just barely managed to withdraw from the battlefield without being killed, and afterward he had fled to Phezzan. There he had sold off his star sapphire cuff links—a gift from the previous emperor, Friedrich IV—to provide himself with temporary living expenses and then set about composing a volume entitled *A History of the Lippstadt War*. His poetry and short stories had always been well received in the salons of the aristocrats.

When he had finished up the opening section, Alfred had triumphantly carried the manuscript to a publisher, only to have it politely rejected.

"Your Excellency's work certainly has a number of fine points," the editor had said to an indignant Alfred. "But it's too subjective, there are inaccuracies, and I have my doubts about what little value it has as a record of events...Instead of using such an ornate style and writing down whatever your passion or romanticism dictates, you should adopt a more restrained style, write calmly and objectively..."

The young count had snatched his manuscript from the hands of the editor, picked up the tatters of his self-respect, and gone back to his temporary residence. It had taken a lot of wine to get to sleep that night.

The next day, his mood had been completely different. No mere chronicler of events was he! He was a man of action. Instead of copying down the past on sheets of paper, shouldn't he be acting in the present and using his own hands to build the future?

It was with thoughts such as these swirling through his mind that he received a visit from Rupert Kesselring, aide to the landesherr of Phezzan. The aide, younger even than Alfred, spoke courteously: "Count von Lansberg, might you be of a mind to offer up your loyalty and passion for the sake of your homeland? If you are, Count von Remscheid is heading up a project I'd like Your Excellency to participate in . . ."

When he heard what the project was, Count Alfred was both surprised and thrilled, and agreed on the spot to participate. Soon after, he was introduced to Schumacher, who was responsible for putting the plan into action.

The former imperial captain was well aware that Alfred had been a friend of the late Baron Flegel. *This might get awkward,* Schumacher worried, steeling himself for the worst.

Alfred, however, had met a lot of captains during the uprising and remembered nothing at all about this one.

"I understand you and I were comrades before," he said, "and starting today we'll be brothers-in-arms. I'm glad to meet you."

The look on Alfred's face was neither discriminating nor doubtful as he held his hand out to Schumacher. As Schumacher reached out to shake it, he could feel alternating bubbles of relief and unease rising to the surface of his consciousness.

Alfred von Lansberg was pleasant enough to be around and had energy and courage to spare, but he did have a tendency to conflate reality with speculation. When Schumacher thought through this scheme's possible outcomes, however, it was hard for him to feel very optimistic.

Could this plan succeed? Schumacher couldn't help but wonder. And even if it did, what was it supposed to accomplish? Would it do anything besides spread the flames of war and create a roadblock on the path to peace? But even as Schumacher was thinking over these things, he still had no choice but to participate, given the position he was in.

In this manner, Rupert Kesselring was making steady progress in assembling the people needed for the plan. He had all the time and money he needed. He was certain the plan would work. And when it was executed, the whole human race would fall over in stunned disbelief. He looked forward to seeing how Duke Reinhard von Lohengramm, a year Kesselring's junior, would react.

When that day came, even Landesherr Rubinsky would have no choice but to recognize his ability . . .

II

Hildegard von Mariendorf, or Hilda, was now assisting Reinhard in the role of secretary to the imperial prime minister. The wealth of political, diplomatic, and strategic sense she brought to the table was thought to be highly prized by Reinhard. However:

"It's not just about her talent."

That observation was the greatest common denominator in the thoughts of all of Reinhard's subordinates—civil and military officials alike. The twenty-two-year-old Reinhard and the twenty-one-year-old Hilda were both rare sorts of beauties, and when they stood side by side, some even likened the sight to that of Apollo and Minerva from the myths of ancient Rome. They did not remark so in public, however—in the empire, the word "myth" was restricted to the ancient Germanic tradition.

Hilda didn't fit the image of the well-bred lady that might be imagined of a count's daughter. Her dark-blond hair was cut short, and when she walked by with that light spring in her step, she looked so vibrant and full of life that onlookers felt more the impression of a young boy. To her father, Count Franz von Mariendorf, Hilda was something of a miracle. She had grown up unfettered by the conventions of the aristocracy, and this had furnished her with powers of reason far exceeding the bounds of her age and station. He felt no regret over having never had a son. It had been thanks to Hilda that even in the midst of the Lippstadt War the count had been able to accurately foresee what lay ahead and lead his family through that time to safety.

Hilda had neither elder nor younger brother. What she did have was a cousin, Baron Heinrich von Kümmel. His silvery-white hair, his attractive but wan facial features, the lack of muscle on his slender frame—he looked more than merely delicate; he looked feeble and fragile. His health was, in fact, quite poor, and as he had to spend most of each day in bed, he had not joined in with the Lippstadt Agreement—one result of which had been his escaping destruction.

By the time he was born, he had already been diagnosed with congenital metabolic disease. From birth, his body had lacked sufficient enzymes, and its development had been hindered by its inability to properly break down or absorb sugars and amino acids. By feeding affected babies a special kind of therapeutic milk for a period of several years, it was possible to cure this condition completely. However, that milk was extremely expensive.

According to the Genetic Inferiority Elimination Act promulgated by Rudolf the Great, children with congenital disabilities were not worth keeping alive. It followed then, that, legally speaking, producing this milk in order to save the weak was out of the question. The real problem, however, had been that children with physical handicaps were born into aristocratic as well as commoner families. A small amount of therapeutic milk had in fact been produced to meet aristocratic demand, but it had been sold at prices that outstripped the purchasing power of the commoners. To the Galactic Empire's ruling class, commoners had no significance beyond their labor and the tax burden they bore to nourish the ruling class. Diligent workers were of course to be praised, but the weak and disabled—those who did nothing but burden others while making no contribution of their own to society—did not have any right to life.

Under ordinary circumstances, Heinrich would have died in infancy. The only reason his life had been extended was that he'd been born to a medium-income aristocratic family. Depending on external factors and the nature of the individual, those in such "privileged circumstances," might find food for deep thought in this, or they might just complacently accept it without criticism. Paul von Oberstein, who had needed artificial eyes since birth, had contemplated it thoroughly and taken action to overthrow a system he viewed as evil, but Heinrich lacked the physical strength for such activity. When he was a newborn, the doctors had said,

"He'll live to be three," and at age five they had said, "Another two years at most." When he was twelve, they had said, "He probably won't make it to fifteen." His cousin Hilda—three years his senior—could never help feeling protective of him and did whatever she could to help her cousin.

To Heinrich, Hilda was not just an older cousin. She was not only beautiful, but also lively and wise—the object of an admiration from him that bordered on worship. Having lost both his parents as a child, he had succeeded to the head of his family with his uncle—Count Franz von Mariendorf—as his guardian. Intellect aside, he had been lacking in age, experience, and health, so his inheritance had been placed under Count von Mariendorf's stewardship. If the count had been of a mind to do so, he could have embezzled the entire von Kümmel family fortune; however, there were very few among the imperial nobility who were as honest and trustworthy as Count von Mariendorf.

Heinrich's tendency toward hero worship was probably only natural. He looked up to a number of people whose accomplishments over the course of a single lifetime had spanned numerous fields: Leonardo da Vinci; political reformer, warrior, and poet Ts'ao Ts'ao; soldier, revolution-ary, mathematician, and technician Lazare Carnot; emperor, astronomer, and poet Rukn al-Dunya wa al-Din Abu Talib Muhammad Toghrul-Beg ibn Mikail.

One day, Hilda asked Admiral Ernest Mecklinger, a subordinate of Reinhard's, to come and meet Heinrich. In Heinrich's eyes, Mecklinger was, in one sense, an ideal human being.

Not unlike the Free Planets Alliance's Yang Wen-li, Mecklinger had joined the military unwillingly. But unlike Yang—whose dossier had "taking naps" written in its "Interests and Hobbies" column—Mecklinger was gifted with fertile powers of artistic expression. In the Imperial Academy of Art's annual art competition, he had won prizes in both the prose poem and watercolor categories, and his piano performances were lauded by critics as "a perfect fusion of daring and delicacy." Moreover, he had displayed reliable ability as a military officer in conflicts such as the Battle of Amritsar and the Lippstadt War, in which he had shone with numerous impressive feats. As a commander, he was more the strategist who observed the tide of battle with a wide view, positioning and committing necessary forces in response to the dictates of circumstance. He could command a large fleet well, but the skill he possessed as an advisor was even harder to come by.

Accepting Hilda's request, the "Artist-Admiral" called on the mansion where Heinrich was living, a watercolor painting of his own creation in hand, and, together with Hilda, spent about an hour with him in pleasant conversation. Heinrich got overly excited and broke out in a slight fever. A doctor was called for, bringing the chat to an end, but Hilda, who had gone to the atrium to see Mecklinger off, asked one question while she was thanking him. When the admiral had entered Heinrich's sickroom, an extremely subtle expression of surprise had passed across his face, and she was curious to know the reason for it.

"Oh, so it showed on my face?" said Mecklinger, smiling gently beneath his brown, neatly trimmed mustache. At thirty-five, he was relatively old among the admirals under Reinhard's command. "Actually, I know a few other people with conditions like his and have noticed that people who can't move around freely often keep pets. Birds, cats, and so on. I didn't see anything like that in Baron von Kümmel's room, however, so I thought, 'Oh, I wonder if he doesn't like animals.' That was all it was."

It was true that Heinrich had never kept any small animals by his side. Did he not need the psychological compensation of enjoying—or envying—the sight of an animal moving about?

Mecklinger's comment reminded Hilda of a doubt that she herself had had once before, though it took less than two hours for her to forget about it entirely.

Both Hilda and Mecklinger were equipped with unusual intelligence and sensitivity. That was probably why she had felt that doubt, although it had been too small a bud to grow into anything more. It would be much, much later that both the count's daughter who served as secretary to the imperial prime minister and the Imperial Navy admiral who was a poet and painter would remember this fleeting conversation. When it came up again, it would come coupled with something bitter.

The plan to move Gaiesburg Fortress, concocted by Tech Admiral von Schaft and to be executed by Kempf and Müller, was not one that Hilda was necessarily in favor of. Put bluntly, she was unambiguously critical of it. What the universe needed now, she believed, were Reinhard's skills as a builder, not his skills as a conqueror. Hilda was not an adherent of absolute pacifism. Like the confederacy of former aristocrats that had represented the late Duke von Braunschweig, there were enemies of reform and unity that must be defeated by military force. That said, military force was not all-powerful. Military force derived its potency from political and economic well-being; if a nation allowed either of these to weaken while only strengthening its military, lasting victories could not be expected. Put in extreme terms, military force was a last-ditch effort to reverse political or diplomatic defeat and was most valuable when not put into action.

The thing that Hilda couldn't understand was why, at this moment in time, it was necessary to invade the Free Planets Alliance's territory. All she could think was that this invasion clearly lacked the element of inevitability.

The plan to move Gaiesburg Fortress was proceeding rapidly under the energetic direction of Karl Gustav Kempf. At the same time that repairs were being made to the fortress itself, twelve warp engines and twelve conventional navigational engines were being attached in a ring formation around it. The first warp test was scheduled for mid-March. At present, 64,000 military engineers were working on the project, and Reinhard had decided to approve Kempf's request to mobilize an additional 24,000.

"I hadn't realized just how tricky a thing warp is," Reinhard said to Hilda over lunch one day. "If the mass is too small, you can't get the engine output needed to warp, but if the mass is too large, the engine's output will go over the limit. And even if you use multiple engines, they have to run in perfect sync—and not sputter out and die, of course—or Gaiesburg Fortress will either be lost forever in subspace or reduced to its component atoms. Von Schaft's full of confidence, but the difficulty of this project is in the execution, not the planning. At this stage, von Schaft doesn't need to be preening about like he is."

"Admiral Kempf's doing good work, though."

"It's not as if he's been completely successful yet . . ."

"I certainly want him to succeed. You'll end up losing a capable admiral if he fails."

"If Kempf dies like that, it will just demonstrate the measure of the man that he is. Even if he were to survive, he would be of no great use." At that moment, Reinhard's voice had gone beyond the bounds of the cool and appraising; it resonated with heartless cruelty.

What would you say if Siegfried Kircheis were alive? Hilda stopped just short of saying out loud. There was only one person in the world who could say that to Reinhard. That was the woman living at the mountain villa in Floren who had the same golden hair as her younger brother and a smile like autumn sunlight, and who bore the title of Countess von Grünewald.

Reinhard moved with a reckless grace as he brought his wineglass to his lips. Watching him, Hilda noticed a kind of danger that this elegant young man carried within him. A wild, winged stallion had made its home inside him and become his driving force. And its reins—did Reinhard hold them himself, or were they in the hands of the late Siegfried Kircheis? That thought haunted Hilda and wouldn't let her go.

III

"On the technical side, there's no reason we can't move the fortress. The problem we have to solve is the relationship between mass and engine output. That's the only sticking point."

Tech Admiral von Schaft concluded his speech confidently, leaving his listeners with no small cause for concern.

The mass of Gaiesburg Fortress amounted to approximately forty trillion tons. How much would it affect normal space when such an enormous mass warped into subspace and then warped back out again? Wouldn't it be lethal if there were a quake in space-time? In the real world, was it even possible to activate twelve warp engines with *perfect* simultaneity? If they were activated with even a tenth of a second's error, wouldn't the million-plus personnel inside the fortress either be atomized or sent to wander subspace for all eternity?

Small-scale experiments were conducted over and over, and research vessels were deployed near the regions of space where the fortress was set to warp in and warp out. When the project had first been set into motion, Reinhard had demanded accuracy "as close to perfection as human beings are capable of," and as Kempf and Müller were both excellent managers, they were employing every means they could think of to bolster the chances of success. Naturally, though, there was no guarantee that this would bring about a perfect result.

Meanwhile, Reinhard was also throwing himself into his work as imperial prime minister. He worked every day except Sunday, spending the first half of the day at the admiralität and the rest of the day at the imperial prime minister's office. The late lunches he would eat at one o'clock marked the dividing point. Hilda often filled the role of luncheon date; Reinhard enjoyed talking to the beautiful young woman. He seemed more interested in Hilda's intellect than her beauty. One day, when the conversation touched on the Lippstadt War of the previous year, Hilda said to him, "Duke von Braunschweig had a larger military force than Your Excellency, but he was destroyed because of three things he lacked."

"Please tell me—I want to hear what those three things were."

"Very well. His heart lacked balance, his eyes lacked insight, and his ears lacked the willingness to listen to the opinions of his subordinates."

"I see."

"Stated backwards, Your Excellency was able to secure victory over a great enemy because you were equipped with all of those things."

Taking note of her use of the past tense, the glint in Reinhard's ice-blue eyes hardened ever so slightly. He set a coffee cup made of paper-thin porcelain down on the table and gazed straight at his lovely secretary.

"It seems you would have words with me, fräulein."

"Only the sort of talk one has over tea. It's frightening to have you look at me like that."

"You shouldn't fear the likes of me . . ." Reinhard gave a wry grin, and for an instant his face was that of a young boy.

Hilda pressed onward. "Nations, organizations, associations—call them what you will, but there's something absolutely essential for binding groups of people together."

"Oh? And what is that?"

"An *enemy*."

Reinhard gave a short laugh. "You speak the truth. Sharp as always, fräulein. So, who might that enemy be whom my subordinates and I require?"

Hilda gave Reinhard the answer he had likely seen coming:

"The Goldenbaum Dynasty, of course," Hilda said. She didn't take her eyes off the young imperial prime minister. "The emperor is only seven, and his age, talents, abilities, and so on present no danger to you whatsoever at this juncture. As the current head of the Goldenbaum Dynasty, and as one who's inherited the blood of Rudolf the Great, he could become a symbol of solidarity for the old forces to rally around. That's the only problem with him—there is no other."

"You're absolutely right," Reinhard said, nodding his head.

What qualities the seven-year-old emperor Erwin Josef might possess were still a matter of unexplored territory. Aside from being a bit irritable, he seemed an utterly ordinary boy at this point, displaying little in the way of sharp wits or reason. Compared to Reinhard at that age, he was lacking both in terms of appearance and of that glow that came from within. Still, even among the great there was such a thing as a "late bloomer," so it was hard to predict how he might grow in the future.

Reinhard had deprived the emperor of nothing materially. It was a fact that he had slashed palace expenses and the number of chamberlains compared to the days of the previous emperor, Friedrich IV. Yet even so, there were still dozens of grown-ups there to wait on him: tutors, cooks, professional babysitters, nurses, dog walkers ... His food, his clothes, and even his toys were luxurious beyond the wildest dreams of any commoner's child. Whatever he wanted was given to him, and no matter what he did there was no one to scold him. Perhaps this was in fact the best way possible to nip in the bud any future greatness he might develop. Even someone with the potential for great wit and reason would probably be spoiled by such an environment.

"Not to worry, fräulein," Reinhard said gently. "Not even I wish to become a murderer of children. I will not kill the emperor. Like you said, I need an enemy. And for my own part, I'd like to be more generous than my enemies and as righteous as is possible..."

"Well spoken, Your Excellency."

Hilda had no sympathy whatsoever for the Goldenbaum Dynasty. She found it a little strange herself that she, born to an aristocratic family, should embrace the kind of thinking a republican might. Even so, she didn't want to let Reinhard become a child killer. Usurpation was nothing to be ashamed of. It was a thing to be proud of, in fact—proof that one's ability had triumphed over authority. But to kill a small child? No matter what the circumstances might be, that would never escape the criticism of future generations...

I∪

Before the test warp was to be carried out, Admiral Karl Gustav Kempf returned briefly to the imperial capital of Odin to make a progress report to Imperial Marshal Reinhard von Lohengramm, commander in chief of the Imperial Space Armada.

"Do you think it'll work?"

A strong, soldierly reply answered Reinhard's question: "It's sure to work. You can count on it."

Reinhard fixed ice-blue eyes on his tall, powerfully built subordinate, nodded, and, softening his expression, recommended he spend one night at home with his family. Kempf had planned on returning to Gaiesburg right away, but instead he changed his itinerary and returned to his official residence. Kempf had a wife and two sons. This was the first chance they'd had in several months to all be together, and with gratitude toward the young imperial marshal, Kempf said to his sons, "Your *vati's* about to go way off into space to take care of some bad guys. Both of you are men, though, so I want you to be good and take care of your *mutti*."

Kempf knew very well that the facts were not so simple, but he believed one should aim for clarity and simplicity when dealing with children. As they grew older, they would naturally learn to comprehend the complications and ugliness of the world. Maybe they would someday come to resent the simple, clear worldview that their father had imparted to them, but it was his belief that when they became parents themselves, the time would come when they would understand.

"Boys, won't you say goodbye to your father?"

At his mother's prompting, the elder of the two, eight-year-old Gustav Isaak, grabbed hold of his father's big, strong body and, stretching up as high as he could, spoke these words to his father: "Bye, Dad. Come home soon."

His five-year-old brother, Karl Franz, grabbed on to the older boy's back. Unsurprisingly, he was stretching too.

"Bye, Daddy. Bring me a present, okay?"

At that, his older brother whirled around and scolded him. "You dummy! Dad's going away to work. He doesn't have time to buy presents!"

But their kindly father laughed, smoothing his younger son's chestnut hair with a large palm as the boy started to sob.

"I'll bring presents next time. But—oh wait, how about this? We haven't visited your grandmother's house in a while. Why don't we go see her when I get back?"

"Darling, are you sure you should be making promises like that? They'll hold it against you if you break them."

"Huh? Oh, it'll be fine. Once I've made this mission a success, I ought to be able to get a little vacation time. We should be able to start sending more money home to your folks, too."

"That's not what I'm—darling, just try to keep safe. Please come back to us safely. That's all I'm asking for."

"That goes without saying. I'll be back."

Kempf kissed his wife, easily scooped up both of the boys in his arms, and smiled once more. With a touch of rustic humor, he asked his wife, "Have I ever gone off to battle and not come back before?"

Hilda wasn't the only one critical of the planned invasion. Wolfgang Mittermeier and Oskar von Reuentahl, deemed the "twin pillars" of the imperial forces, were of a similar mind. Although they had been disappointed at first to learn that someone besides themselves had been tapped to command the mission, regret had metamorphosed into shocked disbelief once they learned that this whole operation had come from the mind of Commissioner of Science and Technology von Schaft. It was plain to see that his motives were extremely personal.

One night at a club for high-ranking officers, the two of them carried a coffeepot into a private room. While playing several games of poker, they let fly with all manner of scathing invective regarding von Schaft.

"Even if he *has* come up with a new tactical theory," said Mittermeier, "he's got things spectacularly backward if he thinks that's reason to press for an attack. This is a *mumei-no-shi*, and as a subject of his lord, he ought to be ashamed of himself for recommending it."

Strong-willed, upright Mittermeier had delivered a stinging critique with those words. *Mumei-no-shi*, an ancient Chinese term that meant "a waste of 2,500 soldiers," was reserved for lawless wars with no high purpose, and of all the terms used for criticizing war, this was the harshest.

Kempf had been named commander in chief for the dispatch, and Mittermeier had been holding back his criticism ever since he had begun working on the project. First of all, things had moved beyond the stage at which criticism was permissible, and secondly, he didn't want people thinking he was jealous of any successes Kempf might have in the field. Still, to von Reuentahl only, he said, "We have to bring down the Free Planets Alliance eventually, but this deployment is pointless and unnecessary. It can't be healthy for the nation to mobilize needlessly and become arrogant because of our military strength."

Mittermeier was a valiant commander—so much so that he was called "the Gale Wolf" as a nickname—but that didn't mean he was unnecessarily aggressive. Nothing could be further from him than to commit wanton acts of savagery or brutality, or to become unnecessarily proud of military strength.

"If Siegfried Kircheis were still alive, I'm sure he could talk Duke von Lohengramm out of this," Mittermeier said with a sigh.

Everyone had been fond of that redheaded youth. He had been selfless to the extreme, and his death has come as a blow to many. With the passage of time, the grief and the shock had lessened, but the sense of loss had only deepened. For those who had known him, it was as if they had found an empty seat in their hearts that should never have been vacated.

And if even I feel that way, how much worse is it for Duke von Lohengramm? Mittermeier thought, unable to help feeling sympathetic.

He and his colleague Oskar von Reuentahl had first met Reinhard four years ago. Reinhard had been eighteen at the time and had already held the rank of commodore. The twenty-six-year-old Mittermeier and the twenty-seven-year-old von Reuentahl had both been captains, and Siegfried Kircheis, following Reinhard around like a shadow, had not yet moved past lieutenant commander.

Since Reinhard had not yet acquired peerage and the family name of von Lohengramm, he had been going by his old name of von Müsel at the time. He had just returned from the Van Fleet Stellar Region, where he had taken alliance officers captive in combat, and the soldiers had felt mildly shocked when they saw him. He was an unbelievably beautiful young man, on whose back white wings would have not been out of place. However, they had felt there was more intensity than kindness in his ice-blue eyes—more intellect than innocence, more sharpness that friendliness.

"What do you think?" Mittermeier had asked. "About the golden brat, or whatever he's called?"

"There's an old saying," von Reuentahl had replied, "'Don't mistake a tiger cub for a cat.' Most likely, that one's a tiger. True, he's the younger brother of the emperor's concubine, but the enemy was under no obligation to lose to him just because of that."

With a forceful nod, Mittermeier had signaled agreement with his colleague's appraisal. The young man known as Reinhard von Müsel was at that time being underestimated by those around him. One reason was that his elder sister Annerose was the emperor's concubine, which made it easy to think that all of his power came from her, but another thing—a slightly strange thing—was that his incomparably good looks were acting as a veil that concealed his true nature. People seemed to think that a sharp mind didn't go together with an excess of physical beauty. Also, the idea of Reinhard's getting ahead due to his own abilities was highly unpleasant to the envious aristocrats, and they had *wanted* to believe that his sister's influence had gotten him promotions he didn't deserve.

Because von Reuentahl and Mittermeier had accurately evaluated Reinhard's qualities from the start, they had never been surprised afterward, no matter how many successes the golden brat achieved or how many times he was promoted. But even for them, it had taken some time to understand the true worth of Siegfried Kircheis. Kircheis had always been following one step behind Reinhard. That redheaded young beanpole's presence had usually been drowned out by Reinhard's brilliance, even though his own looks had been sufficiently eye-catching.

"That is what you call a loyal subject," von Reuentahl had said, though what he had meant at that time was that Siegfried was an ordinary man whose loyalty was his one saving grace. In von Reuentahl's case, it was probably fair to say that his judgment excelled that of the aristocrats only in its respect for loyalty. Whenever the aristocrats hadn't simply ignored Kircheis, they had made fun of him, saying things like, "If the sister is a star, then the brother is a planet . . . and look—there's even a satellite, too."

Without strongly asserting himself, Kircheis had silently played the role of Reinhard's shadow, helping and supporting him. When he had run operations independently during the Kastropf system uprising, many people had learned for the first time of his outstanding abilities . . .

Von Reuentahl may have even been more harshly critical of this mobilization than Mittermeier. To hear him tell it, there was nothing new about von Schaft's proposal at all; it was nothing but a revival of "big ship, big gun" warfare, trotted back out with a new coat of paint.

"What's harder to kill? One giant elephant or ten thousand mice? Obviously, the latter. But what can we expect of a nincompoop who doesn't see the value of the group when it comes to conducting a war?" The young heterochromiac admiral's words were dripping with contempt.

"Still, they might succeed this time. Even if things go as you say in the future."

"Hmph..." Von Reuentahl scratched his dark-brown hair, looking unhappy.

"I'm more concerned about Duke von Lohengramm than that snob von Schaft," Mittermeier said, taking a sip of his coffee. "I can't help feeling he's changed a little since Kircheis passed away. Where and in what way I can't say, but..."

"When people have lost the one thing they can't afford to lose, they can't help but change."

Nodding at von Reuentahl's words, Mittermeier wondered, *How would it change me if I ever lost Evangeline?* Then, hurriedly, he drove that ominous and unpleasant thought from his mind. He was a man of fortitude—one praised in times past for courage on and off the battlefield and for the good judgment that upheld it. In times to come, that praise was likely to continue. But even he had things he didn't care to think on.

The young heterochromiac threw a glance at his colleague's profile, a mixed look that held neither affection nor irony. He held Mittermeier in high esteem, both as a friend and as a soldier, but he couldn't understand the feelings of a colleague who, despite his own personal charm and status, had actively sought to bind himself to only one woman. Or perhaps von Reuentahl only told himself he couldn't understand it. Maybe he just didn't want to understand.

On the day the test warp of Gaiesburg Fortress was to be held, there were twelve thousand military personnel on board, most of them technicians. The two admirals, Kempf and Müller, were with them, naturally, but people had latched on to some peculiar theories regarding whether or not Tech Admiral von Schaft, commissioner of science and technology, would be joining them. One story was that von Schaft had been hoping to be at Marshal von Lohengramm's side at first, looking on with him the moment the experiment succeeded, but instead the handsome young imperial marshal had coolly said, "The command room of Gaiesburg Fortress is the most fitting place for you to sit," and ordered the reluctant von Schaft to board the fortress. Many of those who had heard that story believed it. There wasn't a shred of supporting evidence, but in light of von Schaft's character, they could easily see him saying that he would watch his dangerous experiment from a seat near the VIPs, far from harm's way. Of course, if the experiment failed, the seat next to Reinhard could hardly be called a safe place for von Schaft either.

Reinhard, attended by top officials Mittermeier, von Reuentahl, and von Oberstein, as well as Wahlen, Lutz, Mecklinger, Kessler, Fahrenheit, and three staff officers named Karl Robert Steinmetz, Helmut Lennenkamp, and Ernst von Eisenach, was sitting in the central command room at his admiralität, staring intently at its gargantuan screen. If the experiment was a success, Gaiesburg Fortress would appear on that screen—a silvery-gray sphere suddenly materializing against a backdrop of deep-indigo sky dusted with countless grains of silver and gold. It would be a truly dramatic spectacle.

"However, that will only happen if they succeed." The tone von Reuentahl used to whisper those words to Mittermeier sounded more heartless than ironic. Unlike his colleague, who acknowledged Kempf as a better commander than himself, von Reuentahl's evaluation was scornful. True, Kempf had been ordered to do this, but he was still pouring his heart and soul into something pointless.

Three members of the admiralty—Werner Aldringen, Rolf Otto Brauhitsch, and Dietrich Sauken—had been under Kircheis's command, but after his death they had been placed under Reinhard's direct supervision. The rank of all three was vice admiral. Additionally, Rear Admiral Horst Sinzer had been placed under Mittermeier's command, and Rear Admiral Hans Eduard Bergengrün under von Reuentahl's. These admirals were watching the screen intently from far in the back of the room, together with the other rear and vice admirals.

In the admiralität's central command room were gathered the cream of the imperial military's crop. By simply gesturing with their fingers, they could send tens of thousands of battleships racing across the void. *Right here and right now,* von Reuentahl thought, *you could change the whole direction of the galaxy's history, just by tossing a single photon bomb in this room.* Actually, that wasn't quite correct—there would be no need for everyone here to die. If only one of them, a blond youth of incomparable beauty and intelligence, were to vanish, that alone would be enough to completely change the fate of the universe. That bit of speculation made him feel vaguely apprehensive, yet at the same time, it was deeply interesting. Von Reuentahl was thinking about what had happened half a year ago—of what Reinhard had said when he had reported the capture of then imperial prime minister Duke Lichtenlade: *And the same goes for all of you. If you have the confidence and you're ready to risk everything, go ahead, challenge me anytime.* Confidence! His dark right eye and his blue left eye shifted slightly, and von Reuentahl regarded his young lord. Then, sighing so softly that no one else could hear, he turned his attention to the screen. The voice of the countdown had reached his ears.

"...drei, zwei, eins..."

"Oooh!"

A stir of amazed gasps rose up from the admirals. For a fraction of a second, the image on the screen was disrupted, but no sooner had that impression registered than the scene displayed had changed entirely. Now, the great sea of stars was a wall of light, and with that as its backdrop, a silvery-gray sphere with a ring of twenty-four giant engines appeared, spreading out over the center of the screen.

"It worked!"

Excited whispers broke out all around as everyone stared at the screen, each with his own emotions.

The warp was a success. Gaiesburg Fortress had appeared on the outer rim of the Valhalla system, carrying two million soldiers and as many as

16,000 ships. It was officially decided then that it should embark on the journey to retake Iserlohn. It was March 17, Imperial Year 489.

Duke von Lohengramm, the imperial prime minister, suddenly said, "I think I'm going to go visit Gaiesburg." On the following day, he boarded his flagship *Brünhild*, accompanied by his chief secretary, Hildegard von Mariendorf, and his chief aide, Rear Admiral von Streit. After half a day at regular speed, *Brünhild* reached Gaiesburg, where Commander Niemeller, the ship's captain, pulled her into port with a skill approaching artistry.

The two admirals, Kempf and Müller, came to greet them, and after congratulating them anew, Reinhard waved his hand to the cheering crew and headed off toward the Grand Hall right away.

Kempf and Müller exchanged a glance, both struck with the same surprise.

The Grand Hall was where Reinhard had held a ceremony last year to celebrate victory in the Lippstadt War and where Siegfried Kircheis's incomparable loyalty had cost him his life.

"I'd like to be alone here for a while. Don't let anyone else come in."

So saying, Reinhard pushed open the doors and disappeared inside.

Through the narrow gap in the heavy doors could be seen a wall that had been blasted apart by a hand cannon, left collapsed and unrepaired. Ever the practical administrator, Kempf had decided that repairs need not extend so far as interior decorating. Which was of course true, but now that Reinhard was here, it appeared insensitive to have left the job undone.

Was it only to the dead that Reinhard would open his heart?

Hilda felt a sharp sense of pain flash through her chest. If that were the case, then his loneliness and solitude were far too great for any one man. For what purpose had Reinhard put an end to the old empire, and why was he trying to rule all the galaxy?

This is wrong, thought Hilda. Surely a more fulfilling way of life must be possible for a young man like Reinhard. What should she do in order to bring that about?

Just then, the doors were firmly shut, as if rejecting all the living.

Behind those doors, Reinhard was sitting on the long-neglected steps leading up to the dais. Scenes from half a year ago rose up before his ice-blue eyes. Siegfried Kircheis, lying in a pool of his own blood, had said, "Take this universe for your own...and then tell Miss Annerose...tell her that Sieg kept the promise that he made when we were young..."

> *You kept your promise. And so I'll keep my promise to you, as well. No matter what it takes, I will make this universe my own. And then I'll go and get my sister. But I'm cold, Kircheis. In a world with neither you nor Annerose, the warm light is missing. If I could turn the pages of time back twelve years, if I could go back to those days...if I could do it all over again...then my world might have been something a little brighter, a little warmer...*

Reinhard held in his hand a pendant he had been wearing around his neck until a moment ago. The chain and pendant alike were made of silver. With his finger, he touched an oft-pressed spot to open it, revealing a small lock of slightly curling hair, red as if dyed with dissolved rubies. The blond-haired youth, not moving a muscle, stared at it for a long time.

In a room in the landesherr's office on Planet Phezzan, his official aide Rupert Kesselring was reporting on a number of matters to Landesherr Adrian Rubinsky. After first informing him that the test warp of Gaiesburg Fortress had been successful, he touched on the movements of the Free Planets Alliance.

"The FPA government has summoned Admiral Yang Wen-li temporarily to Heinessen and has apparently decided to subject him to face a court of inquiry."

"A court of inquiry? Not a court-martial, then."

"If it were a court-martial, formal charges would be required to open it. The defendant would have to be given a lawyer, and there would have to be a public record of the proceedings. However, these courts of inquiry have no basis in law—or to put it another way, they're completely arbitrary. Far more effective than an official court-martial, if what you're after is a psychological lynching founded on suspicion and speculation."

"It's just like the alliance's current leadership to do something like that. They extol the virtues of democracy with their mouths, while in reality they ignore laws and regulations, turning them into hollow shells. That's a makeshift—and dangerous—way of doing things. And it's because their authorities have no respect for the law themselves that their societal norms are coming unglued. A symptom that they're entering the terminal phase."

"Even if that's the case, they should solve these problems themselves," Rupert Kesselring said in a tone of pure acid. "There's no need for us to worry ourselves over them. When someone inherits a fortune through no ability of their own, they should face a commensurate test. If they can't endure it, destruction awaits, and that doesn't apply just to the Goldenbaum Dynasty..."

Landesherr Rubinsky, saying nothing to that, tapped his fingers on the top of his desk.

CHAPTER 5:

ON MARCH 9, an order from the government of the Free Planets Alliance was delivered to Yang Wen-li at Iserlohn Fortress, summoning him to the capital.

The order had come straight from the Defense Committee chair, and Yang, on receiving it via the FTL hotline, converted it to text and spent the next five minutes staring at the plate on which it was displayed. At last, he noticed Frederica Greenhill looking at him worriedly and gave her a smile.

"I've received a summons. It says to head for Heinessen."

"What for?"

"To appear before a 'court of inquiry,' it says. Any idea what kinda powwow that's supposed to be, Lieutenant? I can't seem to remember."

Frederica's pleasantly shaped eyebrows drew together slightly.

"I know about courts-martial, but there's nothing in the Charter of the Alliance, the FPA Basic Military Code of Justice, or the regs about anything called a 'court of inquiry.'"

"Aha, something that transcends mere laws and regulations, then."

"Or to paraphrase, something arbitrarily made up, without a legal leg to stand on."

It was said that Frederica, with her superior powers of memory, knew by heart every article in the Charter of the Alliance and the FPA Basic Military Code of Justice.

"You're right," Yang said, "but the fact that this is coming from the Defense Committee chair means it has excellent legal standing. Looks like I gotta head on over to Vanity Fair."

Despite his having been born on Heinessen, the sound of that planet's name summoned a rather depressing image in Yang's imagination: a hotbed of Trünicht faction scheming and power plays. In any case, there was only one man he could leave in charge of Iserlohn while he was away. Yang called in Rear Admiral Alex Caselnes.

After Yang had explained about the order, Caselnes furrowed his brow but was of course unable to tell Yang not to go. "Whatever you do, do it discreetly," he said. "You've got to make sure you don't give them any excuses."

"Yeah, I know. Can you hold the fort down for me again?"

Rear Admiral von Schönkopf, commander of fortress defenses, also seemed reluctant to send off his commanding officer.

"Will you be taking a security detail? I'll be happy to lead it personally if you—"

"No need to go overboard here. It's not like we're sneaking into enemy territory. Just give me one person I can trust."

"It just so happens that you're speaking to a clever and courageous warrior at this very moment."

"But there'll be trouble down the road if I take the commander of fortress defenses off the front line. Stay here and assist Caselnes. I'm not taking Julian this time, either. I've decided to go with the minimum number possible."

For transport, Yang selected a cruiser called *Leda II* instead of his flagship *Hyperion*, along with an escort of ten destroyers that would stay with him only as far as the Iserlohn Corridor's exit point. As he was a commander of vast military forces, he didn't want anyone thinking he was trying to intimidate the government. In his position, Yang had to take all sorts of tiresome things like that into account.

The security guard that von Schönkopf recommended was one Warrant Officer Louis Machungo. With glossy dark skin, upper arms as thick as Yang's thighs, a broad-chested hulk of a body, and charmingly rounded, light-brown eyes complementing a strong jawline, he gave an impression not unlike that of a gentle ox. Those huge muscles could probably unleash a hurricane of overwhelming force the moment he got angry, though.

"Pit him against those weaklings back in the capital," von Schönkopf said, "and he can probably take out a whole platoon one-handed."

"Meaning he's even stronger than you are?" Yang replied.

"I'd take out a whole company."

Von Schönkopf had spoken offhandedly, but afterwards his expression turned a bit mean-spirited as he added, "By the way, will you be taking Lieutenant Greenhill with you?"

"If I don't take an aide, I won't be able to function."

"That's not in dispute, but if you take the lieutenant and leave Julian behind...you'll make the boy jealous."

Having said what he'd wanted to say, von Schönkopf left to go watch Julian's practice on the firing range. When it was over, he said to the boy:

"I'm aware Lieutenant Greenhill has an interest in Admiral Yang, unfathomable as that may be. But how does the admiral feel about her?"

"I wouldn't know..." Julian murmured, smiling slightly. "At any rate, he's the type who hates to have people know what he's feeling, so he rarely says anything that would mean committing himself."

"Which in its own way makes him rather transparent. He's smart and has a simple, honest disposition, and that makes him just a little naive in his personal relations."

"You seem to know all about everybody."

Julian's comment caught von Schönkopf off guard for a moment. "Hey, what's that supposed to mean?"

"Er, nothing. I have to start getting dinner ready, so I'll see you tomorrow. Got to make that Irish stew the admiral likes."

Julian saluted and started walking away immediately.

"It's fine to keep busy," von Schönkopf shouted in a spiteful tone at the boy's retreating back, "but don't wear out those talents of yours making stew."

Julian was genuinely disappointed that he couldn't go with Yang to the capital. Part of it was the talk he'd had with Caselnes; now more than ever, he wanted to stick close by Yang and look out for him. He remembered what Yang had said before he'd been able to express his wishes: "Julian, I'm letting you off from housework for exactly two months."

Julian was unsure whether those words had sprung from the same well as von Schönkopf's parting jab or not. Yang also seemed to be worried about Julian these days—about his apparent lack of friends his own age. Because of this, he might well have been trying to create a chance for Julian to go out and make some friends.

Staying or going, however, this trip to Heinessen would probably not afford Julian any chances to be of service to Yang. He couldn't help the admiral in the same way Frederica could—if she didn't go, Yang's ability to do his administrative chores would plummet.

At any rate, I at least want to make myself useful before he ships out, Julian thought. To that end, he set to the task of making Yang's travel preparations. Yang looked on silently, aware that he'd just get in the way if he tried to help.

As if the thought had suddenly struck him, Yang said, "Hey, Julian. About how tall are you now?"

"Huh? I'm 173 centimeters."

"I thought so. Looks like you're gonna pass me next year. The first time we met, you didn't even come up to my shoulder."

That was all he said, but in those words, the boy felt something like a warm current of air.

II

Travel time between Iserlohn and the capital depended to some degree on conditions along the route, but three to four weeks was standard. Yang had decided to set aside this unexpected blank space in his schedule to do some writing, either on historical theory or on his theories about nations. Even if there wouldn't be enough time to bring a work to completion, he figured he should at least be able to finish a draft. The cruiser *Leda II* set out from Iserlohn, and Yang immediately ensconced himself in his office.

There are two ways to defend a country. One is to possess armaments more powerful than the opposing nations; the other is to render those nations harmless through peaceful means. The former method is the simpler of the two, and the one more attractive to ruling authorities, but it's been axiomatic since modern societies first took shape that an inverse proportion exists between increasing armaments and economic development. Increasing the armaments of one's own nation invites other nations to do likewise, and this goes on until at last this striking overemphasis on armaments warps the economy and society beyond their limits and causes the collapse of the nation itself. This gives rise to one of history's universal ironies: a nation destroyed by the will to defend itself...

Yang looked up from his word processor and slapped the back of his neck with one hand. After revising for a few dozen seconds, he started writing again.

It's said that since ancient times, many nations have been destroyed by external invaders. What demands our attention now, however, is the fact that more nations have been destroyed by internal factors: by launching invasions that result in a counterattack, by corrupting the mechanisms of state authority, by distributing wealth unfairly, and by angering the citizenry through suppression of thought and speech. When societal inequities go unaddressed, when armaments are needlessly multiplied, when their power is abused—internally, to suppress the people; externally, to invade other countries—that nation is on the road to destruction. This is a provable historical fact. Ever since the emergence of modern nations, lawless acts of invasion have inevitably invited defeat and destruction—not for the invaded country, but for the invading one. Without even getting into the morality of it, invasion should be avoided simply because the success rate is so low...

Maybe that part got a little too dogmatic. With a solemn look on his face, Yang thought it over, crossed his arms, and then uncrossed them.

> *What then, specifically, should we do in the present? If we think of all the many ways in which the second method is more practical than the first, the conclusion will become self-evident. We must coexist with the new order within the Galactic Empire. The old order, dominated by the boyar nobility, was not just the enemy of the Free Planets Alliance; it was also the enemy of those whom it ruled in the Galactic Empire—in other words, the common class. And at present, the new order recently established by Reinhard von Lohengramm has the support of the commoners, through which it is rapidly being strengthened. The formation and administration of the new Lohengramm order stands in stark contrast to Rudolf von Goldenbaum's dictatorship. The Goldenbaum system was created through democratic processes governing in an utterly undemocratic fashion. The Lohengramm order, on the other hand, was created through undemocratic processes but is beginning to govern in a more democratic manner. This is not government 'by the people,' but at least for now, it is government 'for the people,' or at least moreso than what came before it. Once we acknowledge that, coexistence with this new order will not be a matter of 'if' but of 'when.' What we must not do, on the other hand, is allow some malignant strain of Machiavellianism to draw us into collusion with the declining old order. The moment we join forces with an old system that is seen only as exploiters of the masses, the alliance will make enemies not only of the new order, but also of the twenty-five billion imperial citizens who support it...*

Yang took a deep breath and stretched his arms. With a slightly irritated expression, he stared at the words he had written. He didn't think the conclusion was wrong, but maybe he should advance it with a bit more demonstrative line of argument. Also, it felt a little rushed and might also draw criticism that he was siding with Duke Reinhard von Lohengramm.

"Duke Reinhard von Lohengramm, eh...?"

The name had such an elegant ring. Yang thought about that young man, as beautiful as some demigod with his golden hair, ice-blue eyes, and porcelain skin. The talents and way of life of that man—a man nine years younger than he—held an undeniable charm for Yang. He was pushing through such drastic changes in the empire that he almost seemed the subject of an experiment to see just how huge an influence a single person could have in the world. Most likely, he would become emperor eventually. Not through bloodline, but through ability. When that came to pass, the peculiar political system known historically as "free imperial rule"—imperial rule without aristocracy, imperial rule supported by the commoners—might be born on a galactic scale.

But if that were to happen, was it possible that the Galactic Empire, under its new emperor Reinhard von Lohengramm, could transform into some sort of tribalistic nation-state? If the citizenry were to conflate their emperor's ambition with their own ideals, the FPA might face attacks by some fanatical "people's army."

Yang felt as if the temperature in the room had dropped suddenly. Of course, it wasn't as if every hunch he had hit the mark, but if he had to break them down into categories, he suspected his bad feelings hit the bull's-eye more often than the good ones. He had felt a similar feeling before the Battle of Amritsar, and before the Military Congress for the Rescue of the Republic's coup d'état as well. It was no fun at all watching events heading straight off in the direction of "Boy, I sure hope that doesn't happen."

My life would've been so much easier if I'd been born in the empire, Yang had once thought. If he had been, he could have run straight over to Reinhard's side, signed on with his organization, and participated gladly and wholeheartedly in wiping out the boyar confederacy and implementing the chain of reforms that had followed. But the reality was, he was alliance born and bred, forced to wage war unwillingly on Mister Trünicht's behalf.

In the end, Yang ended up filling his hours with reading, naps, and

3-D chess, while making no progress to speak of in his literary endeavor.

Three weeks later, the cruiser *Leda II* reached the outer edge of the Balaat system, where Heinessen was located. The crew began to gather in the entertainment room. Several hundred commercial channels were broadcast from Heinessen, and on military and civilian ships alike, trouble would often break out once unlimited reception became possible—as the crew separated into sports fans and music fans.

Yang had a private solivision tank in his office. It was a modest perk. On the first channel he picked, Aron Doumeck—one of the Trünicht faction politicians, just happened to be giving a speech in obnoxious, blustery tones.

"—which is why we must protect our history and tradition. For which cause, we must not begrudge temporary expenditures and the petty lives of individuals. There is no word but 'coward' for those who emphasize only *their* rights as they make no effort to fulfill their duties to the country."

To those in power, nothing was so cheap as the lives of others. That gaffe just now about "petty lives" had probably demonstrated exactly how they thought, and that "temporary expenditures" bit was sure to encompass centuries. It was the average citizen who had to carry the load in either case; all the politicians did was look full of themselves while distributing other people's money.

When Yang couldn't take any more, he changed the channel. In place of the politician's haughty face, there appeared a young boy dressed in impractical-looking garb of some ancient style. It appeared to be some kind of children's action-adventure program; the boy was being called "Prince" by the other characters.

Tales of royal vagabonds—stories with a "wandering prince" theme—were the fountainhead of literature itself. Literature was the medium through which the myths and founding legends of many peoples were transmitted. Popularized versions of such stories existed in countless numbers in every age and in every place. They inspired many artists and had long been supported by a wide range of peoples.

That being said, Yang couldn't help drawing certain associations from this tale: a young prince from a kingdom in space, his birthright stolen by a prime minister depicted as evil incarnate, trying to restore the rightful royal family.

He decided to ask Frederica.

"Lieutenant Greenhill, what company is it that sponsors this show?"

"Some kind of synthetic-foods corporation, apparently. They're backed by Phezzanese capital, but I don't know the details."

"Is that so? For a minute there, I wondered if this was political advertising by the Galactic Empire's old regime."

"It couldn't be," Frederica said with the beginnings of a laugh. Yang wasn't laughing, though, and surprised at just how intent he looked, she put on her serious face as well. "The story could make you think that," she said.

In truth, she was patronizing Yang. If it had been Caselnes or von Schönkopf here, they wouldn't have hesitated to laugh out loud.

But the sound of the word "Phezzan" had been one of the things that sent Yang into deep thought. That name was always in the back of Yang's mind. What was Phezzan thinking? What were they trying to do with all that wealth? Were they hoping for a unified galaxy, or did they want division and strife?

There were a number of historical examples in which economic demands had encouraged unity of government.

One of the primary factors that had allowed Genghis Khan's Mongol Empire to become a vast, unified nation had been the support he had received from merchants traveling back and forth along the Silk Road. Each of the individual oases along that route had been a small, independent nation, and so security had been hard to maintain across the full length of the trading route. In addition, each of those oasis nations had been able to levy trading taxes and passage tolls at will. For the merchants, this had created an untenable situation.

For a time, they had hoped for relief from the Khwarezm Empire, but finding its emperor both incompetent and greedy, they had eventually given up and thrown their support behind Genghis Khan, a man furnished with three valuable qualities: he was religiously tolerant, he had a powerful military force, and he was smart enough to understand the importance of trade between the East and the West. They had provided Genghis Khan with many things—funds, information, weapons and the techniques for producing them, foodstuffs, interpreters, know-how for the collection of taxes—and assisted him in his conquests. It was fair to say that, aside from his purely military actions, these merchants deserved the credit for allowing the Mongol Empire to rise. Among these merchants, the Uighurs deserved special mention for how they dominated the Mongol Empire's finances and economy; they had in effect been the ones running the empire. While it was a Mongol Empire on the surface, it was a Uighur Empire underneath—that was why it was so renowned.

Was Phezzan thinking of becoming the Uighurs of this unified "New Galactic Empire," desiring political reunification of all humanity and working to advance that goal?

That struck him as a more logical, convincing explanation than any other scenario.

Still, people and the groups they formed didn't act solely according to logic.

Though he had no theoretical grounds to say so, Yang could sense a shadow of illogic of sorts in Phezzan's movements. Last year, Yang's prediction that Reinhard von Lohengramm would send agents to incite a coup in the alliance had been right on the mark. This had been because Reinhard's actions had been perfectly reasoned and logical, and Yang had been able to trace his thinking step-by-step. But in the case of Phezzan, he was often unable to read what they were up to. Yang could have simply said that Phezzan had gotten the better of him, and that would have been that. But instead, Yang had a feeling that some unknown element was behind Phezzan's actions—and it was not the kind of element that could be calculated rationally. If someone asked him what kind of element he was talking about, though, all he could say for now was, "Unknown."

"What a terrible mess," Commander Zeno, the captain of *Leda II*, said to Yang while he was lost in thought. While monitoring commercial broadcasts from Heinessen, he had picked up news of an accident. On board a transport vessel carrying spartanian pilots, an elementary mistake by a rookie flight officer had caused air pressure within the vessel to plummet suddenly, and more than ten pilots had died in hard vacuum.

"How much do you think it costs to train a single fighter pilot? We're talking three billion dinars a head."

"That's a lot of money," Yang said, mentally calculating that his own salary came only to about a twentieth of that. Back in Officers' Academy, he himself had undergone training to be what might generously be called a pilot. In the simulator he must have been shot down thirty times, at least. How many times had he shot down his opponent? Twice? Three times, maybe? He remembered the instructor shaking his head and muttering, "Every year we get one or two who should've never enrolled here." Since what he had said had been factually correct, there had been no way for Yang to defend himself.

"You bet that's a lot of money! A pilot is an accumulation of investment and technology. They're a precious commodity, and we can't afford to go losing them this easily. Honestly, if they plan on winning this war, the Rear Service is going to have to get its act together…"

Commander Zeno was practically grinding his teeth.

His anger and grief are perfectly understandable, Yang thought, *but…*

Things had probably been screwed up at an earlier stage than this. After all, the act—the very idea, even—of pouring vast sums of money, knowledge, and technical expertise into a single individual for the sole purpose of murder and destruction could hardly be called a normal thing to do. All that had been pounded into Yang at Officers' Academy, too—not that he'd been a star pupil by any stretch.

Perhaps nations were nothing more than expedients created to justify human madness. No matter how ugly, no matter how despicable, no matter how cruel the act might be, it could easily be excused once the nation had become preeminent. By claiming, "I did it for my country," deeds as vile as invasions, massacres, and human experimentation could sometimes even be lauded. Someone who criticized those actions, on the other hand, might come under attack for "insulting the fatherland."

Those who held fantasies about the things called nations believed them to be guided by brilliant, or intelligent and moral, individuals of surpassing excellence. In reality, however, that just wasn't the case. In the center of a nation's government, any number of people could usually be found who had less developed powers of thought, worse judgment, and lower moral standards than the average citizen. Where they most certainly did surpass the average citizen was in their passion for the pursuit of power. If such passions could have been channeled in constructive directions, they could have reformed government and society, and become the impetus for establishing the order and prosperity of a new age. But were even a tenth of the people in government like that? Whenever he had examined the history of a dynasty, there was nearly always a process at work in which whatever was built in the first generation was eaten away over the next dozen or so succeeding generations. To put it another way, dynasties and nations were extremely tenacious, unyielding organisms that could extend their life spans into the hundreds of years if even one great individual arose every few generations. If they became as corrupt and as weak as the Goldenbaum Dynasty had in the present-day Galactic Empire, however, there was no saving them. If the reforms of Manfred II had been realized a hundred years ago, the empire might have been able to go on for another several centuries, though.

As for the Free Planets Alliance, Yang couldn't equate it with the empire. This was because the very idea of leaving reform up to great individuals who might or might not appear once every few decades ran against the principles of democratic government. Democratic and republican governments were systems designed to make heroes and great men unnecessary—but when would that ideal win out over reality?

⋮ ⋅ ⋅

The cruiser *Leda II* arrived without fanfare at a military spaceport on Heinessen. "Top Secret" had been the order from the chair of the Defense Committee. Yang would've liked to have contacted Cubresly, director of

Joint Operational Headquarters, and Bucock, commander in chief of the space armada, but that would have not only gone against orders, it might also have provoked a clash between the civil and military authorities. In any case, he was never given the chance. The men who came to pick him up at the spaceport had their orders directly from the chairman of the Defense Committee, and no sooner had he landed than he was escorted by them to a landcar and told to get in.

Frederica and Machungo were about to protest, but armed soldiers stopped them, and Yang disappeared from the spaceport. Neither Yang nor Frederica had predicted that such high-pressure tactics would be used in taking him away.

After a ride of about twenty minutes, Yang was let out at one of the military facilities in the area, at which a lone officer in late middle age came out to meet him.

"I'm Rear Admiral Bay. I serve as head of security for His Excellency, High Council Chairman Trünicht. At present, I'm charged with your personal security, Admiral Yang. I promise to take good care of you."

"Much appreciated," Yang replied apathetically. Bay had called his work security, but even a grade-schooler could have guessed it was really sur-veillance. Bay introduced Yang to a personal assistant or some such who was assigned to his quarters—a hulking junior officer with aquamarine eyes as vacant as orbs of glass.

Yang felt immensely let down. It looked like the first thing this court of inquiry had done when selecting his assistant had been to eliminate softness in all its forms—no beauty, no loveliness allowed. There was an extreme emphasis on function over form—and no doubt whatsoever that the functions desired were intimidation and the prevention of Yang's escaping.

Even so, this looks like a pretty unimaginative bunch, Yang thought. *Treat a fellow like this, and any goodwill he might have had toward this court of inquiry goes out the window. As does any chance of him letting his guard down. The only thing left for the subject to do is to assume a defensive posture.*

After he had been shown to his quarters and left alone, Yang looked out the window, but there was nothing to see outside but the building that stood on the far side of a small courtyard. It had only a few windows and was an uninviting bluish gray. Not only had no consideration been made for the appreciation of scenery, contact with the outside world itself had been made impossible. About a squad's worth of soldiers were hanging around in the concrete-fortified courtyard. They appeared to be loitering, but each had a particle-beam rifle slung across his shoulder. That was combat equipment. Yang tried tapping the windowpane. It was about six centimeters thick and made of a special hardened glass. If a brown bear in its prime were to run headlong into a window like that, it would probably do no more than put a hairline crack in it.

The room's furnishings were first-rate, at least, although lacking in personality: a bed, a writing desk, a sofa, and a table. None of them felt like they had been used, though. Yang couldn't even summon up the will to check for bugs and surveillance cameras. Of course they were present, and of course they were well hidden. Hunting for them would just be a silly waste of energy.

"This is house arrest," he said to the empty room.

So what exactly had happened here? He sat down on the bed and sank into thought. The bed cushions were not too soft and not too hard, but that was hardly enough to put Yang in a pleasant mood. On the empty floor, he could see Torture, Brainwashing, and Murder all join hands to dance a gloomy jig. Their choreographer, naturally, was Job Trünicht.

This went beyond the level of mere contradiction. Yang stood on the alliance's end of the battlefield because he believed that a democracy that ordinary people came together to operate—fraught though it might be with detours, trials, and errors—was at least better than the dictatorship of a merciful emperor. Yet here Yang was on Heinessen—a world that was supposed to be the very citadel of democracy—apparently shut up in a birdcage belonging to medieval rulers reeking of corruption.

Don't rush into doing anything too soon, Yang told himself. For the moment, the High Council shouldn't be able to destroy him physically or mentally, no matter how much hate they might have toward him. If they were to do that, the Galactic Empire would be clapping with glee at having a rival eliminated without needing to lift a finger themselves. There were only four scenarios in which Yang could imagine Trünicht or the High Council making the decision to do him harm:

A. A great admiral appears in the alliance with abilities greater than or equal to Yang's, who also feels genuine loyalty to the powers that be.

B. A lasting peace is established with the Galactic Empire, and Yang is determined to be a factor obstructing it.

C. Yang is judged to have betrayed the alliance and taken the side of the empire.

D. The High Council itself betrays the alliance and takes the side of the empire.

Regarding A: Loyalty and submissiveness aside, there was, at present, no one in the Alliance Armed Forces who eclipsed Yang in terms of raw ability. To "lose" Yang in the midst of nigh-perpetual war with the Galactic Empire would be an act of national suicide. Of course, just as human beings sometimes commited suicide, nations sometimes killed themselves as well, but things did not appear to have reached that stage just yet.

Scenario B was just a little on the stupid side. If a lasting peace could be forged with the empire—or a set of circumstances created that would lead to that—Yang would be overjoyed. For him, it would mean retirement and the start of his long-held dream of a pensioner's life. Still, since facts and their perception were naturally separate things, there was every chance the authorities might act based on misunderstandings or distortions.

As for scenario C, Yang had no desire to do such a thing himself, but as with scenario B, the government might resort to extralegal measures with that as their rallying cry.

And regarding scenario D . . .

Just as Yang was about to head off down that lane of thought, the visiphone chimed, and Rear Admiral Bay's face filled the narrow screen.

"Excellency, I'm told the court of inquiry will open in one hour. I'll come to escort you to the Hall of Inquiry, so please get yourself ready to go."

III

The room was needlessly spacious, with a high ceiling. The illumination was kept deliberately dim, just as the air was kept just under the lower limit of the range of comfortable temperatures, creating a chilly, dry sensation on Yang's skin.

As if in accordance with some dark passion, everything here seemed calculated to create an almost palpable sense of intimidation. The questioners' seats were elevated and looked down on the questioned while surrounding his seat on three sides.

If Yang had been the type to put a high value on authority and power, he would have shriveled up in body and soul the instant he stepped into the room. However, all Yang sensed in that room was thick makeup covering a malicious bluff. Although the sight provoked a physical sense of revulsion within Yang's body, he was neither daunted nor afraid.

Nine inquisitors were sitting in the seats above. From Yang's standpoint, that made three in front, three on the right, and three on the left. Once his eyes had adjusted to the low lighting, he was able to make out the face of the middle-aged man who was looking down on him from the middle of the three seats in front of him. It was Negroponte, who now occupied the seat of Defense Committee chair in the Trünicht administration. He was about the same height as Yang but far more heavyset. He had to be the one in charge of the court of inquiry. Of course, he was probably nothing more than a mouthpiece for the true speaker—the FPA's head of state, who couldn't afford to show himself in a place like this.

The thought of having to spend the next several days entertaining Trünicht's underlings here belatedly put Yang in a gloomy mood. Frederica and Warrant Officer Machungo had both been taken from his side, and now a lonely battle was forced upon him. A court-martial would have been vastly more fair, since if they wished, defendants could choose up to three defense lawyers. Here, however, it looked like Yang was going to have to represent himself.

Negroponte stated his name, and then the man seated on his right side introduced himself.

"My name is Eurique Martino Borges de Alantes e Oliveira. I am the president of Central Autonomous Governance University."

Yang saluted to show proper respect. This man was apparently the vice chairman here and probably deserved his respect just for having memorized a name that long.

The other seven inquisitors also gave their names one after another. Five of them were either politicians or bureaucrats in the Trünicht faction, and as such were the sort of rabble Yang hated to go to the trouble of remembering. However, when he picked out the lean, expressionless face of Admiral Rockwell, Director of Rear Service Headquarters and the sole uniformed officer present, he couldn't simply smile politely and forget about him. It was a stark reminder of how the Trünicht clique was expanding within the military. The one other non–Trünicht faction politician here, Huang Rui, looked to be more curious about this court than loyal to it. He left an impression on Yang, although of a different sort than Rockwell. Most likely, he had been chosen as an inquisitor so that Trünicht could keep up an appearance of impartiality, but in the poisonous air of this one-sided farce, he might just play the role of ventilator. It would be a mistake to expect too much of him, but still...

When all the introductions had been finished, Negroponte said, "Well then, Admiral Yang, you may be seated—no, not like that! Do not cross your legs! Sit up straight. You're under inquiry, Admiral Yang. Do not forget the position you're in."

After wisely swallowing the words "It's not like anybody told me how to sit," Yang put together the humblest expression he could manage and straightened up in his seat. In battle, too, timing was everything.

"Well now, let's begin the inquiry..."

It was a solemn declaration, but it made not the slightest impression on Yang. He was just earnestly praying for this to be over soon.

The first two hours were spent going over and confirming Yang's past accomplishments. Starting with his date of birth, parents' names, and father's occupation, his record up until entering Officers' Academy was examined in detail, with comments made as each and every point was introduced. They seemed to know more about Yang than Yang did himself.

What made Yang inwardly groan the loudest were the report cards from his Officers' Academy days that were projected on a wall screen. Leaving aside his 98 points in Military History, his 94 in Strategic Theory (Classical), and his 92 in Exercises in Tactical Analysis, he had a 58 on his practical test in marksmanship, a 59 on his practical test in piloting fighter craft, and a 59 in Exercises in Engine Engineering, for which he had good reason to be embarrassed, since a grade of 55 or less in any subject would have resulted in washing out.

And yet, how different things might have been, both for Yang himself and for the Free Planets Alliance as a whole, if he had flunked out and been expelled. Iserlohn would still be in the empire's hands, proudly impregnable, though on the other hand, the Alliance Armed Forces would have escaped that disastrous defeat at Amritsar. Protected by Artemis's Necklace, the Military Congress for the Rescue of the Republic's coup might have been partially successful, and a state of civil war with the opposition might still be dragging on. And if it were, it was entirely possible that Duke Reinhard von Lohengramm, taking advantage of the civil war, would have sent all his massive fleets at once and been well on the way to fulfilling his conqueror's dream.

As for the impact on Yang personally, he would never have met a young Frederica Greenhill during the evacuation of El Facil, nor would he have gotten to know Alex Caselnes afterward. Without Caselnes, he would have never met Julian or gotten von Schönkopf as a subordinate. He might have been conscripted and lost his life on the front line, or he might have dodged the draft and ended up a fugitive. A human being was nothing more than the smallest component, an atom, of history, but out of all the infinitely branching paths to the future, only one was chosen to become the reality. Was the wonder of fate's deft handiwork to be praised, then, for the countless mutually associating microcosms that were forever taking shape?

"...and, at present, you are both the youngest member of the FPA Armed Forces to have made full admiral and our supreme commanding officer on the front. That's a perfect example of what people mean when they say, 'enviable good luck.'"

The way he said that got on Yang's nerves, popping the bubble of speculation he had surrounded himself with and bringing him back to reality. He hadn't cared much for that expression or the tone in which it had been delivered. If the treatment he was getting really was that enviable, they were welcome to switch places with him. He was the one who had to provide a steady stream of orders while his ship was heaving up one minute and back down the next. He was the one who had to efficiently carry out the work of death and destruction while beams from enemy warships were forming huge swells of light that engulfed his whole field of view. He was the one who had just had a journey of four thousand light-years forced on him the moment things seemed to be settling down—and had traveled all that way to the capital just to be dragged in front of this court of inquiry. He wasn't going to plead for sympathy, but as far as he was concerned, his status was in no way, shape, or form anything worth getting jealous over. Nameless soldiers and their families might be excused for thinking so, but he did *not* need to hear it from this bunch, who were sitting in safety far from the front lines, thinking of nothing but how best to pound down any peg that stood out from the rest.

"In our democratic republic, no one—no matter who they may be—is permitted to take arbitrary action exceeding the norms. In order to eliminate all questions concerning this point, we have convened this court of inquiry today. For that reason, my first question is..."

Here it comes, thought Yang.

"Last year, when you put down the Military Congress for the Rescue of the Republic's coup d'état, all twelve of the satellites composing Artemis's Necklace—satellites constructed with a huge investment of public funds for the defense of the capital—were destroyed on your orders, correct?"

"Yes, sir."

"You'll probably assert that this was a tactically unavoidable measure, but I can't help feeling it was a hasty and roughly handled decision. Was there really no other way besides the complete destruction of our nation's valuable property?"

"I judged that there was none, so I took that action. If you believe that decision was mistaken, I'd certainly like to hear the alternative."

"We aren't military specialists. It's your job to do the thinking at the tactical level. Now that you mention it, though, wouldn't it have been better if you had entered the atmosphere after destroying, say, two or three attack satellites?"

"If I had done it that way, we would have no doubt come under attack by the remaining satellites, and our forces would have certainly taken casualties." As this was an indisputable fact, Yang didn't even raise his voice. "If you're saying that unmanned satellites are more important than the lives of soldiers, then my judgment was mistaken, but..."

Yang hated himself just a little for putting it that way, but without at least this much pushback, Negroponte wouldn't respond.

"Well then, how about this: the conspirators were trapped on Heinessen in any case. Instead of taking such swift, sudden action, wouldn't it have been better to have taken the time to wear down their will to resist?"

"I thought about doing that as well, but there were two factors that made me abandon the idea."

"We'd all like to hear them."

"The first problem was that the coup d'état faction had been psychologically backed into a corner, and there was a danger that they would try to get out of that situation by using government VIPs in the capital as human shields. If they had come demanding concessions with pistols pressed against *your heads*, we would have had no choice but to negotiate with them."

An awkward silence stretched out for several seconds.

"The second issue involved an even greater danger. At that time, the uprising inside the empire was drawing to a close. If we had continued to lay siege to Heinessen and just leisurely waited around for the coup faction to implode, then Reinhard von Lohengramm, gifted war maker that he is, might well have launched a massive invasion, spurred on by the momentum of his victory in the empire's civil war. Aside from its civilians, Iserlohn had only a small security force and some spaceflight control personnel at the time."

Yang paused to take a breath. He would've loved a glass of water.

"For these two reasons, I had to take measures that would liberate Heinessen as quickly as possible and, moreover, deliver a crushing psychological blow to the coup d'état faction. If that's deserving of criticism, I'll resign myself to it. But my own feelings aside, the men and women who risked their lives fighting under my command will *not* accept it unless you can provide a better alternative plan."

Not even Yang was above this much of an implied threat. And it seemed to have worked. A susurrus of low voices passed among the board members, with irritated glances being fired off from their huddle toward Yang. It seemed they had run out of room for more counterarguments. The only exception was Huang, who turned to one side and yawned a little. Finally, Negroponte cleared his throat loudly and spoke.

"Well then, let's set this matter aside for the time being and move on to the next thing. Just before you engaged the enemy in the Doria Stellar Region, you apparently said the following to your entire force: 'Compared to individual rights and liberty, the state is just not worth all that much.' We have the testimony of multiple witnesses who heard you, so there's no mistake, is there?"

IV

"I can't vouch for every word and every syllable," Yang replied, "but I certainly did say something along those lines."

If there were witnesses, there was no point in denying it. But most of all, Yang didn't believe he had said anything wrong. It wasn't like he was always right about everything, but what he had said that day—that had been right on target. If the state were to fall, they could start over and build it back up again. There were plenty of nations that had fallen for a time only to be rebuilt. Of course, far more had fallen never to rise again, but that was because they had already exhausted their roles in history, become corrupt, grown weak in their old age, and lost the value of their continued existence. The death of a nation was tragic in most cases to be sure, but the reason was because of the large amount of blood spilled in the process. What was worse was how that tragedy would turn into the gravest of comedies as many people laid down their lives sure in the belief that they could save an unworthy nation from its inevitable doom—and then with their sacrifices accomplish absolutely nothing. States unworthy of their own existence, jealous of people who did deserve to live, took as many with them as they could in the moment they were cast into hell. Sometimes, the supreme authorities of those nations even lived out their lives in luxury as aristocrats of the enemy nation, forgetting all about the countless war dead who had been crying out their names as they fell on the battlefield. Yang wondered: throughout history, how many of those who were ultimately responsible for wars had actually died on the front lines?

Personal liberty and individual rights—those were the words Yang had spoken to the soldiers. Should he have maybe added "life" to that? But when Yang thought about all he had done up till then and all he was likely to do in the future, he knew there was no way he could have spoken that word. *Just what in blazes do you think you're even doing! There have got to be all kinds of things to do out there that matter more than ordering murder and destruction on the battlefield.*

"Don't you think you made a rather indiscreet comment?" a grating voice was saying.

During his days at Officers' Academy, there had been instructors whose eyes would light up at the sight of a student making a mistake. This guy sounded just like them: a voice like a cat licking his chops in ecstasy.

"Huh? How so?"

The Defense Committee chair, perhaps growing uncomfortable due to Yang's failure to roll over for them, allowed a stern edge to creep into his voice. "You're a soldier with a duty to protect your nation. Young as you are, you wear the title of admiral. You command a military force with numbers equivalent to the population of a large city. So how is it not indiscreet when someone in your position makes a comment that belittles the state, by extension shows contempt for your own duties, and furthermore invites a drop in morale?"

What you need right now, Yang's reason was telling him, *is patience to endure all this vanity and absurdity,* but that internal voice was getting weaker and weaker.

"If I may say a word, Your Excellency," Yang said, controlling his voice as best he could, "I think that statement was unusually discerning for me. States don't divide like cells to produce individuals; individuals with independent wills come together to form states. That being the case, it's clear as day which is principal and which is secondary in a democratic society."

"Clear as day, is it? I see things a little differently. The state has a value to it that makes it essential for human beings."

"Really? Because human beings can live just fine even without any state, but states can't exist if there are no human beings."

"I am . . . shocked, frankly. You sound like some extreme sort of anarchist."

"That's incorrect, sir. I'm actually a vegetarian, though I do bend the rules the minute I see a tasty cut of meat."

"Admiral Yang! Do you intend to insult this court of inquiry?"

The sense of danger in Negroponte's voice edged up a notch.

"No, sir, I have no such intentions whatsoever." Naturally, he most certainly did have such intentions, but there was no need to come out and say so. Yang went silent, neither defending himself nor apologizing, and the chairman of the Defense Committee, perhaps having lost sight of his line of attack, continued to glare at Yang as he drew his thick lips tightly together.

"How about we recess for a little while at this point?" That was the voice of Huang Rui, who hadn't spoken a word since the self-introductions. "Admiral Yang must be tired, and I'm certainly bor—I mean, er, exhausted. I'd be grateful for a little break."

That request probably saved multiple human lives.

After a ninety-minute recess, the court of inquiry reconvened. Negroponte embarked on a new line of attack.

"I understand you've appointed Lieutenant Frederica Greenhill as your aide-de-camp."

"That's correct. Is there a problem?"

"She's the daughter of Admiral Greenhill, who committed rebellious acts of treason last year against our democratic republic. You have to be aware of that, and yet..."

Yang raised his eyebrows just slightly. "Oh? So in my free country, the child bears the guilt of the parent, like in some ancient autocracy?"

"I said nothing of the sort."

"I can't interpret it otherwise, I'm afraid..."

"What I'm suggesting is that, to avoid unnecessary misunderstandings, you need to consider your appointments carefully."

"What's an 'unnecessary misunderstanding'? Could you tell me, with specifics?"

As there was no reply, Yang continued.

"It would be one thing if you had some kind of evidence that cast serious doubt on her, but when it comes to preemptive action against some sort of nebulous 'unnecessary misunderstanding,' I just don't feel any need. Also, the right of a commanding officer to appoint whom he will is guaranteed by law in this case. And furthermore, if I were told to relieve the most capable and trustworthy aide I could ever ask for, that would hamper my ability to use our forces to their fullest extent. All I'd be able to think is that you were deliberately trying to inflict losses on our forces. Is that how I should interpret this?"

Yang's aggressive line of reasoning had clearly beaten the board members to the punch. Two or three times, Negroponte opened his mouth and started to say something, only to close it, unable to think of a comeback on the spur of the moment. Looking for help, he turned toward the president of Central Autonomous Governance University, who was sitting next to him.

The man known as Eurique Blah-Blah-Blah Oliveira had more the bearing of a bureaucrat than a scholar. Of course, Central Autonomous Governance University was a school for cultivating government bureaucrats. Given his reputation for brilliance, Oliveira had no doubt been able to do as he wished at every stage of his life. He was brimming with a confidence and sense of superiority that extended all the way down to his fingertips.

"Admiral Yang, it's going to be hard for us to ask questions if we're being spoken to like that. We are not enemies here. Let's try and understand one another better, using a little more common sense and reason."

As he listened to Oliveira's dry, raspy voice, Yang decided that he hated the man. Negroponte could fly into a frenzy, become confused, and so on, and for that alone, he still had a sense of humanity about him.

"Judging by your words and actions just a moment ago, you would seem to have certain preconceived notions about this court of inquiry, but you are misjudging us. We haven't called you here to criticize you. In fact, you could say that this court of inquiry was opened in order to improve your standing. Naturally, we need your cooperation in order to do that, and we want to cooperate with you in every way as well."

"In that case, there is one thing I would like to request."

"And what would that be?"

"If you've got the answer sheet, could you show it to me? 'Cause I'd really like to know what kind of answers you're all hoping for."

Dead silence filled the room for a moment, and then angry voices churned the air in the room, creating currents of turbulence.

"Let the inquiree be warned! Please refrain from using words and actions insulting to this court of inquiry or scornful of its authority and character!"

The Defense Committee chair managed to rein in his loud voice just before it turned into unintelligible shouting. *If there's anything in this burlesque show you can call "authority" or "character," then by all means, bring it out*, Yang thought. Naturally, it was neither submission nor regret that caused Yang to hold his peace. A thick vein was bulging on the Defense Committee chair's temple. Yang looked on maliciously as Oliveira of Central Autonomous Governance University whispered something in Negroponte's ear.

Finally, Yang was released from day one of the court of inquiry, but that didn't mean there was any improvement in his state of de facto house arrest. Herded into a landcar that picked him up from the meeting hall, Yang was taken right back to his accommodations. As soon as he met the junior officer serving as his personal assistant, Yang demanded to go out for dinner.

"Your Excellency, I'll prepare dinner for you here. There's no need to bother with going out."

"I want to eat out. Not in a bleak, empty room like this."

"You'll need Admiral Bay's permission to leave through the front gate."

"I don't particularly want his permission."

"Whether you want it or not, it's required!"

"Well, in that case, can you put me in touch with Admiral Bay?"

"The admiral is out right now. He has official business at the High Council chairman's office."

"When will he be back?"

"I don't know. So, is that all you needed?"

"Yeah, that about covers it."

The junior officer saluted and went out of the room, and then for a while Yang stood there glaring at the door. Although he knew that bugging devices were present, he couldn't help growling in a low voice, "Do you think you can do this to me?"

Yang flung his military beret down hard against the floor. Then he picked the innocent beret back up, brushed off the dust, and put it on his head. Crossing his arms, he wandered around the room.

I quit. This time, I swear, I'm really gonna quit. He had been thinking that ever since capturing Iserlohn the year before last. These were some of the same people who had rejected his letters of resignation repeatedly—and instead put him in positions of higher and higher authority, expanding his duties and his power.

When he had finally been let go from the court of inquiry, it had not been without a small feeling of pleasure. This was because today, at least, he had secured a tactical victory. He had crushed their false accusations one after another and, difficult though such a thing was, had even managed to embarrass the thick-skinned inquisitors.

However, this tactical victory would not necessarily lead straight to a strategic victory. While he'd be grateful if all those high-ranking officials decided to give up on the court of inquiry, it was very possible that they would instead continue even more obsessively. He had reached the limits of his endurance during today's questioning alone, and it seemed impossible to continue to hold up through tomorrow and beyond. *In which case, there's nothing I can do except quit, right?*

Yang sat down at the writing desk and started thinking about his letter of resignation.

During this time, Frederica Greenhill had not just been twiddling her thumbs while observing from the sidelines. She got to work as soon as she entered her room at an apartment building for female officers and, within the space of three hours, had made fourteen visiphone calls and nailed down the location of Rear Admiral Bay. The moment he left Job Trünicht's office, he was accosted by Frederica, with Warrant Officer Machungo at her side.

"As Admiral Yang's aide-de-camp, I demand to see my CO. Where is the admiral?"

"That is related to top state secrets. I can't authorize any meetings, nor can I tell you where the admiral is."

Frederica was not about to stand for that kind of answer.

"Understood. 'Court of inquiry' must refer to psychological torture carried out behind closed doors, correct?"

"Lieutenant Greenhill, watch what you say."

"If you're saying that I'm mistaken, then I demand that you prove it by publicly disclosing this court of inquiry, allowing lawyers to be present, and permitting the inquiree to see visitors."

"I don't have to respond to such demands."

"Why are you unable to respond?"

"I don't have to answer that."

But Frederica did not back down from the high-handed attitude of the rear admiral.

"In that case, would you mind if I inform the news media that Admiral Yang—a national hero—is being arbitrarily and illegally subjected to a psychological lynching by a handful of high government officials?"

There was a visible flash of panic in the rear admiral's eyes.

"J-just try it. You'd be breaking the State Secrets Protection Act. You'd end up in front of a court-martial yourself."

"There would be no grounds for a court-martial. The State Secrets Protection Act says nothing about any 'courts of inquiry.' Therefore, it follows that even if I made this matter public, doing so would not constitute any crime. If you're bound and determined to ignore Admiral Yang's human rights and force this secret court of inquiry on him, then I too will have to use whatever means are at my disposal."

"Hmph. The apple didn't fall very far from the tree, did it?" the rear admiral spat back, filled with insidious venom.

For an instant, shock—and then fury—flashed across the face of Warrant Officer Machungo, but Frederica didn't bat an eyelash. Only her hazel eyes blazed in that instant, like emeralds bathed in firelight. As Bay turned to go, leaving his cruel words behind him, she made no move to stop him.

Last year, when she had learned that her father was the ringleader behind the coup d'état, she had braced herself to be released from her position as Yang's aide-de-camp. But then Yang, speaking to her in a tone like that of an awkward schoolboy, had told her: "If you're not there for me, I'll have a rough time of it . . ."

Those simple words had sustained her thus far and would likely continue to do so. She turned to look at her large and muscular companion.

"Warrant Officer Machungo, I didn't want to do this, but it's my last option. Let's go see Admiral Bucock and ask him what's going on."

After wasting about a dozen sheets of paper, Yang finally finished his letter of resignation. He had a feeling he wasn't going to be able to look Julian and Frederica, or Caselnes and the others, in the eye after this, but he just didn't think it was possible to go along with the Trūnicht faction any longer. Even if he wasn't around, the empire would have a hard time invading them as long as Iserlohn was still in FPA hands. Thinking of it that way was how he finally managed to calm himself down.

Utterly exhausted, Yang burrowed into bed. He had no way of knowing that, several thousand light-years away, Gaiesburg Fortress was flying across the black void. Neither god nor devil had made Yang all-knowing or all-powerful.

CHAPTER 6:

A BATTLE WITHOUT WEAPONS

IT WAS THE TENTH OF APRIL when a group of sixteen warships, including the battleship *Hispaniola* and the cruiser *Cordoba*, discovered it. This group, under the command of Captain J. Gibson, had departed from Iserlohn on a patrol mission into the corridor.

"If you do encounter the enemy, under no circumstances should you open hostilities. Just withdraw to the fortress and report your findings."

Rear Admiral Caselnes, the acting commander, had given strict orders of this nature to every commander in the Iserlohn Patrol Fleet. While Fortress Commander Yang Wen-li was absent, they were to avoid needless combat insofar as it was possible.

An operator aboard the cruiser *Cordoba* was drinking yet another cup of coffee as he gazed at his instruments. He had lost count of how many cups this made. The present situation was peaceful—and therefore boredom itself. Aside from drinking coffee, there was absolutely nothing he could do to distract himself. His stomach, however, had had about enough of caffeine-triggered stimulation. Suddenly, the operator's eyes lit up, and he violently slammed the cup down on the corner of his console.

"Warp distortion dead ahead," he reported. "Something's about to warp in. Distance: 300 light seconds. It masses..."

The glance that the operator cast toward his mass meter froze there, and he lost the words he was about to say. It took several seconds to get his vocal cords started again.

"The mass is—extremely large..."

"Give me a number!" shouted the captain. The operator loudly cleared his throat two or three times, and then managed to cough up the formless mass of shock that had been lodged in his windpipe.

"Mass is approximately forty trillion tons! This isn't any battleship!"

This time, it was the captain's turn to go silent. After a moment, he shuddered, shook off the choke hold that an invisible pair of arms seemed to have him in, and gave orders.

"Retreat, full speed! We'll be caught in the spacequake!"

Captain Gibson, the commanding officer for this formation of vessels, was also ordering all ships to pull back immediately. The sixteen vessels put distance between themselves and the increasingly warped region of space as quickly as their engine output would allow. Vast undulations created by the spacequake raced after them, bending and shaking space-time itself, squeezing their hearts with invisible hands.

The coffee cup fell from the edge of the console and shattered on the floor. Even so, the operators stared on at the screen, never losing sight of their reconnaissance duties. At last, they saw the shock wave come racing toward them, and a voiceless wail rose up...

A frantic atmosphere was beginning to form in the command room of Iserlohn Fortress. Operators were in constant motion. There was no rest for their hands, their eyes, or their voices. Rear Admiral Caselnes, along with the rest of the executive staff, stood watching the scene unfold.

"A patrol group seems to have encountered the enemy again..."

"The enemy's busy too, these days. Maybe they're trying to earn some overtime."

Idle talk was of course forbidden, but no one could obey that rule when they were uneasy. At last, the chief operator relayed the report from Captain Gibson to the acting commander.

"It's shaped like a sphere or something similar, composed of alloys and ceramics, and its mass is..."

"How much?"

"Mass estimated at over forty trillion tons."

"Did you say *trillion*?!" Caselnes was a man with a quiet, tranquil disposition, but not even he could keep his composure when he heard that figure.

The chief operator continued: "Judging by its mass and its shape, it's likely an artificial planetoid, forty to sixty-five kilometers in diameter."

"You mean . . . a fortress like Iserlohn?" Caselnes said in a low voice.

Rear Admiral von Schönkopf, commander of fortress defenses, cracked an ironic smile. "I don't think the empire's ever sent us goodwill envoys in this form before."

"So was that run-in back in January just a trial run for this?" There was a bitter edge to Caselnes's voice. He had thought the enemy would learn the same lesson their own forces had and be more circumspect in the future. Had he been mistaken all along? "So then, we've got an imperial fleet that's bringing along its own home base this time?"

"You've got to admire their effort," von Schönkopf said, although there was no passion in his praise.

Rear Admiral Murai, ever the serious one, shot a prejudiced glance at the commander of fortress defenses. "Even so, it's an incredible thing they've conceived. To warp here with an entire fortress in tow . . . The imperial military has apparently developed an entirely new technology."

"The technology isn't new," von Schönkopf countered unnecessarily. "They've just upped the scale is all. Breathtakingly, I might add."

"What's certain," Caselnes said, stepping between the two men to bring things back on topic, "is that their forces are vast, and we've been caught napping. What's more, Commander Yang is absent. It's just us while he's away, so at least for the time being, we're going to have to hold the line ourselves."

At Caselnes's words, a wave of tension rolled through the spacious central command room. Understandably uneasy glances were shooting back and forth throughout the room. They had been utterly certain that Iserlohn was impregnable, but now a hairline crack of panic had appeared in the cornerstone of that certainty. Iserlohn had taken every cannon blast that had come its way, but those had been ship-mounted cannons; the output of the approaching fortress's main guns would be on a whole different level.

Soldiers had long joked about "what would happen if you fired Iserlohn's main guns into Iserlohn's defense wall," but it was that very situation that might now be upon them. "Iserlohn," people said, "has four multilayered coatings of ultrahard steel, crystal fiber, and superceramic. It's the sturdiest thing in all of space." After this next battle, however, those words might be spoken in the past tense.

"A duel between fortress cannon and fortress cannon...?" Caselnes could feel an icy, invisible hand running its fingers up and down his neck and spine. When he imagined the unprecedented clash of those vast energies, he couldn't help but feel a chill. If you were to witness a firing of Iserlohn's main cannons with the naked eye, it was said, you would see the afterimage for the rest of your life.

"Just think of the magnificent fireworks we'll get to see," von Schönkopf said. His usual good cheer was a bit lacking at that moment, and it was difficult to call his wisecrack successful. What he was imagining was crossing the line of what frontline soldiers could process as a wisecrack.

"We need to get Admiral Yang to come back from the capital ASAP," said Commodore Patrichev.

No sooner had he spoken those words than a regretful grimace appeared on his face. It was probably a conscious act, done out of consideration for Acting Commander Caselnes. Caselnes, however, showed not the slightest displeasure, and instead signaled positive agreement. He was well aware that he was the *peacetime* commander, just filling in.

Still, even if Yang came running back the moment the FTL reached Heinessen, the distance from there to Iserlohn was simply too great.

"This is a rough estimate," Caselnes noted, "but it looks like we're going to have to hold them off for four weeks. And although that period could grow longer, it's not going to get any shorter."

"That's a fun prediction," Patrichev said, not managing to sound as upbeat as he'd intended. They were going to have to do battle with a force of unprecedented scale—and do it without their commander. It was no ordinary commander they had been deprived of, either, but the undefeated war hero known as "Yang the Magician" and "Miracle Yang."

Fearful shivers ran silently through every nerve in Patrichev's body. He broke out in gooseflesh, and cold sweat dampened his clothing from the inside. It was only natural.

Iserlohn Fortress and its affiliated patrol fleet employed a total of two million soldiers and officers, and even in their present state, with many of the seasoned warriors having been replaced with raw recruits, they still made up the most potent fighting force in the Alliance Armed Forces. That, however, was because they derived their potency from the absolute faith they had in their commander's invincibility.

"What do you think would happen if we lost Iserlohn Fortress?" Rear Admiral Murai forced out in a low voice. "A gigantic war fleet commanded by Duke von Lohengramm would come pouring out of the corridor and into alliance space. If that happens, then the alliance is—"

There was no need to say the word: "finished."

In the past, the Alliance Armed Forces had exchanged fire with the Imperial Navy on any number of occasions when they had launched incursions through the corridor.

However, present conditions were not like those of two years ago. Aside from the First Fleet, the forces they currently had on this side of the corridor consisted of untested regiments of new recruits, planetary security forces incapable of long-range deployments, patrol squadrons with inferior armor and firepower, and units still in the process of being organized—it was fair to say that that was all. The alliance's military security was hinging entirely on Iserlohn Fortress and the Iserlohn Patrol Fleet. This was, in fact, precisely the reason why those serving to the rear of the front lines had time to organize new units and train new recruits.

And yet, at as critical a moment as this one, their frontline commander had been summoned all the way back to Heinessen! And for what? To face a court of inquiry that was neither urgent nor necessary.

Far from the front lines on the capital world of Heinessen, politicos of the Trünicht faction protected nothing but their own hides as they dressed themselves in warm clothing and ate to their hearts' content. When they had gotten bored of that, they had summoned Yang Wen-li and were now amusing themselves playing Star Chamber. When Caselnes pictured their faces, he could feel an urgent fury burning in his stomach. To protect the authority and privileges of those people, frontline troops regularly had to throw away their lives in battle. It had happened in the coup d'état last year, and it had happened before that as well. Caselnes couldn't help feeling skeptical about the meaning of the war.

If there was one thing that lifted his spirits, it was that now Yang would be freed from his pointless battle with the court of inquiry on Heinessen. If he had to fight either way, even Yang would choose to match wits with an enemy force on the vast battlefield of outer space. The duty of Caselnes and the others was to hold Iserlohn until his return.

Caselnes considered the worst-case scenario and took several preventive measures. He had the strategic and tactical computers configured so that all of their data could be deleted at any moment, prepared a system by which secret documents could also be incinerated, and had Iserlohn's civilian population of three million begin preparations for evacuation. The promptness and precision of these measures reflected what Caselnes considered to be his strongest suit.

And so an FTL winged its way from Iserlohn to the rear.

"On April 10, a massive imperial force crossed into the Iserlohn Corridor—furthermore, it is accompanied by a *giant mobile fortress*. Request immediate reinforcements."

II

Also on the tenth of April, sparks were flying in a battle without weapons in the capital of the Free Planets Alliance. Admiral Yang Wen-li was facing off against the court of inquiry, and his aide-de-camp Frederica Greenhill seemed to have somehow made enemies of the entire Trünicht administration.

Yang was not being questioned every day. All of the inquisitors had other work they had to attend to, not least among them Defense Committee Chair Negroponte, who was the chairman of the court of inquiry. Since they couldn't focus all their energies on bullying Yang, the court of inquiry was meeting every two or three days, which meant it was dragging out interminably. Yang's nerves had taken quite a beating, and if he'd had a short temper, he would have exploded long ago. At this point, all Yang could think was that the goal of this court was not to question him and reach some sort of conclusion; it was simply to keep the process of questioning him going.

How do they plan on ending this? Yang wondered. Suppose the goal of the inquiry was to determine whether or not the presence of Yang Wenli was harmful for the alliance. If the conclusion that was that he was harmless, they would have to let him go. If it was that he was harmful, they would need to take some sort of decisive measure—but since the military threat from the empire was very real, they could not, at present, afford to lose Yang. That said, they couldn't just keep the inquiry going forever either. When Yang considered these circumstances, the whole thing seemed both disgusting and ridiculous, and he also took a slight amount of mean-spirited amusement from it as well. Whatever they decided, they would have to let him go eventually, and Yang was by this time of a mind to just wait them out and look forward to seeing what sort of excuse they would come up with to keep up appearances.

He had his letter of resignation in his pocket. If needed, he could whip it out at any moment and shove it up the nose of the Defense Committee chair. He had written it on the first night of the inquiry, and on the following day—when he'd intended to slam it down on the chairman's desk—the court had not convened, and a demoralized Yang had stuck it in his pocket instead. It wasn't as if there had been no chance to tender it since then, but just knowing that it was there and could be used at a moment's notice helped calm him down a little—and also brought out his nastier side: *Let's wait until things get a little more dramatic and then let 'em have it!*

Whenever the court was to convene, Yang would, in his own way, get excited. What was harder on him were the days he had to spend under house arrest in his assigned accommodations. Aside from eating his meals, there was nothing to do there. From the window, there was nothing to see but the courtyard. He didn't even have access to a solivision, and when he tried asking for some books to read—knowing it was a wasted effort—the request was met with the expected hemming and hawing, followed by refusal in the end. When he thought, *Well in that case, let's do a little more writing*, it turned out that he had a pen but not any paper—he had blown through a couple dozen sheets while writing his letter of resignation, using up all that he had. When he fell into bed, he tried imagining himself torturing each member of the court in turn, but he soon grew bored of that.

While all three meals were excellent every day, they were as devoid of individuality as the furniture in this room, and it was no use hoping for something different each time. Breakfast in particular had been exactly the same for days on end: rye bread, butter, plain yogurt, coffee, vegetable juice, bacon and eggs, french potatoes, and salad with onions, peppers, and lettuce. The flavor certainly wasn't bad, and it had to be very nutritious, but if asked, Yang would have described it as "lacking both sincerity and originality." Most unforgivable was their assumption that meals were followed by coffee.

If Julian were here, he would have brewed red tea from fragrant Shillong leaves, and even if eggs were on the menu every day, he would have changed them up, making omelets one day and scrambled eggs the next. And his technique for making rice gratin and rice porridge from the previous night's leftovers had, in Yang's estimation, no equal under heaven. It would be so much better for culture and society if he chose to train formally as a cook and got a license to do that, instead of pursuing a crummy military job that would contribute nothing to civilization or humanity. If he would just do that, Yang could even use his retirement allowance to open up a restaurant for him . . . Of course, it was true that the job of "cook" probably didn't stimulate the boy's youthful romanticism the way "space battleship captain" did.

In this way, meaningless days rolled by for Yang on Heinessen. But it was fair to say that even his circumstances were preferable by far to the hard work that Frederica was doing. Frederica's struggle was one that was literally without sleep or rest.

After receiving that callous response from Rear Admiral Bay, Frederica and Machungo had headed straight to Space Armada Command. The front-desk officer had been a bureaucratic type, wielding regulations, enumerated powers, and organizational mechanisms like a sorcerer's staff. He had wasted a lot of Frederica's time, but at last she had been noticed by a young lieutenant commander named Edmond Messersmith, who had been on his way out the door to head home. He had stopped and tried to help her out. Messersmith had been a student of her father's back when Dwight Greenhill was serving as vice president at Officers' Academy, and for a time her father had apparently had his eye on Messersmith as a prospective groom for Frederica. Frederica had thanked him, and Messersmith had responded with a pleasant little smile.

"Glad to be of service. If you need any help, I'll make myself useful however I can. Say hello to your mother for me. All these years, and you're still just as lovely as ever, Frederica."

Frederica had thanked him, but by the time she was opening the door to the office of Admiral Bucock, commander in chief of the space armada, Messersmith had already been driven from her mind.

"Lieutenant, what in the world are you doing here?"

That was the first thing the seventy-two-year-old admiral said to her. As Frederica had expected, the number two man in uniform had no idea that Yang had been summoned to the capital. It became crystal clear from that question alone just how secretive this court of inquiry actually was.

Frederica gave him a concise summary of what had happened, and by the end of it, Bucock's white eyebrows were quivering, although he held his peace for a long moment afterward. He was not so much surprised as shocked.

"To be honest," she said, "I was very unsure whether I should bring this to Your Excellency's attention or not. Although I would be grateful for any help you can give me in extricating Admiral Yang from his predicament, this could turn into a standoff between the military and the government if things take a turn for the worse…"

"That's certainly a valid concern. But at the same time, that's no longer something we need to worry about."

It was an odd thing the old admiral had said. The bitter, even dark tone in which he had spoken it sounded so unlike the usually affable Bucock.

"What I mean, Lieutenant, is that it's no longer possible for the whole military to come together in opposition to the government."

"By which you mean that the military has an internal split, with two competing factions?"

"Two! There are two factions, no doubt. At least if you can set an overwhelming majority next to the minority and call that two. Naturally, I'm in the minority. Not that that's anything to brag about."

Frederica breathed in softly. She hesitated to say her next words, but she couldn't just stand there and not ask him: "How on earth did such a thing ever happen?"

For some reason, the old admiral seemed as hesitant to answer that question as she had been to ask it. But just as Frederica had been unable to keep herself from asking it, Bucock couldn't stop himself from answering.

"This isn't an easy thing to say, but if I have to point to a reason, it's because of the Military Congress's coup last year. Confidence in the military has plummeted because of that. We have less of a say in things, and the politicians—they've used the opportunity to infiltrate the military with their own people. By manipulating military personnel assignments however they see fit, they've managed to pack the central hub of our leadership with their plants. Neither I nor Director Cubresly was able to do anything during the coup last year, so even when we objected, our opinions were just laughed away."

My face must be white as a sheet, thought Frederica. Once again, her father, Dwight Greenhill, the face of the coup d'état, had appeared before her, standing in her way. It wasn't possible for her to dislike her father. However, if this kind of thing continued to happen, she might well come to hate him.

"For that reason, both myself and Admiral Cubresly are isolated rocks in a wide sea at present. While it's unclear what fundamental motive the politicians had for summoning Admiral Yang to the capital, they're no doubt thinking that, up to a point, they can do as they like without anyone objecting—and anyone who does object, they can simply crush."

"I don't know what to say...I wasn't aware I was putting you in such a difficult position."

"What are you talking about? I'm not in any particularly hard spot myself. I'm just disgusted, is all. All their obnoxious sneaking around's driving me crazy. Actually, this very room might well be bugged. I'd say the likelihood's over 90 percent."

On hearing that, the hulking Warrant Officer Machungo jumped a full ten centimeters into the air. The old admiral laughed himself into a fit of coughing. He stopped laughing, though, when he met Frederica's eyes.

"The reason I'm having this conversation in spite of that," he said, "is that it's already too late to fool anybody about whose colors I'm flying and because any recordings they made with an eavesdropping device would be legally inadmissible as evidence. I, on the other hand, could sue them for infringing on my human rights with their eavesdropping. Assuming the government feels like obeying the Charter of the Alliance, that is."

"The government can't publically trample on its facade of democracy. When the time comes, I think we can use that as a weapon."

"I'm pleased to hear the lieutenant speaking with such wisdom and insight. By the way, to bring this back to Admiral Yang's situation, now that I know what's going on, I'll do everything I can. You most certainly have my cooperation."

"It isn't a problem for you?" Frederica asked.

This time, the old admiral smiled cheerfully.

"You've come here and asked, so it's too late to be worrying about that now. I think a lot of that young man. Oh, but don't tell him I said that. After all, young 'uns can get a big head awfully fast."

"I'm truly grateful for this. And since I know you're a nice person who won't mind my saying so, I think a lot of you too, Your Excellency."

"I'd love to have the missus hear you say that. By the way, there's one other thing..." Here the old admiral's face grew more serious. "No one followed you on your way here, did they?"

A look of shock ran through Frederica's hazel eyes, and she looked over at Machungo. She had been thinking only of the situation with Yang and had given no thought to the possibility of a tail. That had been careless.

Machungo straightened up and answered in a rich bass voice. "I don't have any proof, but I saw more than one landcar that struck me as suspicious. If we were being tailed, I think they were swapping out cars along the way."

"As I thought. It's the sort of thing a weasel like Bay would probably do."

Bucock clucked his tongue loudly, possibly intending for Bay to hear it through his unseen bugs. Bucock was a daring old man.

"Lieutenant, this is the state that the home base of our democracy is in. The rain hasn't started yet, but it's going to be a dreadful sight once these clouds have thickened. We're on an acceleration curve headed from bad to worse, and getting back to clear weather is not going to be easy."

"Sir, we came here prepared for that."

"Very well."

There was a hint of warmth in the man's otherwise brusque tone of voice. "I guess this means we're partners. Generation gap notwithstanding."

III

Although she had wavered before making the decision, choosing to rely on Admiral Bucock turned out to be a great success for Frederica. Bucock was not merely willing to help; his position and reputation were such that not even an "overwhelming majority" could afford to ignore him altogether. Had they been able to, they would surely have relieved the old admiral of his duties as commander in chief of the space armada long ago.

First, *Leda II*, which had been isolated in the corner of a military space-port, was released from surveillance. The crew, who had been forbidden from leaving the ship without being given a reason, were freed and began acting in coordination with Frederica.

As for Frederica herself, she decided to accept the Bucocks' goodwill and stay at their house. This was because the room she had been in up until then was not just bugged and under surveillance—there was even a danger of her being physically harmed if she continued staying there.

Bucock's house was protected by security guards assigned directly to him, and even if it hadn't been, Bay simply could not stretch lawless hands into the home of the commander in chief of the space armada. Mrs. Bucock also welcomed Frederica warmly.

"Please stay as long as you like. Oh, but you can't do that, can you? You've got to rescue Mister Yang and get back to Iserlohn as soon as you can, haven't you? Anyway, just relax and make yourself at home."

"I'm terribly sorry to impose on you like this."

"No need to worry over that, Miss Greenhill. It always seems brighter in this house when a young person comes over, and my husband is thrilled to have a chance to pick a fight with the government. We're the ones who should be thanking you."

Mrs. Bucock's warm smile made Frederica feel envious. Was this what the bond between a husband and wife looked like after they had walked through life for more than forty years together and come to understand one another deeply?

Outside the Bucock household, however, Frederica had to wonder if her nation wasn't losing its right to be called a free country. Frederica was not only concerned about those things that had happened to her personally; she had a feeling she couldn't shake that reason and open-mindedness were rapidly disappearing from the nation and society.

Having made the Bucocks' home her base of operations, she was constantly running in and out, and it was during this time that a certain incident occurred.

There was a civilian organization known as the Edwards Committee. Antiwar activists had joined together to form the organization in honor of the late Jessica Edwards, who had sacrificed her life in the Stadium Massacre the previous year. The committee had raised a certain issue regarding the unfairness of the conscription system.

They had conducted research on 246,000 VIPs in the political, financial, and bureaucratic sectors who had children in the age bracket suitable for conscription, and the results had been utterly shocking. Less than 15 percent of them had children serving in the military, and less than 1 percent had a child on the front lines.

"What do these numbers show? If, as our ruling class never tires of telling us, this long war is essential to bring about true justice, why don't they let their own sons and daughters participate in it? Why use their privilege to dodge the draft? The only answer is that this war doesn't mean enough to them to offer up their own flesh and blood!"

The Edwards Committee sent out a questionnaire in writing, but it went utterly ignored by the Trünicht administration.

Intelligence Trafficking Committee Chair Bonnet doubled as a government spokesman, and all he had to say on the matter was, "We do not recognize the necessity of responding to this." But what angered and frightened the members of the Edwards Committee even more was the fact that this incident went almost completely unreported by the media. E-papers and solivision programs alike rolled out story after story when it came to crime, scandals, and human interest—all completely unrelated to the political authorities—while ignoring the activities of the Edwards Committee altogether.

With no other options, the members of the Edwards Committee decided to take their message out into the streets and go directly to ordinary civilians. When a demonstration involving five thousand members started up, squads of police came out to block their advance. When they turned onto a backstreet to avoid the blockade, they found the Patriotic Knights—a prowar organization—waiting for them, wielding ceramic truncheons. Police officers watched from a distance while Edwards Committee protesters, including women and children, were bludgeoned to the ground one after another by the Patriotic Knights' ceramic clubs. At last, the Knights ran away, and the police moved in to handcuff the bleeding, fallen members of the Edwards Committee. "Staging a riot" was the charge used as a pretext for their arrest. "An internal squabble between members of the Edwards Committee led to bloodshed," explained the police, and most media outlets reported it exactly that way, without ever making mention of the Patriotic Knights...

When Frederica heard that story from João Lebello, a politician of Bucock's acquaintance, she couldn't believe what she was hearing at first. While she knew all too well what had been done to Yang and to herself, her trust in journalism and the system of democracy had strong roots.

Even that trust, however, was being shaken day by day in the course of Frederica's activities. Even with Bucock's public assistance and Lebello's stealthy cooperation, her actions were being hampered by invisible walls and chains. They did at last pin down the building in which the court of inquiry was being held—Lebello had found out by contacting Huang Rui. It was on the grounds of Alliance Armed Forces Rear Service Headquarters, but even when Bucock tried to talk his way in, he was refused entry. They used the phrase "state secrets" like a shield. When Bucock requested a meeting with those involved, that was also refused. Also, Bucock found himself tailed from the moment he left home until the moment he returned, and during his second face-to-face meeting with a witness he had at last discovered, the man had seemed afraid of something and had refused to give testimony.

When for the second time Frederica succeeded in cornering Rear Admiral Bay, he dodged her questions left and right, resolutely refusing to give her a straight answer. Losing patience with his attitude, Frederica decided to try telling him she would go to the media instead. However, Bay's response this time was different from what he had said before.

"If you want to tell them, go right ahead. But you won't find a reporter anywhere who'll pick up your story. You'll just be ignored or, barring that, turned into a laughingstock."

Frederica looked him straight in the eye, and when she did, she saw a faint flash of panic and regret just underneath his skin. He had just said something that he wasn't supposed to say.

Frederica felt her heart go cold. As she had seen with the Edwards Committee incident, the Trünicht administration was feeling a lot of confidence in its ability to dominate and control mass communications. When political authority and journalism colluded with one another, democracy lost its ability to critique and cleanse itself, allowing a deadly infection to take root. Had this country's condition progressed that far already? Were the government, the military, and the media all under the thumb of the same ruler?

It was on the following day that she was reminded of this all over again.

Warrant Officer Machungo had been reading an electronic newspaper, but the moment he caught sight of Frederica, he hurriedly tried to hide it. Naturally, that achieved nothing beyond arousing her suspicion. Frederica asked to see the paper, and Machungo reluctantly handed it over.

There was an article in it about Frederica, which noted in lines of venomous text that even though her father, Dwight Greenhill, had been the "ringleader of last year's coup d'état," she still held rank in the Alliance Armed Forces. It also presented the comments of an unnamed source, speculating that she and her commanding officer—that is to say, Yang—might be involved romantically. Where that article had come from and what sort of intentions were behind it were all too clear.

"This pile of rubbish is nothing but lies," Machungo fumed, but Frederica didn't feel like getting angry. Perhaps nastiness above a certain level had the opposite effect, shearing away the energy one had for rage. Another reason, though, was the impatience and sense of hopelessness she was feeling, unable as she was to find a clear way to get Yang away from that court.

However, a miracle finally happened. One day, an emergency call came in for Bucock, after which the daring old admiral seemed unable to remain calm.

"Big news, Lieutenant. Iserlohn Fortress is under attack by the enemy. The Imperial Navy's invaded."

Frederica gasped. Before her surprise had even halfway subsided, a thought flashed in her mind, and she shouted out: "Then Admiral Yang will be released from the inquiry!"

"Exactly. Ironically enough, the Imperial Navy's our savior this time."

But ironic or not, Frederica was glad. It was the first time in her life she had ever felt gratitude toward the Imperial Navy.

IV

From the very beginning that day, the court of inquiry was pregnant with signs of rough weather ahead. Though Yang had made up his mind to put up with just about anything, President Oliveira of Central Autonomous Governance University, perhaps carried away by academic passion, had begun to lecture him on the raison d'être of the thing called war. According to him, negative opinions of it were nothing more than a product of hypocrisy and sentimentality.

"Admiral, you're a fine man, but you're still young. You just don't seem to have a clear understanding yet of what war really is."

Yang didn't answer, but his attitude did nothing to erode the man's eagerness to lecture a captive audience.

"Listen to me: war is the fruit of civilization and also the most sensible method for resolving both international and domestic conflicts."

Yang wanted to say, *Says who? Who in the world has ever acknowledged such a thing?* But he didn't argue; he figured that asking him would only be wasted effort. Oliveira, apparently interpreting Yang's silence in a manner favorable to himself, expounded on his pet theory boastfully.

"A human being is an animal that can very easily fall from grace. In particular, peace and freedom—two things that lack a sense of urgency— naturally cause people to lapse into complacency. It is war that gives birth to bustling activity and orderly discipline. War itself drives civilization forward, makes the people stronger, and improves them both physically and spiritually."

"A splendid opinion," Yang replied without a sliver of sincerity. "If I were someone who'd never taken lives or lost family in war, I might even want to believe it."

When Yang was in the mood for it, he could sling a lot of snark, even at high-ranking government officials. He had only been refraining here because his chances to do so were so few in number—and above all, the aftermath was sure to be a pain in the neck. By this point, however, Yang had accumulated a critical mass of aggression.

Endurance and silence were not necessarily virtues in every circumstance. Enduring what should be unendurable, not saying the things that needed to be said—that allowed opposing egos to inflate unchecked and let them think that their self-centeredness was acceptable in any situation. Coddling rulers as though they were small children, letting them walk all over you—nothing good would ever come of that.

"Naturally," Yang continued, "that idea probably does have its charms for people who take advantage of wars and try to build their own fortunes on the sacrifices of others. You know, the sort who drape themselves in a love of country they don't feel a shred of in order to deceive the public."

That was when anger first flashed across Oliveira's face.

"A-are you saying our patriotism is a sham?"

"I'm saying that if it's really as vital as you say it is that we be willing to defend the fatherland and make sacrifices for it, how about you do it yourselves instead of ordering everybody else around?"

Yang's tone was almost carefree now.

"For example, you could round up all the prowar politicians, bureaucrats, intellectuals, and financiers, and form some kind of 'Patriotic Regiment.' Then, when the empire attacks, you can lead the charge. But first, you'll all need to relocate from secure zones like the capital and come live on the front line at Iserlohn. How about it? We've got plenty of room for you."

The dead silence that filled the room when Yang finished talking was weighted with both hostility and hesitation. Effective counterargument was impossible, so the wordless interval continued to stretch onward. Yang had known they would have no comeback. He struck again, hard, with a follow-up:

"Of all the things that human beings do, do you know which one is the most brazenly despicable? It's when people who have authority—and the people who flatter them—hide in safe places singing the praises of war; push a patriotic, sacrificial mind-set on the people; and then send them off to the battlefield. If peace is ever going to come to this galaxy, we should eradicate malignant parasites like those first instead of perpetuating this pointless war with the empire."

It was as if the air itself had blanched. No one on the court of inquiry had imagined that the young, black-haired admiral would spew venom to this degree. Even Huang Rui was staring at Yang with a surprised expression.

"By 'parasites,' you refer to this court of inquiry?" Negroponte said. He was putting on a good show of remaining calm and composed, but there was an uneven ripple in his voice.

Yang fired back, making sure it sounded as disrespectful as possible: "Did it sound like I meant someone else?"

Bursting with anger, Negroponte puffed up like a bullfrog, picked up his gavel, and started banging it on the desk violently.

"Baseless insults! Impudence beyond the pale! It seems we've no choice but to impeach the very nature of your character, Mr. Yang. This inquiry will have to be extended even further."

"Objection—" Yang started to say, although the rest of his sentence was drowned out in the continuous pounding of the gavel on the desk.

"I forbid the inquiree from speaking!"

"On what authority?"

"On my authority as chair of this court of—no, wait. I acknowledge no need to respond. You will submit to the order of these proceedings."

Yang put both his hands on his hips and showed them as defiant a face and posture as he could. He had already decided that he was going to explode at some point, and now it felt like the right time had come.

"Can't you just order me to leave the room instead? Because, frankly speaking, I can't stand the sound of your voices or the sight of your faces for another moment. Just kick me out because I didn't pay admission or something. Because my patience is at its absolute limi—"

That was when a chime rang out from somewhere near the Defense Committee chair and made Yang close his mouth.

"Hello? Yes, it's me. What's going on?"

Still glaring at Yang, Negroponte spoke into the receiver in a supremely peeved voice, but then a single phrase from the other end of the line appeared to leave him in utter shock. The muscles in his face became noticeably taut, and several times he spoke, asking for confirmation of certain details.

When he hung up at last, he looked around the table with a panicked expression and in a high-pitched voice said, "We'll recess for one hour. Fellow members of the court, please retire to the next room. Admiral, you wait where you are."

It was obvious that some kind of hairy situation had arisen. Yang looked on without emotion as the board members hurried out of the room. *Political upheaval, maybe?* he wondered. *Or even better, what if Chairman Trünicht has dropped dead . . .*

It wasn't easy to call Yang a gentleman when he had thoughts like that.

One room over from where Yang was waiting, ashen faces were lined up in a row, with Negroponte's dead center. "Massive enemy invasion of the Iserlohn Corridor"—that report was the invisible hammer that had brutally knocked the inquisitors off their feet.

"What we have to do is obvious enough," said Huang Rui, the only one who had kept his composure. "It doesn't even bear consideration. Suspend this inquiry, get Admiral Yang back to Iserlohn, and get him—no, *ask* him—to repel the imperial forces."

"But we can't just do a one-eighty on the spot like that! Up until just now we've had him under inquiry!"

"Well then, shall we stick with our original plan and continue? Until the Imperial Navy comes charging straight toward this planet?"

An uncomfortable silence stretched out in the room.

"In any case, it seems we have no choice," Rui added.

"But we can't decide this at our own discretion," said Negroponte. "We have to ask Chairman Trünicht what he intends to do."

With eyes that pitied him, Huang turned to look at Negroponte's tense features. "Well then, go ahead and do it. It won't take more than five minutes."

Yang had counted to about five hundred when the board members filed back into the room. He could sense a mood about them that was completely different from what had existed just a little while ago. He braced himself mentally, and then the Defense Committee chair spoke to him: "Admiral, an emergency situation has arisen. Iserlohn Fortress is facing the likelihood of an all-out assault by the Imperial Navy. Unbelievable as it may sound, the enemy has apparently attached propulsion devices to a space fortress and brought the whole thing there, together with a large fleet of warships. Reinforcements must be sent there immediately."

"So you're, um, telling *me* to go?"

After ten seconds of dead silence, Yang asked the same question again. His voice and the look on his face were actually kind. Negroponte was visibly embarrassed, but somehow he managed to shore himself up enough to say, "Well, of course I am! You are the commanding officer of the Iserlohn Fortress and Patrol Fleet. You have a duty and responsibility to stop the enemy's invasion, don't you?"

"Sadly, however, I'm away from the front lines and under inquiry. On top of that, I've got a bad attitude, so I might just end up getting fired. What's going to happen to this court of inquiry?"

"It's canceled. Admiral Yang, as Defense Committee chair and as your superior officer, I am ordering you to immediately go to Iserlohn, take charge of its defenses, and counterattack. Understood?"

He had spoken in a ferocious voice, but a tremor in the question "Understood?" exposed the unease that lay hidden in his heart. Legally speaking, he certainly was Yang's superior officer. However, if Yang were to ignore his orders and Iserlohn fell, then the legal grounds that placed him above Yang would collapse, as would the substance of his authority.

Negroponte had finally realized that they had been playing with fire right next to a gunpowder magazine. He could enjoy authority only because a secure nation was there to back him up. He could enjoy his dominance only because others were willing to obey him. Neither he nor anyone else on the court possessed any power that was simply theirs by nature.

"Yes, sir. I'll return to Iserlohn right away—"

Negroponte breathed out a deep sigh of relief at Yang's words.

"—after all, I've got subordinates and friends there. You can guarantee my authority to act freely, correct?"

"Of course. You're free to do as you will."

"Well, in that case, if you'll excuse me."

When Yang rose to his feet, one of the inquisitors called out to him. It was a man from the end of the table, one whose name Yang had forgotten the moment he'd heard it. The shade of flattery in his voice was unmistakable.

"How about it, Admiral—do we have a shot at winning this? Oh, but of course we do. After all, you're Miracle Yang. I'm sure you'll meet our expectations."

"I'll do everything I can."

Yang's tone was offhanded. He had neither the desire nor the intention to string together a bunch of big, impressive-sounding words just to satisfy the members of this court. He could turn out all his pockets and not find a single reason to answer as kindly as he had, but it wasn't just that; at this point in time, he really didn't have any clear plan for dealing with this new attack.

It was the members of the court of inquiry, naturally, who ought to be held accountable for letting this situation occur. Still, there was no point in denying that this tactic of the Imperial Navy's had taken Yang completely by surprise. Call him naive and he wouldn't argue, but still, there were limits on people's powers of imagination.

A fortress to fight a fortress. Attaching propulsion devices to it and making it fly. This was actually a variation on the "big ship, big gun" orthodoxy; hardly the shockingly new tactic it appeared to be at first blush. Still, the fact was it had delivered a serious psychological blow to the alliance's authorities—and in the process done Yang the favor of freeing him from their little farce.

Yang had always figured that if any revolutionary new technology could someday tip the balance of military power between the two nations, it would be the development of a means to warp ultralong distances of 10,000 light-years or more. If something like that became a reality, the Imperial Navy would be able to skip right past the Iserlohn Corridor and send large fleets and all the supplies they needed directly into the heart of alliance territory. One day, the citizens of Heinessen would suddenly look up to see swarms of battleships blotting out the sun. They would stare at them in vacant incomprehension, riveted in place. The authorities would then have no choice but to take an "oath by the castle wall"—the sort of oath you took when you were backed up against it—to surrender unconditionally.

What he would do then was something Yang had never even thought about. Those circumstances would be beyond his ability to deal with. If they tried to make him responsible even in a situation like that, he simply wouldn't stand for it. Yang's public-employee spirit would make him think, *You don't pay me enough for this!*

Yang put his uniform beret back on, brushed the dust from his clothes with obvious deliberation, and with long strides began walking toward the exit.

"Oh, wait, I almost forgot something important," he said, stopping just in front of the door. He turned and addressed the court with a respectfulness bordering on insubordination. "I'm looking forward to eventually hearing an explanation of who's responsible for choosing the exact moment of the empire's invasion to call me away from Iserlohn. That's assuming Iserlohn doesn't fall, of course. Now if you'll excuse me..."

Yang turned on his heel and left the room where he had been forced to endure those miserable and meaningless days. He would have really liked to have observed the inquisitors closely and seen how the flow of blood to their faces changed at his parting remark, but that would have meant remaining in that oppressive space even longer than he had already, a thing Yang had zero intention of doing.

The door swung open, then closed again, leaving nine sets of eyes glaring at it. Defeat was on one face, unease on another; another still was white with rage. Someone growled in a low voice, "Who does that impudent greenhorn think he is?"

The paint had peeled away, exposing the meanness of quality that lay underneath.

"If I recall correctly, he's the hero who saved our country," Huang Rui answered in a tone brimming with sarcasm. "If not for that 'impudent greenhorn,' we would have surrendered to the empire by now, or at best be rotting in cells as political prisoners. We certainly wouldn't have had the luxury of whiling away the hours playing courtroom in a place like this. He's a benefactor to us all. What kind of gratitude have we shown, bullying him here for days on end?"

"But don't you think it's disrespectful—that attitude of his toward his betters?"

"Betters? Are politicians really such impressive creatures? It's not like we contribute a thing to society's output. We're entrusted with the duty of fairly collecting and efficiently utilizing the taxes paid by citizens; that's what we do, that's what we get paid for. And that's all we are, really. At best we're nothing but parasites living off the machinery of society. If we look impressive, it's only a mirage created by advertising. Anyway, instead of arguing over this—" (here the light brimming in Huang's eyes grew a shade more ironic still) "—we've got another fire to put out that's a little bit closer to home, so how about we deal with that now? As Admiral Yang said, who is going to take responsibility for pulling him off the front lines right before the empire went on the offensive? One letter of resignation is going to be necessary. Not Admiral Yang's, of course."

Multiple gazes converged on Negroponte. The Defense Committee chair's thick jowls quivered. The idea of summoning Yang to the capital hadn't been his. Not originally. He had been following the wishes of another. Although not passively, to be sure.

In the minds of the men who surrounded him, the word "former" had already been appended to his title.

When Yang stepped outside into a silent, rich shower of sunlight, he stretched out both his arms wide and breathed deeply, driving the damp, dirty air from his lungs.

"Admiral Yang!"

A slightly trembling voice struck his eardrums and passed straight through them to the bottom of his heart. He turned, looking for the owner of that voice. Frederica Greenhill's slender form was standing there in the sunlight. At her side were Admiral Bucock and Warrant Officer Machungo.

"Lieutenant Greenhill . . ."

I'm finally back in a human *crowd*, Yang thought. Although there might have been times when he had felt otherwise, there most certainly was a place where he belonged in this world.

"I'm sorry to have put you to all this trouble," Yang said, making a heartfelt bow toward Bucock.

"If you've got something to say," said Bucock, "say it to Lieutenant Greenhill. All I did was lend her a hand."

Yang turned toward her.

"Thank you, Lieutenant. I don't what to—I mean, um, there's no way I can thank you enough."

Frederica, holding back a different impulse, gave him a little smile in response. "As your aide-de-camp, I only did what was natural, Excellency. But I'm happy to be of service."

The old admiral's lower jaw made some slight movements. Perhaps he had muttered something along the lines of, *They're both of 'em awkward as middle schoolers*, but no one was close enough to hear. When he spoke up, it was to say this:

"Well now, you may be about to head back to Iserlohn, but we can't send you away empty-handed. I know there're a lot of preparations that have to be made, but first let's all have lunch together. Surely Iserlohn can hold out till we're finished eating."

That was a sound proposal.

João Lebello was waiting at the restaurant called The White Hart. As he was a politician outside the mainstream, he had avoided entering the military facility where Yang had been held. Yang thanked him for his assistance, but after Lebello congratulated him, he grew very serious and began to speak.

"Right now, we're at a point where the people are losing their faith in politics, while at the same time we have a high-ranking military commander who is both highly capable and widely popular. I'm speaking of you, Admiral Yang. These are extremely dangerous conditions for our democratic system. You could even call them greenhouse conditions for the sprouts of dictatorship."

"Does that mean you're calling me a greenhouse flower, Your Excellency?"

Yang had spoken with humorous intent, but it seemed Lebello was in no mood to play along.

"If worse came to worst, Admiral Yang, one could even posit a future history that remembers you as a second Rudolf von Goldenbaum."

"Now…now hold on just a minute, please," Yang said, flustered. He had been called plenty of things he didn't care for in his time, but this had to be the crown jewel of them all. "Your Excellency, I have no desire to become a ruler. If I had wanted to do that, I had the biggest chance I could have ever hoped for during the coup d'état last year."

"That's what I believe, too. That's what I want to believe. But…" Lebello broke off into a gloomy silence and turned a dismal gaze toward the young, black-haired admiral. "…but people *change*. Five hundred years ago, did Rudolf the Great really have ambitions of becoming a dictator from the very beginning? I have my doubts. Aside from a streak of self-righteousness, he may well have been nothing more than a reformer passionate about his beliefs and ideals—at least, until he got his hands on some real power. Then power changed him overnight, and he went straight from utter self-certainty to self-apotheosis."

"So you're thinking that if I were to get hold of some power, it would change me too?" Yang asked.

"I don't know. All I can do is pray. Pray that the day never comes when you're forced to go down Rudolf's path in order to defend yourself."

Yang was silent for a moment. He felt like asking Lebello to whom he would pray, but he knew he would get no satisfactory answer. It was exactly because Yang respected Lebello as a conscientious politician that it made him so uncomfortable to hear these doubts coming from him. When Lebello left early without eating, Yang inwardly murmured, *Oh well*. Frederica and Bucock felt the same. Grateful as they naturally were toward him, a pessimist like Lebello was out of place at this gathering.

After a main course of roast venison had been finished and he had knocked back some melon sherbet as well, Yang was feeling satisfied and full, but on the way out of the restaurant, he met with a most unexpected individual. It was Negroponte, the very man whom he'd been locking horns with in the court of inquiry until just a little while ago.

"Admiral Yang, as a public figure, you're in a position to protect the honor of the state. As such, you won't be making any statements to outsiders that would harm the government's image, will you?"

Yang stared at the man seriously. If he had ever wondered just how brazen a human being could be, the answer was standing right in front of him—dressed in a suit, no less.

"By saying that, you're admitting yourself that that little kaffeeklatsch you threw for me was the sort of thing that could harm the state's image if outsiders knew about it. Correct?"

Negroponte visibly recoiled from this counterattack, although somehow he managed to hold his ground. His job here was to shut Yang's mouth in order to protect Chairman Trünicht's image, so he had come here, enduring the shame.

"I was doing my duty as a public official. That's all. And in spite of that—no, because of that, I'm quite confident I have the right to ask you to do your duty as a fellow public official as well."

"The committee chair is free to be confident of whatever he likes," Yang said. "As for me, I don't even want to remember that court of inquiry, and I have to think about how to win the upcoming battle before anything else."

Saying nothing more, Yang started walking. Such a nice meal, and now it felt like it was about to start fermenting in his gut. Planet Heinessen had had such riches of natural beauty, but the day the humans who now occupied its surface had showed up—! Thinking about winning the battle truly was far better than thinking about those people.

I won't lose to Reinhard von Lohengramm, so I'm certainly not losing to his subordinates . . .

Yang smiled wryly as he caught himself thinking that. It sounded more like conceit than self-confidence.

"Any way you look at it," he was saying to Admiral Bucock shortly afterward, "the government's got a bad habit of tying both my hands and then sending me off to war. Drives me crazy."

Yang figured it would be all right to say that much. It had been like this ever since the capture of Iserlohn. Yang was always being forced to fight in conditions where his authority to make strategic choices was severely limited. He wished he could fight with a freer hand. Contradictory as that may have been with the hatred he felt toward war, that wish certainly did exist within him.

"You're right about that," said Bucock. "No matter what they might be up to, though, there's no choice but to go out and fight this time."

"You said it. After all, ultimately, Iserlohn's my home."

Yang wasn't just exaggerating his own feelings. The place where he was meant to live had never been on the ground.

Although he had been born on Heinessen, he had lost his mother when he was five and come to live in the interstellar trading ship owned by his father, Yang Tai-long, when he was six. Just before turning sixteen, he had lost his father, and although he had entered the dorm at Officers' Academy, in the ten years leading up to that he had not once lived continuously on the ground for a full month. That was why Alex Caselnes had teased, "That Yang! He just doesn't have his feet on the ground."

Julian, of course, was at Iserlohn as well. Most of the people important to him were there.

"All right, Lieutenant, shall we head home, then?"

That was what he asked his beautiful aide.

CHAPTER 7:
FORTRESS VERSUS FORTRESS

"APRIL IS THE CRUELEST MONTH," an ancient poet once declared, and for the soldiers and officers of Iserlohn Fortress, April of IC 798 was indeed a month rife with hardship and suffering. With their commanding officer absent, they were forced to fight alone against a massive enemy force, isolated and without reinforcements.

"Everyone was uneasy at the time. After all, Admiral Yang wasn't there . . ."

That was what Julian would tell Frederica later.

"But by the same token, there was also a feeling that we would be okay if we could just hold out until he returned, and that was a great help to us. That, and . . . This may be a little strange to say, but the anger there wasn't really directed toward the enemy, like, 'How dare you wait till our commander's away!' Instead, way more people were lambasting the government, saying, 'What's wrong with you, calling our commander back to the rear at a time like this?'"

Soldiers could curse the government to their hearts' content, but high-ranking officers didn't have that luxury. During Yang's absence, the acting commander had been Rear Admiral Alex Caselnes, and rest of the core leadership had been made up of Rear Admiral von Schönkopf, the commander of fortress defenses; Rear Admiral Murai, the chief of staff; Rear

Admiral Fischer, the vice commander of the Iserlohn Patrol Fleet; Rear Admiral Nguyen and Rear Admiral Attenborough, division commanders within the Iserlohn Patrol Fleet; and Commodore Patrichev, the deputy chief of staff. Since many of them held identical ranks, a group-oriented leadership structure had been necessary. Acting Commander Caselnes had been merely the first among equals.

This meant that Commander Yang, a full admiral, represented an extremely high peak in the landscape of Iserlohn's leadership structure, with the other high-ranking officers forming a surrounding ridgeline two orders of magnitude lower. Since there was no number two, the Galactic Imperial Navy's chief of staff Paul von Oberstein would likely have opined, "a most impressive organization," had he but known about it.

One other unusual issue was the presence of the commander's advisor, Merkatz, who was being referred to as a "guest admiral." During his time in the Galactic Imperial Navy he had been ranked a senior admiral, but ever since his defeat in the civil war and his defection to the FPA, he had been treated as a vice admiral by the Alliance Armed Forces. That was two ranks below where he had been, but this had been unavoidable. There were presently no marshals in the FPA Armed Forces, and the rank of senior admiral had never existed in it at all. Even Cubresly—director of Joint Operational Headquarters—was still at the rank of full admiral, so obviously the FPA Armed Forces couldn't give a defector from the other side the same rank as their top man in uniform.

Even at vice admiral, however, he was still ranked above Caselnes. If he were to trot out his own rank and demand equivalent authority while Yang was away, it would inevitably throw the organization into confusion. Merkatz, however, was well aware of his standing as "newly arrived guest admiral, not to mention defector," so he always acted with reserve, never cutting in on conversations or even offering his opinion unless he was asked for it.

To Merkatz's aide, Bernhard von Schneider, that was not wholly satisfactory. Von Schneider, the young officer who had advised Merkatz to defect to the FPA, had been a lieutenant commander at the time of the defection. At present, he was treated as a lieutenant. Since his CO had been dropped back two ranks, he had told Yang that the same should be done to him, which would have made him a sublieutenant.

"How about this . . ." Yang had begun when he had answered the young officer.

Personally, Yang had seen no need to demote von Schneider at all, but out of respect for his fastidiousness—or stubbornness—he had offered to compromise with a one-rank demotion.

For von Schneider's part, had he not advised Merkatz to defect, he could have led a peaceful, uneventful life; he had done it because he wanted Merkatz doing meaningful work as a military man. *You could try being a little more assertive*, he sometimes thought of his boss.

Commander Yang, on the other hand, was too soft on the guest admiral and defector, thought Rear Admiral Murai and others in similar positions, harboring doubts as to how well Iserlohn's group leadership structure could function during Yang's absence.

⠿

"Four weeks," Caselnes said emphatically in the meeting room. "If we can hold out for four weeks, Yang will be back." That was all he could say to encourage the soldiers and officers, himself included. While he was regarded highly throughout the organization as a master administrator, his reputation as a combat commander in the face of a crisis was another matter altogether.

When Caselnes spoke in that emphatic tone again, it was to say, "The enemy must not learn Yang is absent." If that became known to them, their attacks would likely become more aggressive and intense, and in a worst-case scenario they might even surround Yang's return route and take him captive.

"Our fundamental policy will be to protect Iserlohn until such time as commander Yang returns. Our strategy will be centered on defense and dealing with enemy offensives as needed."

After he finished speaking, the staff officers looked at one another. While they were not pleased with the lack of creativity and aggressiveness, the fact remained that they had few other options.

"It's fine to focus on defense," said the youthful Attenborough, "but don't you think playing things too passively might invite suspicion from the other side?"

"Passivity in itself might also make them suspect a trap of Commander Yang's," von Schönkopf replied.

"And if it doesn't?"

"When that time comes, Iserlohn Fortress, which we worked so hard to occupy, will simply revert back to imperial control."

Attenborough looked like he was about to say something more, but then a call came in from the communications officer. He said that the newly arrived imperial fortress was broadcasting a signal. For an instant, Caselnes frowned, but then he gave the order to sync it in and headed for the central command room together with the staff officers.

One of the subscreens was switched to video reception mode, and on it appeared a man wearing the uniform of an Imperial Navy admiral—a powerfully built officer in his prime, projecting a confident, bold demeanor.

"Soldiers of the rebel army—or should I say, of the alliance military— I am Admiral Karl Gustav Kempf, commander in chief of the Galactic Imperial Navy Gaiesburg Fortress Expeditionary Force. I wish to say a word of greeting to you before we do battle. If possible, I would prefer that you surrender, although I know you will not. May fortune smile on you in the coming battle."

"Old-fashioned," von Schönkopf murmured at Julian's side, "but dignified and imposing."

Julian found Karl Gustav Kempf's granitelike presence overwhelming. Every inch of the man testified to the admiral's courage...of experience gained and feats accomplished over the course of many battles. *If Yang were standing next to him, he wouldn't look like anything more than a newly minted aide, would he?* Julian thought. And naturally, he meant no disrespect toward Yang in thinking so.

In times to come, when people would ask Julian about his former guardian Yang Wen-li, he would answer them this way:

"Let's see, he never really looked like a very important person. Put him in with a large group of distinguished military officers, and he wouldn't stand out at all. But if he disappeared from that group, you'd know right away that he was missing. That's the kind of person he was..."

"No response from Iserlohn."

Kempf nodded at the comm officer's report.

"I'm a little disappointed," he said. "I was hoping to get a look at Yang Wen-li's face. Soldiers are soldiers, though, so I suppose we should let force of arms serve as greeting."

No reply had come from Iserlohn because Caselnes and the others didn't want to reveal that Yang was not present. There was no way Kempf could have guessed that, however.

"Fortress cannons, energize!" Kempf ordered in a voice that rumbled up from the pit of his stomach.

The main cannons of Gaiesburg Fortress were hard X-ray beam cannons. The beams they fired had a wavelength of one hundred angstroms, an output that reached 740 million megawatts, and could vaporize a giant battleship with one shot. The energy readouts changed from white to yellow, then from yellow to orange, and when the gunnery officer shouted, "Charging complete!" Kempf gave the order in a powerful voice:

"Fire!"

As the order was given, many buttons were pressed by many fingers.

A dozen shafts of white-hot light leapt from Gaiesburg toward Iserlohn. There was such a sense of texture to them that they looked like solid objects, and in the space of two seconds, they covered a distance of six hundred thousand kilometers and gouged into the wall of the FPA forces' fortress. Energy-neutralization fields were powerless to stop them. The mirror-coated ultrahard steel, crystal fibers, and superceramic that made up its four layers of armor resisted for a few seconds and then gave way. The beams pierced the outer walls of the fortress, reached the interior and, in a handful picoseconds, incinerated the surrounding space itself.

Explosions broke out.

The tremors and rumbling shook all of Iserlohn from the inside. All hands in the central command room rose to their feet, though there were some who lost their balance and fell over. Alarms blared out shrill warnings of emergency conditions.

"Block RU77 is damaged!" an operator cried out. Even his voice seemed to have lost its color.

"Get me a damage report!" Caselnes ordered, still standing. "And send rescue teams to get the wounded out of there. Hurry!"

"Life signs negative inside the block. They're all dead. There were as many as four thousand troops over there, concentrated in turrets and armories..." With the back of his hand, the operator wiped away sweat that had broken out on his forehead. "Repair of the outer wall...impossible at present. All we can do with the damaged block is abandon it..."

"There's no choice, then. Seal off Block RU77. Then order all combat personnel to don their space suits. Also, forbid all noncombatants entry into blocks facing the outer wall. See to it quickly."

Von Schönkopf stepped quickly over to Caselnes's side. "Acting commander! What about the counterattack?"

"Counterattack?"

"We have no choice. We can't just sit here and wait for the second fusillade."

"But...you saw what just happened!"

Caselnes was no wilting lily himself, but even his face had gone pale. "If both of us open up with our main cannons, we both go down together!"

"Exactly! If both fortresses keep firing away at each other like this, we'll both be destroyed. So if we can instill the terror of that in the enemy, they'll probably stop firing their main guns so recklessly. If both sides are in a deadlock, that means we can buy time. Now is not the time to show weakness."

"I see. You're right." Caselnes turned toward the gunnery officer. "Power up Thor's Hammer!"

Tension raced through the command room at the speed of light.

"Thor's Hammer" was the collective name for the main cannons of Iserlohn Fortress, and their 924 million megawatt output exceeded that of Gaiesburg. Back when this fortress was in imperial hands, the Alliance Armed Forces had launched as many as six major offensives to try to dislodge them, and every time had suffered massive losses of personnel and ships, allowing the imperial military to boast that "the Iserlohn Corridor is paved with the corpses of rebel soldiers."

"Charging complete! Target locked!"

Caselnes swallowed and raised one hand.

"Fire!"

This time, a gigantic pillar of light rose up from Iserlohn and leapt toward Gaiesburg. It ripped through energy-neutralization fields and multilayer armor plating as though it were paper and caused a massive explosion inside the fortress. On their screens, those inside Iserlohn were able to make out a little white bubble of light that was spilling out of Gaiesburg. That bubble of light was a swell of energy equivalent to several dozen warships exploding at once, and in that instant, several thousand lives were lost inside Gaiesburg as well.

II

This unspeakably fierce exchange of fire between the two main cannons was the first act in this drama. Both sides suffered severe damage, and even more severe psychological shock, and afterward both recoiled from using their main cannons again. If one fired, one would be fired upon. Both would fall together. Because the mutual objective of both sides was to win—not to fulfill a suicide pact—it would be necessary to find another way.

"I wonder what they're going to try next?" Caselnes said, looking around at the staff officers with an exhausted expression.

Rear Admiral Murai replied: "First of all, they have the option of mobilizing their fleet and challenging us to fight them ship to ship, but I don't think the likelihood of that is all that high. If they do bring their fleet out, it will just make easy pickings for our main cannon."

"So then, what?"

"At present, the surrounding region of space is filled with electromagnetic waves and jamming signals. Communications are out, of course, but it also follows that we have only optical means for sighting the enemy. I can imagine them taking this opportunity to slip in close with small vessels and deliver ground troops who would conduct infiltration or sabotage operations."

"Hmm. What does the commander of fortress defenses think?"

Von Schönkopf twirled his empty coffee cup around and around with his fingertips. "I think the chief of staff's opinion is absolutely right. If I could add one thing, however—there's no reason why we should be just waiting for the enemy to come to us. We can do the same thing to them."

". . . Admiral Merkatz, what do you think?"

At Caselnes's words, Lieutenant von Schneider's eyes lit up even brighter than those of Merkatz himself. Just at that moment, however, a chime sounded indicating an emergency communiqué. Caselnes picked up the receiver and, after a brief back-and-forth, turned to look at the commander of fortress defenses.

"It's from Turret 24. Enemy ground troops are beginning to land on the outer wall near that turret. The angle at which they're descending keeps them in a blind spot where we can't pick them off. We're going to have to mobilize ground forces, as well. Admiral von Schönkopf, can you see to it?"

"How did they do that so quickly!" said von Schönkopf, managing to sound both angry and impressed at the same time. He called for Captain Kasper Rinz. Following von Schönkopf's promotion to the admiralty, Kasper Rinz had become commander of the storied Rosen Ritter regiment. He was a young man of functional build, with blue-green eyes and hair like bleached straw.

"Rinz, get ready for some hand to hand. On the double. I'll take command personally."

Von Schönkopf began walking toward the door, still giving orders.

"Wait a minute," said Caselnes. "There can't be any need for the commander of fortress defenses to participate in hand-to-hand combat himself. Please, stay in the command room."

Von Schönkopf merely looked back over his shoulder and said,

"Just going out for a little exercise, sir. I'll be back in no time."

Compared to a planet, Iserlohn's gravitational field was a faint thing indeed, but it certainly did have one of its own, extending from its outer surface to a point about ten kilometers overhead. There was regular gravity on the outer wall, however, due to the gravity control technology that the fortress possessed. At the same time, the outer wall was also a world of hard vacuum and near–absolute zero temperatures—an extremely specialized environment for a battlefield.

It had now become the site of a clash between ground units of both sides. The Imperial Army Corps of Engineers' 849th Battalion and the 97th Regiment of its Armored Grenadier Corps had landed there, with the latter providing security for the former as they got to work rigging a small, laser-triggered hydrogen bomb to the outer wall of Iserlohn Fortress.

The surface area of Iserlohn's outer wall came to 11,300 square kilometers. While there were many enemy-detection systems, gun batteries, cannon emplacements, and hatches that kept an eye on one another, it could not be said that there were no blind angles. The invaders had taken advantage of one of them.

Wave after wave of imperial soldiers landed on the wall, and around the time their numbers passed a thousand, the alliance counterattack began.

Beams of light flared out from laser rifles, and two imperial soldiers collapsed on the wall, writhing in pain. Alliance forces under the direct command of von Schönkopf charged toward the surprised imperial troops. Leaping out of hatches, jumping from the shadows of gun batteries, they fired their laser rifles indiscriminately. Even while panicking, however, the imperial forces managed to return fire. Depending on their respective angles of attack, laser rifles were not necessarily the most effective of weapons, and if an enemy's armored suit had mirror coating, even a direct hit would only be reflected off at some random angle. Because of this, the .18- to .24-caliber recoil-free autorifle made a surprisingly powerful weapon in this situation. The straight-line trajectories of their projectiles trailed rainbow-hued light that drew the eyes of the soldiers. When the distance between the two sides closed even further, primitive hand-to-hand combat broke out, as tomahawks made of highly resilient carbon crystals and long, broad combat knives made of superceramic sucked at the enemy's lifeblood.

Few people could create the illusion that the murderer's craft as practiced on battlefields was one of the fine arts, but Walter von Schönkopf was one of them. Using both hands, he swung an eighty-five-centimeter tomahawk—one intended for one-handed use—up, down, and side-to-side, constructing around himself literal walls of spraying blood. If it were merely a matter of power and speed, any number of enemy soldiers could have surpassed him, but when it came to the balance of these two and the efficiency with which his attacks delivered mortal wounds, no one could match him. Von Schönkopf almost seemed to glide through the chaotic battle, dodging by hairs the mighty swings of enemy tomahawks only to hammer in mercilessly precise counterstrikes on exposed throats or joints.

For the Imperial Army Armored Grenadier Corps' 97th Regiment, it was a battle fraught with misfortune and disaster. Had their opponents been anyone but the "Knights of the Rose" of the Rosen Ritter regiment, they could have probably fought back a little more, but in the end they only underscored their opponents' reputation, that "foes in equal number cannot defeat the Rosen Ritter."

The imperial force took heavy casualties, got caught in a semi-encirclement, and was driven into a corner on the surface of the wall when, from the shadows of the landing craft that had brought them there, there emerged several single-seat walküre fighter craft, which entered a steep descent to attack the alliance forces from overhead.

The beams unleashed by the walküren were ineffective against the outer wall itself but were more than enough to pierce the armored suits of the alliance soldiers. In addition, they rained down antipersonnel missiles. A whirlpool of blinding flashes of light erupted all around, and human bodies torn asunder went flying up into the empty space. After they carried out that one-sided slaughter to their hearts' content, the walküren were attempting a high-speed withdrawal when antispacecraft gun emplacements let loose a soundless roar. Shot through by photon rounds, the walküren started wobbling, lost speed, and at last exploded as they crashed into the outer wall.

Amid all this chaos, von Schönkopf had ordered the firing of a signal flare, and when it unleashed its greenish-white flash of light the Rosen Ritter regiment began to withdraw, disappearing into the fortress through hatches, one after another. An hour and a half had passed already, and they were nearing the limit of how long they could fight while wearing armored suits. This was true for the imperial troops as well, who for a time abandoned their operation, picked up their survivors, and withdrew. The antispacecraft fire, however, continued unabated, ruthlessly inflicting additional casualties all the while.

Von Schönkopf stripped off his armored suit, washed off his sweat in the shower, and returned to the command room.

"Well, we managed to beat them back. I mentioned this earlier, but how about we send engineers and ground troops over there now?"

"No, it turns out we can't do that after all," said Chief of Staff Murai.

"Why not?"

"You've taken a number of their engineers prisoner. What would happen if the opposite happened over there? If they were to use truth serum or torture on our captured troops and someone told them that Admiral Yang wasn't here . . ."

"I see," von Schönkopf said, nodding. "That would be dangerous." Suddenly, the light in his eyes grew harder. His side had taken prisoners, but what about the enemy? Fighting in space, it was sometimes hard to tell the difference between KIA and MIA. Since it was quite common for no body to remain at all, the best you could do in some cases was lump them all together as "Unreturned."

Caselnes tilted his head slightly. "Our side didn't give up any captives, did it, Admiral von Schönkopf?"

"I pray we didn't. But even so . . ."

"What?"

"What should we do going forward? We can't order the troops to kill themselves if it looks like they're going to be captured. Whenever we fight, one or two are bound to get taken alive. It's impossible to prevent that."

"And?"

"It's going to slip out eventually. When it does, our best option will be to use that against them. So how about we try to use that and set a trap for them?"

"No, I'd like to observe the enemy's movements a little longer. If we start with the dirty tricks, the blowback could be a lot scarier than we expect."

There was plenty of reason for Caselnes to be circumspect. Von Schönkopf acknowledged that; when he looked at the image of the enemy fortress on the screen, his own shoulders cringed just slightly.

"Still," said von Schönkopf, "their first attack was big and bold, and their second attack small and crafty. So what form will their third attack take...?"

Nobody gave an answer, but he had not been expecting one. He looked around the room, walked over to his sharpshooting student, and clapped him on the shoulder.

"Julian, get some sleep now, while you can. Soon enough, there won't be any time for sleeping."

In the central command room at Gaiesburg Fortress, Commander in Chief Karl Gustav Kempf and Vice Commander in Chief Neidhart Müller conversed while staring at the image of Iserlohn Fortress on their main screen, six hundred thousand kilometers away.

"So the engineers failed? Well, can't be helped. If everything went the way we liked, this job would be easy."

"And in any case, we're up against Yang Wen-li. Even Duke von Lohengramm respects his skill."

"Yang Wen-li, eh? He's skilled, at least when it comes to running away. The year before last, in the fighting leading up to Amritsar, he ran away from me in the middle of a fight. Just took off, even though he was winning. He's a strange one."

"'A strange one.' That alone means we can't easily guess what kind of tricks he's going to pull."

"But we can't afford to wait around to see. We've got the initiative, so let's press it. Preparations for what we spoke about earlier are complete now, aren't they, Müller?"

"They are. Shall we begin?"

Kempf nodded, and as he stared with a spirited gaze at the image of Iserlohn Fortress, a confident smile spread out across his firm jaw.

III

While tension and unease ate their way into the hearts of the people, events were moving forward. A long lull in the imperial forces' attacks had persisted for eighty hours now, ever since the failure of the engineers' operation. Like lions that had eaten to excess, the enemy was now moving sluggishly.

"They aren't coming out to try anything new. What are they up to?"

Some of those aboard were expressing panic and irritation as well, but since the policy of Iserlohn's leadership was to buy time, any lag between enemy attacks was something to be welcomed.

"With each passing second, Admiral Yang is getting closer to Iserlohn. And the closer he is, the closer we are to victory."

Commodore Patrichev had spoken those words to his soldiers. The rightness of that statement's first half was acknowledged by all, but the second half wasn't necessarily drawing universal support. Some feared that Iserlohn would already be fallen by the time Admiral Yang arrived. Frontline soldiers, however, tended to be geared more toward optimism than pessimism, and even though enemy forces had landed on the outer wall, the fact that they had been repelled played a positive role in improving their morale.

When the next attack came, it came suddenly. There were no obvious warning signs. It was like film skipping a frame: things switched from "stop" to "go" in the blink of an eye. By the time the operators managed to believe what their eyes were telling them, the shaft of light unleashed from Gaiesburg was already piercing the void.

"Energy waves approaching rapidly!"

Before the operator had finished speaking, the outer wall of Iserlohn was ripped asunder by powerful beams of hard X-rays. The fortress shuddered as a series of small explosions went off inside. Those who were in the central command room heard a sound like distant thunder, and their hearts started pounding at a furious pace.

"Turret 79, completely destroyed. No survivors—"

"Block LB29 damaged! Many dead and injured—"

On the verge of screaming, operators shouted out reports in quick succession.

"Abandon the 79th turret! Rescue the wounded in Block LB29 ASAP."

No sooner had the operators' words broken off than Caselnes ordered, "Get Thor's Hammer ready for synchronized firing!" He was grinding his teeth both figuratively and literally. He had thought the imperial forces had given up on settling this with direct exchanges of cannon fire, but that observation had been too naive. If someone were to criticize him, saying that his persistently passive policy had been wrongheaded from the start, all he could do would be to sit there and take it . . .

A few seconds later, the main cannons of Iserlohn Fortress belched flames of vengeance back at Gaiesburg. The fangs of white-hot energy bit into the outer shell of the fortress. Flames of a different color billowed out, but after a few seconds more, a second vengeful beam came racing back toward Iserlohn. Panic, explosions, and a deafening roar filled the air.

"They're crazy," Patrichev gasped as he looked from screen to screen and monitor to monitor. "Do they want us all to go down together . . .?"

Biting his lip, Caselnes said nothing. A portion of his mental circuitry had started to sputter. A bizarre sense of lost equilibrium welled up inside him. Something felt *off*. Something was wrong.

Suddenly, the floor buckled under him. Caselnes and von Schönkopf just managed to stop from tumbling over. The roar of turbulence continued, and two or three monitors went black.

An operator was shouting hysterically, "The wall's been blown open! It was a bomb. Not a beam. Possibly a laser-triggered H-bomb."

"Enemy fleet right behind us!"

"What?!" Caselnes shouted out in bewilderment. "What's going on?"

An instant later, he had his answer. It had been a feint. The exchange of fire between the two main fortress cannons had itself been a diversionary tactic to conceal a fleet mobilization and the activity of military engineers. How had he not realized? From the bottom of his heart, Caselnes cursed his carelessness.

Meanwhile, on the bridge of the battleship *Lübeck*, which had circled around to the rear of Iserlohn, Neidhart Müller was wearing a satisfied smile.

Laser-detonated H-bombs had gouged a gigantic hole into one section of the outer wall. It was about two kilometers in diameter—black depths with a sawtooth fringe—and called to mind the bloody maw of a giant carnivorous beast.

Müller ordered the launch of two thousand walküren. Once they had secured air supremacy within Iserlohn's gravitational field, landing vehicles carrying fifty thousand armored grenadiers were launched to transport the troops to the vicinity of the gigantic hole. From there, the armored grenadiers entered the fortress. Coordinating with attacks from outside, they occupied a number of command and traffic control rooms on the inside. Even without going that far in, they probably could have taken out all communications facilities and transport systems within the fortress.

"If this works, Iserlohn—both the fortress and the corridor—will be ours."

Amid the cacophony of wailing sirens and alarms that seemed to be competing for dominance, Julian was running down the beltway toward a spaceport used exclusively by spartanian single-seat fighter craft. Up until just now, he had been at the Caselneses' home, having been invited to eat lunch with Mrs. Caselnes and her two daughters there. Caselnes, unable to leave the central command room, had quietly asked Julian to check up on his family while he was out. Julian figured that this degree of mixing public and private responsibilities ought to be acceptable.

After all, Caselnes probably could have sent his family back to Heinessen or moved them to the safest place in the fortress any time he felt like it. Leaving his meal behind, Julian had grabbed his uniform beret and run outside through the Caselnes home's entranceway.

"Be careful, Julian!"

The voice of Charlotte Phyllis was still in his ears. *Cute little thing*, he thought. Having her around must be what it was like to have a little sister. One time, Yang, teasing Julian, has said, "Ten years from now, you'll be twenty-six, and Charlotte'll be eighteen. You're rather well matched, wouldn't you say?" Julian, however, could dish it out just as well as he could take it. "Admiral, you're thirty-one years old now, and Lieutenant Greenhill is twenty-four. I'd say you two are matched even better." Yang had only smiled wryly and changed the subject. *When is he going to make things clear?* Julian wondered, trying to imagine himself at age twenty-six...

"Hey, kid, you going out now too?" said a cheerful voice by his ear. At times like these, that voice was utterly devoid of any sense of crisis, although in spite of that, it did convey clearly the toughness and courage of the speaker. Julian stopped running, turned around, and there he was: the young ace, Lieutenant Commander Olivier Poplin. Poplin was also Julian's instructor in spartanian space-combat techniques.

No matter what Yang might say about Julian and the military, he had provided Julian with some first-class instructors in von Schönkopf and Poplin. However, they were also the two biggest ladies' men in Iserlohn. That was the one thing that Julian didn't feel like learning from them.

"Lieutenant Commander, you seem to be taking it easy."

As he spoke, Julian noticed a faint fragrance of heliotrope. He wondered: had Poplin been enjoying the tender embrace of some indeterminate lover since noon? Taking note of Julian's expression and tone, the flying ace gave a short laugh, held up his arm in front of his nose, and breathed in the fragrance of perfume.

"Kid, this is the fragrance of life. Not just your life or mine—I mean of life itself. Any day now, you're bound to figure that out..."

Before Julian was able to share his thoughts on that declaration, the two of them had arrived in the port area. They boarded their spartanians in the hangar and then advanced from the air lock to the runway area. Maintenance crew clad in airtight uniforms were waving their hands. They were hoping for safe returns even moreso than the pilots themselves.

When launching from a mother ship during high-speed flight, one could use the momentum from the vessel, but launching from Iserlohn required a runway. This runway was 50 meters wide and 2,000 meters long, with a gate that was 17.5 meters tall. When a spartanian came out on the runway, it faced points of light stretching out ahead far into the distance. The pilots referred to them as "the whites of the Grim Reaper's eyes."

"Unit 28, into the course!" said the control officer through his headphones. "Launch as soon as you see the signal. Be careful when you get outside."

That was how the space traffic control officer showed affection toward a new recruit.

"Go!"

About a minute later, Julian's fighter flew clear of the "whites of the Grim Reaper's eyes" and out into the void.

"Whiskey, Vodka, Rum, Applejack, Sherry, Cognac: all of your squadrons are assembled, right?"

From his pilot seat, Poplin called out to his subordinates.

"All right, everybody, I want your heads cleared of any pointless distractions like wanting to save the country! That's not your style. I don't want you thinking about *anything* except that pretty young gal you still haven't told you're crazy about, and how much you want to live so you can see her smiling face again. If you can do that, a friendly devil'll be sure to have your back, even if some jealous old god hates your guts. You copy?"

"Roger!" his subordinates answered in unison. Behind his faceplate, the young ace was grinning from ear to ear. "All right, then, follow me!"

Caselnes couldn't make up his mind whether to mobilize the fleet or not. Reports of "ready to mobilize" had come in from admirals Fischer, Nguyen, and Attenborough. It had to be almost unbearable for the crews of space warships to stay cooped up inside the fortress at a time like this, with nothing to do but watch the battle unfold from the sidelines. On the other hand, if the battle became chaotic, it would become impossible for the imperial military to fire their main cannons, at least not without destroying some of their own in the process. Which meant there was the possibility of this coming down to a fleet battle in the end. Intellectually, Caselnes knew that. However, he just couldn't decide on the mobilization's timing.

"Enemy battleships at 0930!"

"Turret 29, open fire!"

Reports and orders cycled back and forth through the comm circuitry until the crews' sense of hearing reach the point of saturation. It was hard to believe that the world outside, just a single wall away, was one where there was no such thing as sound. It was also a strange thing to break out in a sweat that dampened the collars and sleeves in a room that maintained a suitable temperature of 16.5 degrees centigrade.

Rear Admiral von Schönkopf, who was issuing new intercept orders at intervals of *seconds* rather than minutes now, motioned for an on-duty soldier to come near. The soldier, whose nerves looked ready to snap, ran over to him, and the commander of fortress defenses spoke:

"Get me a cup of coffee. Half a spoonful of sugar, and no milk. Make it a little on the weak side."

Von Schönkopf unconsciously opened his mouth and shot the soldier, who was still in his teens, an unflustered smile.

"This might be the last cup of coffee I ever drink. Make it a good one, will you?"

The soldier hurried from the central command room. All the gloss had faded from Caselnes's exhausted face, but he still had energy left for sarcasm:

"If you've got time to waste telling him how you want your coffee, things must still be all right."

"Pretty much. When it comes to women and coffee, I don't like to make compromises—not even if it kills me."

They both smirked at one another, and then a third voice broke in.

"Acting Commander!"

Caselnes turned around at the sound of the voice and found Guest

Admiral Merkatz standing there. The middle-aged defector-slash-guest admiral had a quiet look of determination on his face. Von Schönkopf turned to look at this former lion of the Imperial Navy with unfeigned interest.

"I'd like you to temporarily lend me command of the fleet. I think I know how to make things a little easier for us."

Though Caselnes didn't answer right away, he realized intuitively that this was the moment he'd been waiting for.

"They're in your hands," he said after a pause. "Do it."

IV

Swarthy skin, stiff black hair, medium height with a powerful build, and a mustache along with whiskers on his cheeks—that was a portrait of Commander Asadora Chartian, captain of Yang's flagship, *Hyperion*. How well he could command a fleet of ships was unexplored territory, but at the very least, his leadership and management skills when commanding a single vessel left nothing to be desired, and it was because Yang had been able to confidently entrust Chartian with the operation of the flagship itself that he had been able to focus all his attention on commanding the fleet as a whole during many a difficult battle.

When Admiral Wiliabard Joachim Merkatz and Lieutenant von Schneider headed over to *Hyperion*, this strong and courageous spacer met them with a sharp gleam in his eyes and declared: "I never thought I would ever welcome anyone except Admiral Yang on board this flagship as commander. I do, however, understand my duty, of course. I await your command." His tone, while not exactly rude, showed no restraint either.

That frankness didn't bother Merkatz in the slightest. Chartian had merely expressed what he thought to a high-ranking officer of the fleet.

Merkatz agreed with Acting Commander Caselnes's fundamental policy of assuming a defensive posture and waiting for Yang to come to the rescue. It followed, then, that his duty was to effectively implement that policy at the tactical level. For the time being, that meant having to eliminate the imperial forces trying to land on the fortress. And for that, he was going to need some help.

"I support Admiral Merkatz," Rear Admiral Fischer said.

"I support Admiral Yang. Therefore I support Admiral Merkatz, who supports Admiral Yang," Rear Admiral Attenborough said.

"We have no choice but to support Admiral Merkatz," Rear Admiral Nguyen said.

Merkatz's humble attitude had made a positive impression on all three.

At that time, the imperial forces' walküren corps was maintaining the empire's advantage in the battle, although their dominance of the space above the fortress was a far cry from complete. The alliance forces' spartanian units had proven surprisingly stubborn. In particular, the tactics employed by ace pilot Olivier Poplin's six companies were so sophisticated that the term "diabolical" seemed to fit them. Poplin thought of himself as a natural at space combat—which was absolutely true—but knowing that not just anyone could become a genius like himself, he had drilled group-based tactics into his subordinates, wherein three fighters functioned as a single unit. That meant the sort of tactics where, for example, one fighter might lure an enemy walküre into pursuing it so the remaining two could attack it from behind. Walküren pilots took a lot of pride in their profession, and this kind of tactic made them feel like crying foul. However, the results Poplin's companies got in battle were outstanding, and Poplin himself regularly and daringly downed many enemy fighters in one-on-one engagements himself.

That said, the imperial forces still appeared to have an overwhelming advantage. When Müller briefly returned to Gaiesburg to give a report, Kempf said cheerfully: "Eventually, they'll have to change the name of this place to the 'Gaiesburg Corridor.' Who knows—they might even end up calling it the 'Kempf-Müller Corridor.'"

The angle of Müller's eyebrows tilted ever so slightly at that. The Karl Gustav Kempf he knew was a sensible and respectable warrior—not the sort of man to casually employ that sort of bombast, even in jest. To the eyes of the young vice commander, however, Kempf appeared not so much excited as uncharacteristically flippant and lacking in self-restraint. Marshal Reinhard von Lohengramm would never allow a subordinate to be honored in that way, the late Siegfried Kircheis notwithstanding.

When he returned to his flagship, Müller decided to make some al-
terations to his plan. He had been waiting for the walküren units to gain
complete spatial superiority within the fortress's gravitational field, but
since it looked like that was going to be more trouble than expected, he
decided to seal the gates of the main port and render it impossible for
the alliance's fleet to launch. It should be possible to achieve an effective
tactical outcome, he judged, by making the bold move of crashing six
unmanned destroyers into the port. This wasn't something he had just
thought up on the fly; this was something he had been thinking about
for some time now—a strategy he had hoped to avoid using if at all possible due to the long period of time that the port facilities would be out
of commission following the recapture of Iserlohn.

However, just as Müller finished lining up those six destroyers, Iserlohn's main cannon began belching out tongues of cosmic flame in rapid
succession. The aiming was not precise; those blades of unfathomable
energy grazed a few cruisers and destroyers, annihilating them, but accomplished nothing more. This did, however, force Müller to break up
his tight formation and scatter the fleet for the time being. Afterward he
reassembled his formation in a region of space that the main cannon wasn't
facing, but during that brief interval, Alliance Armed Forces vessels had
come pouring out of the main port's gate.

It had been a very near thing. If the mobilization had come any later,
Müller would have succeeded in sealing the main port of Iserlohn Fortress.
Trapped inside the spaceport, the alliance fleet would have been rendered
powerless. If that had happened, Iserlohn Fortress itself would have lost
more than half its functionality, been reduced to a mere cannon emplace-
ment in space, and suffered a precipitous drop in the value of its existence.

Young Müller stamped on the floor in frustration. Knowing that this
would only set back their ultimate victory by a few days helped him recover
his composure; their overall advantage had hardly been lost. He tried to
intercept the attacking alliance fleet right away. However, the alliance
fleet—the infamous Yang fleet, no less—which could have only come
out in order to fight, changed direction to avoid Müller's sharp thrust and
began moving rapidly along the curvature of Iserlohn's spherical surface.

Müller, anticipating where that curve would take them, didn't make the mistake of pursuing the enemy from behind. Instead, he circled around from the opposite direction, planning to appear in front of the enemy and hit their vanguard formation first. However, a cunning trap had been laid. Müller's fleet had to pass right in front of Iserlon's undamaged battery of antispacecraft turrets in order to do so.

When Müller realized that, he hastily ordered a withdrawal—or rather, he tried to. By the time he was about to give the order, the alliance forces, with stunning speed and orderliness, had already gone on the offense and were effectively cutting off his escape route from behind.

The imperial forces had been caught in a pincer movement between Iserlohn's antispacecraft cannon fire and the Iserlohn Patrol Fleet under Merkatz's command. With beams and with missiles, the patrol fleet, which up to that point had had neither time nor place in the battle, now unleashed all its pent-up vengefulness and aggression, pummeling the imperial forces at will. The imperial forces were caught in a vast net of energy woven of death and destruction. Robbed of their mobility—to say nothing of their means of fighting back—the imperial warships were snared left and right on those blazing strands, unleashing richly colored plumes of flame as they blew apart. Ships that had been smashed and rent asunder burst into fireballs—they glittered like phosphorescent beads, as if to adorn the netting.

The sight could be seen all the way from Gaiesburg. Since firing their main cannon at the alliance forces would vaporize their own force as well, there was nothing Gaiesburg's gunners could do.

"What does Müller think he's doing over there!" Kempf shouted angrily. "This is what happens if you hesitate when there's a decision to be made."

But a decision point was bearing down on him as well: whether or not to mobilize the eight thousand vessels that remained under his own command and send them out to save Müller.

"I can't just stand by and watch while they're slaughtered. Eichendorff! Patricken! Go out and rescue that snot-nosed kid for me."

His two subordinates were surprised at his coarse way of putting it. Still, if they didn't put the order into action right away, their commanding officer's ire would no doubt shift from Müller to themselves. The two admirals headed off to the fortress's main port to take command of their divisions. Along the way, they couldn't help whispering in the elevator. "The commander sure seemed upset..." "Winning here would be an unparalleled achievement, but if he fails, demotion will be the least of his worries—he could even end up getting shuffled off to some do-nothing job." "If it came to that, catching up with Mittermeier and von Reuentahl would be hopeless..."

Exposed to a concentrated assault, the imperial fleet had taken serious damage, but even as it was writhing about in agony, it was through Neidhart Müller's wise command and leadership that it avoided collapsing completely. His flagship raced all across the battlespace, aiding subordinates that were in difficult fights, shoring up ranks that were on the verge of breaking, getting vessels with weak defenses to the back of the formation, tightening perimeter defenses, and waiting for the reinforcements he was certain would soon arrive. When he learned that Eichendorff and Patricken were on the way, he threw the last of his offensive capabilities at a single point and broke through the encirclement.

Merkatz, too, knew when it was time to pull back, and so, avoiding a pointless battle against these new enemies, the fleet returned to the fortress in an orderly fashion. The objective had been sufficiently met.

Julian also returned to port. In this battle, he had shot down three walküren and proven that the kills he had scored his first time in battle had not just been some sort of fluke.

From April 14 to 15, the Imperial Navy's attacks would be successful for about 90 percent of each period of combat, only to end in failure after a sudden change of fortune. For Karl Gustav Kempf, this was maddening, and he started taking out his pent-up indignation on his incompetent—he believed—vice commander.

"You've fought courageously. The problem is, that's all you've done. What have you got to show for it?"

Kempf's remarks cut Müller to the quick. Although he had reflected on his mistakes as well, he was understandably put off when he was told to move back to the rear. It simply was not possible for a man who had been evaluated highly by Reinhard and received the rank of full admiral in his twenties to be entirely free of pride and self-confidence.

Biting back his indignation, he had led the fleet under his command back to the rear of the formation. He was not a man of narrow mind, but in this case, he couldn't help wondering if Kempf might be aiming to keep all the glory for himself.

That was when one of the military doctors came to him bearing a report:

"One of the prisoners has told us something very unusual."

"What is it?"

"He said that Commander Yang Wen-li is actually absent from Iserlohn Fortress . . ."

Bending his upper body slightly backward, Neidhart Müller stared at the doctor. "Really?" he said. It was unclear whether he was asking about the report itself or its content, and that alone was a testament to just how surprised he was.

The doctor calmly replied, "I don't know how credible the claim itself may be, but it's a fact that the prisoner, delirious with fever and on the point of death, let that slip. He's dead now, so there's no way to confirm what he said."

"But is such a thing even possible?" Müller said in a low voice. "Could that bogeyman not even be in the fortress?"

At that, an even younger officer, Lieutenant Commander Drewenz, asked his senior officer, "Is Yang Wen-li really such a frightening opponent?"

After a moment of silence, Müller responded with a question of his own: "Could you capture that fortress without spilling a single drop of your own men's blood? And by using a method not a single person aboard was able to see coming?"

"No," Drewenz said, after thinking about it for a moment. "That would not be possible."

"Well then, Yang Wen-li is someone to be feared. An outstanding enemy commander should be paid due respect, should he not? There's no shame in that."

After he had enlightened the lieutenant commander, Müller again sank into thought. Was it possible that the commander of Iserlohn—a fortress among fortresses—could be away from his post? And at an uncertain time when the imperial military might launch an all-out offensive at any moment? For Müller—and for any soldier with an ounce of responsibility and common sense—that was not an easy thing to believe.

He recalled the visual memory of one of the ships he had seen himself when the alliance fleet had emerged from Iserlohn.

Based on its shape, that battleship had been *Hyperion*—a vessel known these last two years as Yang Wen-li's flagship. Didn't the fact that it came out to fight mean that Yang was present on Iserlohn? Or had that been a trick to camouflage his absence? Was it also possible that this was a complex strategy designed to make them think he was absent and lure them into a reckless assault? In any case, Yang Wen-li *was* a man who had captured Iserlohn without spilling a single drop of his men's blood. It had been such a shock for Müller two years ago, when he had first heard the report. At that time, the infinite diversity of military strategy had really been brought home to him.

Could he truly believe the words of a dying prisoner? Maybe the doctor had been mistaken. Maybe his consciousness *hadn't* been clouded by high fever. Wasn't it just as possible that he had been trying to throw the imperial military into confusion with his dying words?

It was even quite plausible that he had done so on Yang's instruction.

Müller shook his head slightly. *Honestly, though, if he's here, he's here; if he isn't, he isn't. Even so, just look at all the trouble he causes, whether he's here or not. I can see why they call him 'Yang the magician.'*

If Yang Wen-li had been able to hear what Niedhart Müller was thinking about him, he would have almost certainly shrugged his shoulders and said, "Please, don't overestimate me. I'm just a regular guy, big on thrift and low on ambition, dreaming of life as a pensioner. If my own people thought as much of me as my enemies do, I wouldn't have courts of inquiry breathing down my neck."

For Müller's part, no matter how cautiously he behaved, it never felt like he was being careful enough. Müller was anxious for his own sake, to say nothing of whatever clever scheme Yang might be hatching. *Am I on the verge of running amok based on unreliable intel?* he wondered. More than anything, he wished that soldier hadn't died. When it came to captives taken in space, there were usually two kinds: those who were taken when a whole ship surrendered and those who were injured during hand-to-hand combat inside a fortress. In this battle, however, the captives they had taken were extremely few. Moreover, nearly all of them were seriously injured and at present unconscious, so there was no way to confirm what the dead man had said.

They had only been able to interrogate one of them, and his words had only left Müller more confused:

"Admiral Yang ordered Rear Admiral von Schönkopf to say that he isn't there..."

Even so, Niedhart Müller at last made up his mind and gave orders:

"Cast a recon and security net over the whole corridor. We will await Yang Wen-li's return and take him prisoner. If we can do that, not only Iserlohn, but the Alliance Armed Forces as a whole will crumble, and ultimate victory will be back within our reach."

On his orders, three thousand vessels positioned themselves within the corridor. Straining their enemy-detection capabilities to their utmost limits, they filled the whole region with trap upon trap. As they were out to catch Yang Wen-li, a lot of thought went into their positioning.

However, there was one individual whom this decision angered. Commander in Chief Kempf demanded to know why a repositioning of forces was under way without his having given any such order.

Müller had no choice but to try to convince him.

"Last year, Siegfried Kircheis traveled to Iserlohn for a prisoner exchange, and he told me something about Yang Wen-li when he returned—'When I saw the man in person, he looked nothing like a fearless, ferocious warrior. And that right there is probably where his true fearsomeness lies.'"

"And?"

Kempf both looked and sounded displeased, but this was no time for Müller to be giving ground.

"One of the prisoners from Iserlohn said with his dying breath that Yang is not inside the fortress. I don't know why that should be, but it stands to reason that he would have headed straight back toward Iserlohn the minute he learned it had been attacked. If we can intercept him on the way and succeed in catching him, it will be a fatal blow for the Alliance Armed Forces."

After hearing him out, Kempf spat back, "We don't know what kind of unusual tactics Yang is going to use—weren't you the one who said that? The Free Planets Alliance has no strategic base more vital than Iserlohn. Why would its commander be away from his post? His plan, clearly, is to make us think he's not there so we'll spread out our forces. Return your ships to their original positions at once. It is vitally important that we have them here in reserve."

As there was nothing more he could do, Müller backed down, although that didn't mean he was convinced. His wish was to capture that grandest of prizes himself, even if that meant ignoring his CO's orders; still, he felt an uncertainty that was only natural and consulted with his advisor, Commodore Orlau. Orlau's reply went something like this:

"Your Excellency is the vice commander, not the commander in chief. Instead of insisting on your own way, you should follow the policy of the commander in chief."

Müller's silence was worth ten thousand words of eloquent speech in expressing just how difficult it was for him to abandon his plan to capture Yang Wen-li. Even so, he at last let out a little sigh and heeded his advisor's cautioning.

"You're right. A vice commander should follow the wishes of the commander in chief. Understood—I'll toss my ego to the winds. I'll rescind my previous orders."

Just like Yang, Müller was neither omniscient nor all-powerful, and capable though he may have been, there were limits to his insight and predictive abilities.

In this way, all of the traps that for a time had been set to capture Yang Wen-li were removed from his path.

Ultimately, Müller had made the right guess but the wrong decision. In times to come, the empire's historians would criticize him for that, saying that if von Reuentahl or Mittermeier had been in his position, they would have seen their original intentions through to the end and succeeded in capturing Yang. In response, Mittermeier had this to say: "That's nothing but speculation after the fact. If I had been in Müller's shoes, I couldn't have done anything more than he did."

In any case, the combat ground on afterward, with neither side gaining a decisive edge, and in this state of near-deadlock, time passed in the corridor until April was nearly over. It was almost time for Yang Wen-li to be "getting back home."

VI

As Yang Wen-li's subordinates were just beginning to wage their desperate struggle on Iserlohn, Rupert Kesselring, assistant to the landesherr in the Phezzan Dominion, was handling an enraged visitor with the bearing of a seasoned matador.

"Please, Commissioner. There's no need to get so upset."

The young man's hint of a smile, in this instance, was like a red flag being waved at the older man, Commissioner Henlow, and it was driving up his blood pressure.

"That's easy for you to say, Kesselring, but as for me, I can't just stand here and calmly accept this. Following your recommendation, we summoned Yang back from Iserlohn and subjected him to an official inquiry. But then what happened? A massive imperial fleet crossed the border, taking advantage of his absence. Isn't that just amazing, splendid timing? I would really love to hear a detailed explanation regarding this intel!"

"Your tea is getting cold."

"Did I say anything about tea? We followed your advice, and . . ."

"It was wrong of me to advise you."

"It was what?"

"I said that it was wrong of me to advise you."

With an elegant flourish that bordered on ostentation, Kesselring raised a cup of cream tea to his lips. "From the very outset, I had no business telling you that Admiral Yang should be questioned. After all, that counts as interfering in your internal affairs. It was your side, rather, that had good reason to refuse. And yet you failed to exercise that right. All of you voluntarily went along with my impertinent meddling. Yet even so, Your Excellency is insisting that all of the blame lies with this humble son of Phezzan?"

The young Phezzanese watched composedly as the face of the FPA's commissioner changed color by the second.

"But still...judging by the way you acted when we spoke that time before, it's hard to blame us for thinking that if we did refuse, the FPA would fall out of favor with Phezzan."

It was a desperate counterattack, but the landesherr's aide appeared singularly unmoved.

"In any case," he said, "that's all water under the bridge now, so there's really no point in discussing it. The issue at hand is what comes next. Tell me, Commissioner, what do you intend to do going forward?"

"What do you mean, 'going forward'?"

"Oh my, you haven't even thought about it, have you? That puts me on the spot. We here on Phezzan are very concerned about the future—we're thinking long and hard about whose friendship it would be in our best interests to procure: that of the present Trünicht administration, or that of a possible future Yang administration..."

Those words struck the commissioner like the shocking blow of a lash across the cheek. His expression was like that of a badger that had just crawled out of its hole, only to find itself face-to-face with the muzzle of a hunter's rifle.

"A future *Yang* administration? Ridiculous! Er—excuse me, but there's no way such a thing would ever happen. Absolutely not."

"Oh really? You sound quite sure of yourself. In that case, let me ask you a question: three years ago, did you predict that in the very near future a young man named Reinhard von Lohengramm would become ruler of the Galactic Empire?"

The commissioner said nothing.

"That's what the riches of historical possibility look like. That's how the capriciousness of fate plays out. Commissioner, here's something you'd do well to think on at length yourself: to what degree is your personal happiness tied to your unflagging loyalty to the Trünicht administration *alone*? A clever man like you surely knows how important it is to get in on the ground floor when making investments. The present, of course, is of great importance to human beings, but not because it results from the past—it's more because it's the wellspring of the future."

Kesselring took in hand the cup of cream tea he had set down earlier. On the other side of the thinning haze of steam rising up from it, he could see Commissioner Henlow, a man who tossed and turned amid many calculations, with the look on his face of one who had just lost the ability to act for himself.

CHAPTER 8:

THE CRUISER *LEDA II* raced her way back toward Iserlohn Fortress through a vast labyrinth of darkness and stars. The fair lady known as *Leda II* had been accompanied by a bare-bones escort fleet only part of the way on her initial trip to Heinessen; now on her return voyage, she was attended on all sides by deep ranks of lesser and greater knights, numbering 5,500 in total.

"I wonder if the government would've rather sent me back empty-handed?" Yang said to Frederica. This was not speculation; it was bad-mouthing. After all, no matter how great an animus the Trünicht administration might have toward Yang, they still had to provide him with sufficient force strength to repel the enemy. There was no way they would have sent him back empty-handed.

Of course, it was one thing to put together a decent number of ships and another thing altogether to build an effective fighting force. The force Yang had been given was a textbook case of a unit thrown together on the fly. There were 2,200 ships under the command of Rear Admiral Alarcon, 2,040 ships under Rear Admiral Morton, 650 under Commodore Marinetti, and 610 under Commodore Sahnial. All of these were independent units unaffiliated with the main armada, and up until now they had been performing regional patrol and security duties. To an extent, at least, they had weapons and armor.

Admiral Bucock, commander in chief of the space armada, had tried to get the First Fleet mobilized for Yang. The First was at present the only formally organized fleet the FPA armada had that was a match for Yang's Iserlohn Patrol Fleet in terms of firepower, defenses, composition, training, and battlespace experience. It consisted of 14,400 vessels, and its commander was Yang's one time boss, Vice Admiral Paetta. However, Bucock had run into opposition when he had tried to mobilize the First Fleet, not only from the political leadership, but from within the military as well. "What about defending the capital?" they had said. "If the First Fleet leaves for the border, won't that leave the capital undefended?"

"I say this to my shame," Admiral Bucock had replied, "but there were several fleets stationed on Heinessen during last year's coup d'état. And yet the coup still happened, didn't it? Besides, what forces can we realistically give Admiral Yang to lead if we *don't* activate the First Fleet?"

Admiral Cubresly, director of Joint Operational Headquarters, had suffered a setback in his recovery from the wound he had taken earlier, and with him back in the hospital for additional treatment, there was no one to take the old admiral's side. The Defense Committee ordered the First Fleet to devote itself entirely to the defense of the capital, and Joint Operational Headquarters eventually scraped together a force of 5,500 vessels.

"Even Cubresly's gone timid as a lamb in situations like this," Bucock had said. "He's under a lot of pressure, and if he's hospitalized too long, he'll be forced to resign. So finally, I'm just one isolated old man."

"I'm with you, sir." Yang spoke those words from the bottom of his heart.

"I appreciate the thought," smiled the old admiral, "but Iserlohn and Heinessen are much too far apart to be saying that." Truth be told, Yang himself had his doubts about how much assistance he could supply for the old admiral.

Of the four commanding officers, Yang knew little about the two commodores. *I'll be happy if their command skills and basic military knowledge are up to standard*, he just kept thinking.

Rear Admiral Morton he felt he could count on. Lionel Morton had served as vice commander for the former Ninth Fleet. When his CO had been seriously injured during the Battle of Amritsar, he had taken over and commanded the Ninth during the long retreat, managing to prevent it from completely falling apart. He had a solid reputation as a patient, coolheaded commander and a service record that would have surprised no one had it belonged to a vice admiral. In his midforties, he had seen a lot more combat than Yang. He had not come out of Officers' Academy, though, and an excess of self-consciousness about that might have made life hard for him in the organizational hierarchy.

The real problem, however, was Rear Admiral Sandle Alarcon. In terms of skill, there was little cause to doubt him, but his personality demanded caution. Yang had heard a number of unsavory rumors about him: that he was an obsessive military supremacist; that the only reason he hadn't joined the coup last year was the personal feud he'd had going with Captain Evens; that his ideas were even more radical than those of the Military Congress. The thing most abhorrent to Yang, though, was the fact that suspicion had been cast on Alarcon more than once for the killing of civilians and captured soldiers, and on each of the several occasions he had faced a perfunctory court-martial he had been found not guilty, either because of insufficient evidence or because his involvement had been intuited logically, without hard facts. Yang suspected that some mutual back-scratching of a truly disgusting nature had been going on. For now, however, an admiral was an admiral, and a military asset a military asset. All that was demanded of Yang at this juncture was the skill to use Alarcon effectively.

Yang was not going up against Reinhard von Lohengramm himself this time. These days, Duke von Lohengramm was having to devote all his attention to governing. Or to think of it another way, there was not sufficient necessity to bring him to the battlefield in person. That being the case, the level of willpower driving this invasion was probably about on the level of "Hey, won't it be great if we can win?" This battle was not of vital importance to him.

The year before last, von Lohengramm, then still but a count, had invaded the Astarte Stellar Region. He had perfected a tactic for striking separate units of a divided force individually, but that was not the only thing that had made that invasion possible. There was also the fact that Iserlohn had been in imperial hands at the time. It had functioned both as a supply base and as a source of rear guard support, and because he knew it was there behind him, Reinhard had been able to fearlessly plough through the enemy envelopment.

Also the same year, Reinhard had won a great victory at Amritsar. He had allowed the front lines to spread until they reached a breaking point and at the same time destroyed the alliance's resupply capability.

Reinhard's tactics were so spectacular, so dazzling, that to observers he seemed to be wielding some kind of magic. But that was by no means the case. He was a great tactician—a great strategist, even—who would make all the arrangements necessary to ensure victory before he ever arrived on the battlefield.

No matter how brilliant and completely out of the blue Reinhard's past victories might have appeared, he consistently acted with logical coherence and made sure to have strategic guarantees in place.

Reinhard was a man who liked to win on the cheap, and it was on that point that Yang acknowledged his greatness. Winning on the cheap meant preparing the conditions for victory, minimizing the losses to one's forces, and winning the battle easily. The only ones who didn't give Reinhard his due were foolish military and civilian leaders who thought of human lives as an inexhaustible resource.

It was because Reinhard was so capable that so many brilliant admirals had gathered around him . . . although the only one whom Yang had met in person had been Siegfried Kircheis. The day Yang had received word of his death, it had *hurt*—it had felt like he'd lost an old friend of many years. Yang also believed that if Kircheis had lived, he might have become a vital bridge between the alliance and the empire's new regime.

As if responding to his unuttered thoughts, Frederica approached Yang with a question about Reinhard. "Do you think Duke von Lohengramm is going to kill the emperor?"

"No, I don't think he'll kill him."

"But it's obvious he's planning to usurp the throne—surely the emperor would be an obstacle to that."

"All throughout history, there's been no end of usurpers. After all, the founder of a dynasty is by definition a usurper, provided he's not an invader. But as for whether or not usurpers always kill the previous kings after they come to power, the answer to that's a resounding 'no.' There have been plenty of kings who were treated quite well after they were deposed—made aristocrats, even. Furthermore, in cases where that happens, there are exactly zero examples of the deposed dynasty overthrowing the new one and reestablishing itself."

The founder of one ancient dynasty had usurped his throne by having the child emperor of the previous dynasty abdicate, and had treated his predecessor generously, bestowing all kinds of privileges on him and even ordering his successor in his will to sign a contract agreeing to not mistreat those of the old dynasty's bloodline. That contract had been observed throughout the next generation of the new dynasty. Its founder had been a wise man. He'd had the insight to realize that he could win people over by being gracious to the losing side, and that the previous dynasty—having already declined as a system of authority—would, if it were treated as aristocracy, lose its hostility toward the new order and over time grow even less willful.

When Yang looked at the way that Duke von Lohengramm had dealt with the forces of the old noble families—both politically and militarily—he saw ferocity and he saw ruthlessness, but what did not see was heartless brutality. And Reinhard was certainly no fool. Anyone could see that if he murdered a seven-year-old child he would bring down moral and political condemnation on himself. He was not about to go out of his way to make a decision harmful to his own interests.

Of course, the emperor may be seven years old now, but in a decade he would be seventeen, and in two he would be twenty-seven. The future might one day bring about different considerations, but at least for now, Duke von Lohengramm would keep the boy emperor alive. Most likely, he was thinking of how to use him to the greatest effect. Ironically, it was the young imperial prime minister who had to be most concerned for the emperor's safety. If the boy were to die now—even of genuinely natural causes or in some accident—it would nonetheless be viewed as an assassination by many, if not most. Even with the emperor alive, he would pose no great obstacle to the many reforms Reinhard was enacting. Reinhard didn't need the support of those who supported the young emperor.

Five hundred years ago, Rudolf von Goldenbaum had made history's currents run backward. He had dusted off the old garments of autocracy and class society—which humanity had supposedly stripped off and thrown away long ago—and taken the stage before the citizenry. Autocracy and class had been part of a process that civilizations inevitably had to go through on the road from birth to maturity, but the role they had played throughout history had been yielded to modern-day civil society; the old ways should have long since exited the stage. Worse still, the implementation of such a government had created a system by which the many were sacrificed for the sake of a very small number of rulers.

Perhaps Duke von Lohengramm's reforms were nothing more than an expedient for attaining his personal ambitions or were motivated purely by anti-Goldenbaum sentiment. Even so, the path he was walking clearly matched that of history's progress—toward freedom and equality. That being the case, there was no reason whatsoever why the Free Planets Alliance should oppose him. Rather, shouldn't they join hands with him to rid the universe of the dregs of that ancient despotism and build a new historic order? There was no need for the whole human race to be part of a single state, either; what was wrong with multiple nations existing side by side?

The problem was what political process should be used to accomplish that. Should the progress of history and the recovery of its natural currents be left in the hands of an outstanding individual like Reinhard von Lohengramm? Or should the responsibility instead be divided like it was in the FPA—among many people of ordinary morals and abilities, who advanced together slowly through cycles of conflict, anguish, compromise, and trial and error? The question was which way to choose.

Modern civil society, having overthrown autocracy, had chosen the latter. That had been the right choice, Yang was convinced. The rise of an individual like Reinhard von Lohengramm, furnished with ambition, ideals, and ability, was a miracle—or rather, a fluke—of history. He was at present concentrating in one person all the political authority of the Galactic Empire. Commander in chief of the imperial military and imperial prime minister at the same time! And that was fine. He had talent enough to fulfill the responsibilities of both. But what of his successor?

Society gained more by *not* placing excessive power in the hands of mediocre politicians than it lost by limiting the power of great heroes and statesmen who might or might not appear once every few centuries. That was a fundamental principle of democracy. After all, what a nightmare it would be if a man like Job Trünicht became a "sacred and inviolable" emperor!

II

Alarms rang out, and an operator reported:

"Enemy ships detected at eleven o'clock! Enhanced image on-screen." Her voice was so lovely it almost sounded like she was showing off.

It was a small patrol formation made up of one destroyer and a half dozen small escort craft. Surprised by the appearance of an alliance force of several thousand vessels, they were in the process of trying to flee.

"We've been spotted," said Captain Zeno. "No chance for a surprise attack now."

Yang looked over at the captain in disbelief. "Huh? I wasn't planning a sneak attack. Truth be told, I'm relieved that they've gone and done us the favor."

That pronouncement naturally threw the staff officers for a loop, so Yang was forced to explain himself in detail.

"In short, what this means is that the imperial commander's been driven to the point of searching for enemy reinforcements—er, that would be us. I can only imagine how uncertain he's gonna be now. Should he keep attacking Iserlohn with his back side turned toward us, or fight against us and show his back side to Iserlohn? Or should he distribute his forces so they face both directions and fight a two-front battle instead? Should he gamble on hitting us separately, even though that'd be a two-act fight with an intermission between? Or decide that there's no path to victory and withdraw? In any case, he's got his back against the wall, and that alone gives us the advantage."

Yang shrugged slightly.

"As for me, I really hope he settles on option five. If he does that, nobody gets killed and nobody gets injured. And above all, the easy way's always the best way."

The staff officers of this patchwork fleet laughed pleasantly—most likely because they thought Yang was joking. They didn't know him like the core leadership at Iserlohn did. Frederica was the only one there who knew he was speaking in earnest, and she wasn't laughing.

After listening to the emergency report from the patrol that had sighted Yang's forces, Karl Gustav Kempf stared at the screen and considered his options. Deep creases were etched into the fleshy space between his brows.

Just as Yang had supposed, Kempf was now under pressure to make a decision. A few days prior, he had sent a report back to Odin on the progress of the battle—and had had no small difficulty with the wording. He hadn't lost, and he had delivered a psychological blow to the alliance's forces, as well as inflicted considerable physical damage; Iserlohn, however, while damaged, was still very much operational, and he still hadn't managed to get a single soldier inside. Things were not merely at a deadlock; truth be told, the vast fortress called Gaiesburg was a little *too* big for Kempf to handle. Tech Admiral von Schaft had spoken of his own achievement in the most self-congratulatory ways imaginable, but in fact, the difficulties faced by the one who proposed a mission were nothing compared to those faced by the ones who executed it. Even so, there were three different scenarios that might happen if Kempf reported he was having trouble, and any one of them would leave a wound on his pride: he might be dismissed, he might be given orders to withdraw, or a colleague might be sent to reinforce him. In the end, Kempf worded his report as follows:

"We have the advantage."

At about the same time, a massive fleet of over twenty thousand ships was making its way from imperial territory toward the Iserlohn Corridor. This fleet was divided into two divisions—fore and aft—with the forward division under the command of Senior Admiral Wolfgang Mittermeier and the rear division commanded by Senior Admiral Oskar von Reuentahl— they who were praised as the "twin pillars" of the Imperial Navy. Having received sudden orders from Reinhard, they had mobilized rapidly and were on their way to reinforce Kempf's forces.

Mittermeier had looked slightly bewildered while receiving those orders. Von Reuentahl had put the sentiment into words: "I'm honored to receive your orders, milord. Still, if we attack the enemy at this juncture, don't you think Admiral Kempf might mistakenly believe that we're stealing the credit for his successes?"

Von Reuentahl had spoken out of careful concern for the psychology of the frontline commander, but the response this elicited from Reinhard was a low, dry—one might even say lifeless—laugh.

"There's no need for such worries on your part, Admiral. Although that might not be the case were Kempf actually having any successes."

"As you say, milord."

"Don't expand the front any more than necessary. I leave the rest to your own good judgment."

The two admirals withdrew from Reinhard's presence, and once they were walking together in the hall outside, von Reuentahl posed a question:

"What do you think Duke von Lohengramm's really up to? If the fighting has turned into a quagmire, then there's certainly reason enough to send us. But if Kempf is winning out there, there's no need for us to go. And if he's been defeated, this is a waste of time because it's already too late to do anything for him."

"No matter what the case may be, we still have our orders from the imperial prime minister," said Mittermeier, crisply reminding him of their own circumstances. "We'll just have to do as best as we're able. If the situation when we reach the battlefield does demand that we fight, we can decide how to go about it then."

"You're right," von Reuentahl said.

If they arrived and Kempf had won or was winning, there would be nothing to worry about. If things were in a deadlock, they would have to consult with Kempf and his people on-site and decide what to do together. The one thing that Mittermeier and von Reuentahl did need to talk about now was what they should do if they got there and found a defeated Admiral Kempf being harried by pursuers. That matter was settled in two or three exchanges. One could search the empire and alliance both and never find another pair of equally ranked commanders who were as finely tuned to one another's thought processes as they.

After he gave Mittermeier and von Reuentahl their orders, Reinhard was glancing again at the report from Admiral Kempf when Senior Admiral Paul von Oberstein came by and paid him a visit.

"I noticed that you seemed somehow displeased with the update from Admiral Kempf," he said.

"I'd thought Kempf would do a little better than this, but it looks like distressing the enemy is the best he can do. The objective is to render Iserlohn powerless. He doesn't necessarily need to capture and occupy it. In an extreme scenario, it would even be acceptable to crash one fortress into the other and destroy them both."

Light flashed from von Oberstein's artificial eyes. "Still, it was my understanding that Kempf has used Gaiesburg Fortress as a stronghold from which to boldly attack the enemy head-on."

"And that's why I say he's reached his limits."

Reinhard slammed the report down violently on his desk.

His synthetic-eyed chief of staff brushed back his gray-streaked hair with one hand. "On that point, the one who chose Kempf for this mission can't escape the blame either. I myself made the wrong choice in recommending him. You have my apologies."

"Oh? For you that's rather commendable, isn't it?" Reinhard said coldly. "However, I was the one ultimately responsible for choosing him. Although if we want to trace this all the way back to the beginning, everything started with von Schaft and his useless proposal. It would be one thing if we had merely failed to benefit, but now that this has turned out to be damaging, I don't know what to do with the man."

"Still, even a man such as he might prove useful in some way. It's a hard thing to seize the stars through strength of arms alone. I think it's best to gather as many pawns as one can. Even pawns fished from the gutter."

The ice-blue eyes that were fixed on the chief of staff gleamed with a particularly cold light at that moment. "Make no mistake, von Oberstein. I don't want to steal the stars like some cowardly pickpocket—my wish is to plunder them as a conqueror."

"As you wish."

After von Oberstein saluted and left, Reinhard tossed back his luxurious mane of golden hair. His pale fingers were fondling the pendant at his chest.

"Is this what happens when you gain power?" he said. "There isn't a soul left around here who even tries to understand me. Or is that my own fault after all?"

Ice-blue eyes were occluded by clouds of melancholy. This wasn't what he had been searching for. What he had been wanting was something altogether different.

III

"We don't have all that much time," Yang explained to Frederica. Having learned that the Iserlohn Corridor was not yet entirely under his control, Reinhard von Lohengramm was sure to send reinforcements. When they arrived, their numbers would surely be vast; sending a small force would be tantamount to the folly of a piecemeal committal of forces. Yang estimated their odds of victory would plummet to near zero unless the space surrounding Iserlohn could be recovered before the empire's reinforcements arrived.

"So basically, time has been on our side up until now," said Frederica, "but from here on out that won't be the case? If Your Excellency had been the enemy commander, you would have long since beaten Iserlohn, wouldn't you?"

"Pretty much. If it were me, I would've smashed that other fortress into it. One big boom, and down they both go together. Then, with everything cleared out of the way, we could just bring in a different fortress, and that would be that. If the Imperial Navy had come after us with that in mind, there would've been no way to resist, but it looks like the imperial commander hasn't been able to adjust his way of thinking."

"That's quite an extreme method, though."

"Effective, though, isn't it?"

"That I'll grant you."

"And of course, if Iserlohn had already been destroyed by that tactic, there'd be nothing this fleet could do to stop the invasion. That said, though, there is something we can do if they try that now."

As he said these words, the look on Yang's face changed, reminding Frederica of a young boy who had just discovered a new set of moves to use in chess. Yang hadn't changed a bit since ten years ago, when he had commanded the evacuation of the El Facil stellar region. Despite a decade's passage and the promotions received during that time, Yang still hadn't picked up the smell of a military man. During that period, it was the eyes of those watching Yang that had changed. During the escape from El Facil, Frederica—then a fourteen-year-old girl—remembered what the adults had been saying to one another, some in hushed tones, and others in anger: "Are they serious, putting that useless greenhorn in charge of our getaway?"

Nowadays, Yang was the recipient of overwhelming praise—as well as malice that arrived along the same vector. Either way, though, others took a very different view of Yang than he did of himself.

"I think we can safely say that Iserlohn will not be overrun from the outside," Frederica said.

"Well, I wonder about that," Yang said with a slightly bitter look.

Never mind its defensive capabilities as a space fortress; one reason Iserlohn had long been thought impregnable was that the attacking side had always had its hands tied to some degree. The goal in attacking Iserlohn was to gain control of the Iserlohn Corridor and secure dominance over the route between the empire and the Free Planets Alliance. No other goal existed. It was that desire that had led the empire to build Iserlohn

Fortress and that hope that had led the Alliance Armed Forces to attack it on several occasions—always at the cost of countless dead and wounded. That was how high the price tag on Iserlohn was.

In short, the goal in attacking Iserlohn Fortress had never been to destroy it, but to occupy it. And the only one in history who had succeeded in doing that was Yang Wen-li.

Still, that was in the past. If it were possible to establish a combat and resupply base in the corridor *other than Iserlohn*, the empire could then attack Iserlohn with the intent of destroying it. Such an attack would be vastly more intense and ruthless than an attack intended to occupy it.

Yang shuddered to think of such an assault, but the facts didn't seem to be pointing in that direction. The imperial commander appeared to be using the new fortress exclusively as a base of operations from which to retake Iserlohn. That was the most luck that the weakened forces of the Free Planets Alliance could hope for.

Last year's civil war—and above all, the crushing defeat of the year before at Amritsar—had left the combat potential of the alliance military in a weakened state to this day. The alliance military had lost two million soldiers in that fruitless battle. Many capable members of the admiralty had also left this mortal coil.

When he thought about it, Yang had been dealing with fallout from that defeat ever since. The burden on him would have been so much lighter if even one of those brave admirals who had fallen at Amritsar were alive today—Urannf or Borodin, perhaps.

There was no time now, however, to sink into pointless speculation. The dead were never coming back. The problems of this world had to be solved by the living—even though what came next was going to be exhausting, a lot of trouble, and something Yang really didn't want to do.

Meanwhile, the bewildered imperial forces had decided on the direction they should take.

Kempf's plan was as follows:

First, he would execute a rapid pullback from Iserlohn Fortress. When the alliance forces saw that, they would think he was retreating because reinforcements had arrived and come pouring out of the fortress, not wanting to miss an opportunity to catch him in a pincer movement. That was when he would reverse course and hit them. Then the alliance forces, thinking that the "arrival of reinforcements" had been a trap to lure them out of the fortress, would run back to Iserlohn and shut themselves up inside again. In this way, Kempf could confine them to their fortress, reverse course again, and destroy the forces that were on their way here to reinforce Iserlohn. Making good use of the time lag between the two battles, he would destroy both forces separately.

Splendid! Müller had thought when the idea was proposed—and yet he hadn't been able to help feeling uneasy as well. If this operation was successful, Kempf would be lauded as an artist of military strategy, but would the enemy dance to the tune he was playing? This was a plan that called for flawless technique, as well as perfect timing—one misstep, and the imperial forces would be caught in a pincer movement themselves. In and of itself, the tactic of attacking the two forces individually did seem the proper way to go about this, but Müller found himself wondering if it might be better to have Gaiesburg stay behind to keep an eye on Iserlohn, while sending the whole fleet out to destroy the enemy reinforcements first.

Müller offered that suggestion to Kempf. Due to a number of awkward circumstances, it took a bit of courage for him to do that, but Kempf, in a show of broad-minded generosity, made a number of changes to the operation, incorporating some of Müller's ideas.

* * *

"So does this mean reinforcements are coming? Or is it a trap?"

In the central command room of Iserlohn Fortress, the top leadership, centered on Rear Admiral Alex Caselnes, was having trouble deciding what they should do. The Imperial Navy fleet, which until now had blanketed the space around Iserlohn with steady waves of attackers, was pulling away from them like a tide going out from the shore. Gaiesburg Fortress continued to maintain its distance of six hundred thousand kilometers, though. From that range, it could respond to cannon fire at a moment's notice.

"What do you think, kid?"

Von Schönkopf's question to Julian, who had just arrived bringing coffee, was probably meant as a joke.

"It might be both."

That was Julian's answer.

"Both?"

"Yes, sir. Admiral Yang's reinforcements are sure to be somewhere nearby. The imperial forces may know that and may be trying to use that against us a trap. When our fleet departs Iserlohn and runs into an all-out attack, we'll think, 'Oh, it's a trap—get back inside,' right? By making a feint like that, they can make sure our fleet stays here and then go intercept our reinforcements with their full force."

The top leaders of Iserlohn went completely silent for a long moment as they stared at the flaxen-haired youth. Finally, Caselnes cleared his throat and asked him, "What makes you think so, Julian?"

"The imperial fleet's movements are just too unnatural."

"That's certainly true, but is that your only basis for thinking so?"

"Well, it's like this: If this is *only* a trap, what's the objective? To force a surrender? To use our own mobilization as a chance to get into the fortress? It would have to be one of those two, wouldn't it? But even the enemy has to be well aware at this point that our side is focused on defense and won't sortie far away from base. That being the case, they're probably trying to seal us in by *using* our defensive mind-set. That's why it's far more likely that they're counting on us to play safe and stay inside."

"I see," von Schönkopf said after a moment. "It just hit me—this young man was Admiral Yang's finest student before he ever became mine and Poplin's."

Von Schönkopf's words came mingled with a sigh. He turned his eyes toward Caselnes, and the acting commander asked Admiral Merkatz for his thoughts about a countermeasure.

"If that's what's going on, then the answer isn't difficult. We should pretend to be hunkering down like they expect. Then, when they reverse course, we come charging back out and hit them on their back side. After that, if we and our reinforcements are thinking on the same wavelength, we'll be able to catch them in an ideal pincer movement."

Merkatz spoke flatly, and when he had accepted Caselnes's request to take command of the attack, he turned to Julian and said, "I think I'll have you join me aboard *Hyperion*. On the bridge."

The surprise that captivated the veteran strategist was not as great as it had been two years ago, when he had first recognized the brilliance of Reinhard von Lohengramm, yet it was nonetheless a surprise made of similar stuff.

I V

"War can be compared to mountain climbing..."

It was "Griping Yusuf"—Marshal Yusuf Topparole, architect of the Alliance Armed Forces' sweeping victory in the Battle of the Dagon Stellar Region—who had once said those words.

"It's the government that decides which mountain you climb. 'Strategy' means deciding which route you'll take to the top and preparing accordingly. 'Tactics,' then, is the job of efficiently climbing the route you've been given."

In Yang's case, the route he should climb had already been decided for him. That acute longing he sometimes felt to determine his own route by himself was clearly at odds with his distaste for war, but even so...

"Enemy fleet ahead at 1130!"

At the operator's report, tension shot through minds and bodies of crew throughout the fleet. With friendly vessels on the order of five thousand, it was certain that the imperial force was more than double their size. There was no way they could fight them head-on and win. All they could do was wait for their friends from Iserlohn to appear at the enemy's back side.

Yang was just praying that his staff back on Iserlohn would make the right decision. If they stayed inside the fortress twiddling their thumbs,

Yang would lose with his inferior numbers—easy prey for the empire's divide-and-conquer tactics. It was a prerequisite of Yang's operational plan that they be able to carry out a tacitly understood play in coordination with Iserlohn.

Merkatz, a warrior forged through countless battles, was there. Surely he would prove worthy of the faith Yang placed in him. And then there was Julian—Yang remembered once more that handsome-faced youth who was his ward. There was one thing he had stressed whenever he talked strategy and tactics with the boy: when the enemy retreats and the timing seems off, watch out. He had taught him a number of variations on what could happen at such times. Now, would the boy just be kind enough to remember? If he did—no, wait. Wasn't he against Julian joining the military? Wasn't this too much to expect of him…?

"Enemy in firing range!"

"All right, just follow the plan." Yang took a drink of tea from a paper cup. "Pull back! Maintain a relative speed of zero with the enemy!"

Relayed by Morton and Alarcon, his orders were transmitted to every ship in the fleet.

Meanwhile, in the imperial fleet, suspicious eyes were being turned toward viewscreens and all manner of enemy-detection systems.

"The enemy's pulling back. Starting five minutes ago, our relative distance completely ceased from closing."

The operator in the imperial fleet was working hard to maintain a businesslike tone but was unable to conceal a faint tremor of suspicion.

Kempf's huge frame continued to occupy his command seat as he considered the situation. Then, prompted by a certain anxiety, he asked, "There isn't any chance, is there, that the enemy is deployed in long, deep columns and is trying to draw us into the middle?"

Human and electronic brains alike went into overdrive trying to answer the commander's question, until at last an opinion was output: the possibility was extremely low. Their best guess was that enemy fleet arrayed in front of them was all the force strength that they had.

"In that case, they must be trying to buy time. Probably waiting for the fleet from Iserlohn to charge us so they catch us between them. What nerve! Do they really think I'll fall for that?"

Kempf's intuition was, at this time, 100 percent correct. Slapping a powerful palm against his command desk, he gave orders to advance at maximum combat speed, as well as instructions to open fire three minutes afterward. In as little time as possible, he would destroy these reinforcements, turn back around, and reenvelop Iserlohn. And that was only the beginning—by following Müller's suggestion of having Gaiesburg keep Iserlohn in check, they would be able to achieve what up until now had been deemed impossible: passage through to the other side of the Iserlohn Corridor. And that being the case, what was to stop him from continuing onward after his victory and charging straight on through into the alliance's territory?

"The enemy is within firing range."

"All right, then, open fire!"

Tens of thousands of brilliant arrows were unleashed from the imperial force.

For one brief instant, the narrow Iserlohn Corridor became a formless tube carrying a great swell of energy from one side to the other. Eye-catching, colorful vortices appeared as the alliance vessels took a stinging blow, exploding in brilliant flashes of light. Even the ships that had avoided direct hits shook violently in the aftermath—the temporary flagship *Leda II* was no exception.

Yang, who as usual was commanding the fleet from a perch on top of his desk, was tossed off entirely by the agitation and fell hip first into his chair. He had completely forgotten that he was on board *Leda II*, which was 30 percent smaller than the battleship *Hyperion*, and had weaker defensive capabilities as well.

Yang, stuck in his seat, was the very picture of carelessness. Face red with embarrassment, he finally succeeded in standing up. With a concerned expression on her face, Frederica approached him with sure-footed steps; she had apparently developed a far better sense of equilibrium than her commanding officer.

"Formation D..." Yang said. Having failed to learn his lesson, he was climbing back up onto the desk. Frederica cried out, repeating his order:

"All ships: Formation D!"

The communications officer repeated the order as well, transmitting it not by way of the comm channels, which had been rendered useless, but with coded sequences of flashing lights.

Formation D was a type of cylindrical formation, and in its more extreme version could encircle the enemy in what was almost a ring. As the imperial forces attempted to slip through that glittering circlet of shining flecks of light, the alliance forces bathed them in cannon fire from above, below, port, and starboard. That fire was naturally directed from the edge of the ring inward, and by focusing on a single point, its destructive effect was amplified dramatically. Imperial vessels that came charging forward were occasionally pierced by multiple energy beams fired simultaneously from different directions, and the ships looked like they were being cut into circular slices in the moments before they exploded into balls of flame.

When this formation was used in the wide, boundless environment of open space, the enemies that got through could immediately scatter, turn about, and encircle the formation from an even greater radius. Inside this narrow corridor, however, that was impossible. Yang had developed this tactic in order to make use of the specialized topography of the corridor: after the enemy hit them with their first attack, they would turn tail and go on the defensive. And then...

"The enemy is attacking us from behind!" the operator cried out.

As a shocked Admiral Kempf raised his large, muscular form from the command seat, the Iserlohn Patrol Fleet, under the command of Merkatz, was attacking the imperial forces with surprising speed and pressure, both from behind and from directly overhead. If the scene had been viewed from a distance of several light-years, it might have looked beautiful—like a waterfall of light pouring down.

The imperial forces' rear guard had by no means been careless, but unable to shake off the shock, they were being picked off one by one as a high-density barrage of beams rained down on them. Watching from a distance, the crew in Yang's fleet cried out for joy.

"Formation E!" Yang ordered. Although the ring-shaped formation composed of his patchwork fleet showed a bit of disunity in the process, its shape rapidly converged toward the center, completing a transformation into a funnel shape. The imperial forces that were charging onward, suddenly exposed to multiple layers of attacking beams fired from the same direction, disappeared into muddied torrents of white-hot energy. Attenborough, Nguyen, and the rest, carried away by the certainty of victory, were launching frenzied attacks using localized concentrations of firepower—a hallmark of the Yang Fleet's cannon warfare—to guide reluctant imperial forces to their graves.

At a time like this, a foolish commander might have said, "Forward division, fight the enemies in front of us. Rear division, fight the enemies behind us." In fact, such an order might have allowed them to escape from this crisis. Unexpected opportunities for victory did, after all, arise from the chaos of intense battle. As a strategist, however, Kempf had no shortage of experience and pride, and he was not about to give an order that would mean abandoning his duty and authority as commander.

Vice Commander Niedhart Müller could feel black stains of despair gradually eating away at his mind, yet even so, he was resolved to do all he could. The seeds of his regret were beyond counting, but at present it was his urgent duty to prevent the collapse of his columns and rescue his men. Rising from his command seat, he issued the appropriate orders one after another, attempting to get free of the danger zone. He was at an overwhelming disadvantage, though, and his efforts bore no visible fruit, although the speed at which things were worsening lessened.

Even those efforts, however, were about to hit their limits. Both Kempf and Müller had seen any number of their ships erupt into fireballs. The distance between the lines of battle and central command was now effectively zero. Any minute now, the imperial forces were going to fall like an avalanche into the depths of utter defeat.

"Don't retreat!"

As Kempf shouted angrily, beads of sweat went flying from his forehead.

"We mustn't retreat. Just one more step. One more step, and the whole galaxy is ours!"

Even amid these circumstances, Kempf's words were by no means braggadocio. Beyond the defense line of the FPA forces, beyond the exit of the Iserlohn Corridor, there lay a vast sea of stars and planets left practically undefended.

Once they penetrated that line of defense, Kempf and Müller would spur the fleet onward, forcing their way into the alliance's territory. What would the forces guarding the Iserlohn Corridor do when that happened? If they pursued Kempf and Müller, that would leave the corridor wide open. When great admirals of the Imperial Navy like Mittermeier and von Reuentahl, presently waiting in Wave II, came charging in through the corridor, there would be no one there to stop them. The corridor would be cited afterward for the historic role it had played as the passageway through which the Imperial Navy had conquered the galaxy.

That being the case, could Alliance Armed Forces simply ignore Kempf and Müller, and continue to guard the corridor against the second wave that was sure to come stampeding through it? If they did so, Kempf and Müller might go around ransacking alliance territory at will, perhaps even capturing Heinessen. A more likely scenario, however, was that they would establish a beachhead in some nearby star system and wait for the moment—it would not be long in coming—when the second wave invaded the corridor. At that time, they would be able to return to the corridor and, together with their allies, attack the alliance forces there from both fore and aft. For the imperial forces, it was a surefire tactic for certain victory; for the alliance forces, the very thought of it sent an acute twinge of pain into their hearts.

Or it should have, at least—but Yang Wen-li was in no mood for somber worrying. Even if he had been, he wouldn't have thought it his duty to so. This was because even if the nation known as the Free Planets Alliance were to disappear, people would still remain. Not as "the people," but as "people." The ones who would be most put out if the nation came to an end were those who leeched off the state in the center of its structure of authority; you could search to the ends of the universe looking for reasons why "people" had to be sacrificed in order to please them and not find even one. There was no way that Yang Wen-Li alone could have borne full responsibility for the life or death of the nation—not even if it had been his own personal problem.

Among the imperial forces, Admiral Kempf did not believe until the very last that he was going to lose. But even if his entire frame was suffused with an indomitable fighting spirit, the spirit of his soldiers and advisors had already withered.

The blood had drained from their faces at the sight of so many allied ships shattered and in flames on their screens.

"Excellency, it's no longer possible to resist," Vice Admiral Fusseneger, Kempf's chief of staff, advised with pale, quivering cheeks. "At this rate, all that awaits us here is death or capture. As difficult as this is to say, we should retreat."

Kempf turned a blistering glare on his chief of staff, but his reason was not so far gone as to shout him down high-handedly. He took a ragged breath and beheld with an agonized gaze an imperial fleet in its death throes: with every passing second, its numbers were decreasing and its front line contracting.

"Wait a minute, there is still *that option*..." Kempf murmured unconsciously, and Fusseneger sensed something ominous in the color that was returning to the commander's face. "We still have our final option. We're going to use it, and we're going to destroy Iserlohn Fortress. We've lost in the battle of fleets, but we aren't completely beaten yet."

"May I ask what you refer to?"

"Gaiesburg Fortress. We're going to slam that overgrown, good-for-nothing pebble into Iserlohn. Not even Iserlohn could withstand that."

At those words, Fusseneger's suspicion changed to certainty. Even a commander as capable and broad-minded as Kempf could become unbal-anced when backed too far into a corner. However, Kempf had a rather serene sort of confidence when he ordered the retreat back to Gaiesburg.

At last, the Iserlohn Patrol Fleet rendezvoused with Yang's reinforcements.

"Admiral Merkatz, I can't thank you enough," Yang said with a deep bow. Merkatz's grave, dignified face was displayed on the comm screen. Behind both of them, innumerable uniform berets flew through the air as unimaginative but passionate cries of "We did it! We did it!" rang out again and again.

"This is the man who deserves most of the credit," Merkatz said, and pulled a young man into the screen's field of view.

"Admiral Yang, welcome home."

It was a young boy with flaxen hair.

"Julian?"

Yang didn't know what to say. To see the boy in that place came as quite a shock to him. It was just then, however, that an alarm rang out again, and Yang was rescued from his moment of awkward perplexity.

"Gaiesburg Fortress has begun to move!"

There was a ring of awe in the voice of the operator who reported it.

The joy of the alliance forces plummeted back to the ground instantly. Their victory was not complete yet.

"It's heading toward Iserlohn. Impossible—impossible . . . Are they planning to crash themselves into it!?"

"They figured it out . . . but it's too late," murmured Yang. Frederica searched his profile with her eyes. In Yang's voice, she had sensed a note of something like sympathy.

In fact, Yang was sympathizing with the enemy commander. Crashing a fortress into a fortress was not the kind of thing an orthodox tactician would come up with. Outside of Yang himself, it would require either an incomparable genius like Reinhard von Lohengramm or, failing that, a complete amateur who had no idea what he was doing. To an orthodox tactician, a fortress was valuable to use and possess because of the armor and firepower it could bring to bear against the enemy fortress; to think of using it as a gigantic bomb would be extremely unusual, and Yang couldn't help thinking of the mental anguish a commander must feel when driven to the point of such a highly irregular strategic conclusion. Even so, it was still true that the one who had driven Kempf into these dire straits was none other than Yang himself. Some might call his sympathy hypocritical. But on this matter, let people say what they will.

Gaiesburg Fortress, following the remaining forces of the imperial fleet, was closing in on Iserlohn with its twelve conventional engines running on full power—an immense vulture taking silent flight across a void of utter blackness. The sight of it was overwhelming to the alliance forces. On every ship in the fleet, people were staring with their mouths half-open at the extraordinary sight unfolding on their viewscreens.

Inside Gaiesburg were Kempf, a number of his advisors, navigation personnel, and about fifty thousand guards; the rest of its personnel had been evacuated, divided among the ships under Müller's command. Inside the fortress, escape shuttles were waiting on standby, ready to launch at any moment. Filled with a certainty that the tide was about to turn, Kempf looked on as Iserlohn swelled larger, growing nearer by the second. That was when, in the alliance fleet, Yang Wen-li issued a fateful order:

"Ship-mounted cannons are useless against the fortress itself. Take aim at those conventional navigation engines they've got running—at just one of them, actually—concentrate all your fire on the one farthest to port of their vector of advance!"

On every ship, gunnery officers leapt to their consoles, took careful aim, and shouted their orders in unison:

"Fire!" "Fire!" "Fire!"

Hundreds of beams converged on just one of the navigation engines, putting enough of a load on its composite-armor cover to cause it to crack. With the second volley, those cracks immediately expanded. The engine cover burst open, and a white flash blew the whole thing apart.

In the next instant, Gaiesburg stopped moving forward. Its vast bulk turned and began to spin rapidly.

The axis of a spacecraft's engine thrust had to strictly align with the vessel's center of gravity. Whether large or small, the basic shape of a spacecraft was either circular or spherical, to make it symmetrical on both its x-axis and z-axis. In the event that this principle was not followed, the spaceship would lose track of its direction of advance and revolve on its own center of gravity. One could, of course, turn off the engines at that point, but even if it stopped the acceleration, the spinning would continue due to inertia, and during that time all control functions would be paralyzed.

Gaiesburg Fortress spun off course and plunged into the remnant of the imperial fleet; in an instant, several hundred vessels collided with its spinning bulk and exploded. On the comm channels, countless screams superimposed themselves on one another, then stopped, as if cut off by the flick of a knife. Even the fortress itself was damaged by the collisions with those battleships, and what was worse, that was when all of the cannons of Thor's Hammer were fired simultaneously from Iserlohn, stabbing deep into Gaiesburg's outer shell. It struck a fatal blow.

"Did you see that?" The alliance's soldiers were shouting at each other. "*That's* Admiral Yang's magic!"

Like all the other soldiers, Lieutenant Frederica Greenhill was struck with a great sense of admiration for her commanding officer.

If anyone other than Yang had come up with a tactic like this, Frederica would have probably found him terrifying. Yang had been thinking from the very outset that the only way to render the enemy fortress powerless would be to destroy its navigation engines while it was accelerating and throw off the position of its axis of acceleration. This could only be accomplished by causing the fortress to *use* its navigational engines, which could only be accomplished by driving the enemy into such dire straits that they would attempt to crash their fortress into Iserlohn. And Yang had succeeded in doing that—just as he had succeeded on so many battlefields in the past.

Gaiesburg Fortress was convulsing in its death throes. Inside, numerous explosions and fires were breaking out along the paths of its electrical-distribution network, and the heat and smoke overpowered the air-conditioning system and filled the inside of the fortress. Soldiers covered in sweat and grime were coughing as they walked, while at their feet were slumped blood-splattered comrades who weren't moving at all. Even the central command room had been halfway destroyed, and Kempf was sitting motionless at his command desk.

"All hands, abandon ship."

Chief of Staff Fusseneger's voice broke as he replied to that order:

"Excellency, what do you intend to do?"

Kempf gave a painful laugh.

"It's too late for me. Look at this."

Kempf was holding his hands down over his right side, but the blood spilling out from that place could be seen, as well as part of a broken bone that was sticking out. Most likely, his internal organs were severely damaged. A piece of the wall sent flying by the explosion had bored deep into his tall, muscular body.

Fusseneger was filled with silent grief. Last year, the brilliant and undefeated admiral Siegfried Kircheis had met his untimely end in this fortress. Gaiesburg had been the stronghold of the confederated aristocrats' forces. Was some gruesome grudge of its former masters now dragging Reinhard's great admirals down to the grave one after another? Seized by a superstitious fear, the chief of staff shuddered. The ominous life of Gaiesburg Fortress was now drawing to a close.

At last, Fusseneger stumbled his way out of the command room, seen off by the eyes of the dead.

"All hands, abandon ship!" the alarm kept shouting. "All hands…"

Dirty, wounded survivors had gathered at a port used exclusively by evacuation shuttles. One shuttle was about to take off without even half of its carrying capacity filled. Several people were clinging to its hull.

"This is an emergency launch! Get off!"

"Wait—let us on! Don't leave us!"

"I told you people to move . . . !"

The hatch opened. Thinking they were about to be let on board, the soldiers gratefully rushed forward.

And that was when a scream split the air. A soldier who had just boarded that rescue shuttle lashed out with a laser knife and sliced off the hand of the soldier who was trying to come aboard after him. The soldier who had lost his hand lost his balance as well and, writhing in pain, rolled off the boarding gate and fell to the floor. That was when a soldier who had lagged behind the others drew his blaster from his hip and, without a word, shot the man with the laser knife through the face.

That was the beginning of the panic. Terror and desire for survival boiled over, and reason was washed away. Crisscrossing beams of blaster fire leapt back and forth, as comrade blasted comrade down to the floor, then trampled one another under their military-issue boots.

With several soldiers still clinging to its hull, the shuttle began to take off anyway. That was when the roar of a shot fired from a hand cannon was heard, and the cockpit was filled with orange flames. Blown-off arms and legs were carried up into the air by the force of the blast, and the shuttle became a ball of fire that crashed into the crowd of soldiers. The soldiers were mowed down like weeds, and the blood that geysered upward steamed, stuck, and blackened as soon as it touched the scalding-hot floor.

Suddenly, that crimson tableau underwent a dramatic change—it was painted over entirely in white. That was the moment in which Gaiesburg's fusion reactor had exploded.

A blast of immense heat threw everyone still living to the floor and then promptly added them to the rolls of the dead. Suddenly, a great swell of blinding light appeared where Gaiesburg Fortress had been. As the alliance vessels peeled away at emergency speed, their viewscreens' photoflux-adjustment systems pulled out all the stops trying to dim the brilliance, yet even so, not a single hand on board was able to look at that ball of light straight on. The light's invasion lasted for more than a minute. When the last of the explosion's afterglow had faded and space had returned to its primordial darkness, Yang looked at the screen and, still sitting on his desk, took off his uniform beret and bowed his head toward his defeated and destroyed enemies. He felt so tired. Victory always left him feeling exhausted.

VI

The explosion of Gaiesburg Fortress was, for the wounded and worn-out imperial forces, the killing blow. As much as 80 percent of the imperial force remaining from the battle with Yang and Merkatz had been caught in the explosion of that artificial supernova and had met the same fate as their commander. Even among those who were spared, hardly a one had escaped completely unscathed.

Neidhart Müller had been thrown backward several meters by the shock of the explosion. He had crashed into a bulkhead with exposed instruments and parts, and then fallen to the floor. With great effort, he managed to reel back his consciousness, which for an instant had threatened to disappear into the distance. He tried to call out for a medic but was only assaulted by a suffocating tightness in his chest.

Four of his ribs had been broken, and breathing was impossible with their points stuck in his lung. There was no way he could have called out.

Enduring the intense pain and choking tightness, Müller silently, deeply, breathed in. His bones ground, his chest swelled out, and the broken ends of his ribs touched one another again. With his lungs free of pressure, the seriously injured vice commander at last succeeded in speaking to a medic who had come running to his side, in spite of a nasty bruise on his own head.

"How long will it take to recover fully?"

Müller's voice was pained but had lost none of its composure.

"Our vice commander is immortal, is he?"

"That's a good one. I'll have that written on my gravestone. Well? How long will it take to recover from this completely?"

The medic counted off his injuries: "Four broken ribs, cerebral concussion, lacerations, bruises, and scratches, as well as the associated blood loss and internal bleeding. It'll take three months."

Since Müller refused to be carried to the infirmary, a bed furnished with medical equipment was brought up to the bridge. As electrotherapy was applied, blood that had been preserved at ultralow temperatures was transfused and painkillers and antipyretics were injected. Müller met with Vice Admiral Fusseneger, who had just barely escaped from Gaiesburg.

"What happened to Commander Kempf?"

Fusseneger, all cuts and scratches, didn't answer right away, though ultimately he had to say something.

"He's dead."

"Dead?!"

"I have a message for you from Commander Kempf. He said, 'Tell Müller I'm sorry.'"

Müller fell into an electrified silence that was enough to frighten Fusseneger, but at last he grabbed hold of his sheets and squeezed out a low moan.

"As Odin is my witness," he said, "I will avenge Admiral Kempf. With these two hands, I will wring the neck of Yang Wen-li—though I can't do it now. I haven't the strength. The gap between us is too wide . . . but you just watch me, a few years down the line!"

When Müller stopped talking and grinding his teeth, he recovered a little of his composure and summoned an aide to his bedside.

"Get me a comm screen ready. No, on second thought, never mind the screen. Make it so I can transmit audio only."

Even if he was able to control his voice, he couldn't afford to show himself to his troops when he was badly injured. No matter what kind of overblown rhetoric you might use, the soldiers' morale would drop if they saw their commander covered in white bandages.

At last, the surviving members of a pummeled, defeated imperial force listened to the voice of the young vice commander flowing out of the comm channel. Even if it could not be called a powerful voice, it was a clear and lucid one, rich in reason and will, and had the effect of dragging their despair a few steps closer toward hopefulness.

"Our force may have been defeated, but central command is alive and well. And what central command promises is to return each and every one of you to your hometowns alive and well. So hold on to your pride, maintain order, and let's head back home in an orderly manner."

An imperial force that had numbered sixteen thousand when it left home had shrunk to one-twentieth its original size and been set to a pitiable retreat. Even so, it had not completely fallen apart and had been able to maintain order as a cohesive unit. Without a doubt, that success was the result of the sensible command that Müller carried out from his bed.

"Ships approaching from dead ahead!"

At that report, Senior Admiral Wolfgang Mittermeier trained his eyes on the bridge's main screen. His flagship, *Beowulf*, was out in front of even his fleet's vanguard, a position that in itself underscored the valiant reputation of its commander.

All hands were called to battle stations, and a hail was sent out to the approaching vessels.

"Unidentified vessels, you are ordered to stop. If you fail to do so, you will be attacked."

A very busy minute followed, and then Mittermeier learned that the group of ships ahead of them were, in fact, allies set to flight. When Mittermeier had the image on the viewscreen magnified, he let out an unconscious groan at the pitiful sight displayed. His comrade-in-arms Müller appeared on the comm screen, wrapped in bandages and lying in a hospital bed, and after he had explained the situation, the Gale Wolf's shoulders slumped, and he sighed deeply.

"So, Kempf is gone..."

He closed his eyes for a moment in silent prayer for his fallen comrade, then immediately opened them wide again. The urge to do battle was now coursing through every centimeter of Mittermeier's body.

"You may proceed to the rear and report to Duke von Lohengramm. Leave the avenging of Kempf's death to us."

After cutting communications, Mittermeier turned back to his subordinates. In stature, this commander was somewhat on the short side, but at times like these, his men felt overwhelmed, as though in the presence of a giant.

"Proceed ahead at maximum battle speed," the Gale Wolf instructed. "We're going to hit the vanguard of the enemies chasing Müller. We'll take them by surprise, hit them hard, then peel off. Any more than that, at this juncture, would be meaningless. Bayerlein! Büro! Droisen! Carry out your assigned instructions. Got it?"

His staff officers replied by way of saluting and scattered off toward their departments. Next, a transmission leapt across the void to von Reuentahl's flagship.

When von Reuentahl's aide, Emil von Reckendorf, relayed the message from Mittermeier, the young heterochromiac admiral gave a confident nod of his head and issued the same orders as his colleague had.

"So Kempf is gone, is he?" he murmured as well, though his expression and intonation were slightly different from Mittermeier's, sounding somewhat lacking in sympathy. Even if there were such a thing as a victory without a cause, he believed there was no such thing as a defeat without a cause. *Kempf lost because he deserved to lose*, von Reuentahl thought. *I've no time to waste on sympathy.*

Iserlohn Fortress was in such a state of celebration and wild revel that it seemed as if the Alliance Foundation Festival had landed on the same date as Victory at Dagon Memorial Day. What little champagne they had was uncorked, and noncombat personnel returned to their homes just long enough to drop off their luggage before running back out again to go and greet the soldiers. As Caselnes and von Schönkopf gazed at the main screen in the central command room, they took turns drinking from a pocket flask of whiskey.

However, Yang couldn't set foot in his own home just yet. In spite of his strict warning against pursuing the enemy too far, the divisions of rear admirals Nguyen and Alarcon, totaling over five thousand vessels, were chasing the defeated enemy in a relentless advance. With communications not yet fully restored, they had clung to the fleeing enemy's heels, continuing their rapid charge. It was up to Yang to bring them back in.

Intoxicated by the thrill of a perfect victory, Nguyen and the others were not yet aware that von Reuentahl and Mittermeier were standing in their way ahead.

CHAPTER 9:

THE STRUGGLE FOR CONTROL of the Iserlohn Corridor waged from April until May of SE 798 / IC 489 would provide future generations with many lessons and discussion topics when it came to military tactics. Strategically speaking, it was not held to be of any great importance. That said, the course of human history clearly would have changed forever from that point had the empire been victorious. Most significantly, though, this was the year, and this was the battle, in which Julian Mintz first made his presence known on the stage of history. From a historical perspective, then, it was not a battle to be overlooked after all.

The final act of that battle saw the Imperial Navy recover a portion of its wounded honor. Forces commanded by rear admirals Nguyen and Alarcon, carrying out a pursuit even less organized than the fleeing imperial retreat, were led into a trap of exquisite intricacy and daring.

"Enemy vessels attacking from the rear!"

Dreams of victory were dashed instantly by the astonished operator's report. Nguyen stood up from his command seat, at a loss for words. Imperial vessels lurking right on the border between the corridor's zenith and the dangerous, unnavigable region beyond had suddenly swooped down on them, blocking the alliance forces in from behind. These vessels were the cream of the imperial crop, commanded by Wolfgang Mitter-meier himself. Fleeing vessels that Nguyen and Alarcon had thought to be defeated enemies had in fact been a part of Mittermeier's fleet, retreating in order to lure them into the trap.

"This is for Admiral Kempf," said Mittermeier. "Slaughter them. Don't let even one escape."

Mittermeier wasn't so much giving orders as unleashing his subordi-nates on them. Having already secured the tactical victory, he allowed the battle itself to be prosecuted with a natural dynamism, rather than trying to micromanage it.

At the same time, Vice Admiral Bayerlein's division also ceased its fake retreat and turned all its cannons around toward pursuers unable to execute a sudden stop.

It looked as if the vessels of the alliance force were running headlong into a wall of light.

High-energy molecules collided with superalloy molecules at relative velocities just below the speed of light, and half an instant later, the vic-tor between the two had been decided. The empty space was filled by slashed-open shipwrecks and the silent screams of dismembered bodies. As they were vaporized, blown to pieces, or sliced apart and sent tum-bling through space, the vessels of the alliance wove a gorgeous tapestry of death before these imperial forces.

Those who witnessed it were left speechless by a madcap dance of blinding color and overpowering brilliance. It was astonishingly beautiful yet at the same time horrific beyond description. Could such a disconnect really exist between beauty and virtue? Had it always existed?

The imperial vessels attacking from the rear continued to sing an almost entirely one-sided chorus of death. In its first verse, energy-neutralization fields overloaded and ruptured; in the second, ships' composite armor plating was pierced; and in the third, the ships themselves exploded—in this way was a single dirge concluded.

"Take us down! Escape to the nadir," Alarcon screamed. To avoid the withering attack from above, the alliance vessels raced down toward the corridor's nadir, desperate to secure the time and room needed to either flee or launch a counterstrike.

That, however, did nothing but slightly shift the coordinates of their gravestones, for in that direction Oskar von Reuentahl was waiting and ready for them. All of his ships had energized their main cannons already and were awaiting the arrival of their prey with fangs sharpened, ready to rip the alliance vessels apart with cannon fire at the moment their commander so ordered. Their eyes gleamed with aggressive spirit as the alliance vessels came swooping down right in front of them, almost as if begging to be slaughtered.

"Main cannons, three volleys!"

At von Reuentahl's command, merciless cannon fire was unleashed toward the warships of the alliance, which appeared as reflected blips in their scanners. Blades of light slashed them and crushed them, shattering things crafted with purpose into hundreds of millions of purposeless fragments, scattering them through the void.

The alliance forces had reached the height of panic, and their unified chain of command fell apart. They became like a herd of livestock, stampeding wildly as they tried to escape. The imperial forces had greater numbers, superior tactics, and better commanders. They executed a pattern leading to certain victory, rounding up and crushing those doomed to die that day, who would never have the chance to learn from the mistakes that had been made. Leaving behind streaks of light more fleeting than a firefly's glow, they vanished and were gone.

"Are these really Yang Wen-li's people?" the Gale Wolf said to himself, sounding, if anything, disgusted. "His forces were nothing like this when we fought him at Amritsar." Could a military force really be weakened this severely by the absence of an outstanding commander?

Amid a whirlpool of exploding streaks of light, Rear Admiral Nguyen Van Thieu vanished from this world along with his ship. It had been hit by six energy beams simultaneously.

Rear Admiral Sandle Alarcon lived longer than Nguyen, but only by five—or at most ten—minutes. The vessel Alarcon was riding took a direct hit from a photon missile and split in half; the forward part, which included the bridge, collided with a friendly cruiser, and there it exploded.

"Second enemy fleet detected!" shouted an operator on *Beowulf's* bridge. "A lot of them this time—over ten thousand!"

By the time that report had been given, the survivors who remained on the battlefield consisted almost entirely of victors. Mittermeier and von Reuentahl spoke to one another via their comm screens.

"Did you catch that, von Reuentahl?"

"Yes, it seems Yang Wen-li has come out in person. What shall we do? I'm sure you want to fight him."

"I suppose I do. But there's nothing to be gained in fighting him right now."

If the tide were to turn against him, Yang would simply escape to Iserlohn. Besides that, the imperial forces' front line and supply line alike were both nearly stretched to their limits. Both admirals concluded that they should probably get out of there before the main enemy force arrived. A victory as trifling as this one wouldn't make up for Kempf and Müller's terrible loss, but nothing good would come of ignoring their circumstances and getting greedy.

Mittermeier softly clicked his tongue in disgust. "They planned a campaign of conquest thousands of light-years away and sent not just a big fleet but an entire fortress as well. In spite of that, there's been nothing but failure, and the only one to burnish his reputation out of any of this is Yang Wen-li. At least it's over."

"Well, we can't expect a hundred victories out of a hundred battles— that's how Duke von Lohengramm put it. But sooner or later, you and I *will* have Yang Wen-li's head."

"Müller's wanting it too."

"Oh? Then it looks like the competition's going to be fierce."

After exchanging indomitable smiles, the two young admirals signed off and began preparations for withdrawal. They arranged their ships into groups of one thousand, and as each group pulled back, the next group would protect its rear. It was an orderly withdrawal. Mittermeier took charge of the vanguard and got all of the departing ships into line, and von Reuentahl brought up the rear, positioning himself for a counterattack in the event of alliance forces attacking from behind. The withdrawal was executed flawlessly.

So it was that when Yang Wen-li, together with Merkatz and the others, arrived aboard the battleship *Hyperion*, all they discovered were wrecks of allied ships and clustered specks of light receding into the distance. Yang, naturally, did not order pursuit, but instead gave instructions to begin rescue operations and then head back to Iserlohn afterward.

"Do you see this, Julian?" Looking at the flaxen-haired youth, Yang spoke in a voice that sounded like a sigh. "This is how great admirals fight their battles. They come with a clear-cut objective, and once they've achieved it, they don't stick around. That's how it's done."

Nguyen and Alarcon had lacked that quality. Not that this was the time or place for Yang to say so out loud.

He wondered how the imperial military's—or rather, Reinhard's military's—rich store of talent was faring now. If Siegfried Kircheis, that brilliant redheaded young admiral, had been alive, Yang's chances of victory would have certainly been minuscule. Not that he was complaining, of course.

"Lieutenant Greenhill, relay orders to all ships: return to base."

"Yes, Excellency."

"Oh, and Julian, it's been quite a while since I've had any of your tea. Could you make me some?"

"Of course, Your Excellency."

The young boy took off running.

"Julian is quite something," Merkatz said to Yang in a gentle and sincere tone. He related to the boy's unreliable guardian how Julian had seen through the imperial military's tactics.

"So that was Julian."

Yang took off his uniform beret and scratched his black hair. His unruly hair had gotten a little long. During the inquiry, Yang had been the object of some low-level sarcasm—people telling him his hairstyle wasn't very soldierly or suggesting he get a crew cut.

"Maybe you've heard this already," Yang said, "but I don't want that kid to enlist. To be honest, I want him to give up on the idea even if I have to order him."

"That's not exactly democratic," said Merkatz. As he was trying to be humorous, Yang laughed for politeness's sake, but to be honest, that jibe had really hit Yang where it hurt. All sorts of signs seemed to be pointing toward a day when Yang would have no choice but to accept the course Julian would choose.

II

Night had fallen across the capital city of Planet Phezzan. By nature, this was supposed to be a time of rest accompanying men's fear of the dark, but the residents of Phezzan were not simpleminded primitives—even at night, they continued their spirited activities.

The estate of Landesherr Rubinsky, too, remained brightly lit late into the night, with all manner of people coming and going, testifying to the fact that it was one of the hubs around which human society revolved. Rubinsky was neither worshiped like a god nor adored like an angel, but he was respected as a skilled politician.

That night found his aide, Rupert Kesselring, in Rubinsky's study. He was reporting on a shift that had at last occurred in the relative strengths of the three great powers, after more than a century of those numbers remaining unchanged.

"I'll have the exact figures for you tomorrow, but for a rough estimate . . . let me see . . . I'd put the empire at forty-eight, the alliance at thirty-three, and our own beloved Phezzan at nineteen."

With the power of the highborn aristocracy all but purged from the empire, and with talented commoners and low-ranking aristocrats being actively recruited, the empire's workforce was being rejuvenated, and the malaise that had hung over that nation was beginning to dissipate. Also, redistribution of wealth that the aristocrats had monopolized was stimulating the economy, with an accompanying surge in investment. On the other hand, former aristocrats were being driven into poverty. Since an overwhelming majority of the people were benefiting from the changes, however, that this was not considered an issue in imperial society. It simply meant that former aristocrats with no means of supporting themselves were on their way to extinction.

Meanwhile, the drop in the alliance's national power presented such a hideous spectacle that people felt like covering their eyes. The primary factors were the huge defeat at Amritsar two years ago and the civil war last year. In less than two years, their military power had plunged to a third of what it had been, and worse still was the marked weakening of its society's support systems. In every field, accidents were on the increase, and the trust of the citizenry was in decline.

In addition, there was a squeeze on consumer goods. With the trifecta of decreasing production, worsening quality, and rising prices, the FPA was tumbling down a slope toward ruin.

"If not for that loss at Amritsar," said Kesselring, "the alliance's national power would not have fallen this far. It should have been a peace offensive they launched when they occupied Iserlohn. If they had done so, they could have played the empire's old forces against the new and won some favorable diplomatic concessions. Instead, they embarked on a military adventure they had no hope of winning, the result of which is the mess they're in now. The idiocy of those people is positively criminal."

Moreover, their continued opposition to the empire made it impossible to reduce military spending, which meant that they also couldn't shrink their military. That was the root of their present economic distress. Even amid these difficulties, over 30 percent of the alliance's GNP had to be spent on the military.

It was held that during peacetime, no more than 18 percent of a country's GNP should go toward military spending. And in wartime? In the case of a warring nation on the verge of defeat, that number could sometimes exceed 100 percent. This was because their savings had all been eaten up. Consumption had exceeded production, so the only fate for the economy was death by anemia.

"We certainly do want the alliance to stay the course," Kesselring continued. "Once they've bankrupted their economy, Phezzan will be able to completely take over there. And once we've made the empire recognize our rights and interests there, the entire galaxy will be unified under our de facto rule."

Making no reply to his young aide's impassioned speech, Rubinsky looked through the materials in his report and at last said, "In any case, find pawns—lots of pawns. Because the ones who prove useful you can keep around."

"I certainly intend to. I've made what moves that I can. There's nothing to worry about. Incidentally, what should be done with Tech Admiral von Schaft of the Imperial Navy?"

"What indeed? Let me hear your thoughts."

When the question came back to him, the young aide's answer was clarity itself:

"I don't think there's any more use for him. His demands on us only keep growing, too, so I think it's time we cut him loose."

Kesselring closed his mouth for a moment, but observing the landesherr's expression, he grew emboldened and appended this:

"Actually, preparations are already in place for officials in the Imperial Ministry of Justice to receive certain documents through 'natural processes,' which I can set into motion on receipt of Your Excellency's approval. Shall I?"

"Very well, do it now. If you don't flush the waste right away, it ends up clogging the pipes."

"I'll see to it immediately."

Neither the giver nor the receiver of that order seemed to view von Schaft as a human being at all. Their callousness toward a man who had lost his value to them was really quite remarkable.

"And with that, the matter is closed," said Rubinsky. "By the way, isn't tomorrow the anniversary of your mother's passing? Take the day off if you like."

The landesherr's words came abruptly, and his young aide smiled with one corner of his mouth. It wasn't that he'd meant to; it was apparently just a tic of his.

"Well!" he said, "What an unexpected pleasure to learn Your Excellency takes an interest in even my private affairs."

"Of course I do... considering you're my own flesh and blood."

Kesselring's upper body shook slightly at that. After a moment, he said, "So you knew, then?"

"You must think I treated her terribly."

The landesherr and his aide—the father and his son—regarded one another. The expressions on both their faces were too dry to call parent-child affection.

"Did it bother you?"

"Yes, it always did . . ."

"Then Mother will be happy to hear that too in the afterlife. I'll thank you on her behalf. Actually, though, there was never anything for you to be concerned about. You had to choose between the daughter of an impoverished house that didn't know where their next meal was coming from and the daughter of a tycoon who controlled several percent of the galaxy's wealth. I would've made the same . . . Yes; I would've made the same choice as Your Excellency."

A distant look had appeared in the eyes of Rubinsky's son, but it only lasted for a couple of seconds.

"So, was it wholly out of your fatherly affection that I was able to get this important post as your aide, even though I'm nothing more than a greenhorn fresh out of graduate school?"

"Is that what you think?"

"It's what I don't want to think. Since I do have a bit of confidence in my own abilities, I'd like to believe that that was what you were after."

With eyes that had lost all expression, Rubinsky gazed at his son making that confident assertion.

"You seem to be a lot like me on the inside. On the outside, you resemble your mother, though."

"Thank you very much."

"Head of state is not a hereditary position on Phezzan. If you want to be my successor, it isn't a bloodline you need—it's ability and the trust of the people. You'll need to take your time and cultivate both."

"I'll remember. Always."

Rupert Kesselring bowed, but his purpose may have been to hide his face from his father's line of sight. However, that action at the same time kept him from seeing the look on his father's face.

Presently, Rupert Kesselring went out from the presence of his father, the landesherr.

"Ability and trust, eh? Hmph."

Rubinsky's son looked up at the lights of his father's estate and murmured a most disrespectful utterance: "You've committed every outrage one could think of in acquiring those qualities, haven't you, Your Excellency? And you tell me to take my time, even though you never did so yourself. Not very consistent. Never forget, I *am* your son."

Rubinsky saw his son off by way of a monitor screen, which showed him getting into his landcar and speeding away into the distance. Without calling for the maid, he poured himself a full glass of dry gin and tomato juice—a cocktail called a Bloody Catherine.

"Rupert's a lot like me..."

In other words, he had ambition and spirit to spare and also believed that the ends justified the means. He would think calmly, make his calculations, and take the shortest route to his goal. If that meant eliminating certain obstacles in his path, he would do so with no hesitation whatsoever.

Rather than allow such a dangerous individual to operate freely far away, it was better to have him close by, where he could keep an eye on him. That was the reason Rubinsky had appointed him as his aide.

Perhaps Rupert's talents exceeded those of his father. Still, raw talent could not easily make up for the twenty-plus-year difference in experience between them. To fill that gap, Rupert would have to expend enormous amounts of effort. What he would get in return for that was something nobody yet knew.

III

Protected on both ends by admirals von Reuentahl and Mittermeier, the fleet dispatched to the Iserlohn Corridor returned to Odin, having been reduced in the fighting by a scant seven hundred vessels or so. Commander in Chief Kempf had been lost; the mobile fortress Gaiesburg had been lost; more than fifteen thousand vessels and 1.8 million personnel had been lost—it made for a pitiful homecoming.

While the old imperial military was another matter, Reinhard and his subordinates had never suffered such a one-sided defeat before. Even Wittenfeld's failure at Amritsar had been just a small blemish on an otherwise perfect victory. With impeccable tactics, Mittermeier and von Reuentahl had delivered a powerful counterstrike to the enemies who had come pursuing their defeated allies, but they had not been able to salvage the operation as a whole.

It was predicted by many that Duke von Lohengramm's wounded pride would turn to lightning and quickly fall on the head of Vice Commander Neidhart Müller when he came skulking back alive.

So it was that Müller, head still wrapped in blood-tinged bandages, presented himself at the Lohengramm admiralität, and apologized on one knee before Reinhard for his transgressions:

"Though charged with orders from Your Excellency's own hand, it was not within the power of your humble officer to fulfill his duties, and unable as I was to save even our commander, Admiral Kempf, many soldiers were lost and our enemies given cause for boasting. These transgressions are worthy of death a thousand times over, and it is only with the greatest of shame that I have returned here alive, that I may give report of these matters to Your Excellency and await your judgment. As the blame for this loss lies entirely with this humble officer, I ask that you deal leniently with my men—"

He bowed his head low, and a scarlet rill appeared from the lower edge of his bandage, running down the side of his cheek.

For a time, Reinhard stared at the defeated admiral with an icy gaze. At last he opened his mouth and spoke, in front of attending vassals who were holding their breath in suspense.

"The fault does not lie with you. If you can redeem your loss with a victory, that will be enough. Good work on a distant campaign."

"Excellency . . ."

"I've lost Admiral Kempf already. I can't afford to lose you as well. Rest until your wounds are healed. After that, I'll order you returned to active duty."

Still on one knee, Müller lowered his head even farther, then unexpectedly tumbled forward and lay there on the floor unmoving. For a long while, he had silently endured anguish and stress of both the mind and the body, and in the instant of his release, he lost consciousness.

"Get him to the hospital. And then promote Kempf. Make him a senior admiral."

On Reinhard's orders, Captain Günter Kissling, the new captain of his personal guard, signaled his men and had Müller carried away for treatment. Those present breathed a sigh of relief and rejoiced to see that their young lord was a man of such generosity.

But in fact, Reinhard had indeed been furious when he first learned of that miserable defeat. It would have been one thing if the tide had turned against them and they'd been forced to withdraw, but never had he dreamed that they would lose 90 percent of that whole force. When he had heard that news, he had thrown his wineglass down on the floor and sequestered himself in his study. He had intended to come down hard on Müller. But then he had looked in the mirror and seen the pendant on his breast, and remembered the late Siegfried Kircheis. There was no doubting that Kircheis, who at the Battle of Amritsar had pled with him to forgive Wittenfeld's mistakes, would have asked Reinhard to forgive Müller as well.

"You're right," he had said. "A man like Müller isn't easy to come by. I'll not be so foolish as to have him killed over a fruitless battle. Are you happy now, Kircheis?"

Thus Reinhard showed mercy toward Müller, but toward Tech Admiral von Schaft, his attitude was entirely different.

"If you've anything to say for yourself, let's hear it," he said after summoning him. From the very start, he assumed an attitude of condemnation. Brimming with confidence, however, von Schaft responded:

"If I may say so, Excellency, there was nothing wrong with my proposal. Surely, responsibility for the operation's failure lies with those charged with its leadership and command."

And wasn't even Müller forgiven? he was all but saying.

The handsome imperial prime minister turned toward him with a low, cold laugh.

"Don't flap your tongue over irrelevancies. Who said you're being called to account over the defeat? Kessler! Come here and show this fool the charges."

With a sound of booted feet, one of the officers stepped forward.

Admiral Ulrich Kessler, whom Reinhard had made both commissioner of military police and commander of capital defenses that year, turned his sharply angled face toward the commissioner of science and technology and, taking a stern bearing toward the discomfited man, said these words:

"Tech Admiral Anton Hilmer von Schaft, I am placing you under arrest on charges of accepting bribes, misappropriation of public funds, tax evasion, extraordinary breach of trust, and dissemination of military secrets."

Six sturdy MPs had already formed a threatening wall of uniforms around von Schaft.

The face of the commissioner of science and technology changed color until it was like mud mixed with volcanic ash. That look was clearly not shock at being falsely accused; it was the kind of look caused by hidden facts suddenly blown wide open.

"On what evidence…" he started to say, but that was the limit of his bluffing. As his arms were taken by MPs on the right and left, he squirmed, shouting unintelligibly.

"Take him away!" ordered Kessler.

"Why, you filthy—!"

Listening as his shouts faded into the distance, Reinhard spat with disgust. In his ice-blue eyes there floated not a speck of sympathy. Just as Admiral Kessler was about to leave, he called him to a halt and ordered:

"Increase surveillance of the Phezzan commissioner's office. And I don't mind if they notice. That in itself should help keep them in check."

It was not hard for Reinhard to surmise that Phezzan was cutting von Schaft loose as a pawn that had lost its worth. For Reinhard, this provided a perfect opportunity to replace the tired old blood at the Science and Technology Commission. That didn't mean, however, that he could simply overlook Phezzan's movements. Why was von Schaft no longer needed by them? Because Phezzan had achieved its designated goal? Or because some other route had opened up? In either case, something had been gained by them or else they wouldn't be throwing out their trash.

"What are those money-grubbing Phezzanese up to?"

He wasn't worried, exactly, but he had suspicions he could not wipe away. It was not a pleasant feeling to know that some Phezzanese plot or scheme had been allowed to succeed so easily.

IV

The duty of visiting the home of Senior Admiral Karl Gustav Kempf in order to inform his family of his passing fell to Admiral Ernest Mecklinger, deputy manager of Imperial Armed Forces Supreme Command Headquarters. Mecklinger, also an artist, steeled himself and set to his task, but at the sight of Kempf's widow—who, unable to restrain herself, burst into tears, her eight-year-old eldest trying his best to console her—he could feel himself involuntarily flinching from them in his heart.

"Mommy, Mommy, don't cry! I'll get revenge for Daddy! I'll kill that Yang person for you. I promise!"

"I'll kill him!" his five-year-old brother chorused, not really understanding what he was saying.

Unable to bear being there a moment longer, Mecklinger took his leave of the Kempf family. Kempf would be promoted to senior admiral, buried with a military funeral, and given several medals. The family he left behind would never want for the daily necessities of life. Still, no matter what honors and rewards were bestowed, there were most certainly still some things they could never make up for.

Hildegard von Mariendorf understood that Reinhard's heart had an empty space not easily filled. And, difficult though it might be to do so, Hilda was concerned that failure to fill that void might eventually ruin Reinhard's character.

One day at lunch, the young, golden-haired imperial marshal said, "Whether they steal or they build, it's whoever's first who is worthy of praise. That's the natural way of things."

Hilda was in full agreement on that point, so she nodded earnestly.

"But what rights can be claimed," Reinhard continued, "by those who simply inherit power, wealth, and honor through no ability or effort of their own? The only path for their ilk is to beg mercy of those who *are* capable. They have no option but to quietly disappear into the waves of history. The very notion of dynasties based on bloodlines offends me. Authority should be for one generation only. It's not a thing to be yielded—it's a thing to be stolen."

"By which Your Excellency means that your own position and authority will not be left to your offspring, correct?"

The young imperial prime minister looked at Hilda; he appeared surprised, as though someone had just shouted right behind him. No doubt the thought of himself as a father had been beyond the young man's thinking. He shifted his eyes away from Hilda and seemed to be pondering something. Then he said, "My heir will be someone whose abilities are equal to mine, or greater. Also, succession will not necessarily take place after I'm dead."

When he spoke those words, the faintest hint of a smile flashed across Reinhard's handsome face, then quickly vanished. Hilda saw it, and it reminded her of diamond dust, glittering as it danced through icy air. As beautiful as it was brilliant, it was at the same time joyless and frigid—a mist made of minute ice crystals.

"If someone thinks he can stab me from behind and gain everything that is mine, then I welcome him to try. That said, I'll make sure such individuals think long and hard on what will happen if their attempts fail."

Although he spoke in almost musical cadences, something in Reinhard's words sent a chill down Hilda's spine. After he finished speaking, Reinhard drained his glass of rosé. Since losing his redheaded friend, Reinhard's liquor intake had shown a marked increase.

Hilda remained silent. She felt as though his porcelain mask had cracked, and she had glimpsed the loneliness hidden underneath. Siegfried Kircheis, that presence in his life that might have best been called his second self, was gone, and his elder sister Annerose had left him. Those with whom Reinhard had shared the years and his heart were now gone. He had loyal and capable subordinates, but for some reason he kept his heart closed to them. There was even one standing by who considered this a good thing: Paul von Oberstein.

What von Oberstein required was someone who could execute his plots and deceptions with the skill of precision machinery and not get carried away by emotion. Put in extreme terms, Reinhard was just a means to an end for von Oberstein. No doubt he would watch in satisfaction as his "tool" conquered the galaxy, unified humanity, and came to stand at the pinnacle of all power and glory. That satisfaction was probably no different from that of an artist upon the completion of a work made with perfect technique. With strokes of an incomparable brush called Reinhard von Lohengramm, artist Paul von Oberstein would complete his grand historical painting on a canvas woven of time and space.

On the way home that day, Hilda continued to examine the thoughts she'd had during lunch, tracing out their trajectories and following them where they led.

As far as von Oberstein was concerned, the feelings Reinhard had toward his sister Annerose and the late Siegfried Kircheis were probably emotions to be shunned. To his artificial eyes, they bespoke a weakness and fragility unbecoming of a conqueror.

"A ruler should be an object of fear and awe to his subjects. What he should not be is an object of affection..."

Hilda had learned in her university studies of two ancient thinkers who had made that assertion. Their names, if she remembered correctly, were Han Feizi and Machiavelli. Did von Oberstein now wish to become the faithful practitioner of their ideas, though separated from them by several thousand years of space and time? Most likely, he was going to midwife the birth of a conqueror unlike any the galaxy had ever seen. And yet at the same time, he might also destroy the feelings in a young man who had once been very sensitive. If the birth of this new conqueror ended up being nothing more than Rudolf the Great's rebirth on a magnified scale, that would be a disaster not only for Reinhard personally, but for all of humanity, and all of history as well.

Hilda felt the twinge of a mild headache and a sudden shudder, brought on by the thought that she herself might ultimately end up making an enemy of von Oberstein.

If it's a fight that can't be avoided, though, I'll fight it, and I'll have to win it, Hilda thought, confirming her own resolve to herself. *Reinhard must not become "Rudolf II." Reinhard needs to be Reinhard. It's so important to us all that he go on being Reinhard—with all his faults and his weaknesses!*

Later, when Hilda was back at home, she noticed her own slightly flushed complexion reflected in an old-fashioned oak-framed mirror.

"Resolve is a fine thing to have, Hildegard von Mariendorf," she said, directing a solemn question toward the reflection of her blue-green eyes that shone with such vitality and intellect, "but what are your chances of winning? If people can win just by being resolved, no one would have to work as hard as they do. I know what I should do—I should go visit his sister, the Countess von Grünewald. Ah, even so, there'd be no need for the likes of me to stick my nose into this if Admiral Kircheis were still alive."

Hilda's smooth fingers brushed back her short, dark-blond hair. She couldn't call the dead back from Hades's palace, but even so, she had to wonder: how many people both now and in times to come would be moved to murmur those selfsame words because of that redheaded youth who had died so young?

"If only Kircheis had lived!"

 ·   ·   ●
   ·   ·   ·

Baron Heinrich von Kümmel, cousin to Hildegard von Mariendorf, was resting his sickly frame in a luxurious canopy bed. He had been running a slight temperature for some time, and his sweating had been bad enough to necessitate more than ten changes of sheets on that day alone. The maidservant sitting at his bedside was reading aloud from a book of poetry to console her young master.

"Whether my heart hath wings or no . . . I slip from gravity's palm . . . as if bounding across the boundless sky . . . to the homeworld I left, green in olden days . . . though now its birdsong is silen—"

"Enough! Leave me."

So ordered in that fierce yet impotent voice, the maidservant obediently closed the poetry collection, gave a hasty bow, and left the room. Heinrich glared at the door, seething with a frustrated hatred of all who enjoyed good health—and had to steady his breathing after the tiring strain of that alone.

For a while, Heinrich's glassy, feverish eyes were turned toward the mirror on the wall. There was a sickly redness in his cheeks, and beads of sweat were tracing lines down his throat toward his chest.

I won't be here much longer, thought the all-too-young head of House von Kümmel. *It's more of a wonder that I've lived these eighteen years.* As a child, every nightfall had brought with it the terror that he might not live to see the light of the coming dawn.

These days, though, he didn't feel so frightened of death itself. What frightened him was the thought of him gradually fading from people's memories after he was gone. The servants here at this estate, his relatives—even Hilda, that beautiful, clever cousin of his—after he had been gone for a year, would any of them still remember that frail youth named Heinrich?

And what had been the point in his living this long, anyway? Was he only here to eat his meals and wash his face with the aid of his servants? To pay his doctors the fees for his treatments? To come to the end of his short life staring up at the canopy above his bed? Was it simply his lot to meaninglessly fade away, leaving nothing of his own creation in this world, nor any proof that he had ever even lived? He had heard stories of another eighteen-year-old just like himself who had become an admiral at that age, who had been named an imperial marshal at age twenty, had gained the seat of imperial prime minister at age twenty-two, and who even now continued to stride toward a boundless future—so why was it that he had to die yoked to a cruel, unfair fate?

Heinrich pressed a thin, pale cheek against his sweat-dampened pillow. He wouldn't die like this. He couldn't die like this. He couldn't die in peace until he had done *something*—left some kind of mark on history as proof of his having lived.

On the evening of the day of Admiral Kempf's military funeral, Wolfgang Mittermeier downed a single glass of white wine and went to visit his colleague Oskar von Reuentahl at the official residence where he lived alone. Von Reuentahl seemed to have something on his mind, but he welcomed him gladly into his living room and gave him another glass. Mittermeier had been planning on chatting a bit between drinks or something, but his host, oddly enough, seemed to be drunk and blurted out something truly surprising.

"Listen to me, Mittermeier. I used to think we had common goals: putting down the aristocrats, destroying the Free Planets Alliance, conquering the whole universe. I used to think we shared that with Duke von Lohengramm. But now . . ."

"You mean we don't?"

"Lately, I've been thinking—maybe subordinates are nothing more than convenient, disposable tools to that man. Aside from Siegfried Kircheis, of course. But other than him, does anyone in the admiralty mean anything to the duke? Look at Kempf. Now, it's not like I actually feel any sympathy for him, but look what happened—the man was literally used and thrown away in a pointless battle."

"But still, the duke mourned Kempf's death and had him promoted to senior admiral despite his loss. And won't his family be getting a pension to take care of their needs?"

"That's what's bothering me. Think of it this way: Kempf is dead, so the duke cries a few tears, bestows a few honors, and that's that. But what he needs to do is give something more tangible—authority, maybe, or wealth—to the *living*. But I have my doubts about whether that man is capable of it."

Mittermeier, his face now warm from the liquor, shook his head once and then replied, "Wait a minute. Last fall, when Kircheis died and the duke had shut himself off from the world, wasn't it you who said you were absolutely going to get him back on his feet? Were you not serious about that?"

"I meant every word. At that time." Von Reuentahl's heterochromatic eyes flashed, both with their own unique light. "But it's not like I've just made a long string of right calls and right choices every day since I was born. And while it isn't the case right now, the day may come when I regret that choice to help him."

When von Reuentahl stopped speaking, an invisible cage of heavy silence closed in around the two young admirals.

"I'm going to pretend I never heard this," Mittermeier said at last. "You shouldn't be so careless about what you say. If someone like von Oberstein got wind of what you just said, you could even be targeted for a purge. Duke von Lohengramm is the hero of our times. It's enough for us to act as his arms and legs, and to be rewarded accordingly. That's what I think."

At last, his friend left, and von Reuentahl sat down alone on his sofa and mumbled, "Hmph. I can't believe I did that again."

A bitter light sheltered in his mismatched eyes. Just like when he had talked about his mother before, von Reuentahl had drunk too much and told Mittermeier far too much. And this time, he had gone and exaggerated thoughts he wasn't necessarily all that passionate about. Ever since last year, when Reinhard had told him to challenge him anytime if he had the confidence, such thoughts had been precipitating in the bottom of his heart, like silt in the bed of a river.

Von Reuentahl turned his black and blue eyes toward the window. Twilight was slowly, gently falling. In short order, a dark sapphire canopy flecked with grains of gold would spread out over everyone's heads.

To seize the universe in my hands…?

He said the words in his mind, trying them out. From the standpoint of humanity's present level of ability and accomplishments, it was a terribly grandiose thing to say, but there was a strange *something* in those words that set his heart racing.

He had heard that Reinhard von Lohengramm—his young lord and master—had once posed this question to Siegfried Kircheis: "Do you think what was possible for Rudolf the Great is impossible for me?" If he were to amplify that—did he, Oskar von Reuentahl, have the same qualifications? Could he not hope for the same thing that Duke von Lohengramm had hoped? He was still just thirty-one. He held the rank of senior admiral in the Galactic Imperial Navy. The rank of imperial marshal was within his reach. He was far closer to the seat of ultimate power than Rudolf the Great had been when he was thirty-one.

In any case, it had been an extremely disquieting thing he had said. Mittermeier would under no circumstances repeat it to others, but perhaps there was a need for him to make it out to have been a joke sometime tomorrow.

Meanwhile, on his way home, Mittermeier felt like he had drunk some excessively acidic coffee. Unable to wipe away the memory, he was trying to tell himself that those words had just been the liquor talking and not von Reuentahl. Still, he couldn't fool himself.

Did a new age simply mean an age that brought new conflicts? Even if it did, to think that, of all people, his good friend von Reuentahl had been carrying that much dissatisfaction and distrust toward their lord! While that alone would probably not lead to any catastrophes directly, he ought to hold back from doing anything that would get him noticed by someone such as von Oberstein.

Am I just too simpleminded? Mittermeier wondered. While his IQ was high, he didn't really like using his brain for anything other than destroying enemies on the battlefield. Nothing disgusted him more than power struggles between allies. Suddenly, he thought about the enemy. They probably had worries of their own. He wondered what the man known as Yang Wen-li might be doing about now.

Dancing with some beautiful woman at a victory celebration, perhaps?

Mittermeier's guess was wrong.

The hero who had once again saved the Free Planets Alliance from an existential crisis was lying in bed, sneezing over and over. Although overwork was probably to blame, he had become infected with an ineradicable disease: the common cold. Of course, there was a blessing in this—after leaving the victory banquet in the capable hands of Caselnes, Frederica Greenhill, von Schönkopf, Merkatz, and the others, he had been able to go back to his official residence and crawl into bed. Julian, who was set to be promoted to warrant officer, stayed with him. Following his first sortie, Julian had shot down enemy fighters in the string of battles that had followed and, most importantly, had seen through the Imperial Navy's plans, providing his senior officers with ample grounds to recommend his promotion. As for Yang himself, there was the human resources balance among high-ranking officers to consider, so once again he was passed over for marshal and given only a medal instead.

"I'll make you some hot punch. I'll mix honey and lemon with wine and dilute it with hot water. That works best for a cold."

"Can you leave out the honey, the lemon, and the water?"

"No!"

"It wouldn't make that much difference, would it?"

"How about I leave out the wine instead?"

Yang was silent for a moment. "You were a lot more obedient when you came to my house four years ago."

"Yes," said Julian, not missing a beat. "Acting like this was also something I had to learn."

Yang, at a loss for a good rejoinder, turned toward the wall and started grumbling.

"Ah, what a miserable life…A job I can't stand gets foisted on me, I've got no woman in my life, and if I so much as try to drink a little booze, I get snapped at…"

"Don't get all moody just because of a cold!"

Julian had yelled, but that had been to keep his expression from suddenly going soft. It had been more than two months since they'd had a conversation. He felt glad that they were finally able to talk like this again. It had been an essential tradition ever since he had first come to the Yang household. He made the hot punch in the kitchen, then passed it to his patient.

"You're a good kid."

Thoughtless though it was, Yang changed his tune the instant he took a sip. The hot punch that the boy had made him was practically unadorned, pure wine. For a while, the flaxen-haired youth watched the black-haired young admiral sitting in bed while wrapped in his blankets, contentedly sipping his warm cold medicine, but at last Julian spoke up in a tone of resolution.

"Admiral Yang?"

"What is it?"

"I . . . want to enlist. Officially."

For a long moment, Yang said nothing.

"May I have your permission? If—if you're completely against it no matter what . . . I'll give up on the idea."

"Do you want to join no matter what?"

"I do. I want to be a soldier who protects freedom and equality. Not the kind that turns into a pawn to be used in invasions and oppression—a soldier who's there to protect the rights of the citizens."

"You said you'd give up the idea, but what would you do if you gave it up?"

"I don't know. No, wait. If it came to that, I'd become whatever you told me to become, Admiral."

Yang twirled his half-empty cup of hot punch around and around between the palms of his hands.

"It never even occurred to you that you might be told no, did it?"

"That's not true at all!"

"I've got fifteen years on you, kid—don't think I can't see through a bluff that thin."

Yang spoke haughtily, but as he was dressed in his pajamas, Yang's words didn't carry quite as much dignity as he himself believed.

"I'm sorry."

"Well, I guess I can't stop you. How could I say no with you looking at me like that? All right. I don't see you turning into a troublemaker, so be what you want to be."

The boy's dark-brown eyes lit up. "Thank you! Thank you so much, Admiral!"

After a moment, Yang added one more thing. "But do you really want to be a soldier that badly?"

Yang couldn't hold back a wry smile.

In every kind of religion and in every system of law, there were certain points that had been fundamental since ancient times: *Thou shalt not kill. Thou shalt not steal. Thou shalt not bear false witness*—

Yang thought back over his own life. How many enemies and allies had he killed? How many things had he stolen? How many times had he deceived his enemies? That those actions were exempted from censure in this present life was due only to the fact that he was following his nation's orders. Truly, a nation could do anything and everything, except raise the dead. It could pardon criminals and throw the innocent into prison, or send them to the gallows, even. It could put weapons in the hands of civilians who were living peaceful lives and send them off to the battlefield, as well. Within its nation, a military was the largest violent organization.

"Hey, Julian. It's usually not my style to say this kind of thing, but if you say you're going to become a soldier, there's something I don't want you to forget: the military is an organ of violence, and that violence comes in two types."

"Good violence and bad violence?"

"No, not like that. There's violence for the purpose of rule and oppression, and there's violence as a means of liberation. A nation's military..."

Yang drank down the last of his considerably cooled hot punch.

"...is by nature an organization of the former. That's unfortunate, but history proves it. When rulers have clashed with their citizens, it's been rare for the military to side with the people. In fact, in a number of countries in the past, militaries themselves have turned into authoritarian organizations and even ruled the people through violence. Even last year, we had some people who tried to do that and failed."

"But you're a military man yourself, and you opposed that, didn't you? I want to be a soldier like you, even if that's only an aspiration."

"Whoa, whoa! Hold it right there. You know good and well, don't you, that my aspirations don't actually have anything to do with the military?"

Yang believed that the pen was mightier than the sword. In a society where truths were such rarities, that was one of a scant handful of exceptions, he believed.

"Rudolf the Great could not be defeated by the sword. However, we know about the sins he committed against the human race. That's the power of the pen. The pen can indict a dictator who lived hundreds of years ago—of tyrants who lived thousands of years ago. You can't travel back through history with a sword, but with a pen, you can do that."

"True, but doesn't all that really mean is that you can confirm what happened in the past?"

"The past?! Listen, Julian, if we look at human history as something that's gonna continue on from this point as well, then the past is something that goes on accumulating forever. History's not just a record of the past, it's also the evidence of civilization being handed down to the present day. Our present civilization stands on top of a huge mound of accumulated past history. Understand?"

"Yes, sir."

After a brief pause, Yang breathed out a sigh and a gripe together. "That's why I wanted to become a historian. But I had one little misunderstanding at the outset, and my life ended up like this."

"Still," said Julian, "without the people who make history, the ones who write it wouldn't have much to do, would they?"

Yang smiled wryly once more and held out his cup toward the boy. "Julian, that hot punch just now—could you get me another cup of that? It was really good."

"Yes, sir. Right away."

Yang watched Julian as he headed off toward the kitchen, then shifted his gaze up to the ceiling.

"Well, things just don't seem to be going my way—not in my life, and not in anyone else's..."

VI

After deciding to award medals to the leadership of Iserlohn Fortress and the Iserlohn Patrol Fleet—with Yang at the front of the line—the government of the Free Planets Alliance underwent some small-scale reshuffling. Defense Committee Chair Negroponte tendered his resignation, and Walter Islands took over in his place. Due to the strong influence of Chairman Trünicht on both of these politicians, it was safe to say that the chances of there being any changes in military policy stood at zero. The newly appointed Chairman Islands spoke highly of Negroponte for his graceful and willing exit and then declared his intention to continue the policies of his predecessor fully. Whether or not that made Negroponte feel any better was difficult to judge, but on the surface, at least, he had indeed vacated the seat of Defense Committee chair gracefully and then become president of a state-run hydrogen-energy corporation.

The first official act of the newly appointed chairman was to visit Commissioner Brezeli—dispatched to Heinessen from Phezzan—to do a little bid rigging by arranging for kickbacks on the import of military supplies. Once that matter had been safely put to rest, the talk turned to idle chitchat, and Islands told Brezeli about Negroponte's failure when facing Yang Wen-li at the inquiry. As he was doing so, Islands tried to paint Negroponte in the best possible light, saying that his intention had been to stave off military tyranny.

"I've heard a number of different things about this," Brezeli said, "and what it seems to boil down to is that you all would make Yang Wen-li resign if you could just find a reason. That said, it would be a problem for you if he were to go into politics after resigning—he might well start rattling your citadels of power. Does that about sum it up?"

Brezeli had made no effort to dress up his words, pointing out Islands's true intentions with a frankness that seemed rather out of line. Islands, feeling slightly irritated, said he had nothing against Yang personally but did want to suppress soldiers' entry into the political sphere.

"If that's the case, you should just make a law, then. What do you think power's for? It's to make everyone obey laws and regulations that you yourself have created . . . When you feel the pleasure of that—a pleasure that money can't buy—you'll do whatever it takes to gain more power, even if you have to pour a ton of money into doing so. Or am I mistaken?"

"No, it's as you say . . ."

Islands took out a handkerchief and wiped at sweat that had not appeared on his face. This was to conceal a disgusted scowl. What was bothering him so much was that the man's tone was so bald-faced, and that in spite of that, he was on target with regard to a part of the truth. Both of those things nagged at him.

In any case, the Phezzan commissioner's proposal itself had its attractions, so Islands expressed his gratitude and hurried off to inform Trünicht.

Waiting in the next room over, Boris Konev couldn't quite bring himself to spit on the floor, being as it was polished so nicely. Abandoning the urge, he swallowed.

What words could describe a world that was so filled with corruption? While the world he had lived in up to now as a free merchant certainly did have its own brand of bargaining strategy, Konev still believed it was a more straight-talking, fair-and-square kind of world—one where anyone who relied on political power to hobble an opponent would be nothing but a target for insults. This was because he had encountered nothing but this kind of talk ever since he had come to work at the office of the commissioner. He had never planned on putting up with this job for very long, and now he might be about to reach his limits.

One day, as May was drawing to a close, Landesherr Rubinsky handed down a decision on Phezzan.

"Kesselring!" called the landesherr.

The young aide soon appeared and bowed respectfully.

"I take it everything's in place now for that project I mentioned earlier."

Kesselring responded with a slight smile that was bursting with confidence. "I've left nothing to chance, Excellency."

"Very well. In that case, I'm activating the plan. Inform your team."

"As you wish. If I may ask, Your Excellency: when this plan has succeeded and Duke von Lohengramm and Yang Wen-li have brought all their arms to bear against one another, which do you think will emerge the victor?"

"I have no idea. Still, that's what makes it so interesting. Wouldn't you agree?"

"Absolutely. Well then, I'll go and relay your orders to the team."

Relations between the father and son had not warmed in the slightest since that earlier night. Both of them were self-consciously trying to preserve their relationship as supervisor and employee. After retiring to his own office, Kesselring punched the switch on his visiphone, and with video transmission disabled, passed along the orders as soon as reception was confirmed.

"This is Wolf's Den. Fenrir is off the chain. Repeat. Fenrir is off the chain."

What juvenile code words, thought Rupert Kesselring, although his own linguistic sense was irrelevant on this occasion. As long as the message got through to its intended listeners and no outsiders figured out who sent it, that would be enough.

Well now, who's going to be eaten when the unleashed Fenrir opens up his great red maw? The young aide's countenance was colored by a bitter smile. If he had been a wolf and not a dog, he might have even turned on his master.

Leopold Schumacher, formerly a captain in the Galactic Imperial Navy, checked the fake passport he had been given one more time. While it had been officially issued by the Phezzan Dominion, the name on it was not his own.

If this plan succeeded, he was promised not only citizenship and the right to live permanently on Phezzan, but plenty of material wealth as well.

Naturally, though, Schumacher didn't fully trust in the young Phezzanese aide's promises. In fact, he felt an intense skepticism of both the Phezzan Dominion's government and of Kesselring himself, and had no intention whatsoever of changing his mind about that. However, when he thought of the punishment that would be brought to bear on his men rather than himself, there was nothing he could do for now except go along with what they wanted. If Phezzan intended to use him as a tool, he would just have to use Phezzan himself in return. Even so, to think that his doing so would mean walking on Odin's soil once again…

"Ready to go, Captain?"

Count Alfred von Lansberg, who was accompanying him on this journey, spoke in a cheerful voice. Answering him with a nod, Schumacher slowly started walking toward the office at the Phezzan spaceport.

SE 798, or 489 of the imperial calendar, was as yet only halfway finished. Another month yet remained until the event that would send shock waves through both the Galactic Empire and the Free Planets Alliance.

ABOUT THE AUTHOR

Yoshiki Tanaka was born in 1952 in Kumamoto Prefecture and completed a doctorate in literature at Gakushuin University. Tanaka won the Gen'eijo (a mystery magazine) New Writer Award with his debut story "Midori no Sogen ni…" (On the green field…) in 1978, then started his career as a science fiction and fantasy writer. Legend of the Galactic Heroes, which translates the European wars of the nineteenth century to an interstellar setting, won the Seiun Award for best science fiction novel in 1987. Tanaka's other works include the fantasy series The Heroic Legend of Arslan and many other science fiction, fantasy, historical, and mystery novels and stories.

HAIKASORU

THE FUTURE IS JAPANESE

TRAVEL SPACE AND TIME WITH HAIKASORU!

USURPER OF THE SUN—HOUSUKE NOJIRI

Aki Shiraishi is a high school student working in the astronomy club and one of the few witnesses to an amazing event—someone is building a tower on the planet Mercury. Soon, the Builders have constructed a ring around the sun, threatening the ecology of Earth with an immense shadow. Aki is inspired to pursue a career in science, and the truth. She must determine the purpose of the ring and the plans of its creators, as the survival of both species—humanity and the alien Builders—hangs in the balance.

THE OUROBOROS WAVE—JYOUJI HAYASHI

Ninety years from now, a satellite detects a nearby black hole scientists dub Kali for the Hindu goddess of destruction. Humanity embarks on a generations-long project to tap the energy of the black hole and establish colonies on planets across the solar system. Earth and Mars and the moons Europa (Jupiter) and Titania (Uranus) develop radically different societies, with only Kali, that swirling vortex of destruction and creation, and the hated but crucial Artificial Accretion Disk Development association (AADD) in common.

TEN BILLION DAYS AND ONE HUNDRED BILLION NIGHTS—RYU MITSUSE

Ten billion days—that is how long it will take the philosopher Plato to determine the true systems of the world. One hundred billion nights—that is how far into the future Jesus of Nazareth, Siddhartha, and the demigod Asura will travel to witness the end of all worlds. Named the greatest Japanese science fiction novel of all time, *Ten Billion Days and One Hundred Billion Nights* is an epic eons in the making. Originally published in 1967, the novel was revised by the author in later years and republished in 1973.

WWW.HAIKASORU.COM